R

"Bill Kienzle's best yet."

Neil Shine
Managing Editor
Detroit Free Press

"*Mind over Murder* is quite the best of
Kienzle's novels, in what we hope will
be a continuing series."

The Detroit News

Also by William X. Kienzle
Published by Ballantine Books:

THE ROSARY MURDERS*

DEATH WEARS A RED HAT*

ASSAULT WITH INTENT

SHADOW OF DEATH

KILL AND TELL

SUDDEN DEATH

DEATHBED

DEADLINE FOR A CRITIC

*Forthcoming

MIND
OVER
MURDER

WILLIAM X. KIENZLE

BALLANTINE BOOKS • NEW YORK

In memory of Jim Andrews, and
for Fiona, *sine qua non semper*

"The worst of me is known. . . ."

    —J. C. F. Schiller

ACKNOWLEDGMENTS

Gratitude for technical advice to:

Inspector Robert Hislop (Homicide), Sergeant Roy Awe (Homicide), Sergeant Mary Marcantonio (Office of Executive Deputy Chief), Inspector William Brandimore (Fifteenth Precinct), Sergeant Judy Dowling (Fifteenth Precinct), Patrolman Robert Kosinski (Fifteenth Precinct), Detroit Police Department

Robert Ankeny (staff writer), *The Detroit News*
Ramon Betanzos (professor of humanities), Wayne State University

Harry Ford (vice president), First Independence National Bank of Detroit
Jim Grace (detective), Kalamazoo Police Department
Sister Bernadelle Grimm, R.S.M. (Pastoral Care Department), St. Joseph's Mercy Hospital
Lee Hersey (sommelier), Ren Cellar, Renaissance Center
T. G. Litka, life underwriter
Tom Mathes (superintendent), Eric Wolff (crematorium manager), Woodmere Cemetery
Neal Shine (managing editor), *Detroit Free Press*

Blood Found in Abandoned Car

FOUL PLAY FEARED IN CASE OF MISSING MONSIGNOR

By Joe Cox
Free Press Staff Writer

A new development has been uncovered by the Detroit police in the day-old case of the missing Monsignor. Msgr. Thomas Thompson's late-model Eldorado was found early Monday morning parked and abandoned in front of De La Salle High School on Detroit's near east side.

Lt. Ned Harris, head of Squad Six of the Homicide Division, stated that blood was found on tissues in the car's waste receptacle, and a casing from what appeared to be a .32-caliber automatic pistol was found on the car's front seat.

"Investigation of this case as a possible homicide has just begun," stated Homicide Inspector Walter Koznicki. "Until now," Koznicki added, "the disappearance of Monsignor Thompson has been treated as a missing person's case. The discovery of his automobile, the bloodstains, the spent cartridge, as well as several other details I am not at liberty to discuss at this time have moved the case into a full-fledged homicide investigation."

Msgr. Thompson was last seen Saturday evening at Roma Hall on Gratiot in East Detroit. Thompson was attending a wedding reception when, according to witnesses, he was called to the phone. After a few moments' conversation, he was heard to say, "You don't mean it! Where? I'll be right there!"

At first, it was thought that
See MONSIGNOR Page 13A

1

    "SIX HUNDRED THIRTY-NINE DOLLARS AND TWO
cents for liquor? SIX HUNDRED AND THIRTY-NINE DOLLARS AND
TWO CENTS FOR BOOZE! This is unprecedented! This is unheard-
of! This is crazy!"

On this sleepy first Monday in July, June's liquor bill was an
eye-opener for Father Robert Koesler. Until finding the bill
among the papers on his office desk, he had been going through
the motions of beginning another somnolent summer week.

In her office, down the hall from Koesler's, St. Anselm's parish secretary Mary O'Connor half-smiled and half-winced. It
was so unlike Koesler to become excited over anything, let alone
shout, that she was torn between laughter and the natural anxiety
that anger usually generates. Since placing the bill on his desk,
she had expected some sort of audible reaction. But not at this
decibel level.

She heard his resolute footsteps approaching her office.

"Mary . . ." Though he had already offered Mass, including
a brief homily, eaten a light breakfast, and read the *Detroit Free
Press*, for the first time this morning Koesler was fully awake.
"What is the meaning of this liquor bill? Did you see it? *Cases*
of Chivas Regal, Crown Royal, Stolichnaya, Beefeaters, and
Jack Daniel's! We don't stock these expensive brands in the rectory. And certainly not by the case! There must be some mistake!"

3

"There's no mistake," she offered meekly.

"There's no mistake." He wanted to make certain his ears as well as his eyes were functioning. He hoped they weren't, but feared otherwise.

"No, Father, there's no mistake."

"Well, then, who? I certainly didn't order them!" He looked at her quizzically, as if discovering a hitherto undisclosed spend-thrift side to her character.

"Oh, no, Father." His gaze was transparent; the intent behind it obvious. "Not me!"

"Not you?"

"Not me!"

"Then who?"

"Deacon Les."

"Deacon Les?"

"Yes."

He paused to absorb the impact of this news. Deacon Lester Schroeder was in his final seminary years, and theoretically, in his concluding glide pattern toward becoming a Catholic priest. As a practicum, deacons—not those choosing the office as a permanent state, but those passing through it toward the priest-hood—lived and worked in a parish in order to experience what presumably would be their life's work.

Deacon Lester Schroeder had selected Father Koesler and St. Anselm's in Dearborn Heights for his pre-priestly parochial training. Reluctantly, Koesler had accepted him. Reluctantly, because, with weekend Mass help from priest friends, Koesler felt quite self-sufficient at St. Anselm's. In addition, he was not eager for the company of the emerging young cleric who thought he could foretell the future with clarity while knowing absolutely nothing of the past.

"So," Koesler replied, after the reflective manner of Charlie Chan, "it was Deacon Les."

"I'm afraid so."

"Where might I find God's gift to the grape and grain at this very moment?"

"I believe he's in the living room."

"Thank you, Mary."

Koesler turned and strode toward the rectory's living room

with its Chaucerian characters marching along seemingly end-less Canterbury trails on the wallpaper. The design had been selected by Koesler's predecessor. Koesler disliked it but, characteristically, did nothing about replacing it.

There was Lester Schroeder, suave, debonair, with just the proper measure of aftershave lotion to proclaim his presence before one entered it. He was sunk into the overstuffed white couch, feet on the coffee table, assiduously writing on a note-pad.

"Oh, Les . . ." Koesler forced his voice into a conversational tone. It was not easy. He thought he might hurt himself.

"Oh," Les looked up with a winning smile, " 'morning, Bob."

"I'll come right to the point, Les: to understate, I'm upset about this liquor bill for last month."

"Oh?"

"Yes." Koesler consulted the bill. "Six hundred and thirty-nine dollars and two cents!"

"Oh."

"Les, that is approximately what I have budgeted for the parish for at least half a year, if not much longer."

"Oh."

"Do you realize how we are going to have to stretch the booze you ordered?"

"I guess not. It's gone."

"Gone!"

"Well, yes."

"What did you do? Pour it out upon the ground in some exotic ritual?"

"No, they drank it."

"They? Who?"

"My visitors."

"You mean those hirsute, jeans-clad young people I find wall-to-wall on the floor most evenings?"

"Well, yes."

"Les"—it was as if scales were falling from Koesler's eyes—"until now, I thought you were the Pied Piper. But now I see you are the Prodigal Son."

5

"Oh?" Schroeder was uncertain as to whether Koesler was reprimanding or complimenting him.

"From now on, Les, the booze pump is turned off. Your friends can have anything from iced tea to Pepsi. But no hard stuff."

"Not even beer or wine?"

"Not even beer or wine."

"Well, then," Schroeder shrugged elaborately, "that will spell the end to the youth ministry in this parish."

"C'mon, Les. You can do it without leaning on alcohol as bait." In his inner heart, Koesler knew Schroeder couldn't do it.

"I guess I can try," Schroeder affirmed, fanning the embers of his self-confidence.

"Oh, by the way, Bob," Schroeder perked up, "you may get some feedback from something I said in my homily at yesterday's Mass."

Koesler sighed and braced himself. "What might that have been, Les?"

"I told them that as a result of my kerygmatic catechesis, they must respond as the people of God, experience an existential metanoia and become a transcendent faith community." He looked expectantly at Koesler.

There was a pause. "I don't think I'm going to get any feedback from what you said to our 'people of God,' Les," Koesler said, at length. "I don't think anyone understood your trenchant statement."

"Well, if you think not, Bob . . ."

"I think not, Les."

They were interrupted by a hesitant, apologetic knock at the living room door.

"The mail is here, Father." Mary O'Connor spoke just loudly enough to be heard.

"Saved by the mail call, Les," said Koesler as he began the return to his office.

"Whatever you say, Bob."

Koesler fingered through the mail. Almost all of it was junk mail. A company that sold sacramental wine, assuring the purchaser that all company trucks had Catholic drivers. An offer of communion wafers made by contemplative nuns, assuring the customer that the wafers had been touched solely by consecrated virginal hands. Koesler thought it must have been simpler at the Last Supper.

"Damn!" The expletive escaped involuntarily. The envelope's return address was that of the Tribunal, the archdiocesan matrimonial court. Over the years, Koesler had come to associate the word Tribunal with bad news. And at the mention of Monsignor Tommy Thompson—director of the Tribunal—Koesler always heard in his mind the menacing chords that accompany Scarpia's entrance in "Tosca."

Koesler wondered what this bit of bad news could be. Probably, he mused spiritlessly, another notary job wherein the Tribunal would order him to visit some innocent parishioner to ask largely irrelevant, sometimes embarrassingly personal questions regarding a broken marriage involving some relation or friend. The damned inquisitive Tribunal. Forever poking its bureaucratic nose in other people's lives.

With symbolic vehemence, Koesler ripped the envelope from seam to seam.

Slowly shaking his head, he read the contents. The case referred to in this communication was nearly a year old. It had begun when a Catholic woman visited Koesler with the announcement that her husband had deserted her. She wanted an ecclesiastical separation. Koesler had assured her it was perfectly all right for her to continue her sacramental life without permission from the Tribunal. After all, her single state was not of her doing. But, as a member in good standing of the conservative Catholics United for the Faith, she demanded ecclesial permission. Well, to Caesar she had appealed; to Caesar she would go.

Except that, along the red-tape way, her husband had effectively disappeared. Koesler had made several fruitless attempts to locate the husband.

This was the third Tribunal request for information on the status of the case. In response to the two previous requests, Koesler had explained the husband's disappearance and promised that if the reluctant spouse were ever found, Koesler would make sure the Tribunal would be among the first to know. Now,

7

he would have to waste time making yet another written statement to that effect.

At the bottom of the official document, Koesler noted the stamped signature, "Msgr. Thomas Thompson."

The three menacing chords resounded in Koesler's ears.

Father Patrick McNiff pulled his modest silver-colored Fairmont reverentially through the huge stone gates of Mt. Olivet Cemetery.

McNiff had recently been assigned as pastor of Holy Name parish on Van Dyke on Detroit's east side. The parish was almost adjacent to Mt. Olivet. Thus, it was common for many other parishes, especially those on the west side or in the suburbs, to ask the priests of Holy Name to conduct on their behalf the final obsequy—the burial.

Holy Name's cooperation saved these priests enormous amounts of time which, depending on the priest, would be either well-used or wasted. The priests at Holy Name—there were three—put the five-dollar stipend for the burial rite in a common fund that was evenly divided at vacation times.

Prior to his arrival at Holy Name, McNiff's friends and classmates had hosted him at a dinner celebrating his appointment. One classmate, Robert Koesler, had publicly depicted McNiff as sitting forlornly at the stone gates, biretta in hand, chanting, "Bury your dead! Five dollah! Bury your dead."

McNiff took the kidding good-naturedly. His task was most serious, dealing with families frequently at the moment of their greatest grief. In fact, he often remarked he wished society would do away with at least this final funeral rite. The graveside ceremony often demanded too much of the bereaved.

As he cruised the circular drive to await the arrival of the cortege he was to service, McNiff noticed a familiar car parked at the side of the cemetery's central office. A big black Eldorado with silver and red trim and plenty of chrome. Behind the wheel, he noted a man's square-shaped head sporting a trim haircut and red neck. McNiff could almost sense smoke seeping from the ears.

Gliding to a halt behind the Eldorado, he approached from the rear.

"As I live and breathe," McNiff opened, "it's Monsignor Tommy Thompson."

"Eh? What?" Thompson obviously had been startled.

Thompson did not enjoy being startled. In any case, he clearly was not amused.

"Waiting for a funeral, Monsignor?"

"Oh . . . oh, McNiff . . . no, of course not, McNiff. Don't be silly. I couldn't think of anything better to do on a sleepy Monday in July but come out here and direct traffic. *Of course I'm waiting for a funeral, McNiff!* It's just that nothing ever happens in my life."

"How are things at the Tribunal, Monsignor?" McNiff wished he had never begun this conversation.

"Busy. Too busy!" Thompson had not looked at McNiff beyond that moment necessary to recognize him. He looked steadfastly at the gate, watching for the first sight of his cortege. "Everybody wants out of a lifetime commitment. They promise till death do them part; then, at the first sign of trouble, they run. Then they want me to come running and bail them out. Annulment! Annulment! They all want an annulment from me. They think annulments grow on trees. Well, they soon find we grant annulments few and far between."

"Aren't you being a bit all-inclusive, Monsignor?"

"No, I'm not!" Thompson said firmly and finally in his resonant baritone.

A hearse entered the gateway. Thompson's unspectacled eyes peered at the small sign in the driver's side window. Howe-Peterson. Wrong funeral home.

"I suppose," Thompson growled at McNiff, "that's your goddamned corpse!"

"Yes," said McNiff with a bit more verve than necessary, "and you can't have it."

Thompson continued to growl and grouse.

As McNiff took leave to join the cortege, he noted that under his black monsignorial cassock with red piping in all the appropriate places, Thompson was wearing bright green slacks.

So that was it. On top of everything else, Thompson was late for a golf match. I hope, McNiff thought vindictively, that you hit every trap and lake.

Depositing that inoffensive curse, McNiff went forth to bury his dead.

———————

Although St. Anselm's was located in Dearborn Heights and Divine Child was in Dearborn, they were neighbors. Divine Child, founded in 1950, was four years older than Anselm's and offered a complete Catholic education through high school. This was in contrast to Anselm's, which offered only elementary school.

Divine Child was not a populous high school by anyone's standards. Generally, the student body numbered in the vicinity of 350—and always more girls than boys.

A casual glance at the student body was revelatory. The girls of Divine Child looked like—well, high school girls. However, a sizable number of the boys resembled the Incredible Hulk, with massive shoulders, chests, and thighs, and no necks. Most of the other boys were more lithe, but definitely of the split-end, defensive backfield, quarterback variety.

Recruitment was carried on, largely and successfully, by coach Walter Blaszczyk, ably assisted by alumni and several assistant coaches.

It was a breakdown in his recruitment plot that had triggered the conversation now going on between Coach Blaszczyk and Father David Neiss. Father Neiss was the young assistant pastor at Divine Child. And as such, among other duties discarded by priests as they gained seniority, he was athletic director.

"I am telling you, Father, I could not believe it using my own ears and eyes." Blaszczyk removed his tattered baseball cap and scratched his ample head of hair with the same hand.

"Keep it down," cautioned Father Neiss. "School's out, but the maintenance people are around. Someone's bound to hear you."

"I cannot help it, Father. Can you believe it? Two students from over beyond the parish boundaries apply for admission to next year's tenth grade. One of them is Adam Sierminski. A boy

10

whom I have recruited since he played fifth-grade football over by Holy Redeemer.''

"How big is he?"

"How big is he? He could fill your doorway with some left over!"

"That big!"

"He is maybe six feet-five and weighs maybe 280–290 pounds. And he is ready and able to join our summer work-outs.''

"Well," Neiss's attention began to wander to other duties, "what happened?"

"What happened? What happened? You will not believe what happened! But at the same time Sierminski enrolled, so did a goddamn girl. Just your ordinary, everyday goddamn girl!''

"You don't mean—"

"That is my meaning. Sister Mary Patrick took the goddamn girl!''

"But why?"

"Better marks."

"Better marks?"

Blaszczyk simply nodded, confident the enormity of this injustice had registered with Father Neiss.

It had.

"O.K., Walt; relax. I'll get Sierminski in if we have to create an extra place in the sophomore class.''

"That, in point of fact, is precisely what you will have to do. There was only one place left in the tenth grade when Sister picked that goddamn girl.''

"Well, Walt," Neiss laughed somewhat nervously, "one more desk in a classroom is not going to bother anyone, is it?''

Neiss reached up and slapped Blaszczyk on one broad shoulder and walked away. Inwardly, Neiss was not nearly as confident he could convince Sister Mary Patrick to add just one more place. As principal, she guarded her teachers against the slightest over-enrollment like a protective hydra.

Well, he thought, sufficient unto the day is the evil thereof. For now, he was due at the rectory in fifteen minutes for an appointment. He hurried across the parking lot, on three sides of which were the school, the church, and the rectory.

As he entered his office, Neiss turned on the light. That which he did not wish to see on his desk, he saw. A neat bundle of envelopes and a note from his pastor encircled with a rubber band. He yanked the note out from beneath the band.

Father Neiss, the note began. The pastor never used Neiss's first name. *Please address these envelopes to the parish council members, first removing the enclosures and then, after addressing the envelopes, replacing the enclosures. Place a stamp (first class) on each envelope. Seal the envelopes. Mail the envelopes.* It was signed meticulously, *Father Leon Cavanaugh.*

Damn him, thought Neiss; why can't he treat me like an adult?

Mercifully, the front doorbell interrupted the priest's increasingly homicidal reverie. It was Neiss's late-afternoon appointment, one Harry Kirwan, public relations manager at Michigan Bell. Kirwan had visited with Neiss several times. The two had taken an almost instant liking to each other.

Kirwan, a Lutheran, planned to marry Mary Ann McCauley, a Catholic. In addition to the red tape normally involved in a mixed religious marriage—an impediment requiring a dispensation from the Tribunal—further measures were required: Kirwan had been previously married.

Catholic canon law presumes that all attempted marriages are true and valid and lasting until death unless they are proven otherwise.

Kirwan's case was, by far, the easiest to pursue among the red-tape-choked procedures of the Tribunal. It was this point Neiss wanted to explain at this session.

He pushed several items, including the envelopes with their careful explanation, to either side of his desk, thus clearing the center. "Did you bring the documents?"

"Yes, Father. Here's a recent copy of my first wife's Catholic baptism certificate. Her maiden name, Ruth Kukulski, is recorded on it. And, as you told me to get from the priest at her old parish, there is a notation on the reverse that there is no mention of a marriage in her baptismal record. Then, here's a certified copy of our wedding certificate signed by the justice of the peace. And, finally, here's a copy of our divorce decree.

"Is all this satisfactory?"

Neiss, who had studied the documents, one by one, as Kirwan handed them to him, nodded. "Yes, this will do very well."

"Can you explain exactly what this is all about?" asked Kirwan.

"Of course. This is a *defectus formae* case. In other words, we are asking for a declaration of nullity in your first marriage because there was a 'defect in the form' of marriage required by the Church.

"You see, your first wife was a baptized Catholic. By Church law, she was required to have her marriage witnessed by a Catholic priest and two witnesses. If she attempted marriage in any other way, it would not be recognized by the Church. It would be null.

"What we are proving with these documents is that she was, indeed, a baptized Catholic and, at the same time with the same baptismal statement, that she has never been validly married in the Catholic Church.

"How's that?" Kirwan interrupted.

"Because when a Catholic is married in the Church, the marriage is entered in that person's baptismal record and, from that time on, whenever a baptismal statement is issued, the record of marriage is noted on the statement."

"I see."

Kirwan's jaw was setting. But Neiss didn't notice. "So you see," he continued, "we have proven with a recent copy of Ruth's baptismal certificate that Ruth was required to have her marriage witnessed by a priest and, by the same record, that she apparently did not.

"Then, we show how the two of you did get married—not by a priest but by a justice of the peace. And, finally, that your civil marriage has ended in divorce.

"With all of this we prove that your marriage to Ruth Kukulski is not recognized by the Church. It is null and void. Thus, both you and she will be free to marry in the Catholic Church once the decree is granted. She, because she was required to be married by a priest and was not. You, because you married her, who was required to be married by a priest and was not."

Neiss leaned back with a sense of satisfaction similar to that

13

which accompanies the imparting of a carefully constructed syllogism.

Kirwan leaned forward intently. "Now, I want it understood clearly, Father, that neither my first wife nor any of her family is to be contacted on this matter. My visitation rights with my children are chancy enough as it is." He made a wigwag motion with one hand. "Any time anything out of the ordinary occurs, there's the devil to pay, and the children are the prime ones to suffer. If she were to be contacted regarding our marriage, it would be disastrous."

"Nothing to fear." Neiss waved both hands as if signaling a runner safe. "We have all the documents we need. I'll see your mother and brother tomorrow and get their testimony that you and Ruth never had your marriage convalidated by later having it witnessed by a priest. Believe me, that's more than the Tribunal needs."

Kirwan now prepared to leave, relaxed.

Neiss braced his hands against the arms of his chair preparatory to rising. "Well, Harry, what do you think?" The priest was rather pleased with himself in both his careful preparation of the case and with his detailed explanation to the most attentive Kirwan.

Kirwan hesitated. "We're friends, aren't we, Father?"

"Why, yes. At least I consider us friends." Neiss was mildly surprised.

"Well," said Kirwan, "then I'll tell you: I consider this whole process to be a crock. I think if it's possible to insult God with a bunch of ecclesiastical red tape, we're doing it.

"Ruth and I didn't 'attempt' marriage; we were married. It proved a mistake. We didn't grow in our relationship. It stagnated. Over the years we began destroying each other. That's not a marriage. And it's not because there was a Catholic baptism or a missing priest. It's because what we thought was a marriage wasn't. The relationship disintegrated. It self-destructed.

"And, to continue to be frank, Father, if it weren't for Mary Ann's strong wish to be married in the Catholic Church, I wouldn't have participated in even phase one of this operation."

Neiss felt terrible. His pastor treated him like a child. The coach had put him between a rock and a hard place. And now, this man he had quickly come to respect had punctured his Church's balloon.

Seeing his discomfiture, Kirwan smiled and extended his hand. "But we can still be friends. Can't we, Father?"

Weakly but gratefully, Neiss took the hand and shook it with some enthusiasm.

Joe Cox picked up the loaf of Sinai Rye in one hand and hoisted the jug of Gallo Mountain Chianti in the other. He looked soulfully at Pat Lennon and pleaded, "Please pass the Thou."

Lennon giggled briefly but appreciatively. "I think it's sweet of you," she said, "to keep on making passes at me after all these years."

"That's right," Cox agreed, "if we had had a wedding ceremony back in the beginning of all this, we'd be old married geezers by now. Sort of like that couple in 'I Do, I Do.' "

"Well," Lennon demurred, "not that old! What's it been for us—about five years?"

"I guess." Cox spread the red-and-white checkered tablecloth on the ground.

It was the Fourth of July. What better way to celebrate, especially if you lived in a downtown Detroit apartment, than with a picnic at scenic Belle Isle, that gem of an island that rests in verdant lushness between Detroit and Windsor.

Cox and Lennon had met a little more than five years before as fledgling reporters at the *Detroit Free Press*. Shortly thereafter, they had begun living together. The arrangement continued. An enormous amount of interdependent chemistry flowed between the two.

Each had experienced a disastrous marriage. Neither had children. From time to time they talked of children. Perhaps later. Both were in their late twenties. There was time.

Periodically, Cox—never Lennon—would introduce the topic of marriage. Always Lennon shied from it. Sometimes she would treat the subject with lighthearted sarcasm. Sometimes with an emotion nearing panic. Usually, they agreed that, for them, in all probability, a marriage license would also prove to be a death certificate to their relationship.

Cox, sandy-haired, heavily mustached, of moderate height, powerfully built, had become the ace of the *Free Press* reportorial staff. He had begun primarily as a religion writer. But then, in connection with the Detroit religious scene, he had helped solve a series of murders of priests and nuns. For that feat he had received the coveted Pulitzer Prize and rightly won the admiration of the local news media. At least of those who were not frankly jealous of his achievement.

His ultimate and not inconsiderable claim to fame was his ability to coexist, although at several arms' lengths, with the infamous Karl Lowell, *Free Press* executive director. By dint of an infantile grasp for power over everyone, especially those at peer or subordinate levels, Lowell almost single-handedly was destroying a fine *Free Press* staff by maliciously making their work lives unbearable.

One of Lowell's more famous victims was Pat Lennon. She had spurned his casting couch offer, a routine Lowell gambit for all new and attractive female employees. Lennon then steadily learned that hell hath no vengeance like Lowell scorned. He had restricted her reportorial opportunities at every juncture.

Finally, sensing that under Lowell the summit of her journalistic career would be obituary writing, Lennon graduated in opportunity and earnings to the *Detroit News*. In this she followed the well-worn footsteps of many *Free Press* predecessors.

At the *News*, Lennon blossomed. She gained significant local and national prestige for her coverage of a series of murders of evil men whose severed heads were found in various Detroit Catholic churches.

Lennon, a Titian-highlighted brunette, voluptuous, at five-feet-six almost as tall as Joe Cox, easily was Cox's journalistic peer.

They wore well together in complementary ways.

Lennon began displaying the cold cuts, each variety on its sheet of wax paper. Roast beef, turkey, ham, baloney, salami, Swiss cheese, all fresh from the epicurean deli in Ye Olde Butcher Shoppe, which was housed in the shopping plaza of their Lafayette Park apartment complex.

16

Cox put out the paper plates, plastic glasses, and flatware.

With breezy sunny weather and a variety of saucy sailboats tacking the choppy water of the Detroit River, this had the beginnings of a most satisfying picnic.

As Pat reached across the tablecloth to arrange a plate and glass for him, Cox impulsively patted her bottom. Instinctively, she knelt bolt upright.

"Joe!"

"Madam," he said, suddenly a touch more seriously, "I'd like to make you a proposition."

"Always propositions. Never proposals."

"In very fact, Madam, this *is* by way of proposal."

"Joe!"

"I'm serious."

"We've been over this a million times."

"This will be one million-and-one."

"What more is there to discuss?"

"Has it ever occurred to you"—Cox began building a preposterous sandwich—"that it is a little odd that I am the one who, from time to time, is eager to get married? Whereas, traditionally, it is the woman who desires marriage?"

"Or her mother."

"I want to make an honest woman of you, Lennon!"

"You've already done that once for another happy woman."

Cox winced. "Everyone is entitled to one mistake."

"O.K., we've each had our quota; let's not make it a habit."

"I have a theory." Cox had difficulty getting the words out around the mouthful of sandwich he'd bitten off.

"Yes, Sigmund?"

Cox laboriously swallowed and washed the first massive mouthful down with a sip of wine. "It comes," he said more clearly, "from studying you Catholics."

Lennon blushed.

"With you people," Cox continued, "it's once a Catholic, always a Catholic. Now, it's been, what, almost eight, nine years since you've been to confession and communion?"

"About."

"Still, if anyone asked your religion, you would say you're a Catholic, right?"

She hesitated only a few seconds. "Right!"

"Well, I think that's the problem. You figure you can't get married again in the Catholic Church because you were already married in the Church. Right?"

"Ye . . . yes."

"Well, I've been doing a little research, and I think you might just be able to have your wedding cake and eat it too."

"What difference would it make?" Lennon pulled a brittle edge of lettuce away from her sandwich.

"Just this: I think your reluctance to get married is based on what you think is your inability to be married in the Catholic Church. If you can't be married in the Church, you figure, why bother getting married any other way? If it can't be 'the right way,' why make a mockery of it. The way you see it, nonmarriage is as good, if not better, than an 'invalid' marriage."

Silence.

Cox's vibrations told him he had scored heavily. Lennon could find no holes in his argument.

"You know," she said at length, "you may be right. But what's the practical difference? I've gone through a Catholic ceremony, with a Catholic, witnessed by a priest. My options are over."

"Not necessarily."

"Oh?"

"You've told me before about your marriage. Let me see if I've got the story right."

"Shoot, O masterful reporter." Pat tucked her legs beneath her and leaned back against a tree.

Before beginning his narration, Cox decided his sandwich was too heroic. He lifted the strata apart and, with two additional slices of bread, made the whole thing into two sandwiches.

"The multiplication of the loaves and fishes," said Lennon, clearly amused.

"Huh?"

"Nothing. Forget it. Go on with 'This is My Life,' though I don't understand why."

"The reason comes later." Cox took a bite from one of the

scaled-down sandwiches. Better. Now he could eat and talk at the same time.

"This happened about ten years ago, when you were in your late teens," Cox began. Lennon, sipping wine, nodded. "You were about to marry a man your parents disapproved of. And his parents disapproved of you. It was ethnic. He was Greek. Both sets of parents put on so much pressure that, just a week or so before the wedding, you broke it off."

Lennon grew very solemn. The memory was not pleasant.

"Later, you started going with a guy you didn't particularly care for. Your parents didn't care for him either, but they were afraid to pressure you again. You became so nervous you developed a rash. You married him one year to the day after your previously scheduled marriage was called off.

"It lasted three months. Then you separated. Five months later, you were divorced. Right?"

Silence. "Good memory," Pat finally commented. "But what does your accurate recollection of my tale of woe have to do with anything?"

"Suppose you could get your Church to grant a—what do you call it?—a declaration of . . . uh . . . nullity? Suppose your Church stated what is obvious to anyone else: you got married to punish your parents . . . and you managed to punish yourself in the bargain."

Lennon bit a corner from her sandwich. She carefully thought and chewed. "I couldn't. They wouldn't.

"Look, we were both Catholic. We got married in a Catholic church. It was witnessed by a priest. We consummated the thing . . . well, it was more like rape. But as far as the Church is concerned about marital 'rights and duties,' it was consummated. I'm stuck.

"But why bring it up? You're not the type who gets his kicks from pouring salt in wounds."

"It just so happens that I was doing part of a story out at St. John's Seminary and I had some time to kill." Cox started on his second sandwich and poured himself another glass of wine. "I gave an anonymous rundown of your case to Father Leo Clark. Remember him?"

"Remember him! Indeed I do. He was a prime source for that series I did on The Red Hat Murders."

"Would you agree that Father Clark is a reliable expert on religious affairs?"

"Yes, of course I would."

"Well," Cox, feeling a twinge of excitement, rose to his knees, "Clark says there's hope for someone with a case like yours. He says current interpretation of canon law would allow for the emotional strain you were under, and the Church might, after investigation, grant a decree of nullity."

Lennon began twisting a lock of hair around her index finger, a habit when she grew reflective. Suddenly, she looked sharply at Cox. "But what about you? You've been married before!"

"Clark says no sweat. I was married to a Catholic. A judge witnessed it. Clark called it a *defectus* something-or-other. He said it was the easiest of all marriage cases to process."

Silence again for several moments.

"Joe, I'm afraid you don't understand. It's one thing for me to think I couldn't get married again in my Church and another thing to *know* it. If I go into this and find all the doors slammed tight, I don't know—"

"On the other hand, nothing ventured, nothing gained. Maybe we wouldn't get married, but at least you'd know you could."

"How about you, Joe? I just can't see you filling out forms and answering questions. Even if you do have 'one of the easiest cases to process.' "

"Personally, I think the whole thing is a pile of bureaucratic horseshit. But if it will help you, I'm willing to go through with it."

Lennon leaned forward to kiss him. She lost her balance and toppled, taking Cox with her. He glanced from side to side. No one appeared to be looking at them. He slid his hand under her sweater.

"Joe! Your hand's like ice!"

"Right. But isn't it nice I know a place to warm it."

On the Fourth of July, it would be an excellent idea to go on a picnic, thought Father Robert Koesler. And he would do it, he vowed, if only he could get the hell away from St. Anselm's.

At ten that morning, Koesler had conducted a special Independence Day-type liturgy with appropriate prayers, Scripture readings, and homily geared to the theme of responsible freedom.

And, wonder of wonders, Deacon Lester Schroeder had been present. Deacon Les harbored a strange aversion to daily Mass. He seldom attended. Although there was no ecclesial law demanding daily Mass attendance of any Catholic, even a priest, priests were ordinarily expected to offer Mass daily. Schroeder was less than a year from probable ordination to the priesthood, and Koesler, as the deacon's reluctant moderator, wondered mightily about his protégé's attitude.

By now, near noon, Schroeder was long gone on a holiday celebration of his own, as were the approximately seventy-five parishioners who had attended the holiday ritual without benefit of binding law.

Koesler also would have been gone, but he was preparing his third response to the Tribunal's demand for an update on the marital separation case whose status had been quo-ed since Koesler had first alerted the Tommy Thompson gang of the situation.

Koesler finished typing a response to the Tribunal's request for information. The response was almost identical to the two previous communications. The woman's husband had, for all practical purposes, disappeared. Thus, the separation petition was parked solidly in limbo.

The blond, six-foot-three Koesler, in his mid-fifties, and on the slender side of a middle-aged paunch, was at ease in parochial life. As far back as he could remember, he had wanted nothing but to be a parish priest, which he had been for eight years following his ordination. At that point, however, Detroit's Archbishop Mark Boyle had appointed Koesler as editor-in-chief of the archdiocesan newspaper, the *Detroit Catholic*.

He had been editor for twelve years, while simultaneously performing some parochial duties. Now he was simply pastor of St. Anselm's in suburban Dearborn Heights. And happy about it.

As editor, Koesler had been involved with two intensive police investigations of murders that had specifically affected Detroit's Catholic community.

In the first of these investigations, popularly known as The Rosary Murders, Koesler had been instrumental in solving the case. The second series of killings, known as The Red Hat Murders, had remained officially in the category of unsolved crimes.

Irene Casey, formerly woman's editor, had succeeded Koesler as editor-in-chief of the *Detroit Catholic*. The two had remained friends over the years, and it was to Irene's home on the shore of Green Lake that Koesler was headed for his Independence Day picnic. If only he could get this envelope addressed to Monsignor Thompson at the Tribunal. As Koesler rolled the envelope into his typewriter, the doorbell rang. Grumbling mildly under his breath, he rose, smoothed his cassock, and went to answer the door.

It was a woman perhaps his age, perhaps slightly older. Agitated, anxious, perhaps angry.

"May I help you?" Koesler offered.

"Is Deacon Les here?"

Red warning lights went on all over Koesler's imagination.

"No, Deacon Les has gone for the day. I'm Father Koesler. May I help you? I'm pastor here." Just as the doctor has more status than the nurse, he thought she should understand that the pastor may be considerably more effective than a deacon.

"Can we talk?"

"Of course." Koesler led her down the narrow hallway to his office. He and his visitor settled in chairs on either side of the desk. Koesler waited through a short, awkward silence.

"I am Mrs. Leo Cicero." She removed a lace handkerchief from her purse and began nervously running it through her hands. "I've come about my daughter's marriage."

"Excuse me, but is there some reason I don't recognize you?" While Koesler did not claim to know all his parishioners by name, he was familiar enough with them to recognize those who at least attended weekend Mass with some regularity.

"Oh, we're not from your parish, Father. We belong to Divine Child. It's just a few blocks away."

Koesler knew well where Divine Child was. "But if you be-

22

long to Divine Child, why are you dealing with Deacon Les? He is assigned to this parish," Koesler added ruefully.

"Well, you see, Father, there is a problem."

"There is a problem. And Deacon Les is fixing it up for you?" The red warning lights entirely lit up Koesler's imagination. "Might I inquire as to the nature of this problem?"

"My future son-in-law was married before."

"And what makes anyone think he can get married again?"

"Well, you see, he was never baptized. So we're seeking a privilege . . . a privilege . . ."

". . . of the faith case," Koesler completed. "You have petitioned the Holy See to dissolve his previous valid-but-not-sacramental marriage in favor of the sacramental marriage to your Catholic daughter."

"That's it!" Mrs. Cicero brightened.

"Well, that procedure is certainly not unheard-of. But why have you brought this case here? Why isn't it being handled in your own parish?"

"Because of the deadline."

"Deadline?"

"Yes, the youngsters are scheduled to be married on the first Saturday of August."

"Where?"

"Here!"

Koesler excused himself, crossed to Mary O'Connor's office, and consulted the datebook. There it was. Scheduled for Saturday, August 4, at 3 P.M. Dale Worthington to be wed to Anna Maria Cicero.

He returned to his office. "Would you mind running that by me again? The part about the deadline?"

"Well, Father Cavanaugh, our pastor, would not agree to the August 4 date for the wedding. He insisted he would not schedule the wedding until after we got permission from Rome."

"This case is still in Rome?"

"Yes. But Deacon Les—Anna Maria was referred to him by a young man who comes here almost every evening to see him— said that we could set the date and that he would pull special strings to make sure the permission would arrive in time."

23

"But, as far as you know, the permission has not yet arrived?"

"No. That's why I dropped in today. To check that out with Deacon Les."

The red warning lights had become exploding skyrockets in Koesler's mind.

"I see," he said. "If you'll give me your phone number, I'll try to check this out with Deacon Les and get back to you."

"Well, thank you, Father."

Koesler showed Mrs. Cicero out and pondered various torturous deaths he might administer slowly and deliberately to Lester Schroeder, as he finished addressing his envelope to the Tribunal.

Leaving St. Anselm's to the care of its answering service, he took his swim trunks as a last-minute decision. He had not planned on swimming in Green Lake. However, these latest events convinced him he needed a cool place to simmer down.

Father Norm Shanley wondered if the others in his foursome would wait. Nothing separated him from a holiday golf match with three of his priest buddies but a lingering brunch with his pastor, Father James Porter. In any case, if he missed tee time, Shanley knew he would have little trouble finding his friends on the spacious St. John Seminary course.

"Father," Porter worked the first bite of his apple pie free, "did I ever tell you what happened after the very first baptism I ever performed?"

"I don't think so," Shanley answered. "Why don't you tell me about it? I'll let you know if you're covering familiar ground."

Shanley frankly admired Porter. At 69, he was one year shy of retirement. Only a few years back, his right leg had been amputated above the knee. Poor circulation. Now, confined to a wheelchair and burdened with a dozen or so daily pills, he remained a cheerful and dedicated priest.

"Well, sir, Father," Porter chewed his dry, flaky piece of pie, "those were the days when good Catholic women had children—lots of them. Why, even in Imlay City, we could average

24

five to ten babies of a Sunday. Not like today when nobody will listen to the Holy Father.''

"And,'' Shanley was determined to bring Porter back to the point of his story, "what was it occurred on the occasion of your very first baptism, Father?''

At the beginning of their relationship, Porter had insisted on calling Shanley, young enough to be his grandson, Father. And since Porter seemed more comfortable being addressed by title, the two invariably called each other, Father. A bit old-worldly, but habit-forming.

"Well, sir, Father,'' Porter rubbed his hands together and warmed to his tale, "I had no sooner finished baptizing—must have been eight, ten babies—than one of the godfathers comes back into the baptistery. Very excited he was.

"He says to me, 'Father, there's a woman in church with her dress off.'

"So,'' Porter ingested the last of his stale apple pie, "I quick hurried out of the baptistery and looked around. Sure enough, Father, the church seemed completely empty. But there, about three-quarters up the main aisle; there, draped over one of the pews was this blue dress.''

"And then what happened?'' Shanley was finding this one of Porter's more captivating stories.

"Well, sir, Father, I sez to this man, 'Look, why don't you go back there and drape the dress on the woman? I'll just finish putting this away in here and then I'll be out to see what's what.'

"So, I finished in the baptistery and went out into the church. Sure enough, Father, there was that blue dress over the pew again.

"Now, I didn't doubt for a minute that the gentleman had put the dress over the woman. She must have draped it over the pew no sooner than he left.

"Well,'' Porter continued. "I went back to the pew with the dress hanging over it. And there was this lady lying on the pew. But she was wearing a slip and shoes . . . and, I suppose, underthings.'' Porter blushed again.

"Her pocketbook was open near her feet. I looked in. It was filled with prayerbooks and rosaries.

"For a while, I didn't know what to do. Finally, I hurried to the rectory and called the police.

"Well, sir, Father, a crowd the size of a Fourth-of-July picnic gathered in no time. I got back to the church about the same time the police entered. While the chief was getting the story from me, three burly deputies picked up that little woman, stood her on her feet and slapped that dress down over her like she was a mannequin. They slipped her out of there lickety-split. Crowd hung around for a while. But when they saw nothing more was going to happen, they went back to their backyards and lemonade."

Porter puffed contentedly on his cigarette. A smile twitched at his lips as he savored the recollection. He could remember the strong young man he once had been and glory in that image. Those were the days when there was no limit to how many souls he could save. No end to the conquests he could make in behalf of the Holy, Roman, Catholic and Apostolic Church.

Now the limits were painfully clear. One year until the hated retirement. It hadn't been that way before that blasted Second Vatican Council. In the good old days, a priest was expected to die with his stole on, halfway through an absolution. Nowadays, they put you on a shelf when you ripened. All that experience, all that practical knowledge put out to pasture.

"So what happened?" Shanley drew Porter from his reverie.

"What happened?"

"To the lady." Shanley perceived he was not getting through. "What happened to the lady in the slip on the pew who was taken away by the police?"

"Oh . . . oh!" Porter returned to the present. "Her! Well, sir, Father, I heard not a word from the chief. So about a week later I phoned him. And he told me that their investigation had revealed that she was a native of Detroit. And that she had a habit of roaming from parish to parish, poor woman, doing this sort of thing. She had a confusion in her mind about sex and religion."

"Did they hold her? Did you bring charges?"

"Oh, no, Father. Poor woman. We just let her go. But I've prayed for her ever since."

Shanley snuffed out his cigarette and contemplated Porter, lost once more in memories.

Poor guy, Shanley thought; he doesn't know what he's accomplished. He probably thinks his life is a waste. He has no idea of the lives he has touched, changed—changed for the better. Mine, for instance. He has no idea how he has influenced me. His patience in the face of prolonged suffering. His unflagging cheerfulness in the face of one medical discouragement after another.

And the stories Jimmy Porter knew! Stories that could be gathered only after years of experience. But only if one stayed alert and continued to learn from that experience.

Someday, Shanley thought, I'll have a fund of stories like that. Someday—if I live long enough and if I don't fall asleep at the switch.

But now, he thought, as he excused himself from table, for that inexpensive golf course.

"Duck!"

Father Koesler reacted instantly to Joe Casey's Irish tenor warning. The priest did not hear the baseball whiz over his bowed head, but he did hear it plop resoundingly into a mitt some fifty feet away.

Tim and Kevin, two of the seven Casey children, had been playing catch when Koesler had unwittingly become monkey-in-the-middle.

"How's your health insurance, Father?" Joe Casey hollered.

"How's your indemnity?" Koesler shot back. "I think I just suffered whiplash."

Walking more alertly than was his custom, Koesler crossed to the Caseys. Joe and Irene were standing side by side. Welcoming smiles creased their faces; each cradled an open can of Stroh's. All was as it should be. Stroh's was mother's milk to Joe and Irene. To the point where once Irene had returned from the grocery and absentmindedly heated a bottle of Stroh's for the baby.

The three exchanged greetings, which were quickly followed by the placing of a Stroh's in Koesler's hand.

"Golly!" Koesler glanced about, looking for new developments in the terrain or yard equipment. "It must be a couple of years since—"

"—you were here," Irene completed.

A look of amusement played about Koesler's face. "Irene," he said, "you are still completing my—"

"—sentences."

"Yes. Why is that?"

"I don't really know. It must be a bad habit I got into."

"It's a habit," Joe Casey commented, "that predates—"

"—you."

Joe laughed. Joe Casey found humor nearly everywhere. A retired Great Lakes captain and onetime line coach for Notre Dame's Frank Leahy, Joe had long since declared a truce in his battle against weight. At five-eleven and a comfortable 250 pounds, he wore the map of Ireland on his ruddy face. He supervised the daily needs of the two Casey preschoolers, read everything he could get his hands on, and told stories of the Lakes and of football greats of yesteryear.

Irene Casey, in her mid-forties, was fifteen years her husband's junior. Her auburn hair was flecked with gray. Seven children, twenty-three years of marriage, and a successful journalism career had not marred her delicate beauty. She had accepted the position as editor of the *Detroit Catholic* five years before more out of a sense of commitment and dedication than financial need. Detroit's Archbishop Mark Boyle continued to consider Irene's appointment as editor one of his finest moves.

Between Joe and Irene there were as many differences as there were similarities. They were remarkably alike and complementary in their sense of humor while quite dissimilar in temperament. But few would disagree they had one of the world's more secure marriages. Nor was there any disagreement that such a relationship was a relative rarity.

Together, Joe, Irene, and Father Koesler ambled toward the lake and the small rowboat tied to the Casey dock.

"Want to go for a ride, Father?" Irene invited.

"Sure. But I assume you'll do the riding, and I'll do the rowing."

Koesler assisted Irene into the boat, which he then awkwardly entered, nearly tipping it.

Joe untied the connecting rope, tossing it into the departing boat. "Have fun while there's time," he called after them. "Tommy Thompson will be here later!"

"We may not be back," Koesler hollered. "Any advice from Captain Casey, you old salt?"

"Just the word I used to give my old Navy buddies: stay on top of the waves!"

Irene shook her head. She'd heard that one too many times.

Stay on top of the waves, Koesler mused. Then, with the figurative lit bulb over his head, the homograph occurred to him: undulations on the water—or female members of the Navy. Ordinarily, he would not have thought twice about such a remark. But here, in a boat alone with Irene, he blushed. The ancient moralists had stumbled upon something in warning of danger when *solus* was *cum sola*. Or, as one of his long-forgotten retreat masters had noted, between every good man and every good woman should be built a solid brick wall.

After a few self-conscious moments, Irene broke the silence. "I hope you don't mind Tommy Thompson's being here later. He's only going to drop by for a few moments. I used to date his brother and, as a result, I think Tommy considers himself one of the family. It's not so much that I invite him to parties and functions. It's that when he hears about a party, he sort of invites himself."

"Oh, I have nothing personal against Tom. I just wish at least as long as he's going to be officialis—uh . . ." Koesler was not sure if Irene was familiar with the term. ". . . head of the Tribunal, that he would forget I exist. His insistence on the technical niceties of canon law can get on one's nerves after a while."

Koesler rowed easily toward the turn in the lake to the west of the Casey home. His long arms brought unintended acceleration to their progress. As they approached the corner of the lake, Koesler became aware of the enormousness of the lot that embraced the turn. Evidently pie-shaped, the lake frontage appeared to be at least 200 feet wide.

"I didn't know you had an oil sheik living on your lake,

Irene.'' Koesler leaned on the right oar, pulling the boat closer to shore.

''What?'' Irene looked about, bewildered. ''Oh,'' she laughed when she saw the lot to which Koesler alluded, ''that's no sheik, although he must be almost as rich. That's Lee Brand.''

Koesler paused a moment while all the little bells ringing in his head synchronized. ''Lee Brand . . . Lee Brand . . . not the president of the First Standard—''

''—Bank and Trust. Yes, the very one.''

''Does he own that entire lot?''

''He could own all of Green Lake if he had a mind to.''

''And the pavilion that runs the width of the lawn?'' Undeliberately, Koesler was propelling the boat ever closer to shore.

''Better watch out, Father,'' Irene warned, ''or we'll be joining the Brand party. And Liam wouldn't like that.''

''Liam?'' Koesler leaned heavily on the left oar and headed back to sea.

''Liam. Liam Brand. His real name.''

''Liam . . . that's Irish, isn't it, for—''

''—William,'' she said, on the heels of his words. ''Yes, William. Billy Brand.''

''Then why—''

''—Lee? Early on, he determined it had a better ring. That, just between you and me, is the essential explanation behind Lee Brand. He has packaged himself.''

Koesler allowed the oars to drag through the calm water as he and Irene watched uniformed caterers scurrying about the Brand lawn.

''As for the pavilion—Mr. Brand leaves nothing to chance. Even God couldn't rain on his picnic.'' She suddenly pointed to a figure approaching the pier. ''That's him there!''

Koesler peered myopically through the upper portion of his bifocals. ''Oh, you must be mistaken, Irene. I've seen Brand lots of times in photos and on TV. He's a good-looking man. That guy,'' he nodded toward the man standing on the pier, ''is bald, paunchy, and short.''

''Lee Brand sans toupee, corset, and lifts.''

''I'll be darned,'' Koesler exclaimed.

''I told you he has packaged himself. And in his office, behind his oversize desk, he sits on pillows. The number depends on the height of the person sitting opposite."

Koesler chuckled. "No one's head higher than the King of Siam's, eh?"

Just then, a series of piercing shrieks, emanating from the Casey lawn, shattered the calm. Koesler and Irene turned so quickly they almost upset the boat. The fully clothed body of the Caseys' nubile daughter Kitty was just disappearing beneath the surface of Green Lake. She'd been thrown in by several guffawing young men.

"Ah," Koesler reflected, "pity the lot of the pretty girl."

Irene shook her head. "I do hope she gets out of those wet clothes before she gets a chill."

Nothing more, mused Koesler, than Kitty getting out of her wet clothes, would improve the Fourth of July celebration for the guys who threw her in.

"And speaking of pretty girls," Irene returned her gaze to the Brand property, "there's another one."

Koesler located her immediately. In a one-piece swimsuit, she stood near the water, talking with a tall, blond Viking. Koesler, a closet student of such things, would have described her figure as short of voluptuous but clearly sensational.

"They are engaged," said Irene, referring to the couple. "And that is one major fly in the Lee Brand pie."

"How's that? Doesn't he approve of the young man?"

"Not that. The boy's pedigree is without flaw. But he was married before, and Lee insists on a Catholic ceremony for the apple of his eye. Anything else would sully the Brand image."

"Know anything about the young man's first marriage?"

"Episcopalian."

"Both he and his wife?"

"Uh-huh."

"Ouch!" Koesler pulled at the oars. They had been close enough to shore that he had begun to fear the Brands might be able to hear their conversation. "That sounds like a presumably valid, sacramental marriage. At least as far as canon law is concerned."

"That's what I thought, too. But Mr. Brand seems to think

31

he'll be able to talk, or buy, his way out of the jam. The problem is, he's never met Monsignor Tommy Thompson.''

"Maybe," Koesler grinned, "he *will* be able to buy his way out."

"Oh, c'mon, Father. Monsignor Thompson isn't that way."

"When it comes to Tommy, I wouldn't cover any bets."

Irene scooped some of Green Lake and flicked it harmlessly at Koesler. "I've been meaning to ask you if there are any priests left who would . . . uh . . . witness the marriage of a couple like the Brand girl and her fiancé."

"You mean witness a canonically—"

"—invalid marriage," she completed.

Koesler shook his head. "I don't know, Irene. There were a few. But most of them are out of the priesthood now, if not married themselves."

"Nobody?"

Koesler thought for a few moments. "Well, I've heard that young Shanley down at Rosary does that sort of thing." After a pause, Koesler added, "Wait; are you thinking that Brand would—oh, no; he'd never permit his daughter to be married at Rosary! That's a core-city parish. And Shanley would never officiate at such a wedding out here. The only reason he can get away with it now is because he's at an inner-city parish. No one talks and almost no one is interested."

"Well, you never know what sort of port he might be willing to pull into if the weather got bad enough."

"I can't imagine a Brand doing anything at Rosary, except maybe driving past it."

Koesler began feeling the effects of the sun against his head and neck. He began the relatively short trip back to the Caseys'.

Hesitantly, Irene began. "Would you be willing to tell him about Father Shanley?"

"Tell Brand about Shanley?" Koesler was surprised. "Why, I don't travel in Brand's class even when I'm at my charming best!"

"Please?"

"Irene . . ."

"I told the Brands you might drop by later this evening."

Koesler's resistance collapsed. He muttered, "Behind every successful invalid marriage—"

"—there are several mothers."

Like a horse that senses the barn in his immediate future, Koesler rowed for the Casey landing with fresh determination.

"One thing puzzles me, Irene. How do you happen to know so much about the Brand family? The lifts, the corsets, the toupées, the pillows, even the religious persuasion of a future son-in-law?"

"The car pool."

"The car pool?"

"Mrs. Brand and I are in the same car pool. We drive each other's kids to and from school. And she's a real nice gal."

"Oh-ho!"

Irene began waving to someone. Koesler glanced over his shoulder. Monsignor Thomas Thompson was standing on the Casey wharf, hands thrust in pockets, a broad grin on his round face.

"Hi, Monsignor," Irene called. "Get off that pier or someone will throw you in. That sort of thing has been happening today."

But only to pretty girls, thought Koesler.

"Don't worry," Thompson called through cupped hands, "nothing ever happens to me."

If you don't stop sending me stupid requests for useless information, thought Koesler, something might.

———

Father Norm Shanley noticed a strange odor. He got the first whiff on entering the small brick clubhouse at St. John Seminary's golf course. While he couldn't identify it immediately, it definitely was churchy.

A note was taped to the narrow wooden bench: *Rather than get teed off, we teed off. Tee time was 1:30. Why not conduct a search-and-find mission? There's only nine holes.* It was signed, *Bob Morell.*

One-thirty. Shanley checked his watch. Three o'clock. None of them was a good golfer. Shanley himself was the best of the foursome, and anything in the nineties for him was respectable.

33

He made a private wager with himself he would find them on the sixth or seventh fairway.

His olfactory sense led him unerringly to the locker whence came the churchy odor. He opened the door of locker ten. On the metallic shelf near the locker's top burned a small vigil candle. A note taped to the shelf read, *Better to light one little candle than to sit around cursing Shanley.* It was signed, *Bill Cunneen.*

The idiot, thought Shanley. He recalled churches set afire by candles burning seemingly with minds of their own. This might have been the first locker room devastated by an otherwise innocent-appearing votive light.

Shanley quickly changed into attire in which he could either play golf or paint a floor. Golfbag looped over left shoulder, he strode rapidly down the first fairway. He scanned the flat terrain. From his position he could see at least portions of fairways one, two, five, six and seven, as well as the first, fifth, and sixth greens. To the right was an apple orchard. To the left was forest.

Two golfers had just mounted the first green and were about to line up their putts. The full head of dark hair, heavy-rimmed glasses, and nondescript body proclaimed one of the golfers to be Monsignor Joseph Iming. The other had to be Archbishop Mark Boyle. Iming was Boyle's secretary. Shanley had never seen the Archbishop in other than clerical clothing or resplendent vestments. He looked strange, like a bird without plumage.

Beyond them, unmistakably, were Shanley's friends, just finishing the sixth green. One of them must have missed an easy putt; Cunneen's boisterous laughter ricocheted off the trees.

This was developing into a disaster. As far as the official Church was concerned, Shanley tried to maintain the lowest of profiles. He intended to continue dispensing sacraments as he thought best. What the Chancery and Tribunal did not know would not hurt him. If he managed to celebrate his Silver Jubilee, he wanted the Archbishop of Detroit to say of him, ''Who?''

Shanley's friends were approaching the seventh tee, only a few yards removed from the first green. It was unlikely that either Morell or Cunneen would find himself this close to Boyle without talking to him.

Boyle wished to be as uninformed as possible concerning the

core-city ministry. He was aware that for any small measure of success, rules would have to be bent. As long as he did not know which rules were being bent how far, he would not be impelled to punish. He had enormous clout. He did not want to use it. Ordinarily, this arrangement was more than acceptable to core-city priests. Occasionally, however, they would wish an audience regarding such matters as Church taxes, which they could not pay. This was one of those times.

"Who is that coming toward us down the first fairway?" asked Archbishop Boyle as he lined up his third putt.

"Norm Shanley," Monsignor Iming identified. "He's in residence at Rosary and chaplain for a bunch of neighboring hospitals."

Boyle putted and rimmed the cup. "Do you think he wants to join us?"

"No. I'd say he is going to join them." Iming nodded toward the group who had settled in at the seventh tee, one of whom was approaching the first green.

"Oh, dear! That's Father Morell from St. Theresa's, isn't it?" Boyle tapped in the putt.

"That's exactly right. And he didn't even have to ask for an appointment."

Archbishop Boyle sighed audibly. He did not do that often.

"Good afternoon, Excellency!" This was not going to work out too badly, Shanley thought, as he skirted the first green and headed for the seventh tee. Morell would be Boyle's major distraction while Shanley could pass as an unnoticed ship in the night.

Boyle nodded distractedly at Shanley as he directed his full attention at the imminent Morell.

"Hi, Bob." Iming retrieved his cigar from the putting surface and puffed it back to life.

"Hi, Joe." Morell, in single-minded pursuit of his Archbishop, did not bother even glancing at Iming.

"Good afternoon, Father Morell." Formality came naturally to the Archbishop.

"I've got to talk to you, Archbishop."

Boyle, supported by one leg and a putter, retrieved his ball.

"It's about De Porres High."

35

"I assumed it was," sighed the Archbishop.

St. Martin De Porres High School, nearly all of whose students were black, was on the verge of being closed by the archdiocesan school board. Boyle had attended a meeting at which parents of De Porres students had begged for the school's life. Boyle had made no commitment. So, for the past few days, the parents had taken turns camping on the lawn of the Archbishop's Wellesley mansion, much to the distress of Boyle's wealthy neighbors.

"Our parents are really upset." Morell's St. Theresa parish was one that contributed both money and students to De Porres.

"I know that, Father. I see them day and night, and I read their protest posters."

Almost any other bishop would have had squatters such as these long since thrown off the premises. Such an action would have been completely out of character for Boyle. While he fervently wished they would depart, he was far too compassionate a man to have any action taken against these sincere parents.

"They need a commitment from you, Archbishop." Morell thumped his driver against the ground to emphasize his point.

"I cannot make such a commitment, Father. The diocese is strapped for money. As you very well know, our parishes have a most difficult time even meeting their diocesan taxes."

"That's another thing," Morell interrupted, "I wanted to talk to you again about a graduated tax to take some of the burden off the core-city parishes—"

Boyle's heavy black eyebrows nearly met as a supreme frown crossed his still handsome face. "That, Father, is out of the question."

"Well, then, look at the public relations aspect." Morell returned to the point. "It won't look good if we let a school like De Porres close while so many suburban schools remain open."

"I am well aware of that, Father. But we have already subsidized St. Martin De Porres High School to a far greater degree than we have offered aid to any other school in the diocese." Boyle's soft, brogue-tinged voice rose a decibel or two toward the end of his apologia.

"But you can borrow—"

"No, no, Father; we cannot borrow. We have so little collateral. Who would want to buy a church? And we receive no special rate—even though some of our bankers are outstanding Catholic gentlemen.

"Father," he sought to terminate the conversation, "if you had the overall picture of the state of the diocese, you would better understand."

It's the old overall-view ploy, Morell thought; guess who the only one is who has that overall view.

"However," Boyle attempted a measure of conciliation, "if there is anything else I can do . . ."

"You might bring home some barbecue sauce," Morell answered, "your squatters tell me they're running low on it for the ribs."

Boyle merely shook his head. He and Iming started for the second tee. Morell left to rejoin his friends.

"I wish," Boyle sighed, "that all the priests, especially those of the core city, would simply do their jobs without attempting to involve themselves in the administration of the diocese. Like that priest . . ." He gestured vaguely toward the seventh tee.

"Shanley."

"Ah, yes. Father Shanley."

"Well," Father Bill Cunneen asked, "how did you make out?"

"Zilch," said Morell, "retroactively."

Cunneen exploded in laughter. Pastor of Sacred Heart parish in a HUD-leveled area of Detroit, Cunneen was also the founding director of Focus Peace, an organization that procured and distributed goods and services for the needy from government, business, and industry.

"What the pot did you ask him for?" asked Father Mickey Dolan, pastor of St. Elizabeth's, another core-city parish. Dolan, with a Navy background, was slightly older than his companions.

"Help for De Porres," Morell replied.

"Get him to raise the *Titanic* while you're at it," said Shanley.

"I didn't notice any of you guys falling over each other to help me." Morell looked scornfully at one after another of his compadres. "Especially you, Shanley. You walked right by the infamous tableau like the guy in the Gospel."

"You are not a Samaritan. Nor is Archbishop Boyle a thief." Shanley was going through a series of self-imposed calisthenics, trying to overtake the limberness of his already warmed-up friends. "Besides, I just live in my little corner of the world and try not to make enemies needlessly."

"What the pot," observed Dolan, "if the Arch ever gets wind of your marriages, your ass is in a sling."

"I'm celibate," said Shanley.

"You marry everybody!" Sensing he was in a literalness war, Dolan corrected himself. "I mean, you *witness* marriages for *any*body."

"That's not quite true. In fact, I refused a couple just the other day."

Morell's drive sliced sharply. He was fortunate the kidney-shaped fairway afforded lots of room on the right.

Morell glanced back sharply at Shanley. "*You* refused to marry somebody?"

"Couple of kids—eighteen, nineteen . . ." Shanley balanced his Dunlop on the tee. "They never go to church . . . quit completely a few years ago. They just wanted a church wedding for Mama. So I told them to make their statement and get married by a judge or somebody. I didn't want to get involved in a mockery, and I advised them not to either."

Shanley fell silent as he tried to remember all seventeen items the book said were necessary to strike the ball solidly. Forgetting most of them, he hooked to the edge of the forest.

"Gentlemen," said Shanley, searching vainly for the tee the impact of his driver had buried, "I want you to know that at no time during that swing did I see the ball."

"I thought," said Cunneen, returning to the subject, "you married *every*body."

"Only those who really, sincerely want to be married in the Church."

Cunneen's drive followed the path taken by Shanley's, stopping just short of the rough on the left.

"You're gonna get in trouble doing that," Dolan warned as he prepared for his drive.

"I don't think so. I'm just going to stay in my little corner of central Detroit and go about my business. Nobody downtown will even be aware of what I'm doing, let alone care."

Dolan swung so vehemently he nearly fell.

"What the pot!" Dolan cried. "Where is it? Where is it?"

"Up! Up! Way up!" Morell directed.

It was, indeed, a towering drive. If it had cleared the giant oak to the right of center of the fairway, Dolan would have been in excellent position to approach the green. Unfortunately, it did not clear the oak. The ball struck one of the upper branches and bounced back about twenty-five yards toward the tee.

The others laughed. Cunneen broke up.

"You do have a habit of hitting that tree," Cunneen observed.

"Damn!" Dolan commented, slamming his driver into his golf bag. He grabbed his two iron and strode angrily toward the ball.

"You're right in front of the tree, Mickey," said Morell, as Dolan prepared for his second shot. "You'd better aim to the left of the tree and hope for a slice."

"What the pot! If I hit that damn tree one more time, I'm going to pee on it and kill it, and it won't be here when I come back."

With that, Dolan struck his ball a mighty blow. Like a shot, the ball hit the tree squarely in mid-trunk. It then headed directly back at Dolan, who dove—rather gracefully, all things considered—to the ground. The ball whizzed through the space lately occupied by Dolan's head.

"Damn!" shouted Dolan.

Cunneen was on the ground, doubled up in howling laughter.

Dolan rose, looked at the ball now resting on the seventh tee whence all this had begun. He looked at the oak. He looked all around to make sure no one besides his companions was watching. Then he did it.

It was times like this, thought Father Koesler, that lakeside living must be most satisfying.

It was early evening, and Green Lake was like glass reflecting a premature moon. Koesler was seated on a glider near the water's edge. With him were Irene and Joe Casey. The stillness was punctuated by the irregular pop of firecrackers. From the Brand party across the lake came the muffled sound of laughter, conversation, and soft music. It was not an intrusive noise. If anything, it enhanced the hypnotic, drifting mood.

"Judging from the comparatively little noise from the number of guests I've seen wandering in and out of the pavilion, that's a surprisingly subdued party," said Koesler.

"Subdued?" Joe Casey inquired.

"Quiet," Koesler synonymed.

"It won't get louder even in its later stages," Joe observed.

"Oh?"

"No. Loud noise is tasteless. And Lee Brand will not abide tastelessness. So the music you hear comes from strolling violinists."

"But," Koesler countered, "they must be serving liquor. What happens when someone inevitably gets drunk at a Lee Brand party?"

"Most of his guests know enough not to get pie-eyed," said Joe. "However, should one or another violate the pledge, he is given the alternative of leaving, as best he can, or being keel-hauled. Brand runs a tight ship."

The glider rocked gently. Koesler tried to imagine what being a guest at a Lee Brand party might be like. A vision began to form of a group of svelte, soigné people outrageously attired in variations of black and white, not unlike the Ascot Races sequence in "My Fair Lady." All the people in Koesler's fantasy were cautiously tiptoeing over broken glass. Each held a forefinger to his or her lips, needlessly reminding all to maintain decorous silence.

Dominating all this, seated on what appeared to be an infinite number of pillows, was Lee Brand, playing a violin. He was the fiddler, and by jiminy, his guests were going to dance to his tune.

Koesler laughed, breaking the reverie.

"What is it?" asked Irene, startled.

"Oh, nothing. Just an idle idyll that was entertaining me." After a moment, Koesler continued, "I've been meaning to ask you all day, Irene; how are things at the paper?"

"All right, I guess. But circulation continues to drop."

"Badly?"

"No; dribs and drabs mostly."

"Of course, that started back when I was there. Once the Supreme Court ruled there'd be no public aid to parochial schools, then came that dual phenomenon: parishes started pouring funds down the bottomless coffers of Catholic schools, and you got parish councils. And, for the first time, parishioners got to look at the parish books. There was no one to tell them they could not cut funds for parish subscriptions to the *Detroit Catholic*. That's when and why we began to lose circulation."

"I guess you're right," said Irene, listlessly.

Koesler noted the absence of Irene's usual vivacity. "Well, you don't suppose any parish council would try to cut the pastor's salary, do you?"

"No."

His attempt at humor had failed.

"Is there something else wrong at the paper?" Koesler turned as much as he was able in the crowded glider to half face Irene.

She hesitated.

"Go on and tell him," said Joe.

"Tell me what?"

"Well," Irene began hesitantly, "remember that story we ran last week . . . the one about two former priests who have those neat jobs in Mayor Cobb's Human Rights Department?"

"Yes, I remember. I thought it was an excellent story. Just the sort of thing the *Catholic* ought to be involved in. Lots of times, parishioners like to know what's become of the priests who've left. I thought it was decidedly upbeat. What's the matter; did you get some negative feedback?"

Irene nodded. "Father Cavanaugh at Divine Child. He called the other day." She shook her head. "I've always liked him."

"What did he say?"

"He started by saying that he was just going to make a statement, and he didn't want any reply."

"He makes all the rules, eh?" Koesler interjected.

"He said," she continued, "that a story like that didn't belong in a paper like the *Detroit Catholic*. He said it is 'disedifying to the faithful' to read about a couple of former priests who say they are happy and fulfilled. It would be more appropriate, he said, to publish stories of former priests who were suffering or in miserable circumstances. Then he hung up and—I couldn't help it—I cried."

Koesler tried to appreciate the story from Cavanaugh's position. To someone like Cavanaugh, there were no grays. All was black or white. A former priest would be a traitor. Simple as that. Going to hell. Only not fast enough. Should have hell on earth.

All this Koesler could understand, even if he did not agree. But calling Irene—that was too much. Cavanaugh shouldn't have taken advantage of her generous disposition to vent his unsatisfied desire for vengeance.

"Irene," said Koesler, "you can't let him get you down. You did the right thing. Irene, don't ever second-guess a decision you've made as editor. If you do, you'll begin to get queasy about all your decisions. And that, for an editor, is a shortcut to insanity."

"I say," rumbled Joe from the other end of the glider, "he should be keelhauled."

"That," Koesler observed, "should get his attention."

The priest began looking about, apparently searching for someone. "Where," he asked, "has Tommy Thompson gone? I haven't seen him for the past hour or so."

No one could tell in the fading sunlight, but Irene blushed. "Oh," she said, "that's something I've been meaning to tell you: earlier he went over to—"

"—the Brands," Koesler completed, turning the tables.

"That's right."

"Why? I thought you told me—"

"I didn't know. It seems Lee Brand had already called Monsignor Thompson and invited him over today. He just touched base here. What Monsignor really came for was his invitation later in the day at the Brands'."

"Well, that's sort of the emancipation proclamation for me." Koesler symbolically wiped his brow.

"Oh, no," Irene protested.

"But you said the Brands were expecting me. If Lee invited Tommy, he certainly isn't expecting me."

42

ce. Inside the pavilion, she immediately located her
. She hurried to him, dragging Koesler along.

Lee!" she cried, loudly enough to attract the attention
nearby. "This is the one I've been telling you about.
ather Koesler!" She did not inform her husband that he
ll Koesler Bob.

was standing at a table laden with bottles of almost
p brand of liquor known to man.

was the Lee Brand Koesler remembered from all the
Tall, heavy head of grayish hair, tummy tightly pulled
the short, bald, dumpy man Irene had identified as Brand
that day.

is wife and Koesler approached, Brand looked up from
upation of building a drink. His head cocked to one side,
e eyebrow arched elaborately as he gazed pointedly at
r's clothing.

was at a picnic across the lake . . . I didn't know I was
here . . ." It was the doorman revisited.

nd's furrowed brow smoothed. A smile appeared, fol-
by a contagious chuckle. "That's O.K., Father; I've had
ke that. It's cold-shower time."

h, no; I don't need a shower."

e means," Joan translated, "return to the drawing board.
over again."

h."

lay I build you a drink?" Brand asked. "Martini?"

esler nodded.

ry?"

esler nodded again.

e," said Joan, "Irene said Bob here might be able to help
Bunny's wedding."

sler watched fascinated as Brand built the drink. He care-
laced a large ice cube in the glass. He poured in only
dry vermouth to coat the ice. Placing one finger atop
he turned the glass over and shook out the few drops of
th.

t in case we come up with a problem with the ceremony,
w," Joan continued.

"Well . . ." Irene hesitated, ". . . it wasn't Lee. It was Joan,
his wife. And she does expect you."

Koesler shrugged elaborately. "Behind every successful marriage—"

"—there are several anxious mothers!"

———————

It seemed so childish she hated to admit it, but this was an
annual event she eagerly anticipated and almost never missed.

It was the Fourth of July Fireworks Festival. Pat Lennon stood
at the foot of Woodward not far from the Renaissance Center
on the Detroit River. With her was Joe Cox. Arm in arm, they
watched the lavish display of rockets and fireworks.

Three barges were anchored in the river midway between
Detroit and Windsor. Several hundred yards on either side of
the barges, countless power craft and sailboats, large and small,
were anchored, while those aboard enjoyed the display. All
through traffic on that section of the river had been halted.

The festival had begun with a few simple rockets. But im-
posed against the blue-black sky, even they elicited oohs and
aahs from the crowd. Now, almost an hour later, the display was
drawing to a close, and the rocketry became even more breathtaking. Pinks, blues, whites, reds. Pregnant rockets whose explosions had explosions. One could sense the rising exhilaration
of the tens of thousands of spectators.

Cox glanced at Lennon. Her mouth was open in childlike
wonder. She was, he decided again, beautiful in every way. He
put his arm around her shoulder and drew her closer.

It was a good feeling being with Joe. A completed feeling.
Pat had to admit their relationship had stood the test of time.
She also had to admit that Cox had been clairvoyantly correct
earlier in the day when he had uncovered the essential reason
she was reluctant to seal their relationship with marriage. If she
couldn't be married in a Catholic ceremony, she did not wish
any ceremony. And she had been convinced a second Catholic
marriage for her was impossible.

Well, maybe Joe was right. Maybe things had changed enough
so that even she had a chance.

The grand finale. The thunder of explosions multiplied in-

43

credibly. In the vicinity of the river, it was as if daylight had returned. The display ceased, but the rumble of sound echoed through the caverns of downtown Detroit and Windsor.

Spontaneously, the spectators began to applaud, cheer, whistle. The attending boats sounded their horns.

By damn, thought Lennon, buoyed by the excitement, I'll do it!

―――――――

It didn't take long to drive around the curve of Green Lake. In fact, Father Koesler wished it were a greater distance. This was not his favorite type of mission.

He did not like to go where he was not invited and perhaps not even welcome. As far as he could tell, the lady of the house was willing to see him. The gentleman of the house undoubtedly didn't even know he was coming. He did not like to butt into people's affairs. And no one in the Brand family had yet asked him for help. He might be asked to volunteer the name of a young priest who might have very good reason to want not to get involved.

Finally—or at least it was Koesler's final thought as he parked his car several homes removed from the Brand house, which was as close as he could get—he always felt vaguely uncomfortable in the company of the ostentatiously rich.

He did not consider this a virtue. After all, Jesus had seemed at home with the wealthy as well as the common. It was probably, he figured, a reflection of his middle-class upbringing.

Amazing the extent of what he would do when asked by a friend.

A uniformed attendant met him at the door. Koesler wasn't sure whether this was the back or front door. He dismissed the question as irrelevant.

"Your name, please?" The guard did not seem friendly. He had not been hired to be friendly. His job was not so much to greet guests as to exclude gate-crashers.

"Koesler. Robert Koesler."

Using a flashlight, the guard checked a list.

"Is that K-E-S-S-L-E-R?"

"K-O-E-S-L-E-R."

After another moment searching his off the flashlight. "It says here, 'Father priest?" The guard's eye wandered over

"Oh! I was at a picnic today . . . acro why I didn't . . ." Koesler felt foolish. clerical garb. About the only exception he ation. Had he known he was destined to party, he surely would have been in cler reason, he thought, why he should have m Irene's plea.

"You got some identification?"

Koesler found his driver's license and h face so the guard could see his resemblance

The guard nodded, stepped aside, and he

"Thanks." As Koesler entered, he refle most as tough getting in to see Lee Brand as

He was surprised at how few people we living room. Most of the guests must be, h pavilion or at the shore enjoying the delightfu formed waiter offered a tray of cocktail glass some full. He waved them away. This was without trying to balance a glass.

A very tall, very slender, handsome won "May I help you?" she asked.

"I hope so. Irene Casey, who lives across gestured in the general direction of the Casey

"Irene!" she interrupted. "Then you mu Koesler. She's told me all about you. I'm Joa may call me Sunny. Do you mind if I call you

Koesler minded. Especially at a first meet was a Catholic. However, he knew protestati less.

"If you prefer," he said.

"Come. You've got to meet my husban She entwined her arm in his and led him c close she was almost leaning on him.

She was about five-eight or nine. Her p soft, delicate fragrance. Her dress had an

He splashed Steinhager gin over the ice until the glass was nearly full.

"Irene says Bob here may know a priest who would witness Bunny's marriage if all else failed," she concluded.

He cut a peeling from a fresh lemon, rubbed it on the surface of the glass's rim, twisted the peel, and dropped it in the glass. He discarded the rest of the lemon.

"Well, all else is not going to fail." Brand presented the martini to Koesler with just the hint of a flourish. "Not with Monsignor Tommy Thompson a part of our game plan."

"I sincerely hope your prognosis is right on the button." Koesler raised his glass in a toast to his host and hostess.

"Well," said Joan, "you can never be too careful, I always say. Not with Murphy's Law hovering over us all the time."

"I," Koesler affirmed, "am a firm believer in Murphy's Law. And Murphy is as busy within the Catholic Church as he is elsewhere."

"You can't get anywhere with that belt-and-suspenders philosophy. It's damn the torpedoes, full speed ahead, or there's no cream at the top," Brand hybridized.

Koesler guessed that Lee Brand lived by bromide and jargon. Not unlike Koesler's deacon, Les Schroeder.

"C'mon, Father," said Brand. "it's time for you to meet the happy couple, who will, in a few weeks, be married in a Catholic church." He pronounced the last few words in much the same way as God must have said, "Let there be light."

Brand provided the wedge, blocking as he led the way through the crowded pavilion.

"You mustn't mind Lee, Bob," said Joan, as, their arms again entwined, she steered the priest in the wake of her husband's path-clearing. "Lee simply believes he can get anything he wants done. If he can't overcome an obstacle, he figures he can buy it.

"But I'm really worried about this marriage. I've checked with several priests, and none of them was at all hopeful. You see, Richard is Episcopalian, as is his first wife. High Church, mind you. Perhaps you read of their divorce. It was in all the papers."

She looked expectantly at Koesler, but he shook his head. He had never developed a taste for the scandals of the wealthy.

"In any case," Joan continued as she waved to a guest here, presented a cheek to be kissed there, "Richard is not the sort to fiddle with rules and regulations of the 'Roman Church,' as he refers to us. The wedding is scheduled for July 28. That's only a little more than three weeks away. And frankly, I'm getting worried.

"What do you think, Bob? Do you think Monsignor Thompson can pull it off? I mean, given my husband's resources?"

"I really don't know. Some cases are above and beyond the power even of the head of the Tribunal. But I do know that when he wants to be, Monsignor Thompson can be as expeditious as any mandarin."

As they glided through the crowd, exited the pavilion, and neared the lake, Koesler grew ever more self-conscious of his open-necked sport shirt and simple, if neat, blue slacks. He had seldom been among so many chic people.

"Oh," Joan said, "I meant to ask you, do you actually know of some priest who might perform this ceremony if we are unable to get proper Church permission? Sort of a St. Jude-type patron of our hopeless case?" She giggled, as if to discount the possibility of anything's being hopeless to the Brand family.

"Well, I—" Koesler began. But they had reached their target, and Brand was about to introduce his daughter to Koesler. The priest was grateful for the interruption. He had not yet determined whether to drop Shanley's name.

"Father Koesler, this is our daughter Bunny," said Brand. It was obvious Bunny was the apple of her father's eye.

Koesler looked from mother to daughter. Sunny, Bunny, he thought. It figures. "I'm very pleased to meet you, Bunny," he said, wishing she had been introduced by her given name.

"The pleasure is mine, Father," said the bright, blonde, petite, attractive young lady. Then a look of concentrated puzzlement passed over her face. "Say, aren't you connected with the police?"

Koesler laughed. "No. I was somewhat tenuously associated with the Detroit Police Department during a couple of murder investigations. But, in real life—"

"—when you're not being Superpriest?" Bunny broke in.

"—yes, I'm just a pastor in Dearborn Heights."

"And this," Brand led Koesler to an extremely well-built young man an inch or two taller than the priest, "is my soon-to-be son-in-law, Richard Warwick."

Warwick's handshake was considerably more firm than necessary.

He even shakes hands like an Episcopalian, Koesler thought.

"Congratulations," Koesler offered both young people. Then, for the first time, he became conscious of the presence of Monsignor Thompson, who had been standing off to one side of this small group. Thompson held a drink and a scowl.

"You two must know one another," said Brand, gesturing at the two clergymen.

"Tommy."

"Bob."

Each nodded.

A waiter whispered in Brand's ear. He turned to his wife. "Some new guests just arrived, Sunny. Excuse us, folks." They departed, Joan's arm now entwined in her husband's. Koesler was reminded of a vine.

Thompson moved to Koesler's side. "What are you doing here?" he said, in almost a stage whisper.

Koesler smiled. "What do you mean? Do you think we're overpriesting this party?"

The two moved closer to the lake, where they were virtually alone.

"Nobody'll know the party's overpriested the way you look," Thompson chuckled.

"I didn't know I was coming here. I was over at Irene's . . ." Koesler began explaining for the third time. "Oh, the hell with it!"

"So Irene sent you."

"Yes, but I think it was a basic error. By the way, do you think you can do anything about young Richard's first marriage?"

"Don't know." Thompson inserted a finger inside his roman collar and pulled it away from his neck. "Damned uncomfortable uniform, especially in the summer." He returned to Koesler's question. "I talked to him for a while earlier this evening. There may be a *contra bonum prolis* case here."

"Which one didn't want kids?"

"His wife. It would have ruined her tennis game."

"Lots of testimony to gather in a case like that."

"You're telling me! I don't know if Richard's got the patience to go through all the paperwork. I don't know if *I've* got the patience to go through all the paperwork."

"But that's your job," said Koesler, imitating the monotone of "Dragnet," "you're an officialis."

"My job!" said Thompson, disparagingly.

"Do your job well, and they may make you a big fat bishop someday." He would make a good member of the Club, Koesler thought.

"Bishop! Are you kidding? Nothing ever happens to me!"

"Hang in there, Tommy. I have a hunch you're going to be romanced by Lee Brand. And that just might be even better than becoming a bishop."

With that, the two priests parted.

Thompson headed for the liquor table. He was in no danger of being ejected from the party. For one, he had become an intricate element in Brand's latest game plan. For another, his ability to absorb alcohol faultlessly was storied.

Koesler tried to mingle with the guests, but it didn't work. After less than half an hour, he decided to leave. Having joined the gathering unheralded, he felt it was not necessary to seek out his hostess to announce his departure. However, as he neared the door, he was intercepted by Joan Brand.

"Leaving so soon, Bob?"

"Big day tomorrow, Joan."

"Sunny."

"Sunny."

"Before you go, you haven't told me if we've got a clerical St. Jude."

"Oh, could we leave that until or if you've got a bridge to cross? I'd rather not use the man's name in vain without first consulting him. Besides, there's plenty of time for that move."

A slight frown crossed Joan's face. She had not gotten her way. The frown was quickly replaced by a somewhat artificial smile. "Of course, Bob. Now that you know where we live, be sure you stop in again sometime." She hesitated. "But call first."

Koesler nodded and departed. In his wildest imagination, he couldn't envision his returning to the Brand mansion on Green Lake.

She sensed her husband was fighting a foul mood.

"It's just the morning, dear. You'll be able to get to the office by noon," said Pauline Janson.

Fred Janson was driving to Divine Child rectory. Divine Child was their parish. Rather, it was Mrs. Janson's parish. Fred was not Catholic. Nor had the Jansons been married by a Catholic priest. Twenty-seven years before, a kindly judge in Minneapolis had witnessed their consent to marry. It was Pauline's first marriage, and she had wished, with all her heart, that they could have a priest. But it was Fred's second marriage. And so they had had a kindly judge in Minneapolis.

They had raised their children, two daughters, as Catholics. Fred had proudly attended the big occasions: baptisms, first communions, confirmations, marriages, and more baptisms. He and Pauline had endured their children's uncomprehending doubt when parochial teachers had told them repeatedly that their parents were unfortunately headed for hell in the vehicle of an invalid marriage.

Recently, Pauline had been informed by several of her friends that Church court regulations had been relaxed in the wake of the Second Vatican Council. And that it was far easier than it used to be to get a declaration of nullity—that a previous attempt at marriage could be declared null and void. Two weeks ago, she had succeeded in getting Fred to agree, as she had been instructed by the Tribunal downtown, to see her parish priest. They were keeping their appointment this morning, July 5, with Father Leon Cavanaugh, pastor of Divine Child.

Fred Janson was a highly successful corporation lawyer, with offices high in the Renaissance Center giving a breathtaking view of Detroit's east side, the Detroit River spilling out of Lake

51

St. Clair, and that part of Canada that included Windsor and its airport.

Pauline Janson, a small, trim, attractive woman, was as active a member of Divine Child parish as she could be. Any time the church needed cleaning, Pauline was there with bucket and brush. When volunteers were called for almost any task, Pauline was first among them. But no confessions and no communion. And, as party to a canonically invalid marriage, there would likely be a serious problem with Catholic burial.

There was no response to Pauline's observation on the length of time this initial meeting would take. So she tried again. "Try to be patient, dear. This is going to be difficult for all of us."

He reached across and patted her hand. "I know. It's just . . . if I asked you whether you were married to me, would you say no? Maybe? Slightly?"

"We've been over all that, Fred. This is not for us. It's for the Church. So I'll be able to go to confession and communion again."

Fred was well aware of his role in this scenario. He and his first marriage were the sole obstacles to Pauline's reception of her precious sacraments. When he reflected on it, he gained new insights into the suffering of blacks under the implications of being called "nigger." They were not responsible for being black. No more did he consider it his fault he had been involved in a disastrous marriage. No matter; there was a stigma in either case.

"I'll do my best to be cooperative," he said.

She sighed and took his hand in both of hers.

He had parked in the small lot in front of the rectory. Now they were seated in Father Cavanaugh's small office. Fred Janson felt confined. As he was wondering what it would be like working where one lived, Cavanaugh entered. Fred stood to greet him. While Cavanaugh was well-acquainted with Pauline, he had no more than a passing relationship with Fred.

Cavanaugh wore a semi-Jesuitical cassock with large black sash; white French cuffs peeked from the ends of his cassock sleeves. His salt-and-pepper hair was combed flat against his scalp. He had shaved, but a blue shadow of his heavy beard

52

remained. Of moderate height, he had a pronounced paunch, and one shoulder appeared higher than the other.

When all were seated, Cavanaugh took three rectangular pink pamphlets from his center desk drawer. Retaining one, he presented one each to Fred and Pauline. The pamphlet was entitled, "Marriage Annulment Procedures."

This, thought Fred, as he quickly fingered through the pamphlet's six pages, is familiar territory—law.

"You'd have no way of knowing, of course," Father Cavanaugh began, "but the present regulations concerning a possible declaration of nullity aren't what they used to be. But then, nothing is. Church is losing its backbone." His voice had a strong nasal tone.

Pauline made a vaguely supportive noise. Fred continued to study the document and the priest.

"Now, sir," said Cavanaugh, "can you tell me why you think your first marriage might have been null from its beginning?"

Fred shrugged. "To be perfectly frank, Father, I've never perceived it as null from inception. Though for strictly legal purposes I suppose you might contend my wife had to have been in a pre-schizophrenic condition. Of course, none of us knew it at the time, but her condition began to deteriorate shortly after we married. Within eighteen months, she was committed to the Brockport Home in Massachusetts. It's only within the last five years we've been able to keep her at Providence House, an extended care unit."

"And," Pauline added, "Fred has seen to her financial care all these years."

"It really was the least I could do. I loved her. I just couldn't continue to live with her as a husband. No one could. So, a few years after she entered the sanatorium, I divorced her. It meant nothing to Nancy. She was in another world. That's about it, Father."

Cavanaugh adjusted his thick glasses. "Very well, Mr. Janson. Now, let me call your attention to a few relevant considerations you will find in this pamphlet.

"In the third paragraph, 'We believe that your previous marriage, although painful and hurt-filled, is sacred as well.' I point that out to disabuse you of the notion that your case may seem of the open-and-shut variety. The Church considers it 'sacred,' and the burden of proof that it was null from its beginning is upon us.''

''Us?''

''Yes. I call your attention to *d. Mandate*. 'This is the agreement of your parish priest to serve as your advocate (the person who argues for the nullity of your marriage).' So,'' Cavanaugh exhibited what passed as a smile, ''in effect, I am your attorney.''

Janson did not comment but continued to page through the pamphlet. He read aloud: ''The description of the second session of the formal stage states that, 'The Defender of the Bond is present. It is his task to defend the validity of your marriage.' ''

''That is correct.'' Cavanaugh blinked behind his bottle-bottom lenses.

''The title, Defender of the Bond, sounds to me as though it is a trained position. May I assume the gentleman who holds that position is trained in canon law . . . indeed, that he holds a degree in canon law?''

''That is correct.''

''And you, Father?''

''Me?''

''What background do you have in law?''

''Just four years of training in the seminary. But that should be sufficient.''

''To go up against a professional? Father, I think the Church is stacking the deck.''

''You're forgetting faith!'' Cavanaugh had always found that to be the equalizer. If faith could move mountains, it surely could produce justice in a Tribunal.

''Now, another thing,'' he continued, ''from what you've told me, your first wife has had psychiatric treatment.'' Janson nodded. ''And, in that connection, have you had therapeutic counseling?'' Again Janson nodded. ''I will have to write the therapists and the institutions for confidential summaries of the treatment.''

Janson made no comment. He knew that as the number of people who shared confidential matters grew, the less likely

54

were those matters to remain confidential. But once he had agreed to participate in this procedure, there was nothing he could do to prevent this.

"One final question." Many more than one question occurred to Janson, but he could, by now, surmise the answer to most of them. "It states here that if I am granted an annulment, after all this the Defender of the Bond is required to appeal the verdict of the Tribunal to Cincinnati, where the verdict must be affirmed by two appellate church courts before Pauline and I can have our marriage blessed."

"That is correct."

"Isn't that going a bit far to establish nullity?"

"The Church, Mr. Janson, is concerned solely with the protection of the sacraments."

Try as he might, Janson could not understand why sacraments should require protecting. If one wished to believe in them, they were given by God to be used or abused. People profited or demeaned themselves depending on their approach to the sacraments.

Janson began writing the suggested check for $300. "To whom shall I make this out?"

"To the Tribunal. You understand," Cavanaugh hastened to add, "that if you could not afford that, you would pay only what you could afford, or even nothing."

"I understand that secretaries must eat."

Janson and his wife rose to leave.

"By the way, Father," said Janson, "you mentioned earlier that these regulations had been relaxed. How could they possibly have been more harsh?"

"Well, for one thing," Cavanaugh held the door to his office for them, "in my day, couples like yourself were required to promise to live as brother and sister for the duration of their case."

"That's barbaric!" Janson was shocked.

"In any case, Monsignor Thompson allowed the requirement to fall into desuetude. Actually," he almost smiled, "I think he simply couldn't get these young priests to enforce it."

"Monsignor Thompson," said Janson. "Is he the chief judge mentioned in the pamphlet?"

Cavanaugh nodded.

"Why," Janson observed, "he has practically the power of life or death on these cases at every moment. That's an awful lot of power."

"Perhaps," said Cavanaugh as he saw his visitors out the front door. "But they tell me Detroit's Tribunal handles more cases than that of just about any other diocese in the country."

Janson considered that comparable to a pool attendant's telling a would-be swimmer it was safe to get into the pool because the shark in the water was pretty benevolent. The point is there shouldn't be a shark in the pool.

The Jansons departed with Father Cavanaugh's promise that he would mail all the necessary forms and applications to the Tribunal.

2

THOMAS THOMPSON WAS BORN DECEMBER 11, 1927. His father, Gregory, was chauffeur to one of the founders of one of the Big Three auto companies. The Thompson family lived comfortably in the chauffeur's home on the magnate's estate.

Young Tom grew up only a hair's breadth from inconceivable wealth. Regularly, he was the playmate of the magnate's grandchildren. But when play ended, Tommy returned to the modest quarters of the family chauffeur, while the scions retired to the mansion. His carefree older brother Pete took all this in stride. However, the recurrent dichotomy troubled Tommy to his very core.

The tycoon's grandchildren got the best education money could buy. Tom Thompson took the bus to St. Ambrose parochial school in Grosse Pointe. The enormous difference in the lifestyle of his father's employer's family and the Thompsons made a deep and lasting impression on Tom.

After graduation from St. Ambrose High, he entered Sacred Heart Seminary. The fact that Latin had not been emphasized in his parochial education forced him to repeat his senior year. Thus, he had become a classmate of Robert Koesler. They, along with thirty-seven others, were ordained Detroit diocesan priests June 4, 1954.

Father Thompson's first assignment was as assistant at St.

57

Veronica's in East Detroit. In 1959, he was given the special appointment as notary in the Tribunal. The following year he was sent to Rome, where, in 1962, he was awarded a licentiate in canon law. That same year Father Koesler became editor of the *Detroit Catholic*.

Thompson continued at the Tribunal, and in 1965 was named vice officialis, second in command. From then on, it was only a matter of time before he would become head of the marriage court. In 1966, he was named monsignor, a title that carried no additional responsibilities but was very impressive, especially to most lay people. Finally, in 1970 he became officialis.

Almost no one does anything for one reason alone. One of the reasons—although almost a subconscious one—that Monsignor Thompson had become a priest was that the vocation to the priesthood, more than any other, effectively broke down every social barrier. A priest, of whatever color or variety, was at least initially welcome anywhere. He was greeted with missionary openness by the few black Catholics of the inner city. Or he could be treated with respect by the Fishers, the DuPonts, the Rockefellers, or the Fords. It was with these latter groups that Thompson frequently could be found.

He enjoyed the power inherent in the position of officialis. Almost at whim he could make people deliriously happy and grateful or crush their hopes and spirits. Ordinarily, he did not intervene to exercise this authority. He had four priests assigned full-time to his office, and he could call on the services of twenty other priests as judges or prosecutor-advocates. However, from time to time, he would flex his judicial muscles.

The problem with power, in addition to its tendency to corrupt, is its precariousness. No one remains powerful forever. And Thompson knew that just as he had climbed the Tribunal ladder to its peak, so one day would someone else. The prospect of losing his position disquieted Thompson. So he seldom thought about it.

Thompson, like most priests, did not earn much money. A base salary plus fifty dollars per year increment and allowances put his annual income at approximately $7,400.00. By contemporary standards not much. But ordinarily priests do not need much. Room and board are provided. Most priests are not

58

charged for medical or dental services. And the perquisites can go on endlessly. Some priests live with and as the poorest of the poor. And some live as the richest of the rich. The priesthood, more than almost any other calling, is what one makes of it. And there is a rainbow of possibilities.

By almost anyone's standard, Monsignor Thompson lived well. His vehicle was always a late-model Cadillac. He was faithful to clerical black but in the $300-per-suit style. Principally, he had become close friends with several of the movers and shakers of the Detroit scene. Thus, he lived at their level. A ride in a private jet with a GM or Ford executive for golf at Pebble Beach with a tournament professional—all gratis—was not uncommon.

What young Tommy Thompson could only dream—that after the football game he could accompany the tycoon's grandchildren into the mansion—Monsignor Thomas Thompson had accomplished.

The good news was that Deacon Les Schroeder had told Mary O'Connor that he was going to take several days off. The bad news was that neither of them had told anyone else. Thus, the absence was both a surprise and a source of frustration to Father Koesler. He had intended to get to the bottom of this Worthington-Cicero wedding planned for August 4 immediately. Koesler was certain Schroeder had this delicate situation decidedly out of control.

But instead of settling the issue or, at least learning how bad it was, he'd had to cool his heels while awaiting the deacon's return.

Evidently, Schroeder had returned late the previous night.

Between the eight and ten A.M. Masses, Koesler ascertained that Schroeder was in his bed on the screened side porch. Between the ten A.M. and noon Masses, Koesler made arrangements to speak with Schroeder immediately following the baptisms that followed noon Mass.

It was early afternoon. And such a temperate day, rare for a July 8 in Michigan, that Koesler decided to take his deacon for a walk. They began strolling past the church toward the large playground.

"Les, what I really want to talk to you about is this Worthington-Cicero marriage you've got scheduled here."

Schroeder thought a few moments. "Oh, yes," he recalled, "Dale and Anna Maria. Fine young couple."

"Impeded young couple."

"What?"

"Young Dale, Les. He has an impediment to marriage. He's been married before."

"That may be," said Schroeder triumphantly, "but he's never been baptized."

They had reached the playground. A group of eighth-graders was playing a pickup game of hardball. Koesler made a mental note to beware errant line drives.

"Les, that is a major canonical case with major problems. What someone is trying to prove here is that something—namely, baptism—didn't happen. Do you realize how difficult it is to prove that something didn't happen?"

Schroeder pondered the matter in silence. Which was rare.

"Did you prepare this case, Les?"

"No. Somebody—I think it was the pastor—over at Divine Child."

"You don't even know how the case has been presented. You don't know how strong or weak it is. And, worst of all, you don't know its present disposition. Is it on the bottom or top of whose pile in Rome? Does it have the remotest chance of being granted? Finally, might it be refused? Supposing August 4 arrives, and there is no dispensation. Then what?"

Schroeder paused. "I suppose . . . some paraliturgical rite . . ."

"Paraliturgical . . . paraliturgical . . . bullshit!" Koesler exploded. "You may not realize this, but by accepting this wedding and giving it a firm date when Leon Cavanaugh refused them, you have attracted Father Cavanaugh's undivided attention. If that couple gets any kind of Catholic ceremony without a dispensation from Rome, *you* are going to be part of the ecclesial diaspora!"

"Hey, Father! Hey, Father!" called the young pitcher from the mound. "Wanna take a cut?"

"Yeah, c'mon, Father," chorused the others, "let's see ya tag one!"

Koesler couldn't resist. He was so put out with Schroeder he wanted to tag something.

"Well, just one." He removed his watch, sampled several bats, selected the heaviest, and stepped to the plate. "Now, no fooling around," he admonished the tow-headed pitcher. "I'm not standing here to study any curves, sliders, spitters, or screwballs. Just lay one over the middle with nothing on it."

The youngster did just that.

Muscles remembering more than he had any right to hope for, Koesler met the ball solidly. It shot like a bullet over the shortstop's outstretched glove, heading toward the left field foul line. As it neared the left fielder, it took on new life and rose again. It touched ground for the first time just in fair territory near the rear corner of the church and went skipping merrily toward Outer Drive.

The players looked at Koesler with awe. None said a word.

Koesler casually flung the bat onto the pile of baseball paraphernalia, rejoined Schroeder, and departed as if this stroke of luck were routine.

"Remarkable hit," Schroeder observed.

"Nothing to it." The hit had exhilarated Koesler.

"But getting back to old Dale and Anna Maria; they've got to be warned. It may come to a point when there is nothing we can do."

Silence. More walking.

"Les, I'll take care of this under one condition: that you never, ever do a damn-fool thing like this again. Any marriage you handle, as long as you're at St. Anselm's, if it has the slightest hint of a problem, you consult me. Agreed?"

"Agreed," breathed a grateful deacon.

They walked on again in silence.

"Oh," said Schroeder, "I meant to tell you, it turned out like I expected."

"What did?"

"My youth ministry in the parish."

"Oh?"

"Yes. As soon as word got around that we could serve no more booze, I got overwhelming feedback that the gang is not going to show up anymore."

Koesler fought to suppress a grin. "So, now that your booze has run dry, your companions have abandoned you. Does that remind you of anything, Les?"

"What should it remind me of?"

"Les, I welcome you home with the same open-hearted spirit with which the father in the Gospel welcomed home his prodigal son. With one exception."

"What's that?"

"We're not going to kill the fatted calf to celebrate this occasion."

———————

"Ahm fear he gonna die, Fatha. And if he do, we gonna have all kinda trouble bury him in de church."

Leroy Sanders, the object of his wife Elvira's concern, sat impassively alongside her in the office of Father Norman Shanley in Our Lady of the Rosary rectory. Leroy was, as he had been throughout his life, at the mercy of a white man. Short, bald, very black, his noncommittal eyes clouded by cataracts, Leroy was content to wait and see what this white priest would do to him. Experience had taught him to expect nothing but, perhaps, evil.

Elvira, in her sixties, was in a constant state of concern for Leroy, in his eighties. She had been raised a Catholic in New Orleans. Leroy had never even been baptized. They had been married thirty-five years before by a Baptist minister in that birthplace of jazz.

"Now, Mrs. Sanders," Shanley drummed the eraser of his pencil against the desk top, "you say your husband went through a complete set of instructions in the Catholic faith?"

"Oh, yessuh, Fatha. We done dat in New Orleans. But den, when we got done, the Fatha dere he ask Leroy if he ever bin marry before." She chuckled. "Why, he bin marry three time when he young buck. He one time one young strong buck, though he don't seem so now." She gave her husband a playful shove. He looked at her, the shadow of a smile playing briefly at his lips.

"O.K., Mrs. Sanders. Then what did the priest in New Orleans do after he found out that Mr. Sanders had been married three times?" Shanley glanced out the window. It was a gloomy Monday morning. A hard summer rain beat down. Pools of water had been gathering around the feet of Mr. and Mrs. Sanders. Evidently, they had no umbrella.

"Nuthin', not nuthin'." She spread her hands in a gesture of emptiness. "Dat priest, he say Leroy can't git baptized 'cause Leroy livin' with me. Actual', we git marry before dat by dat Baptist minister I tole you 'bout. But dat priest, he say we livin' in sin." She paused and gazed at her hands, now resting in her lap. "He say," she continued, "dat priest, he say he can't baptize Leroy 'cause baptism take all sin away, but Leroy livin' in sin wid me."

Shanley was familiar with the reasoning. As far as Church law was concerned, the New Orleans priest had been on sound ground. He might have looked more carefully at Mr. Sanders's previous marriages to check their validity. Then there was the fact that Sanders had never been baptized. The priest might have instituted a "privilege of the faith" case. But that would have meant considerable trouble and quite possibly might have been fruitless.

Shanley had before him a couple whose union had endured thirty-five years, no small commitment. They were in love. That tested and true love that lasts long past mere physical attraction. They had been true to each other in good times and in bad, for richer or poorer, in sickness and in health. And now they were worried about being parted by death. What was it St. John had written? "God is love. And he who abides in love, abides in God and God in him." These two must be one with God. All they lacked was peace of soul.

"Well, now, Mrs. Sanders. Things have changed."

"They has?" Elvira was apprehensive. She had no idea in which direction the priest was going.

"Yes, they have. I'm sure you have heard of the Second Vatican Council."

"What dat?"

"You haven't. Well, some years ago, the bishops from all around the world got together in Rome for a meeting." He observed she was following him closely, nodding as she understood. He spoke very slowly, trying to select simple words.

"And," Shanley continued, "they changed a lot of rules and regulations so that good people like you and Mr. Sanders could have an easier time of it." Again, agape, she nodded. Actually, thought Shanley, the bishops had not come nearly as far as he had. But they should have.

"So, Mrs. Sanders, to make a long story short, what we can do is we can go over to the church and we can baptize Leroy and that will take care of everything. Leroy will be baptized, and your marriage will be blessed, and everything will be grand. The two of you can go to communion every time you come to church for the rest of your lives."

Tears trickled down Elvira's cheeks. "You means you can do all dat for Leroy and me?"

"That's right!" He had never tried this tack before. But it seemed to be working like magic.

The three made their way through the rectory and the passage to the church. All the while, Elvira was excitedly and repeatedly explaining this wonder to Leroy.

Once in the church, Shanley pulled a surplice and stole over his black cassock, opened the baptistery, took out the holy oil, salt, and cloths, and lit the paschal candle.

Slowly, he went through the ritual of baptism for an adult, pausing to explain each step so Leroy could acknowledge his understanding of what was taking place.

Baptism accomplished, the couple knelt for Shanley's blessing.

"That's it," said Shanley. "All done."

"We is O.K. ?" Elvira asked shyly.

"You are perfect," said Shanley.

Tears now streaming down his craggy cheeks, Leroy grasped with surprising strength Shanley's reluctant right hand, and kissed it.

Mr. and Mrs. Leroy Sanders slowly walked out of Rosary church arm in arm into the rain.

All Shanley could think of was the classic scene of Gene Kelly splashing through a cloudburst. Leroy and Elvira were too old and tired for that now. But Shanley was sure their hearts were singing and dancing in the rain.

Monsignor Thompson reclined in the overstuffed low-slung red chair, nursing a chilled vintage Chablis and his feelings.

He had been a few minutes early for his noon luncheon date with Lee Brand at the superposh Renaissance Club. Now, at a quarter past twelve, Brand still had not arrived.

To Thompson—and, probably to Brand—jockeying for position at a luncheon was not unlike that ritual conducted by prize-fighters before a match. The champion should be the last to enter the ring. But an intimidating challenger will try to outjuke the champ and arrive in the ring last but by no means least.

Thompson contemplated his surroundings. He had not been here before. He was tempted to paraphrase the motto of the State of Michigan: If you seek a pleasant restaurant, look around you. Located on the Renaissance Center's twenty-sixth floor, the club offered cheery decor, comfortable elegance, and a vista that included much of downtown Detroit and a healthy chunk of southwest Ontario. The waiters and waitresses were mostly young and seemed bright, courteous, and efficient.

It was a private club, and Brand belonged to it. Until now, Thompson had read nothing between the lines of Brand's invitation. But as the minutes passed and Brand became more than stylishly late, Thompson began to wonder if this was an exercise in oneupmanship.

Actually, he heard Brand coming before he saw him. The greetings of "Good afternoon, Mr. Brand," and "How are you, Mr. Brand?" grew louder as the subject swept nearer. Finally, he appeared, followed closely by an attentive maitre d'.

"Monsignor," Brand spread his arms expansively, "so sorry to keep you waiting, but I had a live one in the office. Not megabucks, maybe, but definitely a satisfier. Henry," he turned to the maitre d', "our table is ready?" It was more statement than question.

"Of course, Mr. Brand. This way."

Thompson gathered his Chablis and followed to what had to

65

be the best table in the house. It was at a window whose view created the illusion of being over the center of the Detroit River. On the table was a welcoming martini. Thompson noted the single large ice cube and the twist of lemon. Precisely Brand's formula. The other evening at the party, he'd watched Brand build countless martinis of the same mode.

"I trust I didn't keep you waiting too long, Monsignor. Another—what is that—Chablis?"

Thompson nodded, noting Brand's ebullience.

"Henry, bring a bottle for the Monsignor. Monte de Milieu, '77." He turned to Thompson. "Decent but not outstanding." He glanced back at the poised Henry. "And, while we're waiting, another of these." He pointed at the martini.

"Of course, Mr. Brand."

"I hope you didn't mind meeting here, Monsignor. I thought since we both work downtown, and this is a pleasant place . . ." Brand's index finger slowly revolved the ice cube.

"Of course. So, you had a live one." Thompson got Brand's meaning, even though some of his jargon remained in its natural obfuscated state.

Brand swallowed gin with appreciative satisfaction. "Yes, a gentleman I met, for the first time, as a matter of fact, at the party the other night. Talked him into transferring to SB&T on the spot. We were able to candle his assets last Friday. Fellow named Wilson—Jim Wilson. Know him?"

Thompson, in mid-sip, shook his head.

Simultaneously, a waiter arrived with Brand's second martini—Thompson would keep accurate count—and Thompson's Monte de Milieu '77. The sommelier opened the bottle, presented the cork successfully, and poured a sample. Definitely an improvement, Thompson concluded.

"In any case," Brand continued, "Wilson just deposited $400,000 savings, $150,000 checking, and," Brand smiled as a matador delivering the *estocada*, "his wife's account."

Thompson raised his glass. "Then, congratulations."

"Thanks." Brand concluded his second martini. The empty glass was immediately replaced by a fresh successor. "Not megabucks, as I said, but a helluva kick up from psychic compensation. If you'll pardon my French."

Thompson smiled pardon.

"Speaking of the party," said Brand, "what did you think of the kids, Dick and Bunny?"

"Splendid couple."

"Did you get a chance to talk with Dick?" Brand knew very well of their conversation.

"Yes, we talked a little business earlier in the evening." Thompson knew Brand knew. Joining in the game, the Monsignor decided to fudge a trifle.

"Well, what do you think, Monsignor; will it take long to clear this matter?"

Thompson admired Brand's approach. Not, is there any hope? Is it possible? Can you possibly? Just, how long?

"I can't predict that." Thompson refilled his glass, took a breadstick, and wondered when menus would be presented. "I hate to sound like the quintessential doctor, but it is impossible to give any kind of positive prognosis at this time and in a case like this. It's something like asking how long it takes to get to Chicago. It depends. Are you going to walk, drive, fly? And, at any moment, the trip may be canceled."

Two angry vertical lines formed on Brand's forehead. People did not give him ambiguous answers. When he wanted something, people performed.

"What seems to be the problem, Monsignor?" His voice was cold. He pushed the martini to one side.

Thompson caught the symbolism. A friendly luncheon had been tabled until this business matter was resolved. And resolved in Brand's favor. Under the frigid gaze of Brand's blue eyes, Thompson subconsciously wilted.

"Well, now, Mr. Brand," Thompson shifted his wine glass back and forth. "I didn't mean to imply that the boy's case is impossible. Only that the time element is directly related to the cooperation—or lack of cooperation—of the witnesses who will have to be interviewed."

"There are ways of assuring cooperation, don't you think, Monsignor?"

"Well, I'm sure there are in some cases. But sometimes, if a witness wants to be stubborn, there's little we can do about it. We haven't even the authority of civil law."

"When money is no object," Brand was speaking menacingly, so softly Thompson could barely hear him, "there are ways of assuring cooperation. Don't you think, Monsignor?"

Thompson took counsel with himself. He had never considered pouring an unlimited amount of money into a marriage case. But in the final analysis, he had to agree with Brand: he could think of little that money couldn't buy.

"Now that you mention it in that context, Mr. Brand, I'd have to say the prospect of success is considerably enhanced. We'll go back to the drawing board with a lot more enthusiasm."

Brand retrieved his martini. Though not smiling, at least the furrows in his brow had smoothed.

"That's more encouraging, Monsignor. And when this is all over, there will be something for your favorite charity." Brand winked.

Thompson raised his glass in salute. Brand matched the salute and finished martini number three.

The waiter arrived instantly with a fresh martini—Thompson noted it was the fourth—and menus.

Thompson perused the menu. Everything looked good. No prices were listed. A nice touch. Thompson would continue to count. It would be a bottle of Monte de Milieu '77 and a six-martini lunch.

Angela Cicero needed assertiveness training almost as badly as had Genghis Khan, Koesler concluded.

The conversation had begun well enough, especially for a rainy, sultry Monday afternoon. Mrs. Cicero had been calm, almost passive. But as Koesler continued to explain the treacherous ground over which a privilege of the faith case must pass, she grew visibly apprehensive.

He had shown her the Epistle passage on which this case was founded. He explained that canon law considered Dale Worthington's first marriage to be valid but not sacramental, because Dale had not been baptized in order to receive any other sacrament. Thus, Dale, since he had not been baptized, could enter a *valid* marriage but not a *sacramental* marriage. Once the case had been prepared and Rome had approved it, Dale could be baptized and enter a sacramental marriage with Anna Maria. At the moment the sacramental marriage was witnessed, Dale's previous nonsacramental marriage would be automatically dissolved in favor of the sacramental marriage. Thus, a privilege of the faith.

That was the part during which Mrs. Cicero was calm.

Koesler then proceeded to recount horror stories of cases hopelessly buried in Rome. Of cases that, due to Church policy or some hierarchical whim, were refused. There simply was no known way of confidently predicting when or even if a marriage case sent to Rome would be approved and returned. And that, undoubtedly, was the reason Father Cavanaugh at Divine Child refused to give Dale and Anna Maria a firm wedding date.

That was the part during which Mrs. Cicero hit the floor and the ceiling simultaneously.

"What do you mean, no firm date?" Mrs. Cicero leaned forward in her chair in Koesler's small office. "Deacon Les *gave* them a firm date. They are supposed to be married August 4 at 3 P.M. right here in this church!"

"Deacon Les was trying to be kind. But he's young, and he has very little experience, especially in a case like this. Privilege of the faith cases do not come along very often."

"But . . . but we've got the hall rented!"

"The hall?"

"For the reception!"

Strange, thought Koesler, how many weddings were scheduled around the rental of a hall. So much for sentiment.

"I'm sure, in a pinch," he said, "that they would return your deposit."

"That's not the point. That's not the point at all! The hall is rented, the invitations are ready to go out, there have been showers and parties, and we have a firm date here for August 4 at 3 P.M.!"

Mrs. Cicero was an attractive, if momentarily angry, woman in her late forties. Koesler had dealt with mothers who display a special defensive anger when one of their children is threatened or in trouble. This lady was a stereotype.

"Mrs. Cicero, all I can tell you are the facts. This is reality. My advice is that you forget about August 4 and have Dale and

69

Anna Maria wait till they receive the decree from Rome and then set their wedding date."

The set of her jaw clearly showed that she was not about to follow this advice.

"Or," he continued, "you can count on Rome to act before August 4 and bank on the wedding's coming off as scheduled. And that is only twenty-six days from now. But I hasten to assure, if Rome has not acted, we cannot have the wedding. I ask you to consider the grief on everybody's part if the wedding would have to be postponed at the last minute."

He had dismissed the possibility the young couple might turn to a civil ceremony if the Church did not come through. He did not believe this Italian mother would permit such a thing. And his money was on this Italian mother's running this show.

Mrs. Cicero fumbled with the snap of her purse as she agonized over a decision that should not be hers, but was.

"In fairness," Koesler continued after a few moments' silence, "I should tell you I called Monsignor Thompson earlier today. He's the head of the matrimonial court for the archdiocese. I told him about our special problem. He remembers the case. Says it was very well prepared. He promised he would check with Rome on its progress. He also insisted he could guarantee nothing."

Koesler did not think it necessary to mention that Thompson had been initially furious and that only Koesler's good offices had saved Deacon Schroeder from being hung by his testicles until dead, a form of punishment suggested by Thompson.

"We will have that wedding on August 4 if I have to go to Rome and get that permission from the Pope personally!" She said it in somewhat the same manner that MacArthur mentioned returning to the Philippines.

"If that is your decision, Mrs. Cicero," said Koesler. "But let's understand each other: no permission, no wedding."

Actually, normally he would have been willing to bend a few rules, but not after Rome had entered the picture. Rome was prone to take a proprietary interest in cases that made their way to the Vatican.

As Mrs. Cicero was about to leave, she turned back in the

doorway. "This monsignor," she asked, "the head of the matrimonial court; what did you say his name is?"

"Thompson. Monsignor Thompson."

Poor Tommy, thought Koesler; he'll never know what hit him.

"Come on, Father, burn it in there!"

Father David Neiss knew he was scarcely burning it in anywhere. It was just a pickup game of baseball in Divine Child's playground. On his way from the church to the rectory, he had been passing the baseball diamond when a group of eighth- and ninth-graders had invited him to play. For the past hour, during a break in the intermittent showers, he'd been working up considerable sweat as pitcher for the No-Name All-Stars. His velocity was not even of minor league character, but it was sufficient to impress the youth of Divine Child.

"Come on, Father, burn it in there! Hey, batter, batter!" the small catcher chanted.

Father burned it in there. The batter hit a lazy grounder to the shortstop, who shoveled the ball to the second baseman. Attempting to complete a double play, he rifled the ball several feet over the first baseman's outstretched glove.

Tinker to Evers to Chance, thought Neiss. Schwager to Dacey to hell-and-gone.

The priest checked his watch—11:45. Hell! He'd be late for lunch. Failure in promptitude, as far as Father Cavanaugh was concerned, ranked with murder and forgetting grace before or after meals as sins that cried to heaven for vengeance.

"Sorry, gang, I've got to leave now." Neiss dropped his borrowed glove on the mound.

Donny Schwager trotted in and walked the priest to the foul line.

"I've been wondering, Father," said Donny, intently, "how come you priests are so good at sports?"

More often than not, priests are at least moderately acquainted with sports, Neiss reflected. Though that would be more true of the older, macho priests than of the laid-back modern variety.

Arriving at no scientific response, Neiss said the first thing that came to mind. "Donny, we do that instead of girls."

"Oh."

He shouldn't have participated in the game, Neiss told himself as he hurried to the rectory. It was as hot and sticky as a July 16 should be in southeast Michigan. Common courtesy demanded that he shower before lunch. And that would make him even more late.

For a moment, he pondered the fact that, now in his late twenties, he should be so concerned over the wrath of his pastor, who was acting out a bad case of arrested adolescence. But then, he figured, other men and women who worked in large bureaucracies probably had to put up with the same. And he was doing it for God.

"Lunch, Father, is at noon." Cavanaugh did not look up from spooning his soup. "Promptly," he added.

"Sorry." Neiss glanced at his watch. It was only ten after twelve. But, he had to admit, it was not noon. He was washed but still perspiring from the heat of the shower.

Cavanaugh glanced at him sharply. "I do not think it seemly, Father, for a priest to be playing ball all day."

"It was only an hour, Father." The soup, which had been deposited on the table promptly at noon, as was the case with all food whether his chair was occupied or not, was still warm. There were cold cuts and bread on the table. And that was lunch.

"Parishioners who might pass by would think that's all you have to do."

Outside of "busy work" and fairly uselessly ringing doorbells, playing ball this morning was as apostolic a mission as he could imagine. However, he wisely decided to say nothing.

"Did you get my note this morning?"

"Yes, Father." Neiss wished Cavanaugh had not mentioned the note. It had gotten this Monday off to a very bad beginning. That note and its childish detail!

"Did you put the hosts in the ciborium?"

"Yes, Father."

"Did you put the ciborium on the altar?"

"Yes, Father." God, he was repeating the instructions on the note line for line.

"And did you consecrate them during Mass?"

"Yes." He said it more loudly than necessary.

A few moments of blessed silence.

"Another thing, Father." Cavanaugh had finished his soup and was making the single open-faced sandwich that would conclude his lunch. "Sister Mary Patrick told me you've been bothering her about admitting another high school student."

"It's the football team, Father. Coach Blaszczyk is high on this prospect. It would be to our benefit if we admitted him. It's just one more student."

"When the school is filled, it's filled."

"But Father, the football program supports all the rest of our sports."

"When the school is filled, it's filled."

"Father Neiss," Mrs. Blackford, the housekeeper, interrupted, "there's someone on the phone for you. He says he's from the Tribunal. Do you want to take it?"

"Yes." That would be the end of the soup. By the time he returned, it would be too cold to be appetizing. He dreaded facing Blaszczyk should he fail to get the coach's behemothian prospect into school. All over "some goddamn girl." Neiss smiled at Blaszczyk's pejorative term.

"Hi, Dave. This is Ed Oleksiak."

Two years older than Neiss, Oleksiak was a notary at the Tribunal. Some months before, Neiss had been sent a routine notary commission by Oleksiak who, oddly, had misspelled his own name at the bottom of the letter. Neiss had circled the misspelling in red ink, marked the letter "98%" and returned it. Shortly after, there came a phone call pleading that the story not be spread. Oleksiak was informed it was too late for that, that Neiss had already told everyone he could think of. Despite which, the two were fairly fast friends.

"Yeah, Ed; hot enough for you?"

"Plenty. Listen, what I'm calling about is that dispensation case you sent us."

"Which one?" Neiss had sent many.

There was a pause while Oleksiak consulted documents on his desk. "Kirwan vs. Kukulski."

"What about it?"

"The Monsignor wants you to get a B Form on the former wife, Ruth Kukulski."

"A B Form? No, no, Ed; you must be mistaken. That's a defect of form case. You've got all the necessary documents; proof of her Catholic baptism with no notation of Catholic marriage, their record of civil marriage and divorce. You don't need testimony from the wife." While he knew he was correct, he began to feel a nameless anxiety as he recalled the assurances he'd given Harry Kirwan that his former wife would not be questioned.

"New rule, Dave. In cases like this, we need a B Form."

"Why?"

"Polish."

"Polish?"

"That's right. The Monsignor claims that nine times out of ten when a Polish person gets involved in a civil marriage, he or she will have it convalidated. And that's especially true if it's a woman who's in the invalid marriage."

"That's insane, Ed. If she had had the marriage convalidated, there would be a notation of it in her baptismal record and on her baptismal certificate. Look at the date on that baptismal certificate. It was issued just a few weeks ago!"

"Sometimes there are slipups. What's the big to-do about this? All we want is a B Form with her sworn statement that the marriage was never convalidated."

"You don't understand, Ed." Neiss was perspiring freely. It was no longer due to the day's heat. "I promised Mr. Kirwan there would be no contacting his former wife. When anything like that happens, she always manages to make life miserable for him—and their kids."

There was a pause. "I'm really sorry, Dave. But you've got to do it. Monsignor Thompson has made it Tribunal policy, and I know from experience there are no exceptions. You're going to have to get that B Form."

The usually mild-mannered David Neiss exploded. "Like hell I've got to get it. I've had enough of this bullshit! It's a goddamn asinine policy, and I'm not about to do it. Let me talk to Thompson. I want to tell that son-of-a-bitch personally!"

"Now Dave, calm down. I'm going to do you a really big

favor and not let you talk to Thompson. Thus, I will avert two cases of apoplexy. Dave, I know how distasteful this is going to be, but it's got to be done. Do it. Get it out of the way, and your ecclesial career will progress unchecked. Believe me, Dave, there's nothing you can do about this."

There was no reply.

"Dave, I'm sorry."

The phone was dead. Neiss stood motionless, receiver in hand. He would not have a sandwich. He had lost his appetite.

"I think all priests should wear T-shirts," said Father Joe Shanahan, "with some sort of identification stenciled on them. Like 'Thirteenth Century' or 'Sixth Century' . . ."

". . . or 'Twenty-Fifth Century,' " Father Robert Stirling contributed.

Shanahan and Stirling, priests in their early-to-mid-thirties, were lunching in the large ornate dining room on the eighth floor of St. Aloysius rectory.

Downtown St. Al's, as it was popularly known, was unique in the archdiocese. Located just off the heart of one of the busiest sections of downtown, the out-of-place building housed, besides the triple-decked church, the archbishop's office, the Chancery, the Tribunal, and other administrative offices. It also held many residence rooms, most of which were unoccupied.

Shanahan was director of the Catholic Youth Organization. Stirling was a notary assigned to the Tribunal.

One could never be sure who would be at table at St. Al's. There were so many downtown restaurants that the priests assigned to the parish or who worked in the building lunched there irregularly. Then there were usually visitors.

Today's diners, thus far, in addition to Shanahan and Stirling, were Archbishop Mark Boyle, Monsignor Thompson, and Father William Cunneen.

Thompson's was a most rare appearance in this dining room. He had nothing against the food, which fell somewhere between gourmet and so-so. At least there was an attractive variety. One of Thompson's two objections to meals at St. Al's was the absence of any alcoholic beverage, at least at lunch. Lunch or

75

dinner without wine was, to Thompson, barbaric. He could not understand why Boyle, who enjoyed a Rob Roy before and wine during dinner, and who was reputed to have an enormous tolerance for alcohol, did not break this abstemious tradition.

His second reservation involved the table talk. He found it too religious-oriented. He preferred the cosmopolitan flavor of Al Braemar, Vice President of Ford Motor Company, or the in-house gossip of Tony Vermiglio, head of P.R. at General Motors. In either case, conversation was spiced with the presence of high finance. Now he found himself liquorless and listening to a conversation regarding dated T-shirts. It was enough to drive a man to drink. Which he vowed would happen later this afternoon.

"Or, perhaps, 'Vatican Council One,' " suggested Shanahan.

"Or 'Trent,' " Stirling contributed.

"Or 'Council of Jerusalem.' "

"Or 'Vatican III.' "

"What in the world are you guys getting at?" asked an irritated Thompson.

"Oh," Stirling, Thompson's assistant, answered, "Joe and I were talking about some experiences we've each had lately."

"Yeah," said Shanahan, "when you meet a priest these days, you have to sort of feel him out to discover which theology he favors."

"What do you mean, 'which theology'?" Thompson growled. "There's only one theology taught through the ordinary magisterium and protected by the Sacred Congregation for the Doctrine of the Faith."

Cunneen chortled. "That's the happy gang who brought us the Inquisition."

"I wouldn't put that in the past tense, Bill," said Stirling. "They're still chewing up avant-garde theologians."

"Yes," Shanahan said, "and only Henry Higgins preferred a new edition of the Spanish Inquisition to letting a woman in his life."

"Somehow, I knew you would get around to women," Thompson snarled.

76

"Not only are they here to stay, Monsignor," said Cunneen, "but some of them actually want the same rights we've got."

"There you go again with that equality crap, Cunneen." Thompson was growing angry. "What women really want is the license to be aborted anytime they feel like it. I knew this would happen when we began to inform them of the rules and regulations of the rhythm system of family planning. Give the laity information, and they'll abuse it every time. And I've said that before!" He looked pointedly toward the Archbishop, seated nearby.

"Well," said Boyle, who put a fairly high priority on peace in the ranks, "there is more than a modicum of truth in what Fathers Shanahan and Stirling have said. It wasn't always as it is. In a former day, nothing but age, and sometimes not even that, separated the clergy. It was easy to move about in otherwise heterogeneous circles and find a warm, unquestioning welcome in rectories throughout the country. Indeed, throughout the world."

"Those were experiences you younger guys will never have," Thompson snapped.

"I fear that may be so," said Boyle, with a touch of nostalgia. "Nowadays, there is no age gap such as the one in theology. That is true even to a certain extent among bishops."

Thompson, deadly tired of the luncheon conversation, excused himself, prayed a brief, private aftermeal grace, and returned to the Tribunal office.

"Do I have any appointments?" he asked Mary Alberts, the Tribunal secretary.

"Yes, Monsignor; there's a Mrs. Angela Cicero. She has a 1:30 appointment, but she was early. She's waiting in the outer office."

Thompson sighed. An appointment immediately following an uninteresting luncheon. And he was cold sober.

"Do I have anything after that?"

Mary consulted her calendar. "No; you're free after Mrs. Cicero."

Thompson needed only a moment to consider the possibilities. Perhaps an afternoon round of golf at the exclusive Detroit

77

Club, of which he was a member. "All right, Mary; have her come in."

Mary Alberts seemed a fixture at the Tribunal. She had survived five officiales; she knew where all the skeletons were buried, and she easily could have run the Tribunal by herself. Of medium height, a rather full-figured, gray-haired woman in her early sixties, Mary had never married. Her single state might have been an occupational hazard after witnessing an unending procession of broken marriages pass before her in the Tribunal office.

Thompson did not rise as Mrs. Cicero entered his office. She hesitated just inside the door. He looked up from a document he'd been reading. His clear blue eyes quickly studied her. A woman about his age, he guessed, perhaps a bit younger. Salt-and-pepper hair nicely coiffed. Perhaps five feet-five or -six. He was acutely conscious of her full bosom. You never could tell, he thought, whether women really had what their clothing hinted. It was like that song from "Oklahoma!": only when they began to peel could you know if everything they had was absolutely real. Mentally, he began to peel her, as he did with all attractive female visitors.

"Have a seat . . . Mrs. Cicero, is it?"

"Yes. Thank you."

"What can we do for you?"

"It's about my daughter's forthcoming wedding."

"Does it involve a marriage case we have?"

She nodded.

"Do you have the protocol number?"

Angela fingered through her purse and withdrew a sliver of paper. "47956/79."

Thompson communicated the number to Mary Alberts, who brought in the file. He paged through it quickly.

"I remember this case: privilege of the faith; very well prepared; Father Cavanaugh at Divine Child."

"Monsignor, the wedding is only seventeen days away."

"Not if the decree is not granted it's not. Surely a man of Father Cavanaugh's experience and maturity would never have scheduled a wedding with this permission pending."

"The wedding is scheduled at St. Anselm's."

"St. Anselm's . . . Koesler? Father Koesler?" He had long suspected his classmate of occasionally bending a rule or two. But he was genuinely surprised that Koesler would fool with a case that awaited a Rome decision.

"No, not Father Koesler . . . though he's taking care of it now. The one who gave us the date was Deacon Les."

Lester Schroeder. It all came back to him. Koesler's call. His brief note to the Sacred Congregation. Now this woman keeping him from what might have been a pleasant afternoon of golf. Hanging by the testicles until dead was too kind a punishment for Schroeder.

"Father Koesler said he would call you about it," she continued, somewhat dismayed that Koesler might not have.

"He did. It's all coming back to me. A little more than a week ago."

"A week ago last Monday," she clarified.

"Yes; well, I sent a note to Rome the very next day."

"And?"

"And what?"

"What happened?"

"Nothing. I didn't expect anything to happen. At most, somebody at the Sacred Congregation may have moved this case from the bottom of a pile to the top."

"And that's all you're going to do?" She was horrified. "If it's a case of money . . ."

These people! Think that money can solve any problem. It's high time they learned there are some things money can't buy. Especially when they were dealing with someone who is already quite comfortable.

"It's not a case of more money, Madam." Thompson was eager to end this interview. "It's a case of time. And the Church, which has been around for some 2,000 years and will remain until the end of the world, has plenty of time. Your case will be processed in its time. Your mistake was in setting a date for the wedding before the Church acted. This whole mess is not the Church's fault; it's yours!" Thompson was working himself into a rage.

"What do you mean, 'our fault'!" Angela was headed in the same direction. "Those papers are sitting on some flunky's desk.

They can be acted on any time with no waiting. It could happen today if anyone cared."

"It might help, Madam," Thompson leaned toward her, "if you would keep in mind what it is you have petitioned Rome for. It is a *privilege*, not a right you are entitled to. A *privilege*! You are, in effect, begging the Church to grant you a *privilege*. And you know what beggars cannot be. It may be granted, or it may not. In any case, it will be acted upon in the Church's own good time!"

"What nationality are you?"

"What? Oh, I see; my ancestors came from England."

"That's your trouble. You're the wrong nationality."

"What nationality do you think the Pope is?"

"It doesn't matter. Everyone around him, the people who get things done, they're all Italian!"

"What does that have to do with anything?"

"We don't stand around in lines waiting for things to happen. We have a habit of making things happen when we are properly approached. That wedding is going to take place August 4, and we are going to have that stupid privilege.

"You have not heard the last of me, Monsignor. And if I have my way, your superiors are going to hear about how you have treated this whole matter."

"Don't worry about me. Nothing ever happens to me."

"Don't be so sure of that!"

She stormed out of his office. He studied her bottom as she left. It seemed nicely rounded and firm. But . . . who could tell?

At no time had it occurred to either Mrs. Cicero or Monsignor Thompson that this problem was not essentially hers. Somewhere were her daughter and son-in-law-elect waiting to see how Angela would work out their lives.

Lee Brand had arrived at the DAC at five past noon for his 11:45 luncheon engagement with Monsignor Thompson. It was now 12:15, and there was no Thompson in sight. If Brand had not had to use Thompson, he would by now have unilaterally canceled the luncheon and settled on the form of vengeance he

80

would wreak on the Monsignor. Since he needed Thompson to clear the canonical path for his daughter's wedding, Brand contented himself with pacing through the DAC's cavernous lobby thinking dark thoughts and trying to stay calm. Then, he heard what was unmistakably Thompson's booming baritone.

"Al," Thompson cried, "how the hell are you?"

"Tommy! Good to see you. You haven't forgotten our trip to the Costa Smeralda, have you?"

" 'Course not," Thompson replied. "Leaving August 3, aren't we?"

"Right. Going to be a hell of a few days. See you at the airport . . . or should I have you picked up?"

"No, no, Al. I'll meet you at the airport."

"O.K.; see you then."

Brand became conscious that his mouth was hanging open. There was no mistaking it; the gentleman Thompson had greeted as a long-lost buddy was Alvin Braemar, a Vice President of Ford Motor Company and probably the most essential and influential man in that entire organization.

Brand wondered if Thompson had staged the meeting to impress him. He quickly discarded that theory; a man of Braemar's eminence would never stoop to such a charade.

"Well, Monsignor, good to see you again."

"Sorry to keep you waiting, Lee. A last-minute emergency."

Thompson was lying, and Brand suspected as much.

"Let's stop in the bar. The heat of the day has parched the old throat. How about you?" Brand led him toward the first-floor bar.

"Sure thing." This, thought Thompson, was so much better than St. Al's dry luncheon.

In the length of time it took the two men to approach the bar, the bartender had created Brand's own style martini. Thompson wondered how many barkeeps in the world had the proper formula. Thompson ordered a bourbon Manhattan.

"Ever been here before, Monsignor?"

"Sure."

After Thompson's familiarity with Al Braemar, Brand could not doubt the assertion.

"Ever been shown around the place?"

"No, I haven't. Funny, all I've ever done here is eat."

"How about a Cook's Tour?"

"Sure."

Drinks in hand, they saw just about all the DAC had to offer. Huge reading rooms packed with overstuffed chairs, some with overstuffed dozing members; showers, bowling alleys, jogging track, pool. And almost everywhere there seemed to be provisions for serving food and drink. They stopped at the pool.

"Nice," said Thompson. He noted the basketball backboards at both sides of the pool. "Water polo?"

"Yes," Brand replied. He looked rather forcefully at Thompson. "It can be a very dangerous enterprise."

Thompson was uncertain of Brand's import. Whatever it might be, he shrugged it away.

"What's this?" Thompson indicated a curiously outfitted room adjacent to the pool.

"Beaver Club," said Brand. "Sort of a club within a club."

"Are you a member?"

"Certainly," Brand said. "And I'm able to get other members into the club."

They moved on to the dining room. Seated, each began his second drink. Brand elaborated upon his invitation to Thompson for membership in the DAC:

"It is, as you know, Monsignor, a somewhat exclusive club, a whit prestigious. Very good place to bring out-of-town visitors. Quite inexpensive. $1,200 initiation fee, $700 annual dues, $30 laundry fee, and $60 athletic fee. And all these expenses can be taken care of." Brand winked elaborately.

The poor bastard, thought Thompson. I don't have to belong to the DAC, the Renaissance Club, or any other exclusive facility. I have friends who are members of all of them, and they are pleased when I deign to accompany them. I belong to the Detroit Golf Club only for the ease of dropping in for a round whenever I wish. No, Mr. Brand, take back your gold. I will not deign to join the Detroit Athletic Club.

"So," concluded Brand, "how about it, Monsignor? I would be most happy to sponsor you for membership."

"Thank you just the same, Lee. But I don't think it's in the cards for me just now."

"Well, think about it."

They ordered lunch. Brand ordered another martini. Thompson declined. Since each had ordered an Italian dish, Brand selected a Chianti to go with the food.

They were well into the meal when Brand asked, "How goes the battle?"

"Which one?"

"The one that will lead to the Holy, Roman, Catholic marriage for my daughter."

"Not well."

Brand put down a forkful of lasagna. "Not well?" The vertical lines between his eyebrows stretched nearly to his toupée line.

Thompson had been savoring every moment of this meeting. At their previous luncheon at the Renaissance Club, Brand had put him on the defensive. Thompson was determined that would never happen again. He had been deliriously happy at the chance meeting with Al Braemar. He could not have staged a better entrance. He had enjoyed all Brand's not-so-subtle overtures to sponsor membership in the DAC and even to pay the freight. His breaded veal tasted even better now that he was primed to drop the bomb.

"Not well?" Brand repeated. "Monsignor, need I remind you the wedding is only nine days away?"

Thompson elaborately dabbed asparagus tips in hollandaise. "Lee, you simply have no concept of how many witnesses must be called in a case like this."

"I don't care how many witnesses have to be called. Call them. If you have to hire more priests or clerks, hire them. I tell you, money is of no concern." Brand had raised his voice sufficiently that nearby diners began to glance furtively at him, and waiters began to be nervous.

Money again. When would they learn? Money is a telling factor only to those who need it.

"It's not a matter of money, Lee." Thompson sampled a boiled potato. "It's a matter of finding witnesses and getting their cooperation. We don't have any power of subpoena. Just some ancient Church sanctions that no one pays attention to anymore. And, Lee, we are talking abut a *lot* of witnesses.

People who may have knowledge that Warwick's former wife intended not to have children. Witnesses who will testify to the veracity of other witnesses.

"Then there's the former wife herself, Laura Warwick. She's the essence of the case, and we've been unable to get her co-operation." Thompson paused for another sip of wine. "But I assure you, Lee, we will continue to try. You must understand, however, that this is by no means the only case I'm working on. Though I am giving it absolutely top priority."

In fact, Thompson knew that Laura Warwick was living in Chicago, seat of a very efficient and cooperative Church Tribunal. She was reluctant to testify but, Thompson had learned through a private investigating agency on retainer to General Motors, she currently was financially strapped. Apparently, she had spent right out from under her alimony allotment and was deeply in debt. Obviously, there was a good possibility that, for an agreeable sum, she might be willing to overcome her reluctance to testify. That possibility had not been explored.

Nor was Thompson so essential to the daily operation of the Tribunal that he could not make the Warwick case his sole occupation. A great deal more could have been done to expedite this case. It was, indeed, proceeding at approximately the same snaillike pace as all other cases. At this rate, it almost certainly would not be settled by the July 28 deadline.

Thompson was determined to bring Brand to his knees. The decision had not been made at first sight. At the Fourth of July party, when the two had first met, Thompson had given serious consideration to cultivating Brand and making him part of his stable of Very Important Friends. However, he was quick to perceive that Brand was a shameless manipulator of people and that a friendship with him would be as fatal a coupling as the worst of broken marriages that crossed his desk.

Meanwhile, circumstances had forced Thompson to deal with Brand. Thompson saw their relationship as a case of devour or be devoured. Thus, he determined to create the appearance that everything possible was being done, while allowing the case to proceed at a normal snail's pace.

He had no idea where Brand's daughter would be married July 28, but he was quite sure—barring several miracles that might precipitate the case—that the marriage would not be in a Catholic church. Thompson truly didn't care. He was determined only that he would not play lackey to Brand.

His final thought on the matter was that it might work out to be a blessing in disguise. If it was not a Catholic ceremony and the marriage did not work out, it would be simple to get a nullity decree. In which case, Brand would be grateful. There would be no gratitude on the twenty-eighth. Brand would be denied his showcase Catholic ceremony. His anger would be monumental. But Thompson knew from experience he could easily tolerate that.

Something must have clicked in Brand's mind, because his attitude seemed to change sharply. He resumed eating.

"Well, Monsignor," he said, "I'm sure you're doing all you can. The only thing I regret is that you were too considerate to involve me. For instance, I will immediately see about Laura. There must be some way to convince her that it would be best for everyone if she were to testify."

Thompson choked on the Chianti.

"You all right?" Brand seemed concerned.

Thompson nodded as the coughing subsided. So Brand was soon to learn that Laura Warwick probably could be moved by money. Well, so be it. Thompson was not accustomed to needlessly postponing confrontations.

"I don't think," continued Brand, "that in a case like this it is possible to have too many cooks. It won't be disadvantageous if I jump into the middle of this, will it? I don't want to do anything to compromise your position."

"No, no." Thompson finished the veal. "Do what you think is best. Don't worry about me. Nothing ever happens to me."

A tall, distinguished man approached the table.

"Fred!" Brand stood to greet the newcomer.

"Sorry to interrupt, Lee. I saw you just now as I was leaving, and I wanted to remind you that the codicil to your will is ready. You and Joan should come in and sign it."

"Listen, we'll do it. I'll have my secretary call for an appointment." Brand turned to Thompson. "Fred Janson, I'd like you to meet Monsignor Thompson. Monsignor is head of the Archdiocesan Tribunal."

A look of recognition flashed in Janson's eyes. "Pleased to meet you, Monsignor. It's odd we should meet now. I recently had occasion to read something of your operation. You run an interesting court."

Thompson, who had risen to shake Janson's proffered hand, now resumed his chair.

"And Fred should know," said Brand. "He is one of Detroit's top corporation lawyers . . ."

Thompson began to wonder if, as one of Detroit's top corporation lawyers, Janson might be a likely candidate for his Very Important Friends club.

". . . and a very good friend of mine," concluded Brand.

Thompson scratched the VIF concept. Very soon not only the Brands, but their very good friends, would be very angry.

"How did you happen to be reading about our Tribunal?" Thompson asked.

"Oh, it was on a professional basis. We'll have to get together and talk about it sometime." Janson had no intention of exposing to public chatter a situation he considered personally demeaning. Only his abiding love for his wife motivated him to endure a legal process he considered inherently unjust. Otherwise, he wished neither to think of nor talk about it.

"Yes, we'll have to do that."

Neither Janson nor Thompson intended to meet socially. Janson instinctively disliked Thompson, a rare occurrence for a man who did not make snap judgments. Thompson dismissed Janson, as, unfortunately, useless.

So that's the bastard, thought Janson as he left the dining area; he just doesn't look as if he should have all that power at his disposal.

"Bob, I have something I'd like to share with you," said Les Schroeder.

"Les, please don't 'share' anything with me. *Tell* me. Just come right out and tell me," said Father Koesler.

For some reason, Schroeder's jargon jarred Koesler more than if it had come from almost anyone else.

The two were seated in the living room of St. Anselm's rectory. It was mid-morning, Friday, July 20. A pleasant breeze drifted through the building, obviating any need to activate the air conditioner.

"It's this Sunday's homily. I can't seem to be able to work through the kerygmatic catechesis to be able to inspire true metanoia, you know?"

"Please, Les, not when we're alone."

"Huh?"

"Look, Les, the Gospel tells the story of the selection of the apostles and Christ's sending them on their first mission. The Old Testament reading is about the Midrash Jonah and the fish. Why not just develop the theme of our being sent into our world to bring Christ's message of love?

"Just as Jonah went only reluctantly to Nineveh to deliver God's message—so reluctantly that he had to be delivered by a metaphorical fish—so we honestly feel reluctant to deliver the authentic Christian message that has never received a popular welcome. Indeed, we can at least partially measure the message's authenticity by the reluctance of others to hear and follow it."

"Why didn't I think of that?"

"You will. Give yourself time to gain a little experience. But, Les: eschew obfuscation."

"What?"

"Try to avoid being unclear. In other words, try very hard to knock off the jargon."

The doorbell rang. They could hear Mary O'Connor's footsteps against the tile as she went to the door. Schroeder rose painfully from the couch and limped to the window.

"Oh my God!" he said, "it's that Mrs. Cicero. I've got to get out of here."

"Why don't you go out on the porch and work on your homily? She probably wants to see me, anyway," said Koesler. "What's with the limp?" he added.

"Oh," Schroeder hobbled toward the porch, "it's that skiing accident I had last winter. Every once in a while it just acts up. Doctor says I've got a fifty-year-old knee."

Koesler sighed. He had a fifty-plus-year-old body. Yet he did not feel it had to be placed in a cast. He snapped a roman collar around his neck, slipped on his lightweight cassock, and went to meet Mrs. Cicero in his office.

"Now then, Mrs. Cicero, what can I do for you?"

"Have you ever been to Rome?" she asked without preamble.

"Why yes—quite a few years ago. Why do you ask?"

"How long does it take to get there?"

Koesler thought a moment. "It's about a nine-hour plane ride, as I recall. But why . . . you're not thinking of—"

"I've got to get that silly permission. And I'll get it if I have to go right to the Pope and ask him for it."

"Now, wait a minute. Don't you think that is just a bit extreme?"

"The wedding is only fifteen days away. I'm afraid I'm beginning to panic. What I'm really afraid of . . ." she hesitated, close to tears, "is that I'm becoming afraid."

For the first time in the brief span he had known her, Angela Cicero appeared to Koesler as a vulnerable person. Until now, she had come on as Superwoman.

"There may be more time than you suppose," he explained gently. "You have put all your eggs in one basket. In one way, that's admirable. In another, it's dangerous. On August 4, one of two things will probably happen: we will have the wedding here and, because your daughter and her fiancé like him, Deacon Les will preside."

Koesler thought he heard Angela's teeth grind.

"Or," he continued, "you'll have to explain to the guests that the wedding must be postponed indefinitely.

"Between now and then, it *is* possible the Vatican will have given permission. If not, and if you expect anyone over there to respond to an emergency, it has to be a certified emergency. And fifteen days does not qualify. Not with today's standard of communication.

"Now, I'll give you the phone number of a friend of mine, Father Pat Cammarata. He lives at the Villa Stritch in Rome and works at the Sacred Congregation for the Doctrine of the Faith—that's the outfit we're dealing with in this case."

Angela nodded eagerly.

"The phone number," he continued, "once you reach Rome,

is 537-8734. But don't call now. Wait. Wait for at least another week. Wait until you simply cannot wait another moment. Then phone him—remember, Rome is six hours ahead of our time—and explain the problem. Pat is not only sympathetic, he is about the most efficient operator in the Vatican. And, believe me, Angela, there is an abundance of efficient operators in that cloak-and-dagger operation. If anyone can help, he can.

"But the secret is in the timing. We can't wait so long that we've gone beyond a fail-safe moment. But we've got to wait until, even in Rome's view, we've got a genuine emergency."

Angela was conscious of an evolution. As Koesler had been speaking to her, it became no longer "her" problem but "our" problem. By the time he had finished his monologue, she had the comforting feeling she was no longer in this fight alone. And she felt enormously buoyed by that. She felt, in fact, like leaning across his desk and planting a big wet kiss on the priest. His reserve, more than hers, discouraged that.

"So, remember, Angela, at least a week. It's all a matter of timing," Koesler said as he led her to the front door.

"I'll remember, Father. You know, you're the only one who's been a help to me. I wish you were in charge of the Tribunal."

"Don't wish that on me, Angela."

———————

Mary Alberts looked up from her Monday afternoon typing to find a well-groomed, impeccably dressed man pacing before her desk. She thought she recognized him. She had the feeling she had seen his photo in the papers or on TV. She could not quite make an identification.

"Please tell Monsignor Thompson Lee Brand would like to see him." Brand did not return her smile.

"Do you have an appointment?"

"No, but I think he'll see me." If Thompson dared refuse to see him, Brand gave momentary thought to buying the Chancery Building and evicting Thompson along with the whole damn Tribunal.

She announced Brand to Thompson.

"Yes, I'll see Mr. Brand. Send him right in."

Others in Thompson's position might have been frightened

or at least intimidated. It had been three days since their previous meeting. In that time, and with Brand's resources, he had undoubtedly had sufficient time to solve the puzzle. He would now know that, far from having received expeditious treatment, his case had been languishing from inattention.

Thompson found this moment exhilarating. It was the culmination of the little scenario he had been concocting. He had utterly no fear that Brand might cause him any harm. Thompson had far too many Very Important Friends, some of whom were at least of Brand's eminence or loftier. Far from feeling trepidation, Thompson anticipated a certain measure of satisfaction from this confrontation.

To augment the satisfaction, Thompson had merely to recall their luncheon at the Renaissance Club when Brand had overwhelmed him with a figurative full court press. Vengeance is mine, saith Thompson, leaving the Lord out.

Brand entered the office. He did not sit. He remained standing just inside the door. He seemed extraordinarily calm, as if he knew the game was over and he had lost but was unwilling to cry about it.

"It is," said Brand, "as I mentioned at the DAC. You have been too considerate in not including me in the game earlier. For instance, I would have learned that it would not have cost much at all to induce Laura Warwick to testify in this case. If I had bailed her out of debt—and I could and would have—she'd have testified. The only thing I can't quite understand is why you did this."

Thompson neither smiled nor gestured. "Welcome to the world of reality, Mr. Brand," he said sepulchrally. "You have not been mistreated. You have merely been treated the way everyone else is."

"That still doesn't explain why you did it."

"Why I *didn't* do it," Thompson corrected. "What I did do was accept Dick Warwick's case and have it processed in the normal way. What I *didn't* do was give the case any preferential treatment.

"Ask yourself, Mr. Brand, why, in human affairs, anything or anyone is given preferential treatment. It is because someone in a position to accord this preferential treatment finds some

90

reason to do so. In Mr. Warwick's case, I found no such reason."

"But that's just it. You led me to expect that the case would be expedited. That's why I didn't take any active part in it."

"If you thought the case would be expedited, that is your concern, Mr. Brand. Did I ever say it would be expedited?"

Brand didn't answer. Before coming to Thompson's office today he had been quite certain of the direction of their conversation. He had not been mistaken.

"I suppose," said Brand finally, "that it is too late to process the case in the remaining four days."

"Nothing is impossible with God, Mr. Brand. I suggest we all continue to pray. Meanwhile, I assume you have rendered Laura Warwick cooperative by assisting her financially. However, as I explained earlier, there are all those witnesses to be interviewed . . ."

"But," Thompson raised a hand and stood, "I assure you, Mr. Brand, we will continue to work on this case in the very same manner as we would any similar case. Though, bluntly, if I had a last dollar, I would not put it on a July 28 wedding."

"That's something you're not likely to have, Monsignor."

"What's that?"

"A last dollar."

A hint of a smile crinkled the corners of Thompson's mouth. "That's very likely true."

"Our paths may cross again, Monsignor. Only next time, I'll be better on my guard. And," Brand winked significantly, "I'd advise you to be on yours."

"Always. But you shouldn't be concerned. Nothing ever happens to me."

Neither offered a hand as they parted.

———————

Neiss contemplated his day, now nearly over. It had not been aided by Father Cavanaugh's tirade during dinner. Pressed by Coach Blaszczyk, Neiss had continued to suggest to Sister Mary Patrick that one more desk in the high school would not create the havoc she apprehended. She, in turn, regularly reported him to Cavanaugh, who just as regularly delivered tirades.

This evening's tirade had extended sufficiently to prevent him from totaling the petitions, thanksgivings, and special favors placed in the petition box this week. Thus, he would refer to them only vaguely during the upcoming Perpetual Help services. It did not occur to him to fabricate the totals. And thus, he would hear again from Cavanaugh about this abominable lack of preparation.

The organ was playing the intro to "Oh, Mother of Perpetual Help" as he entered the church. He was late. He vested hurriedly.

Perspiring freely during the Perpetual Help services, Neiss reflected that he would have to postpone his ritual appearance at the parish Bingo game to attend to the nadir of this day. It had been hovering over him like a black cloud that this evening he was to meet with Harry Kirwan to inform him that his first wife would have to be interrogated. This despite all the promises and assurances Neiss had given. With this black thought in mind, he hurried toward the back door of the rectory.

"Harry!" She pushed against him rather ineffectually. "Not in front of the church!"

"We're not in front of the church; we're in front of the rectory. See how well I'm doing with my Catholic lessons?"

Harry Kirwan was seated in his car with his fiancée, Mary Ann McCauley. They were necking. It was fun. The only fly in this ointment belonged to Mary Ann and her reluctance to link anything physically sexual with anything spiritually religious. She simply could not reconcile the fact that they were fondling while parking on property belonging to Divine Child parish.

"Church, rectory, what difference does it make?" she remonstrated.

"I know, teacher: A church is where God lives; a rectory is a home for unwed fathers."

"Harry, stop! What if one of the priests or nuns sees us?"

"It might be an education."

"Harry!"

"O.K. All right." Kirwan good-naturedly slid back behind

the wheel. "If it makes you feel better, we'll just talk. What do you think of the Tigers' chances?"

"You're not angry, are you?"

"No. What do you think of the Tigers' chances?"

"Their problem," she said in studied fashion, "is in the left side of the infield. Good glove; no stick."

"I tend to agree. Do you think Ty Cobb will be any help to them this year?"

"You can't kid me. I know Cobb plays for Cleveland."

They broke up. They not only loved each other, they liked each other. They agreed their meeting had been providential. They belonged together, and soon they would be together.

The two had experienced a period of panic when first confronted with the issue of Harry's prior marriage as a possible impediment to their own. That had been followed by an inexpressible relief when they discovered that a declaration of nullity could be rather easily granted in a case like this.

Kirwan had no idea why he had been summoned by Father Neiss. He assumed the declaration of nullity for his first marriage had been granted and that the priest was going to give him an official-looking paper that would so state. He already had papers from Wayne County showing that he had county consent to marry, and a paper from the state certifying his blood was pure enough to marry; now he could collect another paper from the Church clearing the way for a religious ceremony.

"Harry, look." Mary Ann pointed toward the rectory. "The light just went on in Father Neiss's office."

"Lucky thing we quit foolin' around when we did. We might have given him ideas. And I understand there's already a crisis in priestly callings."

Neiss greeted them at the front door.

"I hope you don't mind my bringing Mary Ann, Father," Kirwan explained. "She and I had a date before you and I had a date. In fact, we're squeezing you in between dinner and a movie."

"No, no; of course not," said Neiss. "Come on in, Mary Ann. I haven't seen you since Sunday."

Neiss wasn't sure how he felt about Mary Ann's presence. He didn't know whether she would be helpful or an exacerbation when Kirwan was given the news. In any case, there was nothing he could do about it now, so he showed the couple into his office.

Kirwan and Mary Ann looked at him expectantly. Neiss felt like opening with the hackneyed I-suppose-you're-wondering-why-I've-called-you-here. But though he knew they had a marvelous sense of humor, the matter tonight could become tragic, and he knew it.

"Harry," Neiss opened, "there's been a complication in the process of getting that declaration of nullity."

"What's that, Father?" The specter of having to contact his former wife did not even occur to Kirwan, so confident was he in Neiss's assurances.

The priest cleared his throat. "Well, I got a call the other day from a priest in the Tribunal. They have a new policy. I don't know where it came from. It's never happened to any of my cases before, and I've had many similar to yours. Nor do I agree with the policy. But I've been assured that it is a firm and unequivocal policy."

He himself grew disgusted with his beating around the bush. He took a deep breath and plunged. "They insist that your former wife be interviewed."

He paused. Both he and Mary Ann stared at Kirwan, who said nothing. Kirwan's jaw was clenched, and the color seemed to drain from his face.

"The way they explained it to me," the priest continued, "it's because your first wife is Polish."

An uncomprehending look crossed Kirwan's face.

"And the Polish, according to the Tribunal," Neiss said, "have a practice, more than other ethnic groups, of having invalid marriages fixed up. On that point, I have to agree with the Tribunal."

Neiss paused again. Still nothing from Kirwan.

"I brought up the fact that you had submitted a very recent copy of her baptismal record and that there was no notification of marriage on it. But they said there have been instances when priests have forgotten to send notification, or, on the other hand, have neglected to record it. I can believe that too."

"Did you tell them what would happen if Ruth is contacted?" Kirwan asked through clenched teeth.

94

Neiss, deeply embarrassed, could not look at him. "Yes, I did. They simply stated it was a firm policy and must be followed."

There was another protracted pause.

"I won't have it," said Kirwan, barely audibly. "I won't have it," he repeated somewhat more loudly and firmly.

"Harry!" Mary Ann sounded shocked.

"I've gone through this entire ridiculous procedure without protest," said Kirwan. "You explained all the rules before we began, Father. And I have abided by every one of them. Now that the game should be over, your team is making up new rules. You have no idea, Father, how miserable Ruth can make life when she gets upset. And I can guarantee you this would upset her. And I won't have it!" He was almost shouting.

"Harry," said Mary Ann, close to tears, "can't you agree to just this one last demand?"

"You don't know what you're asking!"

"I'm asking you to do just this one last thing so we can be married in the Catholic Church."

"And I'm asking you to come with me and find a judge and get married. We've got all the papers we need."

"Harry! Harry! I can't do that! I just can't do that!"

She began to sob. Kirwan lapsed into a furious silence. Neiss shifted nervously in his chair.

Finally, the priest said, "Wait. I didn't know it would end like this. There is one more thing I can try. I haven't yet talked to the head of the Tribunal. He is the one who instituted this policy. Let me talk to him. Maybe I can get him to suspend this regulation just once."

Mary Ann dried her tears. Neiss accompanied the couple to the door. "If I were you," he said, "I wouldn't count on my having much success. But it's certainly worth the try."

The couple left in silence. There would be no movie tonight.

Remembering what Irene Casey had mentioned, Father Koesler tried to get a surreptitious glimpse of Lee Brand's chair to see if any pillows had been piled on the seat. Standing, Koesler was several inches taller than Brand, even with the latter's lifts. So the priest suspected there might be pillows. However, Brand's executive desk was so mammoth there was no way, short of circling the desk, that Koesler could check. He concluded that sort of maneuver would be socially awkward.

Brand's office was all Koesler had expected and more. Paneled in what appeared to be authentic oak, one wall was completely inlaid with bookshelves; another seemed to be a self-contained sound system with radio, tape deck, stereo, and television, all connected, undoubtedly, to the four gigantic speakers in the wall; a third wall appeared plain with overstuffed couches and chairs in front of it; the fourth, a window wall, offered a magnificent view of downtown Detroit.

"Very, very nice of you to stop by on such short notice, Father," said Brand. "I'm really strapped for time in four different directions, so I really appreciate your courtesy."

"Not at all, Mr. Brand . . ."

"Lee."

". . . Lee. I can guess how busy you are. I'll be glad if I can be of help."

"I think you can, Father." Brand crossed to the plain wall, stepped between the chairs, and pressed a button. A large panel slid back, revealing a larger-than-life wet bar. "Something to drink, Father?"

"Thanks just the same, Mr.—er, Lee. A little early for me."

Brand dropped several ice cubes in a large glass, splashed a significant amount of vodka over the cubes and filled the glass with tomato juice.

Evidently, Koesler concluded, meticulous attention is reserved solely for the Brand martini.

"I'll get right to the point, Father. It's about my daughter's wedding."

"Yes, your wife explained that earlier this morning when she called and set up this appointment."

A buzzer sounded in the telephone console.

"I'd better apologize right now, Father, for what probably will become a series of interruptions. There's nothing I can do about it. I've got to keep taking calls and messages, or I'll never dig my way out of this day."

Koesler nodded understanding.

Brand pushed a button. "What is it, Cindy?"

"A Mr. O'Brien, Mr. Brand. He's taking out a loan and objected to our prime rate. He says he talked to you about it at the DAC last week. He says he's a member of the Beaver Club."

"O'Brien . . . O'Brien . . . ah, yes, the chalet just outside Zurich . . ." Brand spoke so softly Koesler could barely hear him. Ordinarily, Koesler would make an effort not to overhear another's conversation, but, in this instance, he was completely fascinated by this utterly foreign world of high finance. "Cindy," Brand returned to an unreserved volume, "quote Mr. O'Brien at 8½ percent."

There was a moment of silence, during which Koesler thought he detected a sense of disbelief on the part of the unseen secretary.

"Yes, Mr. Brand," she said finally, professionally dispassionate.

Brand sipped his Bloody Mary. "Father, we've run into a rather bad snag in our plans for Bunny's wedding. It seems we can't clear things through the proper channels—problems with time and testimony and the like."

Koesler suffered a major distraction. He allowed it to simmer on a back burner of his mind. He wondered about the chemistry that must have gone on between Brand and Thompson. Whatever had happened, Brand had evidently failed to get his future son-in-law's case through the Tribunal. My, how the fur must have flown! Koesler surmised that the events that transpired between Brand and Thompson might very well have made grist for a best-seller.

"In any case," Brand went on, "we now find ourselves between a rock and a hard place. But then, Sunny and I recalled that night on the Fourth of July, you mentioned something about a priest who occasionally circumvents more traditional avenues of Church discipline."

Nicely put, thought Koesler. A more euphemistic way to describe breaking Church law did not occur to him.

At that point, the buzzer again sounded.

"Mr. Brand," Cindy announced coolly, "we have a request for a letter of credit from a Mr. James Wilson."

"Why are you calling me about it?" Brand was clearly annoyed.

"It was at Mr. Wilson's request."

"How much and why?"

"It is a $100,000 letter of credit in order for Mr. Wilson to secure an account he's been attempting to acquire for the past seven years. He states he must act immediately, or he will lose the account."

"What's his rating with us?"

"$400,000."

Brand seemed to hesitate. "Wait a minute, Cindy. Call Mrs. Brand and find out if it wasn't Wilson's wife who got drunk at our party this past weekend. I think we had to ask him to take her home."

Brand turned back to Koesler. "So, anyway, Father, do you know such a priest?"

"Well, this is a very delicate matter. I know of a priest who—how shall I put this?—uses his own conscience as well as the stated consciences of those he deals with, rather than canon law, in dealing with sacramental matters."

"Do you think he would consider performing the wedding ceremony for my daughter so she can be married in the Catholic Church?"

"I don't know. He confines his ministry to the core city. That way he operates without any publicity or spotlight. It is absolutely the only way he could continue with his peculiar kind of ministry. However, I did call him before coming here. He said he would be willing to talk to you about it. But I must tell you, he sounded most reluctant."

"But he did say he'd be willing to talk about it?"

"Yes. But reluctantly."

Brand appeared somewhat relieved. "That's very good, Father. I am in your debt."

Koesler hesitated. "Would you like to know his name and where to contact him?"

"His name is Shanley," said Brand with no particular emphasis, "Father Norman Shanley, and he resides at Rosary parish on Woodward at the Ford Expressway."

"But how . . . ?"

Brand smiled broadly. "Father Koesler," his tone was that of a teacher explaining something the pupil should have known, "private investigation agencies are not all the shoot-em-up, cops-and-robbers people you see on TV. Some of them are quite good at quietly gathering information and arranging things that need to be arranged."

"Oh."

"But I did need you to make the initial contact with Father Shanley—break the ice, so to speak. And you've done it, and I'm grateful."

Koesler shrugged away the compliment for a favor he would have performed for anyone.

"One final question, Father. I'd like your opinion as to what might—uh—impress Father Shanley. Perhaps a substantial donation to Rosary?"

Koesler smiled. "No. No, Father Shanley will not be impressed by money no matter to which cause it may be donated."

Brand mulled alternative approaches. The buzzer sounded.

"Mrs. Brand says that Mrs. Wilson is indeed the woman you described," said Cindy's crisp voice.

"Deny that letter of credit."

Koesler, a self-proclaimed foreigner in the field of finance, nonetheless thought this an odd way to do business. Brand, without reference to the denied transaction, returned full attention to the project at hand. "Well, O.K., Father. You really have been a terrific help. The ball is in my court now. I'll take care of things. But thank you."

"Don't mention it."

"Would you like to join me for lunch?"

"No, I really ought to be getting back to the parish."

"Cindy, take care of Father's parking stub, will you?" said Brand as he saw Koesler out of the office.

In the elevator, Koesler again thought of the monumental confrontation that must have taken place between Brand and Thompson.

Well, he thought, Brand is still standing; I wonder about Tommy.

———

Mary Alberts told him she would put him on hold. It was more like "forget." Actually, Father David Neiss was surprised that Monsignor Thompson could be found in the Tribunal on this fine summer afternoon. Neiss had anticipated that Thompson, as well as most area doctors and dentists, would be out on the links or courts. Wednesdays were like that.

However, Miss Alberts had informed Neiss that Thompson was both in and available. That had been five minutes ago. After two minutes on seemingly interminable "hold," Neiss picked up a half-completed crossword puzzle and began to work it. Let me think, he thought, a seven-letter word for genus of stoneworts. . . .

"Yes!"

It was the unmistakable voice of Monsignor Thompson. Except that Neiss hardly ever spoke with Thompson, so he did not recognize the Monsignor's voice. Worse, he had forgotten whom he had phoned.

"Yes?" Neiss ventured.

"Yes!" Thompson was quickly losing what little veneer of patience he had. It was bad enough being boxed in his office on a fine Wednesday afternoon, ordinarily his day off, without being bothered by nincompoops.

"What is it you want?" Only a minuscule portion of patience remained.

"Monsignor?"

"Yes!" Thompson fairly shouted.

Neiss silently cursed himself and the crossword puzzle. This conversation was getting off to a very nasty start.

"This is Father Neiss."

"Yes." Thompson leaned over his desk, fingered through a stack of papers, found the Detroit Catholic Directory, and located Neiss in the alphabetical index. Divine Child parish. With old Cavanaugh.

"I'm calling about a Defect of Form case, Monsignor."

"Yes?"

Thompson was not making this easy.

"Specifically, Monsignor, it's about your new policy requiring interrogation concerning convalidation if one of the spouses is Polish." Neiss had written that sentence before placing the call. He had been afraid his nervousness would cause a major blunder in technical language.

"Yes."

"Well, Monsignor, I've got a case now where such an interrogation would cause a serious problem for a very fine man and for his children. All the other requirements are fulfilled. He says that if his former wife is contacted, she will cause all sorts of trouble. She has in the past."

"Well, then, I guess it can't be helped, can it." Thompson was fast losing what little interest he had in this conversation.

"But I thought . . . wouldn't it be possible for you to make an exception? I mean, this is a very fine man, and we would be making a lot of trouble for him."

"*We're* not making the trouble, Father. We're doing our job making sure we're dealing with an invalid marriage before we officially witness another marriage."

"Monsignor, it's not as if I am unwilling to cooperate with your new policy. As a matter of fact, I assure you I'll never ask for this favor again. But couldn't you make an exception in just this one case? After all, before I knew about this policy, I promised the man his former wife would not be contacted."

"You shouldn't make promises." Thompson was eager to terminate this useless conversation. "And, while we're at it, Father, I'll give you one bit of advice they should have given you in the seminary: don't get involved with these people. You must be coldly objective. Getting emotionally involved, as you obviously have, is just an impediment to sound judgment."

"Monsignor, I'm only asking for one exception."

"Father Neiss," Thompson's voice cut through the receiver like a knife, "if you persist with this nonsense, I will be forced to contact Father Cavanaugh and advise him to remove his delegation from you. Then you won't have this problem again, because you won't be able to witness *any* marriages in Divine Child parish. Is that clear?"

"Yes, Monsignor."

"Very well. Good day."

Damn, thought Neiss; guys like Thompson could take all the joy out of being a priest.

This looks more like a penthouse suite than an office, thought Father Norman Shanley. He had never seen any working space as extravagantly outfitted. He was frankly awed.

Lee Brand had decided it would be more effective to see Father Shanley in the office. It would be too easy for Shanley to refuse Brand's request if the meeting were to take place in Shanley's home court.

Brand opened the panel exposing the bar. Shanley thought he had stumbled upon Shangri-La.

"Drink, Father?"

"Oh, no, thanks."

"Never too early for a Bloody Mary," said Brand, as he followed his own prescription.

"No, no, thanks," Shanley maintained.

Brand led Shanley to a comfortable if spare black chair at the opposite end of the room from the desk. Brand seated himself in an identical chair near Shanley's. This was not to look as if it were a business meeting.

"I understand, Father," Brand swirled his drink in its glass, "that you occasionally conduct 'interesting' wedding ceremonies." His emphasis gave a completely ambiguous meaning to the word "interesting."

Shanley cleared his throat. Somehow, in this spacious office, he was beginning to feel claustrophobic. "That depends on what you mean by 'interesting,' Mr. Brand. What I do, in my little corner of the world . . . well, I try not to let anybody else in on it. It was only reluctantly that I let Father Koesler give you my name."

"I understand, Father. And I'm aware it was only with great reluctance that you agreed to meet with me."

Shanley nodded.

"I appreciate that," Brand continued. "I appreciate that more than I can tell you. But our backs are up against a wall. We've got a wedding scheduled at Our Lady of Refuge in two days, but we can't find a priest to perform the ceremony. And the kids do want so much to be married in the Church."

This was less than half true. Warwick didn't much care where they were married, while Bunny was only mildly interested in a Catholic wedding. However, both had been soundly warned and carefully coached in order to present a united front of people who desperately desired and richly deserved a Catholic wedding.

"That isn't always possible." Shanley shifted nervously in his chair. "Father Koesler mentioned a Tribunal case in this matter. It broke down?"

"Matter of time, nothing but a matter of time. But that is what we ran out of."

"I see. But what exactly do you want of me?" Shanley was quite sure what it was. He hated even to ask.

"We want . . . we'd be most grateful if you would be the missing priest. I'm sure I could fix things up with the pastor of Our Lady of Refuge and—"

"Oh, no. That's absolutely out of the question. I do my work in the core city and only there."

"Because, Father," Brand completed the thought, "you do occasionally witness marriages that can't be or haven't been squared with Church law. And you feel as long as you're in the inner city no one will care."

"That's part of it."

"That's reverse discrimination," said Brand decisively.

"Oh, no. If suburban priests do not include this sort of service in their ministries, that is their decision, not mine. I am assigned to the city."

"Then suppose we come to you."

"What?"

The thought of the Lee Brand family coming to Rosary had not entered Shanley's mind. He had been somewhat prepared for Brand's initial invitation to the Green Lake parish. He had been totally unprepared for the reverse suggestion.

"That, too, is out of the question," said Shanley, attempting to recover.

"Why?"

"Because you're too well known. It—what I've been doing—would get out."

"Now that, Father, *is* reverse discrimination."

"What?"

"I can understand why you would refuse to take your specialized ministry out to the suburbs, but not your refusal to let us come to you. If I and my daughter lived in your parish and if you were convinced we desperately wanted her marriage in the Church, you'd do it, wouldn't you?"

"Probably," he hesitantly agreed.

"So the only reason you're refusing our request is because we are not poor. That, Father, is my idea of reverse discrimination!"

Shanley sat silently thinking it over. Brand quietly congratulated himself on his game plan. So far, everything had gone precisely as anticipated. He had been certain Shanley would reject the idea of coming out to Green Lake. After this setup, he was equally certain Shanley could not oppose the Brands' coming to him.

"But there would be all that publicity." Shanley sensed trouble ahead, but he was now clutching at straws. Brand's ultimate argument, he knew, was beyond his power to refute.

"We can soft-pedal that, Father. You've got nothing to worry about."

"Well, that's one thing I'd have to insist on. Publicity in this situation would be the death knell to my entire approach to dispensing the sacraments. You've got to promise me: no publicity."

"Father, what could I do even if I wanted to? The wedding is only two days away."

"I've got to interview the couple. I've got to make certain they want this as badly as you say they do. This is crucial."

"Of course, Father. I have them waiting for my call. They will come to see you at your convenience."

"This afternoon, then. About two."

"Of course. They'll be there. And if all goes well, the wedding will be this Saturday, July 28. What time would be best for you?"

Briefly, 7 A.M. flashed through Shanley's mind. There was precedent, he thought: old Father Kirkland out in Marine City scheduled all summer funerals for 7 A.M. So they wouldn't interfere with his golf game.

"I guess six in the evening," Shanley relented. "Our regularly scheduled Saturday evening Mass is at five, so this might fit in right after that. But, remember, Mr. Brand, this all depends on my interview with the couple."

"Of course, Father; I understand completely."

Brand ushered the priest out of his office, told Cindy to take care of Shanley's parking, and to get his daughter on the phone. There would be no problem with the kids. They had been carefully coached. He felt exuberant. He was going to beat Thompson at Thompson's own game.

Brand rubbed his hands together vigorously. He had lots to do.

Koesler had offered Mass and brought communion to five shut-ins in the parish, as he ordinarily did on Fridays. He had then returned to the rectory for some coffee and an opportunity to catch up with this day.

Now, cup of coffee in hand, he sat at his office desk, considering the mail. As usual, an enormous proportion was junk. Once in a while there would be a personal letter from a friend— Koesler was a faithful correspondent. But almost always there were the irritants: bills, notifications from the various ecclesial bureaucracies, and invitations to countless meetings.

He fingered through the first-class mail and paused at one envelope. At the upper left corner were the words, "The Tribunal," and its Washington Boulevard address.

Pulling the envelope from the pile, he slit it open. He glanced first at the letter's signature. *Monsignor Thomas Thompson.* Koesler heard in imagination the three "Scarpia" chords.

Dear Father Koesler, were the last friendly words on the page until the closing salutation.

Pursuant to the petition for marital separation, protocol number 715/79, notification of which inception you forwarded to this office several months ago:

This interminable delay cannot continue. Please forward forthwith to this office and to my attention, all documentation you have gathered and assembled. Make certain that each page of the documentation is headed with the proper protocol number.

In Christ,
Msgr. Thomas Thompson
MONSIGNOR THOMAS THOMPSON

Damn! He wondered if "Monsignor Thomas Thompson" was a Tribunal pseudonym for a computer. One which, incidentally, had been badly programmed.

Three times had Koesler patiently explained this case was in a state of suspended animation since the husband, essential ingredient that he was, could not be found. To top it all, Koesler was bone tired.

Well, if Caesar wanted the documents, Caesar would get them!

Slamming the file drawer with unnecessary vigor, Koesler produced the required documents, made certain each page bore the protocol number and stuffed the incomplete documentation in a manila envelope.

He placed the bulging mess on Mary O'Connor's desk.

"Mary, would you make sure this has sufficient postage and send it off to Monsignor Thompson at the Tribunal?"

She hefted it with one hand. "Do you want me to enclose a note telling Monsignor what to do with it?"

"Yeah. Tell him he can—never mind. Just send it, please."

Between the thumb and index finger of his right hand, Father David Neiss held a penny wrapper. As Hamlet contemplating the skull, so Neiss meditated over the penny wrapper, philosophical concepts ranging through his mind.

Had he spent twelve long years preparing for the priesthood for this? Four years of high school, four of college, and four of theological training in order to wrap money?

Yet, this was the order of the day. Before leaving for a vicariate meeting at Sacred Heart in Dearborn, his pastor, Father Leon Cavanaugh, had left his unrelentingly explicit instructions. Father Cavanaugh had determined that since this was the end of the final week of July, all loose currency and change in the safe should be counted and packaged. It reminded Neiss of the decree once issued by Caesar Augustus. All monies shall be returned to their proper denomination, there to be assembled and accounted for.

Neiss glanced again at the note Cavanaugh had left:

Father Neiss:

Empty the safe of all loose currency and coins. Divide the currency into packages of $100 each, maintaining the difference in denominations. Wrap the coins in their proper containers. Forty quarters and nickels to a package, fifty dimes and pennies. Note the total amount, place in leather bag, and leave all in the safe so I may check it.

Fr. L. Cavanaugh

So that was it. A kind of minimal requirement for ordination. The ability to make George Washington face in the same direction and the competence to count to ten, forty, and fifty. This task would take the better part of a Saturday that had begun overcast and steamy but was developing into a dandy day weatherwise.

Since the day seemed to offer him nothing but bleak prospects, Neiss decided to call Harry Kirwan and inform him of Monsignor Thompson's bottom line.

No answer.

He dialed Mary Ann McCauley's number.

"Yes?" Her voice sounded strange, as if she'd caught a cold or, perhaps, had been crying.

"Mary Ann? I tried to call Harry, but there was no answer."

"He's here with me, Father."

"Oh. I wanted to tell him about the Tribunal's final decision, but I can just as well tell you."

"Yes?"

"Well," Neiss fumbled with the penny wrappers for a few moments before continuing, "I'm afraid the final decision is that the Tribunal demands that Harry's former wife be interviewed."

There was a brief silence. Neiss sensed she was dabbing at her eyes.

"Father," she said, "shortly after we saw you, we reached the same conclusion. We knew that was going to be the final decision."

"You did?"

107

"Yes. We've been talking it over ever since. Well, arguing about it. And we've come to our own decision." She hesitated. "Father, we're going to be married in Harry's church in two weeks."

"Mary Ann, wait!" Neiss had not expected this turn of events. "Do you know what you're getting into? You're leaving your Church. You're leaving the heritage you grew up with. Isn't there some way we can talk this out?"

"No, there isn't, Father. Reaching this decision has been the most agonizing effort of my life. I love my Church, but I love Harry, and I'm not going to lose him over some silly rule."

"Mary Ann, a marriage should be a time of joy, a time of great happiness. Listen to yourself: does yours sound like a happy voice, full of joy? Isn't there something I can say?"

"There's nothing you can say, Father. It's our decision, and we've made it." She broke into uncontrolled sobbing and hung up.

Damn! Damn! Damn! Neiss thought. All over some goddamn rule Thompson dreamed up and then made ironclad. All this suffering and sorrow due to Thompson's goddamned rule. All this suffering and sorrow. God! There must be some way of making him pay for it this side of the grave.

In impotent anger, Neiss hurled a roll of coins at the wall. The wrapper broke, spewing pennies in all directions. Swell! Now he could play fifty-pickup and further stew in his growing anger for a man who was further screwing up an already screwed-up system.

———————

It was some sixth sense. Ordinarily, Father Norm Shanley discounted intuition as a vehicle leading to reality, truth, or the knowledge of future events. But there was no doubt he was experiencing forebodings about the Warwick-Brand wedding scheduled to take place in about twenty-five minutes.

Shanley passed on his way to the church at the doorway of the rectory living room. Father James Porter had just returned from offering the 5 P.M. Saturday Mass and was seated in the living room. Shanley would not casually pass by without greeting him.

"So, how was the five o'clock Mass, Father?"

Porter expertly spun his wheelchair around to face the doorway and Shanley.

"The usual. But, say, Father," Porter's expression was a mixture of interest and curiosity, "that looks to be some wedding party that's getting ready for six."

"Oh, were they there before you left the church?" A vague sense of panic set Shanley's adrenaline flowing.

"Yes. Parishioners?" Porter was skeptical. No Rosary parishioners he knew of could afford the sort of preparation he had observed.

"No. Not a parishioner. Somebody who needed some help. Don't worry about it."

Shanley left to hurry to the church. Porter puzzled over what kind of help would be needed by anyone able to afford that show of wealth.

Shanley entered the church. It was worse than his worst fears. The church was filling with people in formal attire. He thought that even in Rosary's heyday, it had never housed *hoi aristoi* comparable to this. Auxiliary air conditioners were being assembled against the walls. He was certain the church's antiquated electrical system could never sustain such a drain. He did not know auxiliary generators had been set up outside.

Strobe lights bounced off an unending series of aristocratic profiles. Huge baskets full of fresh-cut flowers created a funereal fragrance.

And the news media! There they were. He wondered how he could have missed them earlier. They had been outside the church recording the entrance of the elite as well as the presence and open-mouthed amazement of the neighbors, some of whom were sober. Now the TV cameras and their crews entered the church, which was flooded by the bright lights. He counted. Channels 2, 4, and 7. That pretty well covered Detroit and environs.

Near the door were Bunny and Sunny. The former in flowing white, the latter in off-pink. In tux and tails was Lee Brand, greeting guests and appearing to own the church, which, Shanley surmised, he pretty nearly did.

109

Shanley was struck by one overwhelming presentiment. My ecclesiastical ass, he thought, is in a sling.

"Deal!" His fist hit the table, thumb snapped against middle finger, and index finger pointed directly at Bob Koesler. Father Darin O'Day was tolerant of delay to a point, but not when it came to poker. For him, in fact, "deal" was an unexpected utterance. Usually, it was just the thudding fist, the snapped thumb, and an accusatory index finger pointed at the offender, who was left to guess what it was in the game he should be doing that he was not.

Koesler brought his shuffle to an end and began to deal. "Five-card draw, jacks or better to open."

"Anything wild? Anything wild?" asked Father Felix Lasko.

"There'd better not be," warned Father Patrick McNiff.

"No, nothing wild," Koesler reassured.

It was a casual gathering of classmates or at least contemporaries of Koesler. Saturday evenings, each took turns hosting an informal poker party. This evening was Koesler's turn, so the party was located in St. Anselm's rectory basement.

"I can open," announced Monsignor Tommy Thompson. He threw a white chip in the center of the table. "It'll cost you a buck to stay."

There was a clink of chips being tossed into the pot as everyone decided to go one more step. Koesler dealt again.

O'Day's fist hit the table, there was a snapping noise, and his index finger pointed meaningfully at Thompson.

"Oh." Thompson recovered and gave one final quick study to his original two and three freshly dealt cards. "It'll cost you five." He added five white chips to the pot.

Koesler threw in his cards. "Too rich for me. Anyone want a beer?"

"I'll take one," said McNiff.

Whiskey, scotch, gin, vermouth, and a bucket of ice rested on a nearby cabinet. Drinking was relatively light at these Saturday night sessions. The participants had to work the next day.

Father Paul Burk delayed a moment, then threw in five white chips.

110

Koesler went to the refrigerator and got a Schlitz for McNiff.

There was the familiar thump and snap. O'Day was pointing at Lasko.

"Oh, dear," said Lasko, studying his cards. "Is a full house higher than three of a kind?"

"Damn!" said O'Day in a rare display of loquacity.

Throwing in his hand, Koesler announced, "I want to catch the eleven o'clock news." He moved to the ancient color TV set reserved for the basement.

After the last ad of the preceding program, the familiar face of Bill Bonds, Detroit's most watched anchorperson, appeared on screen. "Good evening, ladies and gentlemen. Some of the news tonight: a seven-car Amtrak derailment between Detroit and Chicago. The wedding of the year in an inner-city Catholic church. This and much more coming up on Channel 7's eleven o'clock action news with Diana Lewis, Dave Diles with sports, and Jerry Hodak with the weather."

Pause for commercials.

Wedding of the year in an inner-city Catholic church? What the hell was that all about, Koesler wondered. He paid little attention to the Amtrak derailment. He was waiting for the wedding of the year.

"Hey, will you turn that thing down," called McNiff; "we're trying to play cards."

Koesler turned down the volume and sat only inches from the screen.

Beautiful Diana Lewis had the wedding story.

"Well, Bill," she said, "the wedding of the year, maybe the decade, maybe the century," she shrugged, "took place near downtown Detroit this evening as Richard Warwick wed popular socialite Bunny Brand."

Film showed limousines arriving at the church. The camera zoomed in on the arrivals of banking, utilities, and Big Three auto executives and their wives, couples from Detroit's sports, political, and communications world, as well as such representatives of Detroit's publiciety scene as Ron and Dana Schoonover, heirs to Elsa Maxwell's party-giver's mantle. Also spotlighted were Detroit's hard-nosed but polished assistant police chief and his doll-like but cerebral helpmate. Most of the remainder of Detroit's fabulously famous rounded out the group entering the now-crowded church.

Diana identified celebrities as they appeared. "And," she continued, "they all were there to see *this* couple exchange their vows in a brief Catholic ceremony." On the screen were Richard and Bunny. They were perfect; he a tuxedoed Viking, she shyly but elegantly virginal.

"Our Ven Marshall," said Diana, "was there to cover the event for Channel 7."

There was the familiar square face of Ven Marshall with a beaming Lee Brand. "And here," said Ven, "is the proud father of the bride, Mr. Lee Brand, president of First Standard Bank and Trust. How do you feel, Mr. Brand?"

"Great, just great," said the grinning Brand. "I guess every father thinks there is no one good enough for his daughter. But . . ." He winked. ". . . Richard comes close."

"And here," another shot of Ven Marshall, now with an obviously bewildered Shanley, "is the priest who performed the ceremony. Any comments, Father Shanley?"

"Er . . . no. Please, I've got to leave now."

"Well, that's it, Diana. The reception will be at the Detroit Athletic Club. But I can tell you this," added Marshall, "there is a special sense of pride that a wedding of such magnitude could take place right here in a core-city area instead of a posh suburban setting.

"This is Ven Marshall, Channel 7 Action News, at Our Lady of the Rosary church in the heart of the city of Detroit."

Koesler, conscious that his mouth hung open, closed it. He gave a long, low, all-but-inaudible whistle.

Shanley's ecclesiastical ass, Koesler concluded, is in a sling.

He was internationally known as "The Reverend Charles E. Coughlin, controversial radio priest of the '30s." Although in his *New York Times* obituary, he was identified as "the 'radio priest' of the Depression who was ultimately silenced by the hierarchy of the Roman Catholic Church . . ."

To some of his confreres, he was known somewhat irreverently as "Twelve-Mile Charlie." So closely was he linked with the church he had built on the corner of Twelve-Mile Road and Woodward Avenue. Shrine of the Little Flower and Father Coughlin had a uniquely symbiotic relationship. Coughlin financed the building of his avant-garde church largely from the earnings of his broadcasting and publishing empire. An empire that had required the combined clout of the Vatican, a Detroit Cardinal Archbishop, and the U.S. government to halt and silence it.

Although Coughlin had been retired for more than a decade at the time of his death, Shrine still bore his imprints. Some of those imprints were exiting the church following the Sunday noon Mass.

Each bore, tucked firmly under an arm, the latest issue of *The Wanderer*, a wildly conservative national weekly newspaper that regularly appealed from a weak-kneed Pope (who was, in the editor's eyes, constantly slipping toward Godless atheism) to *The Wanderer*'s God, who, by damn, knew the value of capitalism and the vital importance of the National Rifle Association.

Tight-lipped and beady-eyed, Coughlin's crew strode toward the parking lot where, if one were not careful, one could get killed by autos that played at Dodgem without the playfulness of rubber bumpers.

Frankly, Monsignor Thompson enjoyed helping out at Shrine on weekends. He had done so for several years.

He had just finished offering noon Mass, the final Mass scheduled for Sunday at Shrine. He was "up," with the peculiar exhilaration that comes from having invested a sizable measure of effort in offering Mass and delivering a well-spoken homily.

He stood outside the Church, greeting the parishioners, at least those who would speak to him.

Some of these people reminded him of Coughlin's, instead of Frankenstein's, monsters. Old Charlie had gone a bit far in developing a paranoid community, Thompson thought. Thompson preferred people who, while maintaining a healthy reverence for the cloth, still could be civil to priests. Some of the younger parishioners at Shrine were all right, especially those who had moved in since Coughlin's retirement.

After the final *Wanderer*-bearing couple had passed, Thompson returned to the sacristy, divesting as he went. Having declined an enticing brunch, he drove back to St. David's, his parish of residence on Detroit's east side. If he was lucky and the threatening weather held off, he hoped to get in a little golf.

As he was changing into golfing togs, Thompson reflected on what a seller's market the archdiocese had become. When it came to large metropolitan areas, the priest shortage was at least as critical in Detroit as anywhere else. Thus, instead of receiving assignment letters that began, "For the care of souls, I have it in mind to send you to . . ." priests now could pretty well pick their ministries.

Thompson had selected Shrine in which to donate weekend help partly because the Royal Oak area held a generally wealthy and educated populace, and partly because of its mystique as The House that Charlie Built.

He had chosen St. David's as a place of residence because it was reasonably close to downtown, it was in a mixed but stable neighborhood, and the facilities—downstairs office, upstairs bedroom, sitting room, shower and toilet—were excellent.

But, he thought, as he adjusted his golf cap, if these things change, so can I.

He was passing through the living room en route to his Eldorado, in the trunk of which were his golf clubs and cart, when, for the first time, he saw the front page of Sunday's *News*. He did a double take and stopped dead in his tracks.

On the left side of the front page was a three-column photo, which would not, of itself, have attracted Thompson's attention. However, the related headline read, "Brand Nuptials in Downtown Detroit." The photo displayed Mr. and Mrs. Lee Brand, Mr. Richard Warwick and the new Mrs. Warwick, all grinning merrily.

In the background was a churchlike structure Thompson thought he recognized. Fervidly, he read the account of the wedding. On the jump page were more pictures.

Thompson could not recall when he had been more furious. Brand had got his goddamn way and screwed Thompson in the bargain. As he studied the photo, it seemed to Thompson that Brand was not merely smiling at an auspicous occasion. It

114

seemed Brand was laughing outright at the head of the Tribunal who could not control his troops.

Thompson felt a mixture of humiliation and frustrated fury. He tried to think of some—any—form of revenge. He could not. Brand appeared to hold all the cards. He'd gotten his damned Catholic ceremony, and on the chance the marriage didn't work out, they would have no trouble proving it was invalid, and Bunny would be free to try again. With another damn Catholic ceremony.

Well, that was the bad news. The silver lining was the sacrificial lamb who had performed the ceremony. Thompson referred to the story once more. Father Norman Shanley. The name didn't ring a bell. That didn't matter. What did matter was he finally had one of the inner-city boys under the microscope. Thompson knew those guys were playing fast and loose with canon law, and now he had one of them dead to rights. He had the bastard now! He would make sure the bastard was skewered and left to dangle in the wind.

Golf forgotten, Thompson dialed the private number, known to few, of the Archbishop's residence in Palmer Park.

After a few rings, a soft-voiced Monsignor Joseph Iming answered.

"Joe," said Thompson, "I want to talk to the Boss."

"Yes, I think it's important enough to wake him from his nap."

Thompson, adrenaline still surging, sat waiting, drumming his fingers on the desk. Archbishop Boyle had a tendency to treat such matters as lightly as possible. Thompson was determined to follow this case right through to its conclusion. He would make certain justice was done.

If he couldn't reach Brand, he was sure as hell going to squash this Shanley upstart.

"Hello, Archbishop? I'm sorry I woke you, but this is a matter of utmost importance. Have you seen today's *News*? No? Well, let me tell you . . ."

———————

On this partly cloudy Sunday, Angela Cicero couldn't decide whether to put on more suntan lotion.

115

She and her husband, Leo, were relaxing in deck chairs by the side of the pool at the Dearborn Country Club. The high humidity had been the deciding factor in Leo's choice to stay poolside rather than use the club's manicured golf course.

"So what do you think, Leo," Angela asked, "do you think I need more lotion?"

Leo looked up from his book and over his reading glasses. "You'll be O.K." He admired the fact that his wife had preserved her figure so well. Even after twenty-three years of marriage and three kids, she weighed the same and did not look much different than when they were first married. She was neither thin nor fat, but firm. And she looked great in a swimsuit.

She had done much better than he, thought Leo as he rubbed his tonsure and glanced at the potbelly suspended over his trunks. He again promised himself that one day soon he would get back into shape. He returned to his book.

Angela looked on as their daughter Anna Maria, youngest of the Ciceros, frolicked in the pool with her fiancé, Dale Worthington. A frown crossed Angela's face. Anna Maria, no less than the rest of the family, wanted a big Catholic wedding. Her parents had done everything possible to ensure that event. Now, all their hopes were resting on some bureaucrat's desk in Rome. The wedding was but six days away. Good fortune or an extremely lucky and well-timed phone call was all that stood between the Cicero family and disaster.

Angela retrieved her copy of Sunday's *News*. Her frown was replaced by a puzzled expression.

"Rosary church," she said, "isn't that in the middle of the ghetto?"

"Practically," Leo answered.

Angela reread the wedding article. "Why do you suppose the Brand wedding was held at Rosary?"

"Beats me."

"It couldn't be because Rosary is near the DAC where the reception was held, could it?"

"Nah. What's a few miles to a guy like Lee Brand?"

The silence was broken only by the shouts from the pool.

"Maybe *we'll* end up down there," said Angela, a trace of discouragement in her voice.

"What—at Rosary? Don't be silly." He reached over and patted her arm. "Don't you worry about a thing. If worst comes to worst, you've got that number at the Vatican. You can call good-old Father what's-his-name."

"Yes," said Angela, "it's all a matter of timing."

She put down the paper, pulled on her swim cap, stepped to the pool, and dove flawlessly from the board.

Great figure, Leo thought. One of these days, I'm going to have to do something about getting mine back in shape.

His worst suspicions were confirmed. Archbishop Boyle was disposed to merely slap Shanley's wrist instead of throwing the book at him.

Monsignor Thompson had arrived a little early for his 9 A.M. Monday appointment with the Archbishop. This appointment, as well as the one to follow at ten, with Father Shanley, had been granted only at Thompson's adamant insistence.

Thompson had been arguing with Boyle for forty-five minutes and had won no solid concession. There were only fifteen minutes left before Shanley would have his day in court, and the judge was far from being in a hanging mood.

At no time during this argument had Thompson mentioned his own involvement with the Brand affair. On the one hand, Brand's victory was still too galling a memory and, on the other, Thompson did not wish to cloud the issue with any personal digressions. There was no doubt whatsoever of Shanley's crime. What was at stake was his punishment.

"But Excellency," said Thompson, "it's not only the fact that what Father Shanley did is a flagrant abuse of canonical procedure but that this lawbreaking was flaunted before the public in both our metropolitan newspapers and on radio and television."

"I'm sure, Monsignor, that Father Shanley—from all I know of him—that Father Shanley did not intend to receive such public coverage for what he did." Boyle was unsure how he had come to be placed virtually in the role of defense attorney. Except that Thompson's inability to settle for any but the harshest penalty

117

for Shanley's act seemed to demand a spokesperson for the defense.

"Excellency, it is not a matter of what Father Shanley did or didn't intend. The fact is that his lawbreaking is now as common knowledge as anything could be. Even if he did not intend such publicity, the inescapable reality is that he got it. Everyone in this archdiocese, and with wire services, people throughout the country—the world—know that Father Shanley violated almost the essence of canon law. And they rightly expect a public response from you."

Boyle began toying with the gold chain of his pectoral cross, one of his mannerisms when ill at ease. "Perhaps then, a publicity release or a press conference at which time I could explain the canonical procedure and publicly disavow what Father Shanley did."

Thompson shook his head vehemently. "Not enough, Excellency. You and I both know that this sort of thing is more than common in the core city. The priests there feel free to run roughshod over canon law. They feel that no one in authority will know what they're doing, and, with deference to you, Excellency, they are sure that no one in authority wants to know what they're doing. This is practically a God-given opportunity to get the attention of every priest in this archdiocese by enforcing the strongest ecclesiastical sanctions."

"What do you suggest?"

"Enforced laicization."

"Taking his priesthood from him?" Boyle was genuinely shocked. "No, Monsignor, that is out of the question."

"Then suspension."

Boyle did not reply.

"Excellency, permit me to be perfectly frank."

Boyle, index fingers pressed against his lips, bowed his head in acquiescence.

"Your reluctance to level ecclesiastical sanctions has led to a popular but unanswered question on the part of some Detroit priests. It is a question that has been bandied about behind your back. It is asked only half-jokingly: 'How much can you get away with in the Archdiocese of Detroit?' You will never be in

118

a better position than now to provide the much-needed answer to that question: suspension, at the very least.''

At this point, Boyle's secretary announced Shanley.

Neither Boyle nor Thompson rose when he entered, so Shanley simply took a chair opposite the Archbishop.

Shanley was genuinely embarrassed at being summoned to appear before his archbishop, whom he deeply admired, under these circumstances. Thompson's presence simply confused him.

"Needless to say, Father," Boyle began, "I am deeply disappointed in what you have done.''

"I am sorry for that, Excellency.''

"Do you have anything to say in your own behalf?''

Shanley shifted uncomfortably, as if he were under a spotlight. "Only that the one responsible for that wedding promised me there would be no publicity.''

"Father," said Boyle, "to make matters clear from the beginning, *you* are the one responsible for that wedding.''

"I mean the one who asked me to perform the ceremony promised. He betrayed my trust.''

"And," Boyle leaned forward, "you in turn, Father, betrayed the Church's trust.''

Shanley said nothing.

"Church law has not been abrogated," Boyle continued. "And you as a priest have the duty to apply and enforce this law, Father. You have no authority to change or violate canon laws. Is that clear, Father?''

Shanley did not raise his head to look at the Archbishop. "Yes, Excellency.''

"Do you have anything else to say, Father?''

"No, Excellency.'' The Archbishop's words had a familiar ring. What was tacit was ". . . before sentence is passed.''

"Very well, then.'' Boyle toyed with the episcopal ring on the third finger of his right hand. Another of his mannerisms when ill at ease. "Father, I must suspend you from priestly functions for one month.''

Suspension! Shanley was devastated. He had expected a dressing down but not this punishment. That seemed to answer the question going around the city's priestly circles: how much can you get away with in the Archdiocese of Detroit?

One month's suspension, Thompson thought. Not long enough! Not nearly long enough!

"During this month," Boyle continued, "you will, of course, continue to be a priest. But I will remove my permission for you to function as such. You may not hear confession, offer Mass, preach, or administer any of the sacraments except in cases of emergency."

There was a lengthy pause during which Shanley tried to absorb the ramifications of this unexpected punishment.

"Do you intend to announce my punishment publicly?"

"Ordinarily I would not," Boyle replied. "But in this instance what you have done was so thoroughly publicized . . ."

There was another pause.

"Suspension, Excellency," said Shanley falteringly, "suspension is like excommunication, a special penalty for sin."

The Archbishop, his penetrating blue eyes almost hidden beneath bushy soot-colored eyebrows, nodded solemnly.

"But," Shanley protested, "I do not consider myself guilty of sin."

"Father," said Boyle, "we are not dealing exclusively here with matters of conscience. This is not a matter of the internal forum of the confessional. What you did was in the external forum. And so must be the punishment. If you do not know it is sinful to witness the attempted marriage of a person already in a presumed valid marriage, then you very well should know it."

Shanley thought of all those he had helped by discarding canon law. He thought of Leroy and Elvira Sanders, their canonically hopeless marriage now miraculously healed. How happy they were. If he were to accept this penalty, what would all those people think about their own condition? Would they be thrown back into the nightmare of fear and self-torture laid on by the un-Christian strictures of canon law?

"Excellency," said Shanley, "I must have some time to consider before accepting this penalty."

It was Boyle's turn to be surprised. He began pulling and pushing his episcopal ring off and on his finger. "Time? Very well, Father. One week. No more than that. Your decision must be made,'' Boyle consulted his desk calendar and made a notation on it, ''no later than August 6.''

Thompson could have kissed Shanley. Or, at least demonstrated his gratitude in some manner. He could not have prayed for more. At worst, Shanley would be suspended and the punishment made public. At best, Shanley would refuse the penalty, and Boyle would then have no recourse but to laicize him.

Years before, when Thompson had been Defender of the Bond, he had tried to get the Michigan Attorney General's office to agree to a plan that would have gotten the attention of ecclesiastical law-breakers. The state routinely recognizes as civilly valid marriages all weddings witnessed by bona fide ministers, priests, or rabbis, who are, in turn, recognized as such by their own established churches.

Thompson's plan was to convince the state not to recognize as valid civil marriages those weddings that the various denominations did not recognize as valid religious marriages. If he had been successful, these canonically invalid marriages would also be declared invalid in civil law.

In this he rightly surmised that the few priests involved in witnessing canonically invalid marriages would be discouraged from doing so by the potentially disastrous complications ensuing from civil law.

But Michigan's attorney general, though Catholic, could spot a red herring when he saw one, and had dismissed Thompson's attempt with a negative ruling.

Since then, Thompson had never experienced a better opportunity to get the attention of those violators of canon law than now. And he had capitalized on it. Shanley would become his sacrificial victim. Shanley's head would be mounted on the castle gate for all to see.

Thompson was happier than he'd been since he had been appointed to monsignorial rank.

As Shanley rose to leave the Archbishop's office, the purpose of Monsignor Thompson's presence became clear to him. This was all Thompson's doing. Archbishop Boyle would never have done all this if left alone. He, Shanley, was to become Thompson's scapegoat in the Monsignor's war against violators of canon law.

At Thompson's door, Shanley could lay all his present and impending woe. He had never before felt such loathing for another human being.

He was sure he had committed no sin by disregarding canon law. He was not too certain he was free from sin in his animosity toward Monsignor Thomas Thompson.

———————

It was as if she were back in high school.

Pat Lennon had informed her news editor, with whom she felt comfortable about being open and aboveboard, of her appointment this Monday afternoon at the Tribunal. She had no intention of skipping out of the *News* on the pretext of developing some story. Besides not being the type to dissemble, Lennon could sense she was on the right track toward getting a decree of nullity for her previous marriage, and she wanted everything to do with her case, including her absence this afternoon, to be on the up and up.

This would clear the way for marriage with Joe Cox in a Catholic ceremony. The only way she would have it. All this she shared with her editor, Bob Ankenazy, who was happy for her, told her to take the afternoon off, and wished her luck.

She returned to her Lafayette Towers apartment, showered and perfumed for the second time that day, and dressed in what was, for her, a severe style. She tried to pretend she was dressing for an audience with the Pope. She wore a high-necked white cotton blouse with a blue neck ribbon and a blue-and-white seersucker suit.

It didn't work. Each and every curve insinuated its presence.

She was early for her 2 P.M. appointment, her second with the Tribunal. Her previous visit had been two weeks before, when she had been interviewed by Father Ed Oleksiak. He had listened to her story, taken copious notes, and been cautiously encouraging. It was his opinion that she had entered her marriage out of spite and not freely. Depending on the evidence that could be gathered, Father Oleksiak thought a strong case could be built. At that point, he had been called from the office.

122

Lennon did not know it, but Monsignor Thompson, who had earlier observed her with interest, had quizzed Oleksiak about her case and told him to arrange a follow-up appointment for her with the Monsignor.

Oleksiak had returned and informed Lennon her next appointment would be with the head of the Tribunal. Lennon had deemed that to be a positive sign: her case was going right to the top.

His interview with Lennon had redeemed the day for Oleksiak. It had been the day he had been forced to call his friend Father Neiss and inform him of Monsignor Thompson's Polish policy. That had been as nasty an experience as the Lennon interview had been heartening.

Monsignor Thompson returned from lunch promptly at 1:30. He was so ebullient from his triumph over Father Shanley that morning that he had not even chafed at the parochial pedestrian conversation of St. Aloysius's dining room.

He was well aware that Pat Lennon was sitting, legs demurely crossed, in the Tribunal's foyer. But he spent half an hour studying Ed Oleksiak's notes on her case.

At two, Mary Alberts knocked at his door.

"There is a Patricia Lennon to see you, Monsignor."

"All right, Mary." He did not look up from the notes. "Show her in."

Mary Alberts did not leave immediately.

"Monsignor," she said, "I don't want to alarm you, but someone has been in the files. They are slightly out of order."

She needn't have worried about alarming him. He was convinced she filed her pantyhose each night. Probably one of the notaries being sloppy while rummaging through the files.

"No need to worry, Mary. Nobody wants our files. I'll look into it later."

"Yes, Monsignor."

She directed Lennon to his office.

From the moment she entered Monsignor Thompson's office, Pat Lennon felt a growing sense of disappointment verging on anxiety. She had expected the head of the Tribunal to be a skilled expert, a professional, perhaps even a very ascetic saintly man. Someone who would be able to evaluate the merit of her case

123

quickly and facilitate matters toward a speedy and desirable solution.

However, such was not to be her good fortune. She sensed it almost as she entered the room. It was in the look he gave her. From the top of her head to the tip of her toe, his lingering glance told a pitiful tale she had encountered many times.

She had been lasciviously inspected and mentally disrobed and imaginarily raped by experts. And this Monsignor ranked with the best, or grossest of them.

She had hoped for so much. Yet, she felt as if she had been offered so little. She felt that special sense of despair that one experiences in dealing with a corrupt police officer. To whom do you appeal when the one sworn to protect you attacks you? To whom do you turn when the chief officer of the marriage court wants to bed you rather than judge you?

She had had such high hopes.

They exchanged perfunctory greetings.

"Now, Miss Lennon," he consulted his notes, "according to the testimony you gave Father Oleksiak, you described the consummation of your marriage as a form of rape."

"Yes." She found it difficult to look at him.

"But you were married in a Catholic church, the ceremony witnessed by a Catholic priest?"

"Yes."

"Well, Miss Lennon, it's quite impossible for a husband to rape his wife. She has a *debitum*, a debt, which she must render whenever her husband reasonably demands it. You went to Catholic school, even college; you must have learned that."

"Yes, I learned that in school and then, later, I learned the lessons of reality."

"So, he raped you. You resisted?"

"Of course," she said firmly; "what do you think happens during a rape?"

"Not all women resist, Miss Lennon. Studies show that some women bring it on themselves by their suggestive clothing and actions. You can't tell me these women resist. They enjoy it."

A male chauvinist pig to boot, Lennon thought.

"Well," Thompson continued, "what did he do? Did he beat you? Rip off your clothes?"

124

"Yes."

"Yes to both?"

"Yes." From his tone, Lennon guessed Thompson was, in his imagination, doing to her what her husband had done.

"Did he have to go through this same procedure every time he wanted to have you?"

"No."

"No? Can you explain?"

"It wasn't worth the fight. We stayed together only three months. I couldn't stand him."

"I see." Thompson tapped his pen against the desk. "Was your wedding night the first time you had intercourse with your husband?"

"No." Lennon found herself blushing.

"How often? Frequently?"

"Look," said Lennon, "I don't see what this line of questioning has to do with my case."

"Miss Lennon, leave the questions to me. This is my field of expertise."

I'll just bet it is, Lennon thought.

"So," Thompson repeated, "how often?"

"Once, twice a week. Toward the end of our brief engagement, maybe three or four times a week."

"And where did all this activity go on? The back seat of cars?"

Lennon guessed Thompson was engaged in a form of mental masturbation.

"No, not in the back seat of cars," Lennon said sharply. "Leonard had an apartment."

"Was there foreplay or was it just the act of intercourse?"

"There was foreplay." Lennon felt her blush deepen.

"Was there kinky sex or was it always the missionary position?"

"Monsignor," Lennon was on the brink of losing her temper, "I don't think I am going to answer any more of your questions."

"Very well, Miss Lennon. But I must tell you that your story does not jibe. Why would you have intercourse regularly and

125

willingly and then suddenly on your wedding night accuse your husband of rape?''

Lennon sighed and decided to give it one more try. Though she could not understand why her story had made sense to Father Oleksiak, while Thompson seemed to find it incredible.

''Monsignor, I'm not claiming what I did was honorable, made sense, or was even normal. I'm not at all proud of that period of my life. I didn't even understand it at the time. It was only years after the fact that I was able to sort it all out and, I think, understand it.

''When my original plan to marry was broken up by my parents, I hated them for it. But I internalized the hatred. Then I found a man they could never accept. Only, it turned out, neither could I. I seduced Leonard, I guess. But as soon as I married him and had sufficiently punished my parents, I could no longer stand him. Why, I was so torn up over the whole thing, I developed a rash that disappeared as soon as Leonard and I separated.''

''Ah, yes, the rash.'' Thompson again consulted his notes. ''Was the rash confined to your face or arms or did it cover your entire body?''

His eyes covered her entire body.

''I thought I made it clear earlier, Monsignor, that I did not intend to answer any more of these clinically personal questions.''

Thompson tapped the notes together, inserted them deliberately in a manila folder, and set the folder to one side.

''That, of course,'' he said, ''is up to you. But our hands are tied. It does not seem to me to be a very strong case. You were undoubtedly upset by what happened, particularly when your parents discouraged your first attempt at marriage. But nothing that happened to you could be construed as blocking your free-will decisions.''

They both rose. She noticed his eyes were on the bulge in the jacket made by her breasts.

''Your reluctance to answer questions,'' he continued, ''is not going to do you any good. If you were more cooperative . . .'' Thompson spread his hands at his sides in a gesture intended to convey that it was all up to her.

126

Without a word, Lennon left the Tribunal. She felt demeaned, embarrassed, hurt, and angry. What had begun with so much hope now was heavy with an air of despair. And, seemingly, all due to one monsignorial jackass.

As she reached Washington Boulevard, a thought came. She found a pay phone and dialed the number of Father Leo Clark, whom she considered her primary source in any question having to do with religion. The operator at St. John's Seminary informed her that Father Clark had returned to his native Idaho for summer vacation.

Next, she dialed Father Koesler, her secondary source. Fortunately, he was available at St. Anselm's. Pat explained, dispensing with the more lurid details, what had transpired in her two visits to the Tribunal.

"What I want to know, Father," she concluded, "is, can he do it? I mean, Father Oleksiak was so kind, so understanding, and helpful. And then this bastard—pardon my French, Father—comes along and messes everything up. Can't I go back to Father Oleksiak and forget about this clown?"

Koesler, standing next to his desk, shook his head. " 'Fraid not, Pat. I'm sorry, but a case as complicated as yours would never get through without Monsignor Thompson's knowing about it. Now that he's taken a personal interest, there's just no way to get around him."

"What if I took it to another city?"

"No good. The relevant court is Detroit. You live here, and you got married in this archdiocese.

"I'm sorry, Pat. I know how frustrated you must feel. Why don't you just live as a Catholic without going through the Tribunal? Nobody's going to stop you."

"It's not that easy. I've got a live-in. If this had gone through, we were going to get married."

Koesler felt bad. Also useless. "I am sorry, Pat. But remember, it's a matter of your conscience. No one can form that for you but you. If your conscience tells you you're doing the best you can, that's the best you can do."

He was conscious his words were of little practical value, but he could think of nothing more to offer.

Lennon thanked him and hung up.

Suddenly, like a light bulb flashing on over her head, a new thought occurred. Thompson's final words. If she would be more cooperative . . . the son-of-a-bitch wants to go to bed with me! God bless us, if it isn't Karl Lowell, it's a Catholic monsignor. That bastard! I could kill him!

The basement was a mess. At least its southwest corner was in shambles.

The Ciceros were in the midst of redecorating and remodeling their basement. Ladders, tools, buckets of paint and mortar, piles of bricks were everywhere. Anna Maria, her fiancé, and several of their friends were busily and noisily painting the stuccoed walls, while Leo and Angela were working with the bricks and mortar. They were closing off the basement's southwest corner to be rid of an eyesore and add to the room's symmetry, since a previous owner had bricked off the northwest corner.

"Thank God for central air," said Leo.

"Even with air conditioning, this is pretty hot work," said Angela dabbing at her forehead.

The two worked smoothly together, she spreading and smoothing layers of mortar, he placing the bricks and tamping them.

"One thing for sure, though," said Leo, "we'll never be done in time for the wedding."

"It doesn't matter. That's why we hired a hall for the reception."

"The hall." He fumbled a brick. "For a moment I forgot the hall. And the deposit. When's the latest we can cancel the hall and get our deposit back?"

"We've already passed the fail-safe time. The deposit is not ours anymore."

Leo put down the brick and sat on the small stool inside the enclosure they were creating.

"Are you sure you shouldn't be calling Rome now? I mean, supposing everyone's on vacation. The Pope spends lots of time during the summer at that place—what's it name—Castelgandolfo—doesn't he? What if he's out of town? It *is* the Pope that has to give permission, isn't it? Or does one of his flunkies rubber-stamp it? Shouldn't you be moving on this?''

"Calm down, will you." Angela smiled. "If you don't take it easier, *you* won't be around for the wedding."

"How can you be so calm about it? This is Monday evening and the wedding is scheduled for next Saturday afternoon. We've got to get permission from Rome, and we don't know when or if it's coming. Between us and disaster are four days of mail delivery and a phone number. And we haven't even got a backup plan!" Leo's concluding sentence was delivered so loudly the others paused briefly in their painting and glanced at him.

"I check every day with that nice Father Oleksiak to see if they've gotten the document. Thank God for him. He never gets impatient. He even encourages me to call. If it weren't for him, I'd have to deal with that Monsignor Thompson. And that would be impossible."

"But what if it doesn't come?"

"Then I've got the phone number." She handed him a brick. She was getting too far ahead of him. "And Father Koesler said to trust my instincts to know exactly the right time to make the call."

"But you never called Rome before!"

"So, what's that? You dial the number, you get the party, you explain the problem, you get the answer."

Leo shook his head. I wish I were as sure of this as you are."

"So do I."

Angela could not let her husband know, but she was not at all that self-confident. For the past several days, she had spent nearly every waking moment worrying about the wedding and doubtful about the timing of the phone call.

Monsignor Thompson could have been a substantial help in this, but he was not.

She would not forget.

———————

"You mean all those weddings were invalid?" Father James Porter seemed to be pleading for a negative response.

Since his confrontation with Archbishop Boyle and Monsignor Thompson the day before, Father Shanley had been dreading this moment when he would have to tell all to his pastor.

"No, no," Shanley reassured, "by no means were all the weddings I performed here invalid. Just a few of them."

"A few of them!" The old man rubbed his head. "*One* would have been too many."

It was no use. Shanley had explained his opposition to canon law and the ratiocination that had led him into a sacramental approach that now had been condemned. He also had told his pastor about the meeting of the day before and the dilemma he now faced.

But, as Shanley had feared, Porter found none of it credible. Worse, the old man appeared to be personally offended, something Shanley had never intended.

"I just don't know how you could do this in my parish, in my church." The old priest pounded his fist against the arm of his wheelchair with as much force as he could muster.

"Father, I had to follow my conscience."

"Not when it conflicts with Church law, Father. And not in *my* church!"

Shanley made no response.

"Well, Father," Porter half-turned his chair, indicating the conversation was at an end, "I do not know whether you will accept the Archbishop's discipline. But I do know one thing: you will have to find another residence."

"Father!"

"I'm sorry, Father. I would never be sure if you were validly administering a sacrament or following your conscience. I am truly sorry, Father. I thought we could be . . . friends. But my mind is made up on this."

"All right, Father. Whatever else happens, I'll make arrangements to move as soon as I can." Shanley went to his room and sat at the writing desk.

His small world had tumbled around his ears. He tried to think of how he might have done things differently. From earliest memory, he had never seriously planned any calling other than the priesthood. Yet, shortly after he was ordained, he knew he could not enforce the prescripts of canon law. He then decided to supplant Church law with the law of Christ as he understood

130

Christ's law. He could not believe he had done any wrong save in one thing—getting caught practicing Christ's law.

A new thought occurred. There was an alternative. He did not necessarily have to choose between accepting or rejecting the penalty of suspension. He could leave the priesthood.

God, what a choice!

His only blame lay in having followed his conscience. Nor could he fault Father Porter's reaction. That dear old man was, after all, to the bone a loyal son of the Church.

Shanley found it difficult even to blame Lee Brand. He was a man of the world getting what he wanted any way he could. Besides, Brand had an irrefutable argument of reverse discrimination if Shanley had refused to witness the marriage.

Then there was Thompson. There had been no purpose in Thompson's presence the day before except that he had pressed the Archbishop into levying this extreme ecclesiastical punishment.

No doubt about it: of all the roles in this scenario that had brought Shanley down, Thompson's was the one most freely and deliberately exercised.

There should be some way of making Thompson answer for his un-Christian reprisal even before he met God in judgment.

Shanley sat at his desk and thought.

———————

Three A.M., Friday, August 3.

It was time.

Angela Cicero had not retired for the night. She sat in a fairly uncomfortable chair near the phone. She had spent the past several hours rereading Edgar Allan Poe, a particular favorite among the mystery writers. She had fought to stay awake, and she had succeeded.

It was now 9 A.M. in Rome. Angela visualized the Vatican routine. Up around six; Mass, prayer, breakfast, preparation for the day, and now at nine about ready to leave.

Carefully, she dialed Rome's area code, followed by the Villa Stritch number. The phone rang, seemingly interminably. With each ring, her level of self-confidence further waned. Could this be the wrong time? Had she waited too long? Was it too late to make the round-trip?

"Pronto," a deep baritone said.

"Hello?" Angela tried.

"Oh, hello," the voice, now sounding very American, responded.

"Hello. Is this Villa Stritch?"

"Yes."

Thank God, Angela breathed. Now to push my luck one step further. "May I please speak with Father Patrick Cammarata?"

"Speaking."

Thank God. It was becoming less an expression and more a prayer. "My name is Angela Cicero—Mrs. Leo Cicero—and I'm calling from Dearborn, Michigan. That's a suburb of Detroit."

"I know where Dearborn is, Mrs. Cicero. You're very fortunate. I was just heading out the door. A few minutes earlier and nobody would have been in this room. A few minutes later, and I would have been gone for the day."

Thank God. Now it was a prayer, pure and simple.

"What can I do for you, Mrs. Cicero?"

Angela detailed her problem. Father Cammarata asked her to repeat the case's protocol number. He must be taking notes, she thought. She finished her explanation by emphasizing the fact that her daughter's wedding was scheduled for tomorrow afternoon. There was no hiding the element of pleading in her voice.

"Mrs. Cicero, anyone who would call me at—what time is it there?—three in the morning deserves my best shot. If the papers on Dale Worthington are as well prepared as you say—and there's no reason to think they're not—then they have to be in the files somewhere. I'm headed for the Sacred Congregation now. I'll tell you what I'll do: I'll find the papers and personally make sure that Cardinal Mangiapane takes them with him. He's scheduled to see the Pope today. All that's needed is for the Pope to give his approval. And that, once the Cardinal presents the documentation, is routine.

"Now, Mrs. Cicero, this next part is very important. Tell your officialis—who is the head of the matrimonial court there, do you know?"

"Monsignor Thompson." Instinctively, she feared his involvement, especially now when triumph seemed so imminent.

"Oh, yeah, Tommy Thompson. O.K., tomorrow is Saturday, so we can't use the office. I'll get his residence number from the Catholic Directory. Tell Monsignor Thompson that he is to hold himself in readiness for a call from me at any hour tomorrow. He is to consider this an order from Cardinal Mangiapane himself. Once I have all the papers properly prepared and signed, I'll call Monsignor Thompson, and he can get in touch with your parish, and you can have your wedding."

Angela Cicero was nearly beside herself. "You're sure everything will be all right?"

"I can't see any hitch. By the way," Cammarata sounded as if he realized he was running late and had to move alone, "where'd you ever get my name and number?"

"Father Koesler."

"Bob Koesler! Is he still editing the paper?"

"No, Father. He's a pastor now."

"Give my best to him, Mrs. Cicero. And I'll get on your case right away."

"Oh, thank you. Thank you. Thank you."

She was too excited to sleep. She decided to stay up and continue reading until it was time to call Monsignor Thompson. She could hardly wait to make that call. This time she held all the trumps.

———

"You've been in a blue funk since Monday," complained Joe Cox.

"I can't help it," protested Pat Lennon. "It was one thing when I just took it for granted I couldn't get married again in the Catholic Church. I told you I was afraid of how I'd feel if my worst suspicions were confirmed. But," she said with a combination of grin and grimace, "I'll get over it. Just give me time to get back on an even keel."

The two were breakfasting in their jointly leased apartment in Lafayette Towers on the fringe of downtown Detroit. Breakfast, as it was generally, was cold cereal, self-served.

"It's not a *fait accompli*, Pat. It's just one dirty old man's opinion."

"Something more than that when the dirty old man is the head of the court."

"I've already offered to punch him out for you."

"It's not going to do either of us any good to have you locked up for battery."

They munched in silence.

"Thompson's not going to be in that job forever," Cox said finally.

"Fine. We can get married in wheelchairs right after I locate our teeth."

"No, really; I've been asking around. That's not the kind of job a guy dies in."

"That's too bad."

"I'm serious." Cox poured each of them a cup of coffee. "The average term of duty as head of the matrimonial court is from ten to fifteen years."

"Which means?"

"Which means, my despondent beauty, that Thompson figures to leave the court in from one to six years. After which, the post may be occupied by a human."

Lennon spooned the last of her Wheat Chex. "One to six years. Sounds like a prison term." She shook her head. "No, Joe, I'm not going to psych myself up again. It's over. Waiting for the right person to inhabit the right office—that way leads to insanity."

"Maybe God'll get him."

"More likely the devil." Lennon began putting the breakfast things away and the dishes in the dishwasher. "It's not so bad for us. We can go on with business as usual. But Thompson is messing up the lives of a lot of people." She added thoughtfully, "Something ought to be done about him."

"Speaking of business as usual, I know you want to get to work on time, but you're getting me into bad habits. My punctual arrival each morning is baffling poor Nelson Kane. And it doesn't help city editors to begin their mornings in a state of bafflement."

Lennon began to smile conspiratorially. "Didn't you mention

last night that you have to start today at the City-County Building? And they don't know what time you check in there."

It was fortunate they had not yet gotten dressed.

Nine A.M., Friday, August 3.

It was time.

Angela Cicero dialed 371-7770.

"St. David's," Mrs. Dearing, the housekeeper, singsonged.

"I'd like to speak to Monsignor Thompson."

"Just a moment; I'll see if he's still here."

Angela suffered a sinking moment. What if he was gone? What if he couldn't be reached? Could Thompson, even in this passive role, still ruin all her plans?

"Hello." It was the unmistakably resonant voice of Tommy Thompson.

"Monsignor, this is Angela Cicero."

"Who?"

"I'm the woman whose daughter's fiancé's marriage case was lost someplace in Rome." She paused.

There were an abundant number of cases like that, the Monsignor thought.

"Protocol number 47956/79," she intoned.

Does this crazy broad think I memorize protocol numbers, he wondered.

"It's a privilege of the faith case," she further clarified. "I've been in to see you a couple of times. The case was prepared by Father Cavanaugh, but the marriage is scheduled for St. Anselm's parish. As a matter of fact, tomorrow."

Remembered and noted. "Ah, yes, Mrs. Cicero. Lucky you called when you did. I'm leaving for the weekend in just a few minutes."

God really was smiling down on her, Angela thought.

"I'm sorry," Thompson continued, "but to the best of my knowledge the papers have not been returned from Rome. So I'm afraid there won't be any wedding tomorrow." He sounded smug.

"You may be wrong," said Angela in muted triumph. "I've been busy." She went on to tell him of her call to Rome and the

135

affirmative response she had received. She concluded by explaining his part in all this. Her explanation was followed by silence wherein Thompson attempted to assimilate the disconcerting details of her story.

"Are you sure?" was his initial response. This was not the Rome with which he was familiar. Rome did not react to hysterical phone calls nor, ordinarily, to situations deemed by their victims to be emergencies.

"Yes, I'm sure."

"But that can't be." He was slipping close to a state of shock. "I'm supposed to be on the Costa Smeralda tomorrow. Today, in fact. That's where I was headed when you called."

He sounded near tears. That pleased her.

"I can't help that, Monsignor. I was told to tell you to be available at all times for a call from the Vatican. This was to be understood as a direct order from Cardinal Mangiapane."

"Whom did you say you spoke with?"

"Father Cammarata."

All the names were correct. Could she possibly have actually pulled this off?

"And what number did you call?"

"547-8734."

He checked it in his directory. It was the number for Villa Stritch.

"Who gave you that number?"

"That's not important, Monsignor. What *is* important is that you remain here and are available to the Vatican call."

Thompson evaluated the alternatives. It didn't take long to arrive at the least common denominator. If he were to continue climbing the ecclesiastical ladder toward a bishopric and beyond—and he fully so intended—there could be no question of his fidelity to Vatican demands. Costa Smeralda might come and go, but a personal call from the Vatican was no diurnal occurrence. He would be attentive when the Vatican called, no matter the reason.

"Very well, Mrs. Cicero. I will be available throughout tomorrow and when the call comes through, I'll relay the information to the appropriate parties."

Angela hung up. She had won, but she was surprised: she felt no exhilaration. And she sensed that in battles with Monsignor Thompson the underdog rarely emerged victorious.

But somehow, this wasn't enough.

Harry Kirwan was abidingly angry. At the moment, he was trying to determine the proper target of his anger. As to the cause, there was no doubt.

It was as Father Neiss had told Mary Ann. On the occasion of her marriage she should be deliriously ecstatic, overjoyed, at least extremely happy. Marriages might, and frequently did, deteriorate. But by and large they usually began on an upbeat note.

However, Mary Ann's attitude as she approached her wedding, now only a week away, might be optimistically described as guardedly pleased.

There was no question of her love for him. But the fact that her marriage would be outside the Catholic Church was more than a fly in the ointment. It was more like an important contest she had not only lost, but had barely survived.

More than once, empathizing with Mary Ann's unhappiness, Harry had wavered from his objection to the Tribunal's insistence on questioning his former wife. However, his vacillation was met by unexpected resolution on Mary Ann's part. Yield to this arbitrary regulation, she argued, and where do you draw the line?

Independently, she had arrived at the opinion that it would be intolerable to allow the Church, or any third party, to control the private areas of one's life. As fervently as she desired a Catholic wedding, she was just as determined that Harry not give in to the Tribunal.

Harry perceived himself squarely in the center of Mary Ann's dilemma.

And who was to blame? Surely neither of them. They had fulfilled every legitimate Church requirement in good faith. Surely not Father Neiss. Harry was convinced the priest felt as bad as they did about this turn of events. He was no more than a functionary. In his position, he could do no less than carry out the orders of his superior, no matter what Neiss thought of those orders.

Ah, but the superior, the one who originated the Polish regulation, *he* was the responsible party. Single-handedly, he had managed to all-but-completely ruin their wedding. He had refused to budge even after Father Neiss had explained their special circumstances. Mary Ann's misery at what should be the happiest moment in her life was a monument to Thompson's bullheaded intransigence.

Harry had taken it upon himself to investigate the life and lifestyle of Monsignor Thomas Thompson. It was remarkable the amount of information that could be gleaned about a person by someone at Harry's level in the telephone company. Calling in his markers, Harry termed it, from well-informed people he dealt with in the police department and in city and state government.

Harry had no specific purpose in gathering this information. It was just that when contemplating evening a score, it is good to know as much about the object of one's potential retribution as possible.

———————

Omnia parata—all was in readiness—as canon law would put it.

The foyer of St. Anselm's had become a staging area for chaos. Guests for the Worthington-Cicero wedding collided with bridesmaids, attendants and, of course, the proud parents. Anna Maria Cicero, a picturebook bride in white Empire gown and ten-foot train, made last-minute touchups in makeup, assisted by her maid of honor. These latter two were ensconced in the ushers' room off the foyer. Outside, the groom, the best man, and several ushers nervously made poor but ribald jokes.

Earlier in the day, a game of ecclesiastical Australian tag had been played out. The Pope had consented to the protocol 47956/79 case. Cardinal Mangiapane had so informed Father Cammarata. He had phoned Monsignor Thompson. Who had phoned Father Cavanaugh. Who had phoned Father Koesler. Who had told Deacon Schroeder. Now, within the hour, an invisible miracle would take place. At the moment Dale Worthington exchanged consent with Anna Maria Cicero,

Worthington's former marriage would be dissolved in favor of his present endeavor in "the faith."

There would be no Mass, just a simple wedding ceremony embellished by several songs, a couple of readings from Scripture, and a homily. Since there was to be no Mass, Deacon Schroeder was competent to conduct the wedding without benefit of higher clergy. Nevertheless, Father Koesler had come over to the church to make certain that all was properly prepared. Deacon Les was not noted for attention to detail.

It was 2:45. Fifteen minutes to nuptial ignition and counting. All seemed well. The candles were lit, flower badges attached to pews, white runner at the foot of the sanctuary rolled and ready, and a couple of dozen guests clustered in noisy cliques. In the choir loft, a soprano, utterly bereft of vibrato, was giving "We've Only Just Begun" a whirl. It was just about what a wedding should be, Koesler thought: vaguely happy, a curiosity, clichéd, and pretty much an echo of all the weddings that had preceded it.

Someone touched his arm and brought him, somewhat startled, out of his reverie.

"I beg your pardon, Father."

Angela Cicero was stunning in a sleeveless aquamarine chiffon dress that nicely set off her dark, gray-flecked hair.

Koesler smiled. "Congratulations. Your day of triumph. You've conquered the highest level bureaucracy. Not many have pulled that off."

Angela returned the smile, though there was a hint of nervousness in it. "I couldn't have done it without you, Father. So, thank you."

"You're welcome, Angela." Koesler sensed there was something troubling her. "Is there something I can do?"

"Well, yes, Father, if it isn't too much trouble. I'd like to go to confession."

"Of course." Koesler led her to one of the confessionals in the rear of the church.

He settled in the metal folding chair, slipped the slender violet stole around his neck, opened the sliding door on Angela's side, and closed the opposite door. Strange how in the darkness and silence of the confessional sounds were amplified. He could hear the rustle of her dress as she knelt, her elbows hitting the resting board, even the brushing sound made when she flicked a hair back into place. Her Bal à Versailles wafted through the grill. No doubt about it, Koesler concluded, women smelled better than men.

"Yes?" Koesler began. It was always a mistake to assume the penitent knew the priest was ready.

"Oh. Bless me, Father, for I have sinned. It's been . . . oh . . . several months—I don't know exactly—since my last confession. I was angry with my husband and children several times. I missed Mass once, but I was very ill. We're remodeling our basement, and it's hard work, and I lose my patience a lot. And . . ."

"Is there something more?" They always save the biggies for last.

"Yes. I'm ashamed of it, but I'm angry at a priest. Monsignor Thompson. He almost ruined Anna Maria's wedding, and he was very rude and unkind to me . . ."

They also usually have excuses and extenuating circumstances for the biggies.

". . . and, I'm sorry, Father, but I hate him. I hate him so much I think I could kill him."

And they usually exaggerated the biggies, making sure they don't cop a plea with God.

"Well, killing is a little extreme, don't you think?"

"Maybe. But I am damn mad!"

Profanity used in the confessional usually connoted maximum emphasis.

"Well, are you sorry for your anger at Monsignor Thompson?"

A substantial pause. Koesler was aware that the time for Mrs. Cicero's procession down the middle aisle was impending.

"No, I can't say I am."

Another pause as Koesler tried to find an immediate solution to this dilemma.

"Well, are you sorry you are *not* sorry for your anger at Monsignor Thompson?"

Another pause.

"Yes, I guess I am."

"I guess that's enough. For your penance, say five Our Fathers and five Hail Marys."

Angela began mumbling a prayer of contrition while Koesler mumbled absolution.

She emerged from the confessional as the soprano was beginning the second verse of "We've Only Just Begun," just in time for her escorted trek down the middle aisle.

Koesler stayed in a rear pew through a reading from Kahlil Gibran and one from the Gospel according to John. One verse of John was worth three pages of Gibran, thought Koesler. He then suffered through a flat rendition of "A Bridge Over Troubled Water." Then it was time for Deacon Schroeder's homily.

"It is a distinct pleasure," Schroeder began, "for me to address the faith community today."

Koesler moaned inaudibly.

"It was the late, great Pope John," Schroeder continued, "who called us all to the spirit of *aggiornamento*. And, if we really hear what he was saying, then we must look upon marriage as the occasion for the ultimate *metanoia*."

Koesler moaned audibly. He rose and headed back to the rectory. Oh, Les, he thought, somehow I've got to convince you that the vernacular of this country is *not* Greek.

NEWLYWEDS
HUDSON/VAN PATTEN

Dawn Hudson, daughter of Mr. and Mrs. Walter Hudson, will become the bride of Doug Van Patten of Philadelphia at a candlelight nuptial Mass at St. David's parish, Saturday, August 11, at 8 P.M.

Msgr. Thomas Thompson, head of the Archdiocesan matrimonial court, will preside at the wedding and be the principal speaker at the banquet to follow at Roma Hall in East Detroit.

The couple will honeymoon in Hawaii.

The announcement was there in the *Detroit News's* August 5 issue. It was there for everyone to see.

3

"I DON'T SUPPOSE YOU'D BE INTERESTED IN A little golf." Joe Cox leaned against the bedroom doorjamb.

"Are you kidding?" Pat Lennon sneezed and blew her nose resoundingly, murmuring imprecations.

"Gesundheit!" Cox was unsure of what, if anything, to do for her.

"Where did the idea for golf come from?" With extreme effort, Lennon was able to open her eyelids to approximately half-mast.

"That was Freddie Collins from the composing room on the phone just now. You remember Freddie, don't you?"

Lennon nodded.

"Well, Freddie invited us to join him and maybe Nelson Kane for nine or eighteen, whatever the traffic allows, at Chandler Park." Cox sat on the bed after rearranging huge Sunday editions of the *News*, *Free Press*, and *New York Times*.

"Careful," Lennon warned, "don't knock any of those off the bed. I intend to go through everything today. This is one Sunday I'm going to read *all* the papers.

"Chandler Park!" she reacted tardily. "Whoever thought of Chandler Park on the second Sunday of August? That place will be more a shooting gallery than a golf course!"

Cox chuckled. "That's part of the attraction. I'm looking forward to watching Nellie hit the ball, then duck. I can't wait to see the storied Kane temper build to an eight on the Richter Scale.''

"Well, you run on without me, lover. If I can just stay in bed all day, I should be up and at 'em tomorrow." She paged through the *Times* magazine to the crossword puzzle.

Cox shook his head. He never ceased to be amazed at Lennon's ability to not only complete each week's difficult *Times* puzzle successfully, but to do it in ink.

"A summer cold!" he said. "How could you ever have let yourself in for a summer cold? Where did you go last night, anyway?"

"Out!" Lennon responded firmly. "And what did I do? Nothing!"

"Aha!" he intoned dramatically, "playing the femme fatale, eh? You're sexy when you become a mystery woman."

"Don't get any ideas today, my gold-plated stud. Either you'll get my cold, or I'll break and disintegrate, or both."

Cox smiled and patted her knee. He sensed she had been developing a story last night when she caught cold. She had been somewhat secretive for the past several days. Usually a manifestation of working on a story. He retreated from further prying. The two had mutual respect for each other's exclusives.

Cox began assembling his golfing togs.

"By the way," he said, "Freddie mentioned that your friend didn't show up for church today."

"My friend?" Lennon didn't look up from the puzzle.

"Monsignor Thompson. Freddie goes to Shrine parish. He said Thompson didn't show up for noon Mass."

"Maybe he's on vacation."

"No." Cox searched through a bureau drawer for a sportshirt. "Freddie said that Mass started late, about a quarter after twelve. But today the pastor did it—started late and skipped the sermon."

Cox did not continue, nor did Lennon comment for several seconds.

"Maybe he was sick," she finally offered, still without digressing from her puzzle.

"If he is, he's very sick. Freddie, good newspaperman that he is, asked the pastor after Mass. He said Thompson's absence was unexpected. And that he'd gotten no answer when he phoned Thompson's residence.''

There was another extended period of silence.

"Maybe he was just suddenly called away.''

"Freddie doesn't think so. He says the pastor said that Thompson is very careful about his assignments and wouldn't miss a Sunday Mass without telling someone beforehand.''

After another pregnant pause, Lennon said, "Hell, maybe he died! Who cares?''

Cox chuckled.

However, he thought, there is something here. His investigative instincts were tingling. If anything, he was surprised that Lennon had dismissed so out-of-handedly the prospect that there might be a story here. He could only attribute it to her illness.

Almost on a whim, Cox decided to wear his dress slacks and blazer and pack his golf clothing. A plan was forming in the devious portion of his mind, and he wanted to be prepared to carry it off if the opportunity arose.

He zipped his duffel bag.

"Hit some line drives for me,'' Lennon called out weakly.

"Darling,'' said Cox as he departed, "I dedicate the entire match—including the nineteenth hole—together with the ears and tail of Nelson Kane, in your honor.''

"Of course you'll stay for dinner. Won't you, Father?'' Wanda Koznicki asked the question as she admitted Father Koesler.

"Oh, I hadn't thought of that,'' demurred the priest. "That would be an imposition. Please, no. But thank you.''

"Nonsense, Father,'' said Wanda. "We usually eat about four on Sundays. That's just about half an hour from now. And at the rate my brood eats, one more mouth to feed will make no great difference. Let me just get you with Walt.''

"You're sure it's no imposition? I don't want to disrupt your Sunday.''

"Oh, no, Father. Walt's been expecting you ever since you phoned.''

Wanda and Koesler entered the study. Replete with overstuffed furniture, it had a lived-in look. The walls were covered with citations, certificates, and awards. Recorded music was playing softly. Koesler recognized a Brahms symphony. The Fourth. Nice.

As they entered the study, Inspector Walter Koznicki, head of the Detroit Police Department's Homicide Division, stood to greet the priest.

"How good it is to see you again, Father. You'll stay for dinner, of course." Koznicki exchanged a knowing glance with his wife.

"Good to see you again, Inspector. Yes, Wanda has been kind enough to extend the invitation."

Though they had become fast friends over the years, Koesler and Koznicki scarcely ever used each other's first name. Theirs was a mutual if unexpressed intent to maintain a respect for each other's profession.

Well over six feet tall and big-boned, Koznicki generally dwarfed everything and everybody around him. It was not merely his considerable physical size; he seemed to exude large-ness. He was one of those people usually described as being larger than life.

The priest and the police officer had been thrown together quite accidentally some five years before in a homicide case known popularly as The Rosary Murders. In the meantime, they had become friends, and at least every few months became each other's guest at either Koesler's rectory or Koznicki's home.

"It is always good to see you, Father," said Koznicki. He turned down the music's volume, and the two men sat down. "But what brings you here now? Trouble with your deacon?"

Koesler smiled. Once previously he had unburdened himself to Koznicki about Deacon Lester Schroeder. Koznicki had been nicely professional. He had simply sat with widened eyes as Koesler ranted and raved and became slightly profane as he loudly complained about Schroeder in particular and the current crop of seminarians in general. Koesler had felt much relieved after that unburdening.

"No, not Deacon Les this time. Though there are times when I'd like to wring his neck."

"Don't do that, Father. Detroit's homicide detectives are too good."

146

"Don't I know that! No," Koesler grew serious, "what I wanted to talk to you about is Monsignor Tommy Thompson."

"He is the archdiocesan chancellor?" Koznicki stabbed, trying to remember.

"Head of the Tribunal," Koesler clarified.

"Ah, yes."

"Well, he was missing today from his assignment for noon Mass at Shrine of the Little Flower."

"That is significant enough to bring to the attention of the police?"

"I think so, Inspector. Monsignor gave no notice that he would not be at the parish for his assigned Mass this afternoon. And that is utterly out of character for Tommy Thompson."

"What alternatives have we?"

"Not many, Inspector. Monsignor has not been away on vacation. He was in perfect health. But he apparently did not spend last night at his residence. I phoned the pastor of St. David's. He checked, and Monsignor's bed had not been slept in.

"It seems the last anyone saw of him was at a wedding reception last night. He got a phone call and left immediately after that."

A look of amusement crossed Koznicki's face. "Well, Father, you've done some excellent investigating. But tell me, why were *you* specifically informed of his absence from noon Mass?"

There was an embarrassed silence.

"Monsignor Thompson and I are classmates," Koesler said at length. "The Shrine pastor, Father Ed Rausch, knows this. He also knows I'm one of the few people who would care enough about Tommy Thompson to look into the matter."

Koznicki leaned forward, for the first time specifically interested. "He is that disliked?"

"I'm afraid so."

"Why would so many hate a monsignor?"

"Well, it isn't totally Tommy's fault." Koesler shifted in his chair. "He is, after all, administering some pretty bad and antiquated Church law. But then, on top of that, he sort of has a habit of running roughshod over people. I think, in all objectivity, Tommy has left a record number of unsatisfied customers in his wake."

Koesler paused a moment. "I would not have mentioned this to anyone, but I am genuinely worried about him."

"You say he was last seen at a wedding reception last night?" Koesler nodded.

"It's a little early to make a report, but under the circumstances, I think a report is warranted."

A feeling of gratitude swept over Koesler.

Koznicki phoned Missing Persons and authorized the report. Then he handed the phone to Koesler for a description.

"Monsignor Thomas Thompson. St. David's rectory, 8141 East Outer Drive." Koesler answered successive questions. "Male, white, age—uh, 52; I don't know the exact date of birth; light complexion, blue eyes, dark hair, a touch of gray, a little jowly. Last seen wearing a lightweight black silk suit, roman collar—like priests wear—black shoes, black socks. Last seen at Roma Hall in East Detroit about 10 or 10:30 last night. He received a phone call and left the hall immediately.

"As far as I know, he is in good health, and there is no good reason for his disappearance. Yes, as far as I know, this is the first time he's ever been reported missing. Yes, thank you, sergeant."

As the priest hung up and turned from the phone, Koznicki handed him a glass of port.

"That missing person report will be on the teletype of every precinct by tomorrow morning," said Koznicki. "And you can be sure, since it's a monsignor, every officer will be alerted. We don't lose that many monsignors."

"And you're sure we're not being premature?"

"Not at all. It never hurts to be cautious, especially in a case like this."

They heard Wanda call.

"Come along, Father." Koznicki motioned the priest toward the dining area. "Come eat with us and our kids. But don't be bashful, or you'll find this experience a spectator sport."

———

He was afraid it would be dinnertime. But a call from a public phone in Chandler Park to St. David's rectory revealed that there were no priests present—not peculiar for a sunny early Sunday summer evening.

Monsignor Thompson was still unaccounted for—very peculiar—and Mrs. Bovey, the housekeeper, was too upset to prepare a meal for herself—very understandable.

Joe Cox considered Mrs. Bovey to be overly communicative. He certainly did not object. Reporters regularly encountered people who would not talk, or if they would, would not do so for the record. Mrs. Bovey, however, seemed the type who would tell anyone anything. Even an anonymous caller who was prying into the absence of priests at the dinner hour, a missing monsignor, and her immediate plans.

Well, good for her. Her nicely cooperative attitude might just make the next ploy work. Sometimes it worked; sometimes not. But it always worked better with someone who, like Mrs. Bovey, was a dedicated communicator.

With these thoughts in mind, Cox parked on East Outer Drive, directly in front of St. David's rectory. For the first time that day, he was grateful the nine holes of golf had been so backed-up and slow. He had not perspired greatly, so he was fairly comfortable wearing a jacket. Only Nelson Kane's fury—at his own game, at everyone else's game, at the tee-to-greens crowds—had saved the day. Kane's anger was instantaneous, monumental, and fun to behold as long as it wasn't directed at you.

Cox pushed the doorbell but heard no chime or ring. After some moments, he knocked. Seconds later, a yapping dog hit the door. Cox heard some commotion, and the yapping grew faint.

The door opened. A small, rather attractive gray-haired woman stared at Cox with wide inquiring eyes.

"The doorbell's broken," she explained.

Mrs. Bovey, he presumed. She had put the dog in an office adjacent to the front door whence the animal continued yapping.

Cox opened his wallet and exhibited his police and fire department press card. It was an impressive green; his picture adorned one corner, and the word "police" was fairly prominent. Mrs. Bovey looked at the card only briefly, then nodded.

"The other officers were here earlier. Didn't they get everything they wanted?"

Surprise! Cox had been unaware the matter was under formal investigation. He was growing more and more sure there was a story here.

He flipped shut his wallet and pocketed it. "I'm from a special detail, ma'am. The other detail, they searched . . ." Cox let his voice trail off as he looked expectantly at Mrs. Bovey.

"Oh," she said, after a brief pause, "Monsignor's suite upstairs and his office just down the hall here."

"Yes, ma'am," Cox essayed a Jack Webb monotone, but feared he sounded more like Bela Lugosi. Pat critiqued all his attempts at imitation as resembling the late Dracula specialist. "If you'll just show me where those rooms are, I'll get on with my work."

She indicated the office at the end of the hall, then showed Cox the second-floor suite. He assured her she need not attend him; he would go about his business and show himself out.

Mrs. Bovey shuffled down the hall to her quarters in the rear of the rectory. Well, she thought, if you can't trust a police officer, who can you trust?

Not bad, Cox thought. A modestly sized bedroom and sitting room, separated by shower and toilet facilities. Very stylishly furnished, including a display cabinet filled with the finest Waterford.

Toothbrush, paste, and shaving equipment were in place in the medicine cabinet. The Monsignor didn't appear to have packed for even an emergency trip. The closets seemed full. Thompson obviously had decided to buy black. There were several black suits, each silk and, Cox estimated, each in the $300 neighborhood.

The boys who searched earlier had been neat. Nothing seemed out of place. Nothing, also, seemed to be a clue. Cox felt doubly disappointed that, after his press card ploy had worked so well, he could find nothing in Thompson's living quarters that might help solve the mystery.

With little expectation, he approached Thompson's office on the first floor.

The shelves were filled with books. Several were theology

150

textbooks, but most were commentaries by various experts on canon law.

He tried the desk. The main drawer held nothing of interest. Rulers, pens, pencils, stationery. He tried the side drawer. It was locked. But there was a key in the main drawer. He tried it. It worked. He opened the side drawer.

Bingo.

A diary. A new one. Going back over only little more than a month. Cox couldn't think of a single adult who kept a diary. But he thanked all the gods that be that Thompson had kept one. He paged through it quickly. Even a cursory reading revealed matter that Cox would term hot stuff. He wondered how, and indeed if, the cops who had been here earlier had missed the diary.

He also wondered, for at least eight to ten seconds, whether he should take the diary. After this hasty deliberation, he tucked the diary under his arm and, as he had promised Mrs. Bovey, let himself out.

Suddenly Nelson Kane's golf course rage, once the salvation of a sleepy summer afternoon, faded into insignificance.

————————

At the bottom of page three—the *Free Press*'s "Second Front Page"—was a story by-lined Joe Cox. It was headlined, "Few Clues in Case of Missing Monsignor," and ran a scant six inches. At that, Cox had had to argue long and hard with Nelson Kane to get the item in at all. What tipped the scale in favor of running the story was Cox's possession of Thompson's diary. That and the possibility that the story might burgeon. And if it did, the *Free Press* would have gotten on board first. A not inconsiderable advantage in combat journalism.

Cox had returned to the *Free Press* just before six the previous evening. He had worked out his story on the VDT. It was simple and unornate, merely narrating Thompson's unaccounted-for absence from his weekend assignment, the consternation and lack of explanation on the part of those diocesan officials Cox had been able to contact, as well as the neat and complete condition of Thompson's personal effects, evidencing the absence of even a last-minute emergency trip.

Cox had then phoned Kane and, after reluctantly agreeing to trim eight inches from his story, eventually won the argument. He was able to complete the story, argument, and trim in plenty of time to make the met. Thus, it would appear at least in the late-night edition, and, more importantly, in the early Monday editions.

Cox's story did not mention the diary, because he did not yet know if there was any connection between the diary and the disappearance. He mentioned neither the diary nor the story to Pat, because she represented the competition and, far more pointedly, because she appeared in Thompson's diary. At this stage, he was not at all sure how he was going to handle that.

Now, on this bright, warm, Monday morning, Cox sat by Nelson Kane's desk while the city editor paged through the Thompson diary, pausing to read slowly the passages Cox had underlined. Occasionally, Kane would utter a low whistle, mutter, "bastard!" and make a note on his legal pad.

"Near as I can figure," Kane's lip rolled a gone-out cigar from one side of his mouth to the other, "this Thompson royally screwed at least five people over the past . . ." he checked his note, ". . . little more than three weeks."

Cox nodded. "Remarkable performance."

"Either," Kane continued, "he hit an especially fertile streak, or he's been an extraordinary bastard to an awful lot of people for an awful long time."

"I'll bet on the latter."

"If he shows up alive and well, you're going to have to see this gets back in his possession." Kane rolled the cigar butt back to its former position.

"If he shows up dead . . ."

"If he shows up dead, or just doesn't show up, we have our hands on a document that would throw tons of suspicion on a lot of people."

Cox sat up straight. "Do you think one of these people might actually have killed him?"

Kane removed the cigar from his mouth. "If he had treated me the way he treated them, I'd give it some consideration."

"Well, what do we do now?"

"You, my friend, drag ass over to police headquarters and give yourself up."

"What?"

"Xerox the diary, dummy, then give the original to the police. Tell them that in your abiding interest in the good Monsignor's welfare, you borrowed it. But now you want them to have it just in case they're going to conduct an investigation into his absence."

"You think they'll buy that?"

"They won't go to the mat over a diary. On the other hand, they just might get damned angry if you kept it."

"O.K." Cox started to rise, but halted as Kane continued.

"Then get back here and find out what happened to those people . . . that Mrs. . . . ." Kane again consulted his notes, ". . . Cicero, for instance. We know Thompson shit on her, and she got some measure of revenge by making him stay home, forcing him to cancel his vacation. But we don't know from the diary what happened to the Cicero kid. Did she get the permission? Did she have a church wedding? The answers might have something to do with how Mrs. Cicero felt about Thompson. She might have ended up feeling they were even.

"There are several similar questions raised by that diary. And we ought to have answers just in case we get to pick up this story and run with it."

"And that raises another question," said Cox, hesitantly, "what about Pat Lennon? She's in the diary."

"Is she ever!"

"Well," Cox seemed embarrassed, an extremely rare occurrence, "you know how it is with us . . ."

"How it is with you? The entire city of Detroit knows how it is with you two!"

"Well?"

"Look, kid, either you're playing hardball or you're not. In case something's wrong, she's one of five known possible suspects. You've gotta make up your mind: either she's treated the same as everyone else, or you're off the story."

Cox simply nodded, picked up the diary, and headed first for the Xerox, then for headquarters.

Hardball, Kane had termed it. Cox thought a confrontation

with Pat Lennon over what was in that diary would be more like Russian roulette.

Things were pretty dull in the Fifteenth Precinct. Which was bad news for the bad guys and good news for the police.

The blue-and-white Plymouth rolled slowly through familiar streets. Gunston, Barrett, Roseberry, Annsbury, Kilbourne, Glenfield. Atop the car were blue and red lights mercifully at rest. Inside, the car resembled a tank. Exquisite electronic equipment was everywhere; tucked near the floor on the passenger side was a shotgun.

In the car were patrol officers Judy Duby, black, on the force one year, and Robert Stopinski, white, and a ten-year veteran. They were laughing over an incident that had occurred the previous Saturday night. They had been just about to go off duty when they had received an accident call for a house on Westphalia.

It was an elderly couple, neither of them spoke English. And Stopinski didn't understand enough Polish to comprehend what the woman was trying to tell them. She was the only one talking, as she had wrapped her husband's head entirely with gauze, which pretty well precluded his even opening his mouth.

Duby had begun to unravel the gauze so the man could breathe more easily when the woman began to point frantically at the man's right ear. So Duby had left the bandage around the top of his head and covering his right ear. In which condition the two officers had delivered him to Saratoga General and, leaving him in Emergency, had gone off duty.

"But did you hear what they found was actually wrong with him?" asked Duby.

"No; what?" Stopinski was driving.

"They had been sitting on their front porch, minding their own business, when a moth flew into the man's right ear." Duby began to laugh. "Well, the woman tried to coax the moth out. When it wouldn't come, she put a mothball in his ear and wrapped up his head!"

Both laughed. But as they cruised the familiar streets, their eyes were never still. They looked for overt trouble or anything

154

out of the ordinary. Anything that would waken alarm bells buried in their training or experience.

"Did the doctors get it all out?" Stopinski asked.

"Yes, finally. The mothball was in good shape. But the moth was somewhat the worse for wear."

Again they laughed.

"Things are seldom what they seem," Duby quoted from "H.M.S. Pinafore."

"Like that, for instance." Stopinski nodded toward a solitary car on the lot behind De La Salle High School.

They had just turned from Conner near the entrance to Detroit City Airport. Duby scanned the area several times before discerning the object of Stopinski's concern. It was, indeed, suspicious. School was out for the summer, and if any of De La Salle's faculty or staff were going to be in the building—which was highly unlikely—they would probably not be there this early in the day.

The fact that a single auto was parked on a school lot in the middle of the summer did not necessarily indicate anything wrong. It was out of the ordinary. Duby marveled at Stopinski's ability to perceive a possible problem so quickly. At the time he had spotted the car, from his angle of vision, he could not even have seen the entire vehicle.

Stopinski rolled the squad car to a stop to the rear and off to one side of the parked car. Both officers remained inside as they surveyed the scene. The parked vehicle was going nowhere, while they wanted to study every possible detail cautiously and carefully.

"The locusts have been here," said Duby.

"Yeah."

All four tires were gone. The car rested on three cinder blocks.

"Somehow, I hate to see that happen to a Caddy," said Duby.

"Yeah," Stopinski again agreed. "Vandalism always looks more appropriate when perpetrated against a junk heap. But then again if it hadn't been a Caddy, maybe they would have left it alone."

It was a late-model—practically new—Eldorado, obviously well cared-for. The paint seemed intact, and the abundant chrome was in a highly polished state.

"I wonder," said Duby, "why they didn't strip the chrome?"

"I've got a hunch we're going to find out that and a few more answers shortly."

Stopinski punched out the license plate number on his Mobile Data Terminal. He waited a few moments; data began spelling itself out on the MDT screen.

"Does that name ring a bell?" Stopinski moved the MDT so Duby could see the impressive amount of information called forth by a mere license number.

Duby studied the name for only a few seconds, then whistled. "Holy smoke! It's the missing Monsignor!"

Stopinski smiled at her oblivious use of "Holy Smoke" with reference to a monsignor.

Not only had Monsignor Thomas Thompson's disappearance been included in the morning report, Inspector Mike O'Hara of the Fifteenth had called it to everyone's special attention. Thompson's missing person status had been given similar treatment in all Detroit police precincts.

The two officers put on their hats as they exited their car. Each circled the Cadillac gingerly, from opposite directions.

"Looks pretty much in one piece," said Stopinski, standing near the trunk.

"Uh-oh," said Duby from in front, "I think they forced the hood." There was a broken strip of metal where the hood, which was ajar, met the body. She assumed that with an automatic hood lock in the interior of the car the thieves had had to pry the hood open. She tried to lift the hood. Suspicion confirmed.

Peering into the engine compartment, she called to her partner, "Whatever else they got, they took the battery."

"I wouldn't touch anything else if I were you," Stopinski was looking through the closed side window and standing several inches farther than necessary from the car. As if trying to avoid even the semblance of adding an extra fingerprint.

Instantly, Duby released the raised hood, which fell against but did not lock into the chassis. She rapidly came alongside Stopinski and squinted with him through the side front window. After a few seconds, she saw the metallic bullet casing resting against the black leather upholstery of the passenger seat. So riveted was her gaze on the shell that she had not yet noticed the car's portable waste receptacle. It was overflowing with white tissues . . . white tissues marred by splotches of red.

Stopinski, who had seen both shell and red-tinged tissues, returned to the squad car. He called the precinct station and received some terse commands that translated into, stand there and don't do anything, and don't let anybody else do anything.

The precinct inspector then called Homicide.

It was a familiar feeling.

Father Robert Koesler, at the invitation of Inspector Walter Koznicki, stood in a large office in the Homicide Division on the fifth floor of Detroit Police Headquarters. He wasn't so much standing as shifting. A continuous procession of men, most of them large, all of them wearing guns, moved about the room. In almost every instance, their destination seemed to be where he happened to be. If he was standing in front of a filing cabinet, an officer would need to open it. If he stood near a desk, a detective would have to squeeze by. He was ill at ease. But it was a familiar feeling.

As he moved about the office, unerringly selecting a spot that soon would be desired by another body, Koesler reflected on the great number of occasions when a priest was a fifth wheel. It was always awkward when going to, say, the theater with a couple. The priest with no date was something like a period in the middle of a sentence. At more formal parties when the hostess attempted a boy-girl-boy-girl seating, the priest would derange her math.

As a result, people at times felt sorry for the priest and his constant companion, celibacy.

What these people could not understand is that the unmarried state can be habit-forming. There were times when even Koesler felt a bit sorry for the younger priests. Their seminary training had not prepared them—as well as his had him—for a woman-less life, especially in those early years when one is in his twenties and thirties. This, perhaps, helped to account for the fact that young priests were an endangered species.

But, as far as he was concerned, like Henry Higgins, he was a confirmed bachelor. And this even in his early fifties. If there

157

were to be an Eliza Doolittle in Koesler's domestic future, he did not believe he had yet met her.

Walter Koznicki, in his office, which was adjacent to the room in which Koesler waited, was occupied with one of his lieutenants. Koznicki had invited Koesler for at least two reasons. After their conversation the previous day, it had occurred to the Inspector that since they were dealing with a monsignor, Koesler might be helpful, as he had been in two previous homicide investigations that had had religious implications. Also, Koesler had never participated in a missing person investigation, and Koznicki thought the experience would be educational for the priest, if he was going to continue to dabble in crime investigations.

Koznicki, as soon as he was done with his lieutenant, intended to escort Koesler to the Missing Persons Division so he could familiarize himself with the branch's procedures.

It was not to be.

The first diversion was perpetrated by Joe Cox.

It was not Cox's fault, actually. He had attempted to rid himself of Thompson's diary in the office of Chief of Police Frank Tany. However, never one to accept a buck if it could be shifted elsewhere, Tany had his secretary ascertain who had instigated the Thompson investigation. Missing Persons, taking a page from the Chief, identified Inspector Koznicki as the officer at whose initiative all this had begun. So, off Cox was sent to see the Wizard.

Even then, Cox tried one more time to avoid Koznicki. Walking through the corridors of the Homicide Division, Cox stopped at Squad Six's door. He glanced in and spotted Lieutenant Ned Harris talking to several detectives. Cox, counting on Harris' being somewhat distracted, attempted to dump the diary on him.

It was not to be.

"What have we here?" Harris interrupted Cox's mumbled explanation, "a new Pulitzer Prize novel?"

Cox sighed and, while the other detectives looked on in obvious amusement at his embarrassment, tediously explained the history of his possession of the diary.

On hearing Cox's explanation, Harris, a muscular, six-foot, stylishly dressed black with short, straight hair, knew that the diary belonged with Missing Persons. He also knew he didn't have clout enough to force that division to deal with and accept the diary.

"Come along, my main man." Harris led Cox toward the one who had the clout. "We'll just check this out with Inspector Koznicki."

Great Caesar's ghost! thought Cox; I'm going to have to tell this goddamn story again.

Harris tapped lightly on Koznicki's door. Koznicki—like the genie in the bottle—appeared. Cox looked up at the Inspector in the manner of a sheepdog. He attempted a confident smile. He feared all he had achieved was a silly grin.

While Koznicki paged through the diary, Cox did, indeed, have to tell the goddamn story again. After which, he had to answer questions.

No, he had not known of the diary's existence before finding it. No, he had not impersonated an officer to gain access to St. David's rectory. Yes, he had shown the housekeeper his press pass. Yes, she may have thought it was a police credential. But what control could a reporter have over what someone thought?

"Besides," Cox attempted to reverse things and go on the offensive, "your guys passed right over it earlier in the afternoon. Why should I think it was important to you, when your guys left it sitting right there in the desk drawer?" He stopped short of mentioning the drawer had been locked.

"Our guys?" Harris asked.

Koznicki shook his head. "Must've been a team from the Fifteenth."

Father Koesler, who had been leaning against a file cabinet, which, miraculously, no one wanted to get into, smiled throughout the exchange. He was familiar with the participants in this conversation. He had worked rather closely with Koznicki and Harris in two previous criminal investigations. And he knew of Cox both through those investigations and also, slightly, through Koesler's journalistic tenure at the *Detroit Catholic*. The priest considered it appropriate, turnabout being fair play, that a reporter should be grilled from time to time.

"I see you have underlined certain passages," said Koznicki, continuing to page through the diary.

"Yeah," Cox admitted. There was no point in implying the underlining might have been done by Thompson; why would he underline his own diary? "It helps me concentrate."

Koznicki, who was certain that Cox had photostated the diary pages, was about to conclude this discussion and make sure the diary went to and stayed with Missing Persons, when a detective caught the Inspector's eye and beckoned him aside.

Cox carefully studied Koznicki's face as he received the brief whispered message. At one point, a bushy eyebrow arched—for Koznicki a show of significant emotion.

Koznicki whispered to Harris, who immediately left the room. Without so much as a goodbye for Cox, Koznicki then left the room, motioning Father Koesler to follow.

Odd, thought Cox. Odd that Koznicki would terminate so suddenly a conversation for which Cox alone was responsible. Odd that Koznicki would take the priest with him. Odd, come to think of it, that the priest was here at all. Odd that Koznicki had taken the diary with him. Indeed, after Koznicki had received the whispered message, he had seemed to clutch the diary more firmly.

Cox went to a pay phone on the first floor of headquarters and dialed his paper.

"City desk," the familiar voice barked.

"Nellie, I think something's cooking here at headquarters. But I'm in a kind of awkward position to find out. What with going all over the building trying to get rid of the diary and all."

"Who's got the diary?"

"Koznicki. I gave it to him, somebody came in, and then he left in one hell of a hurry. I've got a hunch it's got something to do with that Monsignor—Thompson."

"Where are you?"

Cox gave him the number.

"Stay there," Kane ordered.

Kane then phoned Brian Fogerty at the chaotic press office on the third floor of headquarters.

"Fogerty!" There was no need for the caller to identify himself. "Find out if Koznicki is working on the Monsignor Thompson case and call me right back."

For what seemed a long time, Kane sat drumming his fingers

against his desk as he chewed an unlit cigar. Finally, his phone rang.

"That's right," Fogerty confirmed, "he's on the Thompson case."

"He *is*."

"Yeah. They think the guy may have been iced."

"Iced?"

"Axed."

"Axed?"

"Wasted."

"Wasted? Whaddya mean, 'iced, axed, wasted'?"

"You know—killed."

"Well, for crissakes, *say* killed!"

Damn kids, Kane thought as he slammed the phone in its cradle. Put them on a police beat, and they think they have to talk tougher than the cops.

He dispatched Cox to De La Salle's parking lot, the location Kane had gotten from Fogerty before shattering his eardrum with a slam-dunk hang-up.

Kane rocked back in his chair. He liked it when things were humming. And, by God, so far this was a *Free Press* exclusive.

———————

Anyone seeing the parking lot early Monday, looking away, then looking back again, might have thought the single police car had given birth.

What had begun as a quiet summer morning in the residential neighborhood that bordered City Airport and surrounded De La Salle High School had developed into a day the residents would remember and talk about for a long time.

Now, just past noon, there were seven blue-and-whites from the Fifteenth Precinct on or around the parking lot. In addition, there were several vehicles used by various police experts from the Central Photo, Scientific, and Identification branches. Lieutenant Harris and two of his sergeants from Squad Six were there. Teams of detectives and patrol officers of the Fifteenth were there, fanning through the neighborhood searching for possible witnesses. Standing near the abandoned Cadillac were Inspector Koznicki and Father Koesler.

161

Ordinarily, Koznicki would not have come. But he was aware of the personal concern of his friend. This concern and their friendship had brought Koesler and Koznicki to this now-busy parking lot.

The experts were engaged in their fields of expertise. Koznicki was lecturing, something he enjoyed, to an audience of one.

"This, Father," Koznicki said with some solemnity, "is the most important moment in any investigation. This," he gestured at the various police officers engrossed in their tasks, "the scene of an alleged crime."

Koesler looked about. All he saw was an abandoned car and a goodly number of working officers. The scene was beginning to flesh out with the arrival of press photographers, television crews, and reporters. He noticed Joe Cox had arrived. There was also a reporter from the *News*; Koesler could not recall his name.

"All you've got is an empty car." If he had to guess at when an investigation became important, Koesler would have thought all would do their best once these initial steps were completed and the investigation got on the road, so to speak.

His reaction was to be expected. Bob Koesler had never been particularly attentive to fundamentals. As a very young boy beginning piano lessons, he had eschewed scales, arpeggios, and other nonmelodic practices in favor of simplified versions of the classics. His mother, an accomplished pianist, had accused him of building windows without foundations. It was true. Thus, he was better suited to the flamboyant guess that might solve a mystery than the dogged endeavors on which sound police work was based.

"We've got much more than an empty car." Koznicki smiled. "What you are looking at is silent evidence. No matter how careful criminals might be, they may leave behind fingerprints, footprints, hair, clothing fibers, blood; all these and more can accuse them.

"This evidence does not forget; nor can it change its testimony. It does not get excited or confused. *We* can make a mistake. *We* can misinterpret evidence. But physical evidence cannot be wrong, cannot commit perjury . . . and it cannot be entirely absent.''

Koesler was impressed.

"For instance," Koznicki continued, "because of the physical evidence initially found at this scene, what had been a missing person case is about to evolve into a full-fledged homicide investigation.''

Koesler looked at the Inspector and telegraphed curiosity.

"A spent cartridge shell from what appears to have been a .32-caliber automatic pistol was found on the front seat passenger side of the automobile, and tissues blotted with a bloodlike substance were found in the disposal container.''

Koesler was about to say something but stopped short as Koznicki continued.

"Lieutenant Harris and a couple of detectives from his squad are coordinating the investigation. Let's go over and see what they've come up with so far.''

Throughout Koznicki's monologue, Koesler had been peripherally aware that officers were constantly reporting to Harris, who made notes of each report. Now, Harris had nodded to Koznicki, and the Inspector and the priest approached.

"What have we got, Ned?" Koznicki asked.

"Confirmed .32, no prints. Confirmed blood on the tissues; we'll have to wait on the type. Tissues apparently from the dispenser on the floor midway between driver and passenger seats.

"Officers Stopinski and Duby from the Fifteenth found witnesses across the street who saw the vandals, four of them, teens, at about the time they were removing the fourth tire. One witness yelled at them. Nothing. Then, he brought out his handy rifle, and they split. Probably why they got only tires and battery. Scared away before they could get serious about stripping this mother—uh . . .'' Harris became conscious of the priest's presence, "sorry, Father.''

Koesler nodded forgiveness. Koznicki suppressed a smile.

"Prints?" Koznicki asked.

"Amazingly clean car. Must've been washed Saturday, after the rain. Not all that many prints on it. For one thing, we're likely to pick up some small-time thieves, if not a homicide.''

The word homicide in connection with Monsignor Thompson, a man Koesler knew well and considered terribly vital, sent a shiver through the priest.

"There are some prints on the interior. Probably the owner's," Harris continued. "Funny thing: turns out the Monsignor was one of those honorary Wayne County Deputies. We've got records of his prints and blood type." Harris smiled. Even small victories for the good guys Harris considered worth celebrating.

"And then," said Harris, "we come to the bad news. There are no prints on the steering wheel or gearshift."

"The rear-view mirror?" Koznicki asked.

"Clean."

"Professional," Koznicki commented.

A precinct officer beckoned, and Harris moved to receive his report.

"Oh," said Koznicki, suddenly aware of the priest's unasked questions, "the assumption now is that someone other than the Monsignor drove his car to this lot. There is no reason to assume the Monsignor would wipe off his own fingerprints.

"The rear-view mirror without prints adds another dimension. Almost everyone before driving a strange car will adjust the rear-view mirror. Since no two drivers sit at exactly the same height and position in a car, the rear-view mirror is never at just the correct angle. Most run-of-the-mill thieves forget they've adjusted the mirror; they clean all their prints except those on the mirror. In this case, however, the mirror is clean. Which means not only was the mirror adjusted by a driver other than Monsignor Thompson, but it was wiped clean. Very professional."

"Uh . . ." Koesler was reluctant to break in on Koznicki's ponderings. "I was going to mention a little while back: Monsignor Thompson carried a gun."

"What?"

"We were driving together some place several months ago, and Tommy asked me to get something from the glove compartment. When I opened it, there was this gun."

"What did it look like?"

"Well," he tried to find a way of describing the gun without comparing apples and oranges, "it didn't seem as large as the guns most of these uniformed officers are carrying."

e of a diary, as well as the way those who
through Thompson's diary spoke of this
t contained the writer's innermost thoughts
was no question in Koesler's mind that the
was an invasion of Thompson's most pre-
question raised by Koznicki concerned the
g that privacy.

esler, throughout the day, kept finding ex-
reading.

nt attendant to finding Thompson's car that
d lunched with Koznicki at a small restau-
which bordered police headquarters. During
ually able to forget the missing Monsignor

cer and priest parted, like a persistent in-
in burned its way into Koesler's conscious-

s were usually filled with cleaning up the
-completed weekend liturgies and the very
or next weekend's liturgies. From time to
Koesler that parishes, especially suburban
ly for weekend liturgies. During the week,
ortance took place. Of course, there were
s of councils, commissions, and commit-
ere was a lonely soul to counsel or console
ady processions of panhandlers. Clearly,
y of parishioners thought of their parish
nce-weekly Mass of obligation.

t he would be unable to sustain a Monday
or was he yet willing to delve into Thomp-

d to visit Betty Hardwick, a parishioner
rebral palsy and was presently hospitalized

rely drive out Michigan Avenue to Wayne
ital, more popularly known as Eloise, af-
n it was situated. Once there, Koesler was,
ed by the number, size, and complexity
ildings. After getting directions at the in-

"Smaller than a .38, then. Did it have a cylinder like the ones
you see on these guns?"

"No."

"An automatic. That could be it. Of course, if the Monsignor
had the gun registered, we would have found out about it eventually. But it doesn't hurt to know early."

"Judging from the way Tommy related to law," said Koesler,
"he probably had the gun registered."

Koznicki moved quickly to consult with Harris.

It was the opportunity for which Joe Cox had been waiting.
From the time he'd been ushered in to be quizzed by Inspector
Koznicki, Cox had been curious about the presence of Father
Koesler. Why would the priest be at headquarters? Even more
curious, why would he be here, at the probable scene of a possible crime? Cox moved quickly but, he hoped, inconspicuously
to the priest's side.

"Joe Cox, *Free Press*," he introduced himself.

"I know," said Koesler.

That pleased Cox inordinately. Nobody remembered reporters. On-camera TV personalities were probably among the best-
known people in town. Columnists whose likenesses appeared
with their columns were moderately well-known, particularly if
their photos resembled reality. But nobody knew reporters. It
was rare when people even recognized reporters' names from
their by-lines. Woodward, Bernstein, Jimmy Breslin, that was
about it. But Koesler recognized Cox. What a Pulitzer will do
for a guy!

"I've been wondering, Father," said Cox, "to be blunt, just
what are you doing here?"

"I'm a friend. Just a concerned friend."

Recalling what he had read in Thompson's diary, Cox thought
there probably wouldn't be many willing to identify themselves
as a friend of the Monsignor.

"You're sure you're not here as an expert consultant?" Cox
pushed his interrogation another notch.

Koesler smiled. "No. No. What would the police want with
a suburban pastor?"

"If memory serves, Father, you were pretty useful back in
the days of The Rosary Murders."

"That! That was luck. No, I'm just a friend of the Monsignor's. Just concerned about his welfare."

Cox ripped a corner from a sheet in his notepad and scribbled his name and phone number on it. He handed it to Koesler.

"Here, Father; just in case anything occurs to you about this case while it's being investigated, give me a call, would you?"

Cox noticed that Koznicki was returning, accompanied by the burly, white-haired head of the Fifteenth Precinct. Cox wished to avoid any further contact with Koznicki this day. Better to wait till the furor over the diary was forgotten.

No matter what the priest disclaimed, Cox was certain the police would use Koesler as a consultant in the disappearance of the Monsignor. Cox vowed to be included in whatever light the priest might shed on this investigatiion.

Koznicki introduced Inspector Hara to Koesler.

"You'll also be investigating this case, Inspector?" Koesler asked.

"Ah, call me Mike, Father." Just a trace of brogue. "Yes, since the good Monsignor's car was found in our precinct, we'll be workin' on the case too." He smiled. "But since it's a possible homicide, I'll be workin' for big Walt here." He playfully cuffed Koznicki's arm.

"It's anybody's guess who will be working for whom." Koznicki returned the smile.

O'Hara grew serious. "Only thing I can't figure is, who'd want to harm a good monsignor?"

If only you knew, Koesler thought. Matter of fact, if O'Hara investigates, he'll discover the "good Monsignor" had managed to accumulate more than a fair share of enemies.

"Finding out what happened to the 'good Monsignor' should keep us both pretty busy for a while," said Koznicki.

"At least we're starting this investigation even," said O'Hara.

"Not quite," replied Koznicki, "your people found the car."

"Ah, yes, but you're the one who turned in the missing person report."

"I guess you're right, Mike. We start even."

With that, and a tip of his hat to Father Koesler, O'Hara left. Koznicki led Koesler to the Inspector's car. "I want you to have

a copy of this d
made for you at

"Oh, no; than
tively, Koesler sh
Thompson.

Koznicki stop
Press undoubted
our investigating
a copy. If we ar
signor Thompso
may be able to l

"If you put
course."

During the re
the repartee be
minded him of t
priests. And w
similarities. B
staffed by male
tion. And both
American life.

There was a
as far as Bob K

He concurr
among secrets
confession, fol
simple confide
others measur
ability, Koesle
He'd always b
a setting wher
secrets. His d
to confession

So it was
Xeroxed copy
spector Kozn
indeed, study

By the very na
had read or glanc
one, Koesler knev
and feelings. The
reading of this dia
cious privacy. The
necessity for invac

Nevertheless, K
cuses to postpone

After the exciter
morning, Koesler
rant in Greektown,
the meal, he was g
for the moment.

But as police of
truder, the diary ag
ness.

Monday afterno
nitty-gritty of the ju
remote preparation
time, it occurred t
parishes, existed sc
relatively little of ir
interminable meeti
tees. Occasionally,
and the slow but s
however, the majo
solely in terms of a

Koesler sensed t
afternoon routine. I
son's diary.

Instead, he deci
who suffered from c
with arthritis.

It was a long, lei
County General Ho
ter the village in whi
as always, overwhe
of the institutional t

formation desk, he began an extended trek through huge, seemingly identical wards.

In some of the wards housing the elderly, it was sometimes difficult to discern where a chalky emaciated body stopped and the white sheet began. It was also sometimes difficult to tell whether a patient was alive. At one point, a white-haired woman sitting in a chair, but chained to her bed, reached out and grasped Koesler's hand, frightening him momentarily. "Pray for me," she pleaded, "I am insane." Probably not, thought the priest as he continued his journey. Probably her behavior is merely sufficiently different from the rest of ours that we feel uncomfortable having her around. So we've locked her away.

Finally, he found Betty Hardwick, who seemed overjoyed to see him. She was another whose appearance made others uncomfortable. So she had few visitors whether she was in or out of the hospital.

It was difficult to understand her until one became used to her speech defect. And occasionally, she drooled. But she rambled on, unself-consciously telling Koesler how she spent her days visiting with other patients, cheering them up and finding silver linings for some realistically dark clouds.

As always, Koesler marveled at how beautiful a soul was housed in that broken body. He was forced to remember Tommy Thompson. How many opportunities a man in his position had to lighten the burden of troubled people. Koesler was aware that his classmate was not noted for benevolence; he feared the diary he would soon be forced to read might well expose exactly the opposite.

Betty, on the other hand, was rare if not unique. Koesler had known a few, a precious few, chronically ill people who were able to sublimate their illness in favor of a genuine concern for others. As always, his visit with Betty cheered him and as he blessed her, he realized that she had bestowed on him a greater blessing.

There was no time for the diary on his return to the rectory as the day's mail was yet unopened, and Mary O'Connor handed him an impressive list of phone calls to be returned.

After picking up the pieces of Monday, Koesler dined alone.

Deacon Les Schroeder was out somewhere making sure the world was safe for the Church.

He was tempted to begin the diary after dinner. But he remembered that two women were scheduled for instructions, at seven and eight, respectively. Requests for instructions to become Catholic were extremely rare. In the case of these women, each was the only member of her family who was not Catholic, and since their high school children were attending catechism instructions on Monday evenings, the ladies had decided to give official Catholicism a whirl.

As it turned out, neither instruction had been either demanding or controversial. The first woman's only nagging problem concerned the details surrounding Mary's visit to her elderly cousin Elizabeth.

Mary, pregnant with Jesus, came to help Elizabeth, who was carrying the baby who would become John the Baptist. Describing the meeting of these two women, Luke wrote that when Elizabeth heard Mary's voice, her baby leapt in her womb. And Luke quotes Elizabeth, "The moment your greeting sounded in my ears, the baby leapt in my womb for joy."

Mrs. Donahue, who with five kids was no stranger to intrauterine kicks, found it difficult to accept Elizabeth's interpretation of her baby's activity. Mrs. Donahue patiently explained to Koesler, who needed all the help in this field he could get, about the prenatal calisthenics of infants. Elizabeth, Mrs. Donahue reasoned, probably was excited when she heard her cousin. When she unconsciously passed that excitement along to her baby, he kicked more as a reflex action than out of joy. Mrs. Donahue concluded she did not think she was going to be able to accept this incident as a miraculous event.

Father Koesler explained to Mrs. Donahue that acceptance of John the Baptist's early punt as a religious mystery was not crucial to the deposit of faith and that it was a matter she could pretty well decide for herself.

The second woman, usually reflective and quiet, had only one question this evening. Who, she asked, buttoned the priest's shirt up the back? Seeing Koesler's roman collar and clerical vest with no buttons visible, she had supposed the article of clothing must be buttoned in back. With this premise, the ques-

"Smaller than a .38, then. Did it have a cylinder like the ones you see on these guns?"

"No."

"An automatic. That could be it. Of course, if the Monsignor had the gun registered, we would have found out about it eventually. But it doesn't hurt to know early."

"Judging from the way Tommy related to law," said Koesler, "he probably had the gun registered."

Koznicki moved quickly to consult with Harris.

It was the opportunity for which Joe Cox had been waiting. From the time he'd been ushered in to be quizzed by Inspector Koznicki, Cox had been curious about the presence of Father Koesler. Why would the priest be at headquarters? Even more curious, why would he be here, at the probable scene of a possible crime? Cox moved quickly but, he hoped, inconspicuously to the priest's side.

"Joe Cox, *Free Press*," he introduced himself.

"I know," said Koesler.

That pleased Cox inordinately. Nobody remembered reporters. On-camera TV personalities were probably among the best-known people in town. Columnists whose likenesses appeared with their columns were moderately well-known, particularly if their photos resembled reality. But nobody knew reporters. It was rare when people even recognized reporters' names from their by-lines. Woodward, Bernstein, Jimmy Breslin, that was about it. But Koesler recognized Cox. What a Pulitzer will do for a guy!

"I've been wondering, Father," said Cox, "to be blunt, just what are you doing here?"

"I'm a friend. Just a concerned friend."

Recalling what he had read in Thompson's diary, Cox thought there probably wouldn't be many willing to identify themselves as a friend of the Monsignor.

"You're sure you're not here as an expert consultant?" Cox pushed his interrogation another notch.

Koesler smiled. "No. No. What would the police want with a suburban pastor?"

"If memory serves, Father, you were pretty useful back in the days of The Rosary Murders."

"That! That was luck. No, I'm just a friend of the Monsignor's. Just concerned about his welfare."

Cox ripped a corner from a sheet in his notepad and scribbled his name and phone number on it. He handed it to Koesler.

"Here, Father; just in case anything occurs to you about this case while it's being investigated, give me a call, would you?"

Cox noticed that Koznicki was returning, accompanied by the burly, white-haired head of the Fifteenth Precinct. Cox wished to avoid any further contact with Koznicki this day. Better to wait till the furor over the diary was forgotten.

No matter what the priest disclaimed, Cox was certain the police would use Koesler as a consultant in the disappearance of the Monsignor. Cox vowed to be included in whatever light the priest might shed on this investigatiion.

Koznicki introduced Inspector Hara to Koesler.

"You'll also be investigating this case, Inspector?" Koesler asked.

"Ah, call me Mike, Father." Just a trace of brogue. "Yes, since the good Monsignor's car was found in our precinct, we'll be workin' on the case too." He smiled. "But since it's a possible homicide, I'll be workin' for big Walt here." He playfully cuffed Koznicki's arm.

"It's anybody's guess who will be working for whom." Koznicki returned the smile.

O'Hara grew serious. "Only thing I can't figure is, who'd want to harm a good monsignor?"

If only you knew, Koesler thought. Matter of fact, if O'Hara investigates, he'll discover the "good Monsignor" had managed to accumulate more than a fair share of enemies.

"Finding out what happened to the 'good Monsignor' should keep us both pretty busy for a while," said Koznicki.

"At least we're starting this investigation even," said O'Hara.

"Not quite," replied Koznicki, "your people found the car."

"Ah, yes, but you're the one who turned in the missing person report."

"I guess you're right, Mike. We start even."

With that, and a tip of his hat to Father Koesler, O'Hara left. Koznicki led Koesler to the Inspector's car. "I want you to have a copy of this diary, Father,'' said Koznicki. ''I'll have one made for you at headquarters.''

''Oh, no; thank you, but I don't care to have a copy.'' Instinctively, Koesler shrank from prying into the private life of Tommy Thompson.

Koznicki stopped and faced the priest. ''Cox and the *Free Press* undoubtedly have a copy. We will make some copies for our investigating officers. And I think it important that you have a copy. If we are going to find out what has happened to Monsignor Thompson, his diary may just prove to be the key. You may be able to help us. Will you?''

''If you put it that way,'' Koesler said resignedly, ''of course.''

During the return drive to headquarters, Koesler reflected on the repartee between Inspectors Koznicki and O'Hara. It reminded him of the kind of familiar kidding that went on amongst priests. And why not? The two professions shared not a few similarities. Both were either completely or preponderantly staffed by males. Both demanded an extreme degree of dedication. And both were completely outside the mainstream of American life.

———————

There was a sense of the sacred associated with all secrets, as far as Bob Koesler was concerned.

He concurred with the notion that there was a hierarchy among secrets. At the top of the list was the storied seal of confession, followed by the professional secret, on down to the simple confidence that one person places in another. Where others measured these secrets in terms of their range of revealability, Koesler's attitude was that all secrets were to be guarded. He'd always been somewhat uneasy even hearing confessions in a setting wherein the penitent voluntarily reveals most intimate secrets. His discomfort stemmed from the subtle pressure to go to confession that many Catholics had experienced.

So it was with genuine reluctance that he had accepted the Xeroxed copy of Monsignor Thompson's diary, along with Inspector Koznicki's charge to read it, familiarize himself with it, indeed, study it.

By the very nature of a diary, as well as the way those who had read or glanced through Thompson's diary spoke of this one, Koesler knew it contained the writer's innermost thoughts and feelings. There was no question in Koesler's mind that the reading of this diary was an invasion of Thompson's most precious privacy. The question raised by Koznicki concerned the necessity for invading that privacy.

Nevertheless, Koesler, throughout the day, kept finding excuses to postpone the reading.

After the excitement attendant to finding Thompson's car that morning, Koesler had lunched with Koznicki at a small restaurant in Greektown, which bordered police headquarters. During the meal, he was gradually able to forget the missing Monsignor for the moment.

But as police officer and priest parted, like a persistent intruder, the diary again burned its way into Koesler's consciousness.

Monday afternoons were usually filled with cleaning up the nitty-gritty of the just-completed weekend liturgies and the very remote preparation for next weekend's liturgies. From time to time, it occurred to Koesler that parishes, especially suburban parishes, existed solely for weekend liturgies. During the week, relatively little of importance took place. Of course, there were interminable meetings of councils, commissions, and committees. Occasionally, there was a lonely soul to counsel or console and the slow but steady processions of panhandlers. Clearly, however, the majority of parishioners thought of their parish solely in terms of a once-weekly Mass of obligation.

Koesler sensed that he would be unable to sustain a Monday afternoon routine. Nor was he yet willing to delve into Thompson's diary.

Instead, he decided to visit Betty Hardwick, a parishioner who suffered from cerebral palsy and was presently hospitalized with arthritis.

It was a long, leisurely drive out Michigan Avenue to Wayne County General Hospital, more popularly known as Eloise, after the village in which it was situated. Once there, Koesler was, as always, overwhelmed by the number, size, and complexity of the institutional buildings. After getting directions at the in-tion made some sense. However, Koesler assured her that the answer, as was the case with what if anything was worn beneath the kilt, would have to remain a secret revealed to a precious few.

It was 9:30. For all religious purposes, St. Anslem's had settled down for the night.

He could avoid it no longer. He made a rather firm scotch-and-water and settled into a comfortable black leather chair in the living room, the Xeroxed copy of Monsignor Thompson's diary on his lap.

The barely legible scribble brought to mind the notes Thompson had occasionally passed to him in the seminary. At first, he had complained to Thompson that the notes were deliberate obfuscations and that Thompson was preparing for the wrong profession. He should become a doctor and write prescriptions only a pharmacist could decipher. As the years progressed, Koesler had accommodated himself to the inevitability of Thompson's scribble and learned to lived with it. Thus, Koesler would have an easier time reading the diary than had the others who had copies in their possession.

Koesler shuddered. He was about to enter his classmate's mind.

For a first reading and for the sake of dispatch, he decided to scan only those sections that were underlined. The first such passage was under the date, "Wednesday, July 18."

Lunch today with Boyle and the Chancery children. Dull to the point of boredom. No one is running this diocese. It is just happening. If Boyle would take a page from the Tribunal, things might shape up. But what the hell difference does it make? The Archdiocese is Boyle's concern. The Tribunal is mine. But I do think Boyle is beginning to notice how efficiently and well the Tribunal is being run, like a tight ship. If Boyle hasn't thrown my name in to become a bishop, he certainly soon will.

Angela Cicero was early for her appointment.

Koesler was jolted. He was surprised to find someone he knew in Thompson's diary.

When will these people learn to come to the Church on their knees rather than thumping a table! Imagine, setting a wedding

171

date for a case that's in Rome! Foolish people! Angela Cicero will pay the price. She hasn't a prayer of getting the dispensation. And Koesler will not dare act on his own while Rome has the case.

So even he himself was in the diary.

I wish I could be there August 4 to witness the inevitable conclusion of this case. Fortunately, I will be tanning on the Costa Smeralda. Meanwhile, back here, everyone will be all dressed up, and no one will have anywhere to go. The Church and her sacred law will win again, as, in the end, she always does.

But I think I was successful in convincing her I could do something to expedite the case if I were willing. She offered me money. Silly woman. Now, had she offered herself . . . we'll just never know. As a future bishop, I could not broach the subject. But if she had offered . . . God, it would have been tempting. Just to see if she's got the boobs and hips she seems to have. She is what the praise of older women is all about. In middle life, held on to a terrific figure, not a tight-assed kid; voluptuous, and with all her experience probably terrific in bed. It would have been quite a temptation. She just might have gotten her privilege if she had given me the privilege.

Nothing further in that passage was underlined.

Koesler shook his head and sipped his scotch. He felt shame for Thompson and mortified that others could read these words.

And where *was* Thompson? At this moment he could be in danger, or pain, or even dead, while strangers had access to secret thoughts that were utterly unworthy of anyone who represented Christ's Church.

Steeled by another sip of scotch, Koesler read on.

Thursday, July 19.

The very next day.

What outrageous good luck to have Al Braemar leaving the DAC just as I was entering. I could tell that Lee Brand overheard us. It had to impress that bastard that I need neither him nor his money nor his influence. It got our luncheon off on just the right note. It was a real challenge to turn around our earlier luncheon at the Renaissance Club.

172

Koesler paged back through the diary looking in vain for a mention of the Renaissance Club, much less a luncheon there with Lee Brand. It had to have been entered in a previous volume.

I think Brand finally got the point—that I am not going to expedite his intended son-in-law's case. God, it felt great dumping on Brand. With him, it's just a case of who dumps first. And I'll bet he hasn't been beaten that often. When he lost his control and his temper—it felt almost like an orgasm.

The only problem I can foresee is that I'm sure Brand sensed that we were doing nothing out of the ordinary to get testimony from Laura Warwick. Well, that was unavoidable. We'll just have to see what comes of it. One thing for sure: there's no way in hell Brand's rich-bitch daughter is going to be married in a Catholic church.

Koesler added some ice and water, diluting the scotch, and read on.

Monday, July 23

How sweet it is! I'll wager not many people have beheld what I saw today. A Lee Brand completely defeated. All his money, all his influence, all his power, and I defeated him. I wonder where his Bunny (what a ridiculous name!) will have her high-society wedding? The Anglican Cathedral, perhaps? Some sleazy justice of the peace?

The real kick is that at every turn I outsmarted the brilliant Lee Brand. I tricked him into believing I had expedited the case without my ever having said so in so many words. And I kept him hanging until even with all his money, it was too late.

This is one of those times I wish I had a woman. One would like to follow up a figurative screwing with a physical one.

It was like reviewing last week's newspaper. You read all these stories that were developing but because the time for their development had passed, you knew how they all concluded. Thompson's firm conviction that Brand was defeated was, of course, mistaken. And, oddly, Koesler had played a role in that drama.

Thomas Thompson, Koesler thought, I wonder if you ever had any misgivings about keeping a diary.

Wednesday, July 25

It is, as I have always said, the rabbit punches of life that really take the toll. Today was relatively problem-free. All in all, I would have nothing to complain about if it hadn't been for that call from Neiss.

Koesler assumed this was a reference to Father Neiss at neighboring Divine Child parish. He could not anticipate in what way the ordinarily mild-mannered Dave Neiss could have upset the supercilious Tommy Thompson. But for the first time in the underlined sections of Thompson's diary, at least he, Koesler, did not appear to be involved.

Neiss's problem is symptomatic of the shortsightedness of most of the priests in this Archdiocese. He has no overview of the problems of the Tribunal . . . none of them has. If any of them had to deal with as many possibly convalidated marriages as we do, they would understand the necessity for my Polish policy.

Whatinhell, Koesler wondered, is a Polish policy? It couldn't be a rotten ethnic joke; Thompson wasn't the type, especially when formulating Tribunal policy.

Besides, Neiss is a fool to get involved with his clients. Some of them are bound to get hurt. It's in the nature of the enforcement of laws and regulations. Police would be useless if they got involved with the people they deal with. Doctors would be emotional wrecks if they got involved with their patients. Priests are no different.

Neiss claims my policy is hurting a friend. The truth is, Neiss shouldn't be handling the case of a friend.

I have strong suspicions that Neiss is going to continue to prove himself a troublemaker. And if he is, I will carry through my threat to him and see that his faculties to administer the sacraments in this Archdiocese are withdrawn.

While the diary was not particularly explicit, Koesler got the impression that Neiss was easily as angry with Thompson as vice versa.

Koesler rose, stretched, and once more diluted his drink with ice and water. Then he returned to the diary.

Sunday, July 29

I've got the bastard now!

*After getting over the initial shock this afternoon of reading
that Brand got his goddamn Catholic wedding after all, the
beauty of it hit me. There is no way this bastard Shanley is going
to get out of this. I can lay the pictures, the stories, on Boyle's
desk. There is no way the Old Man can avoid this confrontation.*

*I will settle for nothing less than suspension for Shanley. And
I'll get it. I've got all of canon law behind me. Shanley couldn't
have helped me more. Witnessing a prima facie invalid, illicit
union. Giving communion to non-Catholics—even Jews, probably. Giving notorious scandal. All blatantly recorded by the
news media! I almost love the bastard.*

*Shanley's punishment will be warning to ALL those bastards
out there who are playing fast and loose with canon law. I would
be very surprised if we don't have a flood of cases that used to
be illegally "solved" in parishes come through our office now.
Once again, the Tribunal will enjoy its rightful place in the Archdiocese.*

*And last, but by no means least, when I get Shanley, I will
also get Lee Brand. He had his day in the sun. I will make
certain everyone knows it was an illicit day of glory. The whole
Archdiocese, the whole city will know that his precious Bunny
is, as far as her Church is concerned, an adulteress and a whore.
I want to see Brand's face as I wipe the smirk off it.*

*And all of this I'm going to accomplish over the ecclesiasti-
cally dead body of Father Norman Shanley. Father Shanley, all
who are about to die salute you!*

Koesler reread this passage. He recalled the Saturday night
poker game during which he had seen the TV account of the
Brand wedding. He remembered thinking at the time that Shanley was in a lot of trouble. Koesler had had no concept of how
much trouble Shanley had courted and how much trouble Shanley had created for others. All through the good offices of Monsignor Tommy Thompson.

Koesler found himself amazed at the degree of revenge of
which Thompson was capable. Evidently, the Monsignor put
little stock in the Biblical admonition, "Vengeance is mine. I
shall repay, saith the Lord."

Koesler returned to the diary.

Monday, July 30

No two ways about it, Pat Lennon is a sexy bitch. Today is the second time I've seen her. The first time, when she was waiting to see Oleksiak, I couldn't take my eyes off her. From the top of her curly hair to her well-turned ankles, she is a series of curves, each in the right place. It didn't hurt at all that she was wearing a light clinging summer dress.

But today she was dressed more modestly than the average modern nun. And still the curves were there. All that and a beautiful face to boot. She is almost—not quite, but almost—enough to exchange a bishopric for.

I think I can keep her coming back. She has a very workable, if not terribly strong, case. People are bound to keep telling her that. So she should keep returning to the Tribunal. Eventually, she will realize that it is I who hold the carrot at the end of the string. And before she gets the carrot, she'll have to give something first.

It shouldn't take her long to realize it's a quid pro quo situation. Or, in this case, tit for ass. She's been married once and is living with a man now. She's probably had any number of sexual partners in between. It would be great to tap all that sexual expertise.

I think she goes for me, too. There was a lot of hostility there today. But it's not that difficult to turn anger into another more pleasant form of passion.

I wouldn't count on that, thought Koesler, as he recalled the phone conversation he'd had with Pat Lennon immediately after her interview with Thompson. After learning Lennon's reaction to Thompson, it was odd and a bit creepy reading Thompson's lascivious reaction to Lennon.

Koesler paged through the remainder of the Xeroxed sheets. There was only one other underlined passage. He decided to reinforce the scotch into a potent nightcap. He anticipated a difficult drift into sleep after the trauma of rummaging through Monsignor Thompson's frequently un-Christian thoughts.

He settled back for the final dairy venture of this evening.

Friday, August 3

Murphy's Law was working overtime today. Somehow that

crazy bitch Angela Cicero was able to get through to Rome. Her luck is phenomenal. She was able to get through to Pat Cammarata and convince him he should become her guardian angel.

Again, thought Koesler, I enter the scene. He wondered if Thompson knew it was he who had given Mrs. Cicero Cammarata's name and number. Had he not read these excerpts from the latest volume of Thompson's diary, Koesler would never have guessed at his involvement in and impact on Thompson's life.

The silly broad probably didn't know what she was doing. She actually set the wheels of Rome in motion. Ordinarily, Rome moves when Rome feels like it. She made Rome feel like it. Now Rome is moving over me. I've got to pass up that great weekend on the Costa Smeralda and sit on the phone waiting for Cammarata's call.

Of course, I could have accomplished what she did. Far more easily than she did. She would be a fool not to know that. She probably thinks she got the last laugh.

Well, she's wrong. Nothing ever happens to me. Tomorrow I will prove to be the most cooperative officialis Rome has ever known. When Boyle presents my nomination for bishop, I want as many Romans as possible to be familiar with Monsignor Thomas Thompson and his good work.

Koesler tapped the Xeroxed sheets into alignment and carefully placed them in the folder the police had provided.

He downed the last of his elongated scotch and water. A pleasant dullness began to invade his consciousness. Sleep was not far off.

He decided, en route to his bedroom, to take a shower. Ordinarily, he showered in the morning. But tonight he felt soiled both by the act of reading another person's diary and by the sordid outpourings of Thompson's paranoid and defensive mind.

Koesler could not imagine any possible way he could be of help in this police investigation. But he vowed to remain ready to respond to any call from the police as well as any unlikely entrance of divine inspiration.

———

Blood Found in Abandoned Car

FOUL PLAY FEARED IN CASE OF MISSING MONSIGNOR

By Joe Cox
Free Press Staff Writer

A new development has been uncovered by the Detroit police in the day-old case of the missing Monsignor. Msgr. Thomas Thompson's late-model Eldorado was found early Monday morning parked and abandoned in front of De La Salle High School on Detroit's near east side.

Lt. Ned Harris, head of Squad Six of the Homicide Division, stated that blood was found on tissues in the car's waste receptacle, and a casing from what appeared to be a .32-caliber automatic pistol was found on the car's front seat.

"Investigation of this case as a possible homicide has just begun," stated Homicide Inspector Walter Koznicki. "Until now," Koznicki added, "the disappearance of Monsignor Thompson has been treated as a missing person's case. The discovery of his automobile, the bloodstains, the spent cartridge, as well as several other details I am not at liberty to discuss at this time have moved the case into a full-fledged homicide investigation."

Msgr. Thompson was last seen Saturday evening at Roma Hall on Gratiot in East Detroit. Thompson was attending a wedding reception when, according to witnesses, he was called to the phone. After a few moments' conversation, he was heard to say, "You don't mean it! Where? I'll be right there!"

At first it was thought that
see MONSIGNOR Page 13A

Joe Cox had no trouble writing the second-day story. It almost wrote itself. At this point, the *News* and the *Free Press* were approximately neck and neck in their coverage of The Case of the Missing Monsignor.

The *Free Press* enjoyed a slight proprietary lead, since Joe Cox had broken the story exclusively in the August 13 Monday-morning edition. The *News* was able to add the dimension of a homicide investigation as it introduced its readers to the case, on Monday afternoon. Cox's second story appeared late Monday evening as well as Tuesday morning. Virtually a tie.

But Cox held the tie breaker in the copy he had made of Monsignor Thompson's diary. While the police were all but certain he had copied the diary, only Cox and Nelson Kane knew for sure.

The *News* was soon to learn that Cox had an advantage. It would be a while before they would be able to discover just what it was.

Cox, for his part, was eager to get his investigation under full throttle.

There was only one fly in his investigative ointment. How could he handle a serious interrogation of Pat Lennon? He did not believe it possible that the woman he loved could be capable of murder.

Nevertheless, this was a possible murder investigation, and Pat Lennon's name did appear quite prominently in Thompson's diary.

Until this investigation was complete and Thompson—or his body—was found, all bets were off.

4

THE ANNOUNCEMENT WAS THERE IN THE Detroit News's August 5 issue. It was there for anyone to see. Monsignor Thomas Thompson would be at a wedding reception at Roma Hall in East Detroit on the evening of August 11. It was unlikely that any of his cronies would be with him. He would be unguarded, unprotected, among strangers, virtually alone, vulnerable.

Angela Cicero read the announcement perfunctorily. She routinely scanned wedding news for about the same reason she read obituaries: to see if anyone she knew was involved. Fresh from her daughter's wedding the previous evening, Angela found herself reading the Newlyweds column with slightly more than usual interest. Her attention, of course, was riveted by the mention of Monsignor Thomas Thompson. He had played such a crucial if potentially disastrous role in her daughter's wedding that he was not far from Angela's consciousness. Especially since the Monsignor had been the substance of her confession yesterday.

For all intents and purposes, Angela thought, he's out of my life now. There will be no more marriages, tribunals, or last-minute-granted privileges from Rome.

But what of those who would follow? In Angela's fantasy there appeared an endless parade of young people waiting to be manipulated and maltreated by Monsignor Thompson.

It wasn't fair. It wasn't Christian. Somebody should do something about it! But who? What? Apparently, the institutional Church was unconcerned. From the reactions of Fathers Cavanaugh and Koesler and Deacon Schroeder, all knew what Monsignor Thompson was doing, but no one could or would do anything about it.

More and more, as she considered the problem, she began to consider the possibility of volunteering her own involvement. It was typical. Part of her creed was, if you are not part of the solution, you are part of the problem. It explained what she had been doing in the middle of her daughter's wedding. Under normal circumstances, Angela Cicero would have been most content to be seen only on the sidelines as the passive, happy, tearful mother of the bride.

However, there had been a problem. Her daughter Anna Maria wanted a Catholic wedding. Some silly regulation threatened to prevent the Catholic ceremony. It was only natural and normal that, at that point, Angela had gotten involved.

It was the way she had been reared.

Angela Bonfiglio was the tenth of twelve children. Her father, a hulking construction worker, ate spaghetti and meatballs for dinner every night of his adult life while quaffing a cornucopia of Chianti. After which he would yell at his wife and throw things at his children.

Her mother, rotund and submissive, was self-conscious of her Sicilian heritage. While she would yell at her children, she never challenged her husband.

For some inexplicable sibling reason, it was little Angela who became proficient at two things: interceding with her father on behalf of her brothers and sisters, and dodging pots and pans. From her earliest memory, Angela had been the one who took charge and got things done.

Nor did she lose that quality when she became an adult and married. She made certain her household was the antithesis of the home in which she had been raised.

Leo, her husband, was kept supported and fulfilled. Her children were encouraged to develop their individual personalities and talents. Far from becoming submissive and rotund, Angela quietly but expertly steered her family through every crisis while maintaining a dazzling figure as she neared middle age.

Now, seated in the shadowed coolness of her living room, contemplating the announcement that Monsignor Thompson was scheduled to appear at a wedding reception the coming Saturday evening, Angela once again felt impelled to get involved.

A plan began to form.

She had never even dared to think of anything like this before. But desperate circumstances demanded desperate measures. For the good of the nuptially troubled of the Archdiocese of Detroit, someone would have to put a stop to the machinations of Monsignor Thompson. And, in a burst of responsibility rarely found in others, Angela once more substituted herself rather than be satisfied with the amorphous and ineffectual "someone."

But this, her most ambitious intervention thus far, would require meticulous and fail-safe planning.

As she sat very still, she could envision the coming week. She picked up her Edgar Allan Poe anthology, found the selection she sought, and began to read.

MONDAY, AUGUST 6, DINNER

Angela Cicero had spent a couple of hours this afternoon preparing coq au vin. It was time well spent. The house was filled with the aroma of browning chicken, simmering wine, and sauteing vegetables.

Leo Cicero caught the aroma even before opening the door to the kitchen area from the adjoining garage.

"Hi, hon." He leaned over to kiss her nape. He didn't have to ask what was for dinner. He patted her bottom appreciatively.

She smiled and continued to assemble a tossed salad.

"Hard day?" she asked.

"No worse than usual. Hot, though!"

Shedding jacket and tie, he draped them over a dining room chair and loosened his collar.

"Dinner will be ready in about fifteen minutes," she called from the kitchen.

He made each of them a martini and marveled at how satisfying certain routines could become. Coming home about the same time each working day. Being greeted by this terrific woman who always had everything, including the kids and the food, under complete control. Sharing a predinner martini. Evenings, nights, weekends, vacations with his wife. Life, he concluded, a blissful smile creasing his face, had been good to him.

"Well," she asked as they began the meal, "how does it feel now that the last kid is gone?"

"Good." The chicken fell from its bone at the touch of his fork. "And that surprises me. I thought I'd get lonesome with all the youngsters gone. But I'm not. Matter of fact, I'd almost forgotten how good it was to be alone with you."

"I'm glad. I feel that way too." She tasted the chicken and approved.

"Now that we're alone," she continued, "don't you think it would be good if you picked up some of the sports you've let drop over the years?"

"Oh, I don't know. It was tough enough giving them up to be with the kids more and fix up the house and things. But they're gone now. I don't miss them anymore."

She reached over and patted a tummy that prominently expanded above and protruded over his belt line. "This," she said, "misses the sports activity."

He felt a rush of sheepish embarrassment. For years, he had been growingly conscious of the marked disparity in their physical conditions. His wife kept her figure by working at it. He knew she did it for him, and he was grateful. The unfairness of having let himself slip physically overwhelmed him.

"You're absolutely right, hon," he admitted. "I owe it to us." He rested his fork and picked up his half-finished martini, counterproductive to his latest resolution. "Remind me next week to call some of the gang and find out what's going on."

She laughed heartily. "Oh, no. You're not going to get away with this 'next week' business. I called 'some of the gang' earlier today. 'What's going on' is that your old bowling team is mired in last place with their summer season just about over. They've been one man short for the past few weeks. They want you back for what's left of the season. They agree that in their present standing, you can't hurt them."

They both laughed.

"O.K.! All right! I'll get in shape for the harsher demands of sports by bowling. When is bowling night?"

"Saturday."

"This Saturday? Do we have anything on the calendar?"

"No," she replied emphatically. "It's perfect. You get in there and bowl your little heart out. I'll be waiting by the home fires with the rubbing alcohol."

Smiling, he returned to his attack on the coq au vin.

Somehow it seemed right that he was going to resume what had been for him a rather active athletic avocation. And he was pleased that his bowling team wanted him back and—characteristic of them—that they would couch the invitation in a joke.

"Oh, and by the way," she said, "I know you're a creature of habit. So it's best that you know I plan for us to finish the basement Friday evening."

"Friday evening? Why so late?"

"Because of our schedules: I have to go to a shower Wednesday evening, and you have a K of C meeting tomorrow and a St. Francis Home meeting Thursday evening."

"But what if we don't finish Friday night? There's quite a bit left to do. I don't want to get into bricklaying on the weekend if I can help it."

"Stop worrying," she reproved. "If we don't finish it Friday, I'll work on it Saturday night while you're out smashing pins."

"I don't want you working while I'm out bowling."

"Don't worry," she assured him. "It'll be a pleasure.

FRIDAY, AUGUST 10, EVENING

"Don't get me wrong," said Leo Cicero, "I like a brew as well or better than the next guy, but aren't you going in the wrong direction?"

"What do you mean?" Angela Cicero replaced an emptied Budweiser bottle with a freshly opened one.

"This." Leo indicated the full bottle. "I thought the idea was for me to lose some weight and get back in shape. I don't think I'm going to get there very fast on an unending series of beers."

Angela squatted on the floor of the basement and alternately applied mortar and bricks to the facade they were constructing.

"Listen, sweetie," she said, "anytime you want the series to end, all you have to do is either drink the beer slowly or quit drinking."

"You don't understand the Italian mind even though you're Italian."

Angela looked up at him quizzically.

"You can lead an Italian to booze, but you can't stop him from drinking," he explained.

Leo carefully inserted the brick that linked the current section to the ceiling.

Angela laughed. "Oh, it's not going to hurt you that much. You've been perspiring all evening. And besides, tomorrow we'll go to the club, and you can take a sauna and swim a bit. Then, tomorrow night there's bowling."

"Just the same," he said, "I think I'll just call it quits on the beer for this evening. I'm getting a little bleary-eyed."

"I wasn't going to mention that your bricks have not been going in all that straight for the past half-hour."

Leo stepped back and appraised his handiwork.

"You're right," he declared. "It'll hold together, but it is definitely not a professional job."

"Why don't we quit for the night?"

"But we've got only a few rows to go, and it'll be finished."

"Leave them. I'll finish them tomorrow night while you're bowling."

"I don't want to stick you with that job."

"Don't worry about it. It'll be a snap. It'll give me something to do while you're gone. Besides, maybe we'll think of something we'll want to stick in there behind the false wall. Something like a cornerstone laying."

"Yeah," Leo reflected, straightening up and putting things away. "What do you suppose we'd want to put in there, anyway?"

Angela cleaned a trowel in the sink. "Oh, I don't know. Something no one would miss for the next hundred years, I expect."

The Ciceros had returned from the country club rather late in the afternoon. It had been a glorious hot day with low humidity and a gentle breeze. Perfect for lounging poolside and occasionally diving into the cool water. Leo, true to his resolve, had undergone a lengthy sauna and had swum for a total of nearly an hour broken into fifteen- to twenty-minute segments.

Angela had served a hearty spaghetti and meatball dinner at approximately 7:30. At this point the most important consideration was timing. She planned to get her husband to his 9 P.M. bowling date just about on schedule. She knew from years of experience as a bowling widow that the nine o'clock league would not begin on time. Nine on the dot, then, would be a good time for Leo to arrive. He would have time to renew acquaintances, but not enough time to exhaust talk of the good old days. That way, with a few beers and more talk after league play, it would easily be one or two in the morning before Leo would return.

The next bit of timing would be more delicate. But, fresh from her triumph in timing her call to the Vatican the previous week, her self-confidence was high.

Her call to Roma Hall must be placed at just the right moment.

The wedding was scheduled for 8 P.M. Figure an hour-and-a-half for the wedding Mass, photographs afterward, and the trip to the hall—9:30. Another half-hour for greeting guests, getting settled at the tables, a blessing, and toasts to the newlyweds—10 P.M.

Ten P.M. is the moment to call.

SATURDAY, AUGUST 11, 10 P.M.

"Roma Hall."

"I'd like to speak with Monsignor Thomas Thompson."

"I'm sorry. He's with a wedding party, and they have just begun eating."

Perfect.

"I need to speak with him only briefly, and it is very important. I'm sure, as a priest, he would be willing to accept this call."

A few moments of hesitation.

"Oh, very well. Hold on, please."

Several minutes passed, during which Angela could hear the muffled sound of a large gathering of diners talking, laughing and, by tinkling their glasses, encouraging freshly connubial kissing.

"Monsignor Thompson." His tone betrayed a mixture of pleasure, probably from the fun of the party, and annoyance, undoubtedly from being called away to the phone.

"Monsignor, this is Angela Cicero." Of greatest importance now was to afford Monsignor Thompson no opportunity to speak until her entire invitation was offered. So, Angela took a deep breath and began to talk nonstop.

"You may remember me from last week. My daughter was married after we received a privilege of the faith from Rome through your good offices. Now I know we didn't seem to hit it off. But I want you to know that as far as I was concerned, that was just on the surface. Actually, I admire a man like you who has the courage of his convictions. All the time we seemed to be at each other's throat, I was secretly admiring you. A guy like you, if you don't mind my saying so, really turns me on. Now, the reason I'm calling is that my husband is gone and won't be back until tomorrow. I'd like you to come over now and just let's see if something—you know—develops."

"Uh . . ." He almost said something.

"If you're worried about dinner," she cut in, "I have plenty here if, after all, you prefer dining to me. This is our one chance to find out if the chemistry I detected between us is really there. I can promise you this, Tom," she dropped her voice seductively, "you won't be disappointed."

"You don't mean it!" he said enthusiastically. Several nearby waiters glanced at him.

"But I do mean it, Tom. Come on. No strings attached. Let's just see what happens."

"Where?"

She gave him her Robindale address, and added, "If I were

187

you, Tom, I wouldn't park out front. Neighbors, you know. Somewhere along the way, get a cab.''

"I'll be right there!"

Two waiters looked at each other and shrugged as Monsignor Thompson hurried from the hall after murmuring an excuse to the bride and groom.

Outside Roma Hall, the parking valet took Thompson's stub and dashed off to retrieve his car. The young man knew exactly where it was. He had been somewhat startled when a clergyman exited an Eldorado with, the valet noticed while parking, everything in it but a CB radio.

He located the car at the rear of the lot, just where he'd parked it. He got behind the wheel and began searching on the floor for the ignition key. Instead, he felt something cylindrical. He raised it to the light and saw that it was an empty cartridge, the sharp edge of which had cut his finger rather badly.

Muttering empty curses, he tossed the cartridge on the passenger seat, pulled several tissues from the handy dispenser, and tried to stanch the flow of blood. Finally, finding the key, he started the car, then drove it to a rocking stop just short of Monsignor Thompson, stuffing the bloodstained tissues in the car's disposal box as he braked.

Thompson gave the valet a quarter and drove off too quickly to hear the young man's lush imprecations, all of which were variations on a theme describing someone who was parsimonious and illegitimate.

As he drove down Gratiot toward the Ford Freeway, Thompson remembered there were always cabs at Detroit City Airport, which was practically on his way. He would leave his Eldorado at De La Salle. There it would be safe and inconspicuous.

Before leaving his car, Thompson noticed some stains on the steering wheel. Slightly sticky, they appeared to be blood. Probably that damned valet. If there were bloodstains on the wheel, there must be . . . yes . . . on the gearshift and rear-view mirror too. Thompson took an immaculate handkerchief from his pocket and wiped them clean.

188

When she saw the cab stop in front of her house, Angela Cicero went to the front door and waited for the sound of footsteps on the porch. She heard nothing till the doorbell rang. He must have tiptoed, she thought. She opened the door.

Neither the porch nor hall lights were on. By the light coming from behind her in the living room, Thompson could see Angela silhouetted through a diaphanous gown. Evidently, she could deliver on the full-figured voluptuousness she had promised when fully clothed. He began to perspire profusely. He was grateful he had splashed on the Brut liberally.

Silently, she took his suit jacket and hung it in the hall closet. Quickly, he removed his clerical collar and vest and tossed them on the closet shelf.

She led the way into the living room. He followed very closely. They sat on the couch. She looked at him. It was clear he was unsure of the next move.

"I'll just get us some wine," she said, and patted him lightly on the knee.

He watched her leave the room. Her filmy gown caught against her body as she moved sinuously. He took out a fresh handkerchief and mopped his brow and the back of his neck. He noticed that all the shades had been lowered. He felt more at ease.

She returned with two glasses of wine. As she bent to place them on the table in front of the couch, she revealed more than a hint of two large, rounded, firm breasts.

As she sat next to him on the couch, he lunged at her. She was able to get both arms up and between them. She managed to hold him off, although only inches separated them. God, he's clumsy, she thought.

"Just a minute, lover," she said, "don't you want some wine?"

He just sat there, clutching her, his mouth ajar.

"You're ready, aren't you?" she said. An obvious evaluation of the situation.

He nodded.

"All right," she said, "but not here. Everything is prepared downstairs."

She led him to the basement door and opened it.

There were only four steps to the first landing, where the staircase took a sharp, right-angle turn descending to the basement floor.

Thompson put his hands against either wall to steady himself. As he took the first step he thought this might be the first time he had ever gone *down* to paradise.

Angela picked up the short, heavy two-by-four she had earlier placed near the door. She tried to recall all the times in the movies or on TV she had seen someone fictitiously slugged. The operation, as far as she could remember, called for hitting the victim at the point where neck meets shoulder.

With a silent prayer for beginner's luck, she swung from the heels.

She hit him exactly where she intended.

He crumpled and fell in a heap on the landing.

She was elated. Everything was working just as planned. She retrieved his jacket and clerical collar from the closet, then tugged his heavy body down the remaining steps.

SUNDAY, AUGUST 12, 12:15 A.M.

I have a serious pain in the neck, was Thompson's first thought. Next, he became conscious of a cramped feeling throughout his body. Several layers of tape covered his mouth. His hands were tied and fastened tightly to the straight-backed chair on which he sat, as were his feet.

He tried to look about as panic welled within him. It was dark. He seemed to be in an extremely small space. He looked up to a small opening through which shone a narrow shaft of light. He stared at the opening as he tried to clear his mind and figure out what had happened.

Suddenly, a pair of eyes appeared in the opening. They looked vaguely familiar. They belonged to Angela Cicero.

One of the eyes winked, there was a grating sound as a brick slid into place, and all was blackness.

Angela cleaned her hands, then returned to the living room.

She stretched out on the couch. She felt tired but fulfilled. The way, she thought, an avenging angel might feel.

She decided to read herself to sleep or till Leo's return, whichever came first. She picked up her Poe anthology, which fell open to "The Cask of Amontillado."

Father Koesler sat in the dining room of St. Anselm's rectory, sipping his morning coffee. He was the only one he knew who ruined instant coffee. He could bracket this nonskill with the general run of mechanical skills, none of which, for him, was a strength. At least the brew was hot.

He was reading the morning *Free Press*. He had just finished Joe Cox's story on the missing Monsignor Thompson. It recalled the excitement of yesterday's police investigation, as well as last night's depressing reading of Thompson's diary.

The memory of those events so distracted him that he found himself turning page after page without paying attention to what he was reading.

At this point, the pajama-and-bathrobe-clad Lester Schroeder passed through the dining room en route to the kitchen.

" 'Morning, Les."

"Mmmff." Schroeder opened the refrigerator.

"Want me to make you some coffee?"

"No! No, that's O.K. !" Schroeder responded as one suddenly roused from a sleepwalker's trance.

Koesler smiled. He had prepared instant coffee for Schroeder in the past. Once.

Schroeder sleepily made his way back to the dining room and sank heavily into a chair opposite Koesler. He clutched a glass of orange juice as if it were a life preserver.

Koesler chuckled as he read the sports section. "It says here," he read, "that if the University of Michigan punter had a drug habit and tried to kick it, he would miss."

"Mrrfsk." Schroeder rubbed his hand across his mouth, muffling whatever brief comment he had made.

Koesler looked up momentarily to contemplate the sight of a tousled Schroeder rubbing his eyes with the heels of both hands. The priest read on.

"Says here," Koesler continued, chuckling, "that if Billy Ford took over the Ford Motor Company there'd be a lot of holding on the assembly line."

Silence.

Koesler raised his gaze again, only to see Schroeder staring vacantly back. "Either what I'm reading to you is funny, or," Koesler pointed to his cup, "somebody put something in my coffee."

Again the vacant stare.

"Don't you get it?" Koesler asked. "Billy Ford is the owner of the Detroit Lions football team, which is frequently penalized for holding. So that if—"

"Oh, I get it all right, Bob," Schroeder interrupted. "It's just that I'm kind of tired."

Koesler checked his watch. Nine o'clock. He had been up since seven and had already said Mass for the nine or ten faithful daily communicants. But, he had to concede, nine in the morning represented the shank of the night to Schroeder.

"What are you doing up so early, Les?"

"Oh, I wanted to talk to you before you went out today."

"About what?" Being wide awake, Koesler knew he had Schroeder at a distinct disadvantage.

"Well, I was thinking about what the faith community needs to broaden their world vision."

"And what might that be, Les?" Koesler reflected that if jargon were amputated from Schroeder's vocabulary, the Deacon would be struck mute.

"Flags! Flags of all the United Nations!" Schroeder was warming to the exposition of his plan. "Each flag on its own pole and the poles placed around the large square between the church and Outer Drive!"

"Flags," Koesler repeated flatly.

"And a pagoda—a Chinese pagoda with a bell in it!"

"A pagoda."

"Yes. In order to internationalize and Orientalize our faith community and impress them with the truly catholic dimensions of the world family."

Koesler looked long at his deacon. The priest tried very hard to keep from laughing.

192

"I think we can give this the amount of study it deserves," said Koesler, "under one condition."

"What's that?"

"That you agree at the outset that you will arise each and every morning at six, go to the pagoda bell, and ring the Angelus."

The import of this prescript began working its way slowly into Schroeder's matutinal consciousness.

The phone rang.

"I'll get it," Koesler said unnecessarily.

Schroeder was trying to comprehend why an alarm clock would ring in that fashion.

It was Inspector Koznicki.

"I was wondering, Father, if you have had time to read the diary?"

"Last night. But I only had time to read the marked sections. I plan to read the entire diary—or at least as much as we have of it—sometime today."

"There's no hurry. But when you do get around to reading the rest, I think you will agree that Mr. Cox selected those passages judiciously. You have read the essence of it, Father. What do you think?"

"I am embarrassed and shamed for him."

"I can understand that, Father. But I would prefer it if you would see the diary as we do. As another, perhaps very valuable, piece of evidence. As a result of having this diary, we have the names of five people who had every reason to be very angry with the Monsignor. Perhaps angry enough to have acted out his or her frustration."

Koesler hesitated. "Wait a minute, Inspector. Why do you want me to view the diary the way you do?"

"Frankly, Father, I think you could be of significant help to us in this case. Now, wait; hear me out before you speak." Koznicki correctly anticipated objections from the priest. "We feel that Church law as well as clerical procedures and protocol will figure heavily in this case. It seems clear that it was in his interpretation and administration of canon law that Monsignor Thompson appeared to provoke these people. Also, there is a good deal of priestly interplay going on. We feel we may be limping badly in the investigation of this case due to the significance of these matters and our lack of familiarity with them.

"Frankly, Father," sensing he had addressed most of Koesler's more serious objections, Koznicki breathed more easily, "I have every confidence that you understand these circumstances at least as well as anyone else and that your coolly logical approach to matters that can become ambiguous will be an asset in this case."

Koesler had to admit that his friend had marshaled more than adequate arguments to enlist his aid. As a Christian, let alone an ordained minister, Koesler felt an obligation to do what he could to help the police and, perhaps, his classmate.

"One thing more—" it was Koesler's final objection. "How much of my time is going to be required? I am a full-time pastor, you know."

"In an investigation like this, Father," said Koznicki, "we tend to think in terms of days. With the substantial leads we have, we should pretty well know what happened within a week. If we do not wrap this up in approximately a week, we'll ship you back to your parish."

"I don't know . . ." Koesler was weakening.

"Father, you told me yourself that you hadn't planned on using your full three weeks vacation this year. You can use a week of vacation to join our homicide investigation and accomplish what you claim is your favorite avocation—learning more about humanity."

"You never forget, do you?" Koesler was smiling.

"The Polish mind never rests. Besides," Koznicki added, "you may learn enough to write a book."

"Don't be funny; who would want to read a book by a priest about a missing monsignor?"

"May we see you soon?"

"I'll be downtown directly."

Koesler now faced an agonizing decision. Could he possibly leave Lester Schroeder in charge of this parish? There seemed no alternative. It would be an obvious insult not to appoint Schroeder caretaker. And, in truth, the ranks were thin. There was no one else available whom Koesler could think of. He had no choice but to bequeath St. Anselm's parish to Deacon Schroeder for at least the next few days.

"Les," Koesler approached Schroeder, who was still pondering the insanity of rising at six to ring an Angelus, "do you know what the briefest canon in the code of canon law is?"

Schroeder looked up inquiringly. He had no idea which was the briefest canon, the longest, or anything in between.

"Sede vacante, nihil innovetur," Koesler intoned.

Schroeder smiled and retained his quizzical visage. He vaguely resembled *Mad* magazine's Alfred E. Neuman.

"It means," Koesler explained, "when a See is unoccupied, let nothing new be introduced."

"But that refers to a diocese!" Tuesday was beginning to happen to Schroeder.

"In this case, it is a parish. *This* parish. I've got to be away from the parish more often than not for the next few days. I'll try to get a Jesuit from the University of Detroit to cover morning Mass. And I'll be here, of course, for the weekend liturgies. But in between, Les, just be around to pick up the pieces of little problems that may come up. Mostly, don't get in Mary O'Connor's way. Left to her own devices, she can run this parish as well as anyone."

"Gotcha!" Schroeder was brightening as the morning progressed. "You want me on deck in case there's a kerygmatic - crisis."

"Les, just babysit the parish for a few days."

"Babysit?"

"Make sure the parish does not become a mother."

It was with considerable trepidation that Koesler departed for police duty.

"I can't take it. And I can't tell you why."

Pat Lennon was close to tears, and that, for her, was completely out of character.

Bob Ankenazy, a young news editor at the *Detroit News*, felt a familiar frustration. Married and the father of two girls, he was among the first to confess that though he was virtually surrounded by women, he did not understand them.

Pat Lennon, in the two years she had been at the *News*, had become recognized as one of the very best and most reliable reporters in the newsroom. In story conferences, editors regularly vied to have Lennon assigned to their stories.

And when Lennon was given an assignment, it was a thing of journalistic beauty to watch her develop it. Over the years with first the *Free Press*, then the *News*, she had gathered an impressive group of reliable contacts. Depending on their fields of expertise, they were useful in developing leads. She faithfully touched all bases, was fair and aboveboard with her sources, was capable of getting the story's essence in the opening paragraph, and seldom required more than incidental copy editing. She brought her stories in on time, and they were invariably at the very least satisfactory.

She was, in a word, that person with whom it is most desirable to work, a professional.

These considerations made it all the more difficult for Ankenazy to understand Lennon's present reaction.

He had just presented her with what he thought could develop into a top-notch story. The disappearance of Monsignor Thomas Thompson could be anything from an embarrassment for the good Monsignor to a gruesome homicide. But gossip or murder, it looked tailor-made for Lennon.

Yet, unaccountably, when he had given her the assignment just a few minutes ago, she had grown ashen, and he'd noticed a slight tremor in her hands. And she had flatly refused the assignment. When he pressed her for a reason, she would give him none. She just repeated her refusal.

And she seemed close to tears. All in all, a scene Ankenazy had trouble handling. Staff writers, particularly those of the highest rank such as Lennon, did not turn down assignments. Especially without good and adequate reason. In addition, weeping women always unnerved him. When women cried, he never knew what to do with his hands. It always seemed that his hands should be doing something. But he never knew what.

"Pat," Ankenazy said somewhat awkwardly, "I've got to know why you refused this assignment. London is going to have to know."

It had been Leon London, managing editor, who, through Ankenazy, had assigned the story to Lennon.

"Tell him I've got female problems."

"Oh, come on, Pat, you know I can't tell him that. You try to cop a plea like that, and you'll be writing second-string obits or covering the Living Rosary on Belle Isle."

"Bob, I just can't. I'm too close to it."

She thought a moment. In the past, she had trusted Ankenazy with confidences of varying import. To her knowledge, he had never betrayed a confidence, no matter how insignificant.

Perhaps she could reveal at least part of the story.

"You remember," she asked, "back a couple of weeks ago when I told you I was going to have my first marriage annulled? What I haven't been able to bring myself to tell you was that the whole thing fell through. And Monsignor Thompson was the main reason for the failure."

She paused to let that sink in.

"I can't be objective about Thompson," Lennon continued. "So I know I couldn't be objective about the story. I'd mess it up. I know it. That's why I can't do the story. If you need something for London, tell him I'm trying to fight off pneumonia. Besides, it's the truth; I can't seem to shake this cold. Even if I took the Thompson story, like as not I would probably be forced to go home and collapse in the middle of it."

Ankenazy looked at Lennon with greater sensitivity. Her ordinarily pert nose was swollen and red. Her eyes were barely open and carried bags. She looked as if she was close to collapsing even now. He wondered why he hadn't noticed it before. He guessed he was so used to dealing with Lennon the professional that he simply took it for granted that she would bring in an assignment as long as there was breath in her. He had to admit that Lennon, like Shylock, was as human as the rest of humankind. Prick Shylock and he will bleed. Hit Lennon with a king-size summer cold, and she will fold.

Ankenazy nodded agreement to Lennon's assessment of her own condition.

"When you finish what you're working on," he said, "why don't you go on home?"

Lennon shrugged and accepted the reprieve gratefully.

Ankenazy returned to London, giving Lennon's debilitated condition as the reason she could not accept the assignment. He did not mention her personal involvement with Thompson. Her ill health was ample excuse.

From time to time, London peered around Ankenazy to confirm what he was saying. Each glance more than verified the tale of imminent disintegration. Lennon sat at her desk, blowing her nose and dabbing at her eyes. Only a minuscule portion of this was an act.

Having convinced London that Lennon was under the weather, yet certain the Thompson story had significant potential, Ankenazy found himself doing something he rarely did. He volunteered himself for the assignment.

"Are you sure?" London arched an eyebrow. "I don't want you off your editor's desk for any extended period."

"No chance of that, Leon. This may or may not turn into a blockbuster, but, on the face of it, it's just a missing person who may have died or have been murdered. Seems like I've covered this story a million times."

"I don't know . . ." London scratched his head.

"Besides, it'll give me a chance to get back in the trenches. Always good to keep your hand in."

"Well, O.K. But don't get in over your head. If you need help on this, yell. I don't want you spending too much time on this one story. There's too much other stuff going on in this town."

"No problem." Ankenazy fastened the top button on his shirt and tightened his tie. "Let's see; it's just noon. I'll get over to police headquarters and get this show on the road."

Ankenazy picked up his notepad and headed for the door. He did not know he was about to step into a journalistic mousetrap that was baited and set to snap.

"Let's see; it's just noon. I've got plenty of time to write this story and get it in the one-ball." Joe Cox spread his notepad on the table and rubbed his hands together.

He and Nelson Kane were in a booth in the Press Pantry on the main floor of the Free Press Building. They had ordered sandwiches and coffee. Cox wanted to tell Kane about his in-

198

terview earlier in the day with Angela Cicero. And Kane wanted to hear about it.

"How'd it go?" Kane blew the steam from his coffee, then sipped it.

"Good. Not great, but good."

"Promise her anonymity?"

"Yeah. That was a great move. Thanks for suggesting it."

Kane grunted; the coffee had burned his tongue.

"We would never have been able to use her name anyway," Cox continued. "There's no way the cops can charge her with any crime, and we would have burned our ass if we had violated her right to privacy. But it really loosened her up when I promised her anonymity."

"Damn right." Kane, having determined his tongue would survive, bit into his sandwich.

The restaurant began to fill.

"I didn't tell her about the diary. Just that I had certain sources that linked her name with Thompson's. I told her the police would be calling on her."

Kane caught Cox's eyes with a sense of challenge.

"I told her the cops' sources were at least as good as mine," Cox explained. "But then I told her this was her chance to put her side of the story on record. And then I repeated the promise of anonymity.

"She bought it. She told me how Thompson had treated her and her family and how she had reacted to it all. Of course, as she tells the story, it's just the reverse of the diary. Thompson is the ogre, and she is the innocent victim. Somehow I prefer her version."

"Motive?" Kane spoke the way he wrote, in lean prose.

"She's got plenty of motive. If Thompson had treated me the way he treated her, I would at very least have kicked him in the balls. Maybe worse."

"How about an alibi?"

"She's got a problem there, and the cops are going to jump on it. As far as I can see, she can't account for her whereabouts Saturday night. But that's *her* problem—hers and the cops'."

"Wait a minute," Kane hesitated as he was about to bite into

199

his sandwich, "what makes you think the cops are going to follow you through the Cicero door?"

"I figure we're using the same guide—Thompson's diary. The logical thing to do is take the people mentioned in the diary in chronological order." Cox placed his sandwich on the plate and consulted his notepad. "That would be . . . uh . . . Angela Cicero, Lee Brand, Father David Neiss, Father Norman Shanley, and, finally, Pat Lennon."

"What about Lennon?" Kane asked, sharply. "You sure you can treat her the same as the others?"

"Like you said, Nellie: we're playing hardball."

"Damn right."

"All we need, Nellie," said Cox, animatedly, "is for the cops not to find the bastard for at least a few more days. We've got a five-parter that'll end with a big wrap-up for our Sunday morning edition. By then, we'll have published the profiles of five people, each of whom has ample reason for killing the bastard.

"We will have used none of their names. But the readers will be playing the game with us: which one of these anonymous characters had the best reason to do away with the Missing Monsignor? Then, if we're really lucky, the cops will find the body and the murderer. And we tell our readers, see, it was number three—and identify him or her.

"Boy, Nellie, this is going to be one helluva story. Like a whodunit that actually happened."

"I can see the lead now," Kane was catching Cox's enthusiasm, " 'While Detroit police search for a missing monsignor, they don't have to look far for a motive behind his disappearance.' "

"Yeah." It did not come close to the lead Cox had planned. But since this lead had come down from the mountaintop, he knew he would have to incorporate it into his story.

"Oh," Cox seemed to be looking out of the coffee shop toward the elevators, "there's Breslin. I've got to see him for a minute."

Cox rose abruptly and hurried from the coffee shop toward the elevator area where there was no Breslin. He left behind an empty sandwich plate, a cup with a residue of cold coffee, and the bill for his lunch.

It was several minutes before it dawned on Kane that he had been stuck with the lunch tab.

———————

Police headquarters was just as he remembered it. It had been almost thirteen years since Bob Ankenazy had been assigned the *News* police beat. But virtually nothing had changed.

The exterior was unmistakable. A huge, square, dull gray building that created the impression of an impervious object in the midst of an area teeming with crime, suffering, despair, frightened as well as cocky juveniles, first-time offenders, and three-time losers.

Inside, one was struck by the overwhelming presence of impersonal marble. Police officers, in uniform or plain clothes, with prominent identification tags, were ubiquitous.

The sundries counter was familiar. A warning that a microwave oven was in use was new.

Ankenazy entered an elevator and pushed the button for the fifth floor. Once again he was struck by the apparent utter lack of security in a building where one might expect maximum security.

On the fifth floor, he followed the signs leading to the Homicide Division. He passed many officers he had never met, further emphasizing the time that had elapsed since he had last worked this building full-time. He almost passed an open office door, but, recognizing one of the room's occupants, he stopped. The officer he recognized was Ned Harris. Ankenazy could not recall Harris's rank now. He had been a patrol officer with plenty of promise when Ankenazy knew him.

He entered the room and stood just inside the doorway until Harris looked up.

"Yes?" Harris looked at the intruder noncommittally. Gradually, recognition dawned.

"Ankenazy! Bob Ankenazy! What are you doing here, slumming? I mean, who are we that an executive of the *Detroit News* should show up on our doorstep?"

"Easy, Ned." Ankenazy laughed. "I'm hardly an executive.

I don't even have a key to the executive washroom. Hell, I don't even know where it is.

"And you—you're a sergeant?"

"Lieutenant, sir. You should read your own paper more often. I been in it."

Ankenazy felt sheepish. Undoubtedly, he had read of Harris's promotions. Assuming their paths would not again cross, Ankenazy had not deposited in his memory bank any of the information on Harris's advancing police career.

"But back to square one," said Harris. "What brings you here?"

"I'm on the Monsignor Thompson story."

Harris nodded. Obviously, he was familiar with the case. Ankenazy's spirits lifted slightly. Until this moment, since entering headquarters he had felt like a stranger in a remotely familiar foreign land. Now, he had found someone he had known fairly well. And that someone was familiar with the story on which he was working.

"I wonder," Ankenazy continued, "if you could tell me who's active on that case?"

Harris nodded again and consulted a loose-leaf binder. "Sergeants Dean Patrick and Bill Lynch from Squad Six."

Ankenazy wrote the names in his notepad. "And where," he asked, "can I find Sergeants Patrick and Lynch?"

"They're on the street."

Ankenazy smiled. He recalled the first time an officer had told him a cop was "on the street." Ankenazy naturally had pictured the officer literally pounding the bricks, walking the pavements.

"On the street," at least as far as Detroit's Homicide Division was concerned, was the equivalent of Blue Cross's or Michigan Bell's describing one of their employees as being "in the field." The phrase revealed the officer to be out of the station but did little to pinpoint his or her exact location. That—the simple designation that an officer was "out"—was precisely what the Police Department intended to convey.

But Ankenazy wanted much more specific information.

"Exactly where might I find Patrick and Lynch?"

"Sorry," Harris answered, "I'm not at liberty to say."

In the time it took to ask two questions, Harris had become professionally uncommunicative. Ankenazy had hit his first brick wall in The Case of the Missing Monsignor. There would be more.

After an exchange of valedictions, Ankenazy found the General Assignments Unit office, which was also on the fifth floor of headquarters.

Sergeant Terri Scanlon of GAU was a friend of Ankenazy's, owed a few favors and, as luck would have it, was in. Ankenazy explained the nature of the desired information.

"How about it, Terri; can you get me the name and address of whomever it is Patrick and Lynch are questioning this afternoon?"

Scanlon looked ruefully at the pile of forms on her desk that needed filling out and filing. "I suppose so, but it'll take a while."

Ankenazy looked at her questioningly. Her willingness to help had been his only uncertainty. Once she agreed, he couldn't understand why the enterprise need be time-consuming.

"If I were looking for this information for myself," she explained, "I'd just go get it. Since you're going to use it, eventually Homicide is going to know you got the information from somebody. I don't want them to tie it to me. So, I've got to get this in a roundabout way."

"Be devious," he urged as she left the office.

Robert Ankenazy, with a full head of dark brown hair, salt-and-pepper beard, of medium height and build, in his early forties, was one of those rare people whose life was progressing almost exactly as he had planned it.

He had a degree in journalism from the University of Michigan. He'd married a sensitive and brilliant woman with whom he had two children. He had paid his early dues doing virtually all the jobs needed to put out a newspaper at a succession of suburban journals. Almost twenty years ago, he'd landed a job with the prestigious *Detroit News*, working his way from the City-County Bureau to the police beat through general assignment writing to the news editor's desk. There seemed no reason he would not continue to climb. In unguarded moments, he occasionally slipped into a smug mood.

A good half-hour passed before Terri Scanlon returned. Ankenazy was surprised it had taken her so long.

Wordlessly, but conspiratorially, she slipped him a piece of paper on which was printed Angela Cicero's name and Dearborn address.

Ankenazy, preserving the mime tone, smiled, bowed low, and left headquarters. He aimed his car at Dearborn. He was unaware of Joe Cox's involvement in this story, nor was he aware of the existence of an important diary, from knowledge of which he was singularly excluded. So, for at least the next three-quarters of an hour, he was able to enjoy a fine summer day.

———————

There was a consensus. No one was comfortable with the priest's presence.

Angela Cicero had been shocked, confused, and embarrassed when, after she had answered the door, detectives Patrick and Lynch identified themselves. She also felt a sense of humiliation. She had never experienced anything like this. She had seen police officers show their badges and identify themselves. But that was always fiction on a stage, in a movie, or on TV.

All these negative, nervous feelings, especially that of humiliation, were intensified by the presence of Father Koesler. The detectives had explained that he was attending only in a consultative role and that the presence of a priest during their interrogation should not affect or disturb her. But it did.

Patrick and Lynch themselves had been less than enthusiastic when Lieutenant Harris had informed them that Koesler would accompany them during their investigation of the Thompson case. At least he was expected to be present while they interrogated the suspects mentioned in Thompson's diary.

Harris tried to allay their objections to Koesler's presence; however, both Patrick and Lynch could not help but feel their professional integrity was being compromised. They wanted Koesler aboard about as badly as a big brother wants his little sister around on his first date.

Completing this negative unanimity was Koesler himself. Secretly, he was pleased that he'd been called upon as a consultant. But this feeling was more than displaced by the sense of being

204

an unwanted and amateur trespasser into another's field of expertise. While they were faultlessly polite, the negative vibrations sent out by Patrick and Lynch were all but palpable. And, Koesler reasoned, why not? How would he feel if the Archbishop assigned a couple of detectives to see that the priest was offering Mass correctly?

After all, it was common knowledge the seminary offered no training in criminal investigation. Koesler had long been convinced there was a very definite limit to the number of ex officio appointments a person could accept while being able to contribute anything concrete to any of them. There was no doubt in Koesler's mind that he was once again a fifth and easily disposable wheel.

Thus, it was with a feeling of discomfort that the four—hostess and three visitors—were seated in the Cicero living room.

Angela Cicero perfunctorily offered coffee. All politely refused.

"Mrs. Cicero," Patrick observed, "you seem nervous."

"Who wouldn't be?" she responded. "It's not every day a simple housewife gets a visit from a newspaper reporter, then two police officers—and," she added almost as an afterthought, "a priest."

Patrick exchanged glances with Lynch. So Cox—utilizing the diary—had already been here.

"Mrs. Cicero," said Lynch, "we're just trying to find out what happened to him. We thought maybe you could help us."

"How could I possibly help?" she protested. "What possible connection could I have with Monsignor Thompson? He's not our parish priest. Never has been."

"You mean the reporter did not mention the diary?" Patrick asked.

"What diary?" She seemed genuinely surprised.

"I'd like you to look at this," said Lynch. He handed her several sheets on which had been copied only those passages in Thompson's diary that had reference to her.

As she read them slowly and carefully, the color rose in her cheeks. She was angered that Thompson had written so pruriently of her and horrified that others had read it. Was there no evil foreign to that man?

205

"What has this to do with anything?"

"Well, ma'am," said Patrick, "it indicates that there was a relationship of sorts between you and the Monsignor and, as far as he was concerned, it was a significant relationship."

"Do you mean to imply that I had something to do with his disappearance? That I did something to him?"

"No, ma'am." Patrick's manner was that of a concerned friend, eager to clear up a mystery, but anxious not to offend his hostess. His blue eyes could be frighteningly penetrating on occasion. Now they were smiling, and crow's-feet crinkled their corners.

"As you may have read in the papers or heard on the news, Monsignor Thompson disappeared last Saturday night under rather suspicious circumstances. We're just trying to find out what happened. So we're looking for anyone who might be able to help us. Since your name appeared in his diary . . ."

Patrick let the observation drift into a rather uneasy silence. The intent was that no one would break the silence until Angela did. Though Koesler was tempted.

"I don't know how I can help you," Angela Cicero said at length.

"Well, for one thing, ma'am, you can tell us about your contacts with Monsignor Thompson from your own point of view. Up to now, we have nothing but what he wrote." Patrick smiled broadly. "We don't even know what happened to your daughter's wedding. The Monsignor's diary reads like a mystery story without a conclusion. We've got him waiting for a phone call from Rome. But we don't even know whether he got it."

Koesler, of course, knew what had happened to Anna Maria Cicero's wedding. It had been solemnized at his parish. But no one had asked him. He resolved at some future moment to get a word in edgewise. These two detectives ought to know that he could, occasionally, be of some help.

Angela shrugged and began an understated narrative of her daughter's premarital canonical problems and the role played by Thompson. She omitted any reference to her emotional reaction to Thompson's manipulation of the case. At the mention of Koesler's critical role in the drama, Patrick glanced at the priest, suggesting a new appreciation of the reason he had been included in this investigation.

When Angela began her narrative, Bill Lynch had excused himself and let himself out the front door.

She concluded her story with a brief description of her daughter's wedding at St. Anselm's.

"Well," said the smiling Patrick, "I guess all's well that ends well."

There was no comment. The three sat in silence while Patrick finished writing his account of Angela's response.

"One thing more, ma'am," said Patrick, "can you account for your time last Saturday night from about nine on?"

An odd expression crossed Angela's face. "No, I don't think I can. I got my husband off to his bowling league about 8:30. Then I got a phone call from someone who said my daughter Anna Maria had been in an auto accident at the corner of Jefferson and Grand Boulevard—that's near the Belle Isle bridge . . ."

Patrick nodded.

"So I got in my car and drove over there."

"Did you find the accident, ma'am?"

"No. No sign of one. I drove all around the area and asked several people, but no one knew anything about any accident."

"Did you get the name of the person who phoned?"

"No. He sounded as if he were a passer-by."

"Did he sound like a black man?"

"No, white. But it was hard to tell. I was so upset."

"There was no one at the site of the alleged accident who could identify you?"

"N . . . no."

"What time did you return home, ma'am?"

"I don't know. It must have been before 1:30 Sunday morning. That's the time my husband got home from bowling, and I was here when he came in."

"Did you tell your husband about the call and your wild-goose chase?"

"Yes." The worried look on Angela's face turned to one of indignation. "Should I call my lawyer?"

"Oh, no, ma'am." Patrick's smile returned. "As I said, we

207

are merely asking questions to try to find out what happened to the Monsignor. No need for you to be concerned about a law-yer—unless you think you need one. As a matter of fact, we're pretty well done for the day. We'll just be going now.''

As Patrick stood, so did Koesler and Angela.

''Just in case we need to ask some more questions, ma'am,'' said Patrick, ''you hadn't planned to leave town, had you?''

Angela felt as if a trap were tightening about her. ''No. At least not till the end of this month. My husband and I had planned a short vacation.''

''Yes, ma'am. Well, thank you, ma'am.''

Koesler stayed behind for a few moments to offer Angela a few reassuring words.

As he prepared to leave, for the first time he noticed on the shelf beneath the coffee table an Edgar Allan Poe anthology. Himself a mystery buff, he suddenly felt a special kinship with Angela Cicero. He was about to ask which of Poe's stories she was reading. But, with the seriousness of this visit, the question seemed inappropriate. He noticed a bookmark tucked into nearly the exact center of the volume. He resolved, just for kicks, to consult an identical volume he had at the rectory and see which story she was on.

Sergeant Lynch had that rare ability to fall asleep almost anywhere at almost any time, given half an opportunity. Thus, Sergeant Patrick was not surprised to find his partner in the passenger side of their unmarked police car, head resting against the seat back, mouth open, snoring.

Patrick got behind the wheel and slammed the door loudly enough to waken Lynch. Koesler got in the back.

Lynch yawned and stretched. ''She must have told you the story of her life.''

''Not really.'' Patrick laughed. ''You haven't been asleep that long.''

Lynch checked his watch. ''Oh.''

''What did you get from the neighbors?'' Patrick asked.

''Not very much,'' said Lynch. ''Sort of a mixed bag.'' He took a notepad from his jacket pocket and consulted it. ''Two ladies think they saw Mr. Cicero leave sometime before nine. One puts it at 8:30. One of them thinks she heard a car door slam about 1 or 1:30 Sunday morning. She assumes it was Mr. Cicero returning home.

"That's about it."

"Did anyone report seeing Mrs. Cicero leave that evening?"

"No. But a lady who lives five doors down thinks she saw a cab drive by. She says it could have stopped in front of the Cicero home. But she really doesn't know for sure. She did think it was odd; they don't get many cabs on this street. Everybody here drives."

"We'll check it out with the cab companies," Patrick said, "but Mrs. Cicero said she took her own car when she went out."

"She claims to have gone out Saturday night?"

"So she says."

"Doesn't prove she didn't go out, but none of the neighbors seems to have seen her . . . how's her alibi?"

"From very poor to nonexistent. If she ever has to lean on that story of what she did Saturday night, she'll fall flat on her face."

"What do you think?"

"What do you mean?" Patrick bounced the question back.

"Plenty of motive and no alibi. Think she did it?"

"She's sure a live one. We'll undoubtedly be back checking out Mrs. Leo Cicero."

"One thing, though," observed Lynch.

"What's that?"

"If she did away with Thompson, and if she didn't leave the house, what did she do with the body?"

"Maybe," said Patrick, "she's building a Panama Canal in her basement like that crazy nephew in 'Arsenic and Old Lace.' "

Both detectives laughed. Patrick turned to Koesler. "We've got to go ask some questions at Roma Hall, Father. This won't involve anyone mentioned in the diary, so you won't need to come along. We'll drop you at headquarters, if that's all right."

Until then, Koesler thought they had forgotten he was in the car.

He bit into a Superburger. He had a love-hate relationship with fast foods. On the one hand, Bob Ankenazy thought, it was some kind of crime to call this amalgam of thin beef, aging lettuce, gooey sauce, and casual condiments food. On the other hand, it *was* food.

Ankenazy had arrived at the Cicero house just before two. Parked in front of the house was an unmistakable—to the practiced eye—unmarked police car. A solid blue Plymouth four-door Fury One, police radio aerial in the back window, four black-wall tires and, providing the solemn oath that this was indeed an official vehicle, a 1978 license plate with no expiration date and a small 'x' dividing the numbers.

Ankenazy had not lost his practiced eye.

He drove in ever-widening circles, not wanting to return to the Cicero home too often or with any noticeable frequency. Finally, since he had skipped lunch, he decided to stop for some food.

Eventually, when he returned at about 4 P.M., the police car was gone. If there were no unforeseen difficulties, he should be able to finish his story by the 6 P.M. deadline for the State edition. Surely by the 7:30 P.M. deadline for the morning street edition.

When Angela Cicero answered his ring, Ankenazy exhibited his press credentials. She reacted as though she was going to slam the door. Then, apparently thinking better of it, she showed him in with a resigned air. All this Ankenazy took to be her reaction to being subjected to a reporter after having been grilled by the police.

"I'm sorry, Mrs. Cicero," he began, "I know the police were here and their questions must have tired you, but I have a story to write. I'll try to be as brief as possible."

Angela Cicero slumped into a chair and pinched her forehead tightly between thumb and index finger. "It's the whole darn thing. It's . . . when is this going to end? First the reporter from the *Free Press*, then the police, now you."

A cold feeling of dismay turned his stomach.

"Another reporter? From the *Free Press*? He was here? Before the police?"

Angela nodded.

"Do you remember his name?"

She shook her head.

He knew he soon would find out which *Free Press* reporter. He would need only to see the first edition, look for the story, and read the by-line.

But how, he wondered, did whoever it was manage to get there before the police? Could he have a source in Homicide? If so, who?

For the moment, Ankenazy knew he would have to put all such speculation out of mind and concentrate on this interview.

He did not promise her anonymity, as had Cox, as a ploy to win cooperation. Rather, he explained the simple fact that the *News* would withhold her name because, at least at this stage in the investigation, the paper could not violate her right to privacy.

It might not have worked. But she had told her story twice already this day. Once more could not hurt.

So, in an unemotional and uninvolved tone, she recounted again her contacts with Monsignor Thomas Thompson.

Without Thompson's diary to guide him, Ankenazy could not ask the penetrating questions nor appreciate the ironic flavor of her statements, as had Cox and the police.

In fact, as he concluded the interview, Ankenazy wondered why the police had questioned Angela Cicero in connection with the disappearance of Monsignor Thompson.

Ankenazy decided he would develop his first installment describing this anonymous woman as being among the last to have had professional dealings with Thompson. Seemingly, these professional dealings were most unsatisfactory and perhaps even most unprofessional. He would lead the reader to speculate that it may have been someone similarly displeased with Thompson who may have "done him in." Tune in tomorrow for more speculation.

But what, damn it, did whosit at the *Free Press* have that gave him an edge?

Whatever it was, Ankenazy would have to get it by hook or by crook.

Walter Koznicki did not approve of "marriages" between members of the Homicide Division.

"Marriage" was his term for steady partners. The lieutenants in charge of Homicide's seven squads were supposed to guard against the formation of such partnerships. In practice, the ban was a policy the lieutenants seldom enforced.

To Koznicki, "marriages" encouraged sloppy work and a tendency to overlook mistakes, indiscretions, or worse, on the part of one's partner.

To many officers, a partner became more dependable than the random officer, and it was more comfortable working with one whose habits and approach to an investigation were familiar.

As often as they could, Sergeants Dean Patrick and Bill Lynch teamed during an investigation. Although they seldom fraternized outside working hours, they found they worked well together. So, in an investigation such as this one involving a missing monsignor, which was assigned to two officers rather than an entire squad, Patrick and Lynch would maneuver themselves into position to work together.

Lieutenant Harris understood their game, but in his estimation, they were too good at their job to fall into any of the bad habits Koznicki foresaw.

Lynch was the taller of the two detectives, both of whom were slightly more than six feet. Lynch, the more slender, was quiet almost to the point of being laconic. His deep brown eyes usually appeared sleepy. This was deceptive. Actually, he was among the most alert, astute, and aggressive officers in Homicide. Criminals frequently took the image he created for reality. But they paid for that mistake.

Patrick, with a full head of salt-and-pepper hair, was the extrovert of the pair. He had a quick and engaging smile and expressive blue eyes. Not a flashy dresser, and occasionally fighting a slight weight problem, still he was a commanding figure. Whenever the two detectives interrogated a suspect, Patrick invariably made the greater impact.

Now, late Tuesday afternoon, they pulled into the parking lot of Roma Hall. It would be their final business of the day.

Roma employees were gearing up for the evening banquets and receptions.

The two officers waved off a parking attendant. Patrick, who was driving, flashed his badge, and parked near the entrance to the hall. Lynch observed that the attendant was Hispanic and that his eyes bulged with nervous alarm as he caught sight of the police badge.

They sought out the manager immediately. They found him, one Frank Trupiano, standing at the reservation desk, checking details of the evening's schedule.

Trupiano, darkly handsome, appeared to be a suave, wordly-wise gentleman in his late fifties. Yet even *his* eyelashes flickered when the two identified themselves as homicide detectives. It was a not uncommon reaction to the mystique created by the nature of their work. Homicide was the ultimate crime. Homicide detectives, then, solved the ultimate puzzle: Who would dare take another's life—and why.

Trupiano had read of the Monsignor's disappearance, had been shocked that his hall had been the last known public place where Thompson had been seen, and had been expecting a visit from the police. But not from Homicide.

Trupiano showed them the area in the huge hall where the Van Patten Wedding reception had been held.

"The guests mingled quite a bit before the meal was served?" Patrick repeated Trupiano's statement in the form of a question.

"Yes." Trupiano found himself replying to his own statement. "It's very common. There was an open bar and, particularly at wedding banquets when families get together for one of their infrequent meetings, people tend to stand around and socialize. We do all we can, after a decent interval, to get them seated. The waitresses like to get home as soon as they can, you know."

"I see," said Patrick. "What time would you say the guests were seated?"

"About . . . sometime between 9:30 and 10. I think it was close to 9:40."

"And then?"

Patrick was taking notes. Lynch, hands joined behind his

213

back, was taking in the scene. He did not appear to be paying attention to the dialogue.

"Then," Trupiano continued, "there was a prayer and a toast delivered by Monsignor Thompson. The salad course had just been served when the Monsignor was called to the phone."

"Who was the waiter who overheard the Monsignor's half of the phone conversation?"

"That would be Sanchez. He's in the kitchen now. Do you want me to get him for you?"

"Later. What happened next?"

"Monsignor said something to the bride and groom; then he left the hall."

"What did he say to them? Do you know?"

"Just that he was sorry, but he had to leave to take care of an emergency."

"He said nothing to anyone else?"

"Not that I know of." And then, almost as an afterthought, "Unless he talked to the parking valet."

"Fine. We'll see that waiter now."

A brief conversation with Jesus Sanchez revealed nothing more than Thompson's three responses. The detectives learned it had been Sanchez who had called Thompson to the phone. And, no, the waiter had been unable to tell whether the caller was male or female. The voice, he said, was muffled. He had had difficulty understanding who it was the caller wanted.

Next, the detectives checked with the head of the parking attendants, a man with a preposterous beer belly and the stub of a cigar between his teeth.

"Monsignor Thompson's car? Sure I remember it. A black Eldorado, not a spot or wrinkle on it, and everything on the inside. You don't forget a car like that, especially when a poor parish priest steps out of it. Lemme see, I think . . . yeah, Ruiz handled that."

Carlo Ruiz, it developed, was the young man Patrick had waved off when the detectives had driven into the lot.

Carlo, eighteen years old, was not a wetback, but he had the frame of mind of one. He had been programmed to fear police. When white cops talk to a brown- or black-skinned person, he had been taught, they are only one short step from putting that unfortunate-hued individual in jail, or breaking his skull.

So when his boss called Carlo to the parking booth, the young man felt a stab of fear. It turned to panic when he saw the two white policemen waiting, one smiling, the other impassively studying him.

"Hi, son," Patrick opened. "Your boss here tells us you handled a black Cadillac last Saturday night."

"What Caddy? I park lots of Caddys."

"You know, Carlo," said his boss from around the cigar, "the black Eldorado. We talked about how it was loaded, and a priest was driving it."

Ruiz's eyes flicked nervously from one inquisitor to the other. Which was noted by Lynch.

"Oh . . . oh, yeah. The Eldorado. So?"

"Did you notice anything unusual about the car or the priest who was driving it? Did the priest say anything to you?" Patrick asked.

"No, no, nuthin'."

"He didn't say anything?" Lynch asked. "Not when he left his car with you or when you got it for him?"

"No, he didn't say nuthin'." At least that part was true. It *was* unusual to find a cartridge in a car. And the fact that he had bled in a stranger's car also was unusual. But Ruiz had no intention of volunteering that kind of information. All the police needed was to link a Chicano with a bullet and blood in a white man's car and, Ruiz was positive, next came the cuffs, and then they'd lock him up and let him rot.

"Did the priest give you anything?" asked Lynch. "A tip?"

"A crummy quarter."

Not only nasty, but cheap too, thought both Lynch and Patrick.

"O.K., son" said Patrick. "If you think of anything else that happened that night with respect to the priest, give me a call at this number." Patrick handed Ruiz a calling card.

The two detectives entered their car and left.

It was a very attractive calling card. It gave Patrick's name, rank and division, address, and phone number. Lightly imprinted in gold next to Patrick's name was the official shield of the State of Michigan.

The two officers were barely out of sight before Ruiz crumpled the card and tossed it in the waste receptacle.

———————

"Nervous," said Lynch.

"Yeah," Patrick agreed. "Like lots of folks, he's scared of the police."

"It was more than that, Dean. He knows something. I think if we give him a few days to stew—just enough time for him to get plenty spooked, then figure we've let him off the hook—then we pop back into his life."

"And when will that be, O great swami?"

"I don't know yet. But when the time comes, I'll know. And I'll let you know." Lynch slouched and closed his eyes. The hint of a smile played at his lips.

5

THE ANNOUNCEMENT WAS THERE IN THE *Detroit News*'s August 5 issue. It was there for everyone to see. Monsignor Thomas Thompson would be at a wedding reception at Roma Hall in East Detroit on the evening of August 11. It was unlikely that any of his cronies would be with him. He would be unguarded, unprotected, among strangers, virtually alone, vulnerable.

Lee Brand read the announcement with mounting interest.

He was seated in a lawn chair only a few yards from the softly lapping waters of Green Lake. On the ground around the chair were the littered sections of the *Free Press, News, Chicago Tribune* and *New York Times*. The scattered debris, particularly the *Times*, brought to mind the wag who claimed that New York's pollution problem would be solved if anyone knew a way to dispose of discarded copies of the Sunday *Times*.

Normally, Brand did not read wedding announcements. He supposed he was reading these because of his daughter's recent wedding. An event about which he still had decidedly mixed emotions.

Although he was a fierce and dedicated competitor in everything in which he was well-versed, from golf to big business, still Brand managed to be a good if infrequent loser at golf or tennis. Those, after all, were games that combined skill with youth, strength, physical endurance, and a healthy measure of

217

luck. Brand realized he was no longer a kid. A younger man or one with a better run of luck might best him in sports. But Brand was unwilling to concede victory to anyone in the realm of wheeling and dealing.

Monsignor Thompson had bested Brand at his own game. And the bastard had stood there in Brand's presence and gloated. It did not matter that Brand had, perhaps, the last laugh. He had been bested. It was a sore spot at the center of his ego. Whenever Thompson came to mind, Brand's soul ached.

Thus, Brand was surprised when he became aware that, triggered by that announcement in Sunday's paper, he'd been thinking about Thompson for several minutes without hurting.

For the first time since that day of confrontation at the Tribunal a couple of weeks before, Brand was able to look upon Thompson as fair game once more. Until this moment, Brand had considered the Thompson affair an unfortunate, indefeasible stalemate.

However, Brand found intriguing the fact that, with a full week's warning, he could know precisely when and where Thompson could be found next Saturday evening. Suddenly, Thompson's image became transformed from a burr under Brand's saddle to that of a sitting duck.

Brand let the *News* slip from his lap to the ground. Parallel vertical lines appeared in his forehead. His fingers formed a cathedral ceiling pressed against his pursed lips. He plotted.

At first, he had been inclined to dismiss this opportunity to not only even the score, but win the whole enchilada. He and Sunny were scheduled to take a late-summer Alaskan cruise. They would be aboard the *Alaskan Queen*, which would be sailing just hours before Thompson would arrive at the wedding reception.

But then, as Brand's fertile mind began working the facts against the possibilities, his presence aboard the ship began developing into an advantage rather than a liability.

He entered the house and rummaged through the desk drawers in his study until he found the cruise schedule. Returning to his lawn chair, he pushed his sunglasses firmly against the bridge of his nose and carefully studied the itinerary.

218

As Brand sat very still, he could envision the coming week forming.

MONDAY, AUGUST 6, 9 A.M.

"Cindy," Brand spoke into his intercom, "get my travel agent on the phone, would you?"

He fingered the stack of mail on his desk. Jackie, his secretary, had sorted and opened all but the personal letters. The intercom buzzed.

"Rob Rix here, Mr. Brand. What can we do for you this morning?" The travel agent's tone was the special bright, brisk one reserved for his very best customers.

"Yeah, Rob. You know that Alaskan cruise Sunny and I are taking this week?"

Rix did not have to consult his files. "Yes, sir. Two weeks. From Los Angeles, on the *Alaskan Queen*."

"I want another cabin."

There was silence as Rix caught his breath. He knew Brand was not joking. Brand never joked in serious matters.

"You mean instead of the one you have? Or in addition? You know there aren't any more cabins, Mr. Brand. That cruise has been sold out for nearly a year. If Mrs. Brand hadn't booked as early as she did, I doubt I could have gotten you anything at all."

It was as if Rix had not spoken.

"We're in cabin 424 on the Upper Deck. I'd like the neighboring cabin, 426. I know it's late in the game, Rob. But if you can't get 426, make sure the one you get is either a Superior or Luxurious category."

"I'm afraid you don't understand, Mr. Brand. There are no cabins available. Perhaps on some future sailing . . ."

"Rob, I am about to say four words. After that, I want you to take the ball and run with it." He spoke deliberately: "Money is no object."

"Oh."

"Now, this is the game plan, Rob. Talk to the steamship company. Find a couple who is booked say, in an outside double. Make up whatever emergency comes to mind. Offer them three or four times the total ticket cost. By passing up this cruise, they'll be able to go on three or four cruises. What could be fairer?"

"Yes, Mr. Brand." Rix was already planning his fabrication.

"Then, Rob, find another couple who've booked over their heads. Somebody who is really stretching to be in a Superior or Luxurious. Somebody who has requested a cheaper cabin, but had to take a more expensive one because the cheaper cabins were already sold out. Talk them into accepting the cheaper accommodation for consideration of, say, half the fare."

"Yes, Mr. Brand."

"Think you can do that, Rob?"

"I think your four magic words will enable me to do that."

"Good. Call me in a day or so when you get this set up, will you?"

"Yes, sir." A day or so. Lee Brand wants his miracles yesterday.

Lee Brand sat at his desk smiling smugly. The remaining preparation this week would be easy coasting. He could even concentrate on bank business. He just loved wheeler-dealer plans that fell into place like pieces of a jigsaw puzzle. Only a few more arrangements needed to be made before Brand would be ready to make The Phone Call.

SATURDAY, AUGUST 11, 6:30 P.M. P.D.T.

With tugs pushing and pulling fore and aft, the *Alaskan Queen* was leaving its Los Angeles pier.

Among those standing on Promenade Deck watching this busy and precise procedure of getting the luxury liner underway were Lee and Joan Brand.

As often as they had observed the sailing or docking of giant ships, the Brands were always fascinated by the precision of movement of gigantic equipment, the very size of hawsers and anchors, the babble of tongues of the Eurasian or Indonesian crews, the nonchalant free-and-easy attitude of the average tug captain.

220

The *Alaskan Queen* was approximately one hour late in weighing anchor. There was nothing extraordinary about this; only those unused to the leisurely cruise life would be anxious about the tardy departure.

Dinner had just begun for those scheduled for the first sitting. They had just finished getting settled in their cabins, renewing acquaintances from previous cruises, or enjoying potent pre-prandial drinks.

The Brands had chosen the later meal sitting. Thus, there was an hour and three-quarters before they would be seated at 8:15. They leaned against the railing absorbing the soft, warm, salty Pacific breeze.

Joan Brand entwined her arm with her husband's. "As often as we do this, I'm always surprised at how the cares slip away as the ship leaves the shore."

Lee smiled and nodded agreement.

"And this time," Joan continued, "we don't have to take Bunny with us or worry about her either. She's off on her honeymoon, a happily married woman."

"Yup, a happily married woman." As he repeated his wife's phrase, Brand remembered the canonical invalidity of his daughter's marriage. If it doesn't work out, he thought . . .

"Lee," Joan seemed suddenly concerned, "what will happen to that nice priest, that Father Shanley, who married Bunny?"

"He's being helped."

"Helped?"

"He accepted the penalty of suspension. It's no more than a slap on the wrist. It amounts to a month's vacation. I'm making sure it is a month the likes of which he has never seen. For a change, he'll live on our level instead of his."

She frowned. "I feel a little guilty about him. He's a priest . . . maybe he chose not to live on our level. I mean, it's just too bad he has to be penalized just for doing us a favor."

"That's the choice he made. We have to live with the consequences of our choices. I am making it as easy for him as I can."

Brand checked his watch. He'd been doing this with increasing frequency during the past half-hour.

Joan covered the dial with her hand. "C'mon now," she scolded in jest, "this is vacation. We're going to forget time and appointments and schedules. You've got to begin to relax."

Brand attempted a smile. However, he obviously was preoccupied. "Don't mind me, Sunny. I've got just one more item of business, and then it's school's-out time. You just excuse me for a few minutes and wave good-bye to L.A. for me."

Giving her hand a brief squeeze, he slalomed his way through a disarray of deck chairs, past the salt water pool, into the interior of the ship to the elevators.

He waited alone for an elevator. Half the ship's passengers were eating. The other half were preparing for dinner. Few were traveling through the ship.

He took the elevator up two levels to the Navigation Deck. He angled through a narrow corridor to the Wireless Room. He had already arranged for this ship-to-shore call. He checked his watch. It was exactly 7 P.M. Pacific Daylight Time. Ten P.M. Detroit time. He placed the call.

SATURDAY, AUGUST 11, 10 P.M. E.D.T.

"Monsignor Thompson." His tone betrayed a mixture of pleasure—probably from the fun of the party—and annoyance—undoubtedly from being called away from the party to the phone.

"Monsignor, this is Lee Brand. I can tell from your voice this is not too good a connection. You're probably having difficulty hearing me. The reason is because this is a ship-to-shore call."

The quality of the call was indeed poor. Thompson had almost hung up the phone in disgust at the outset. Only the name Lee Brand had stayed an abrupt terminating action. Intrigued that Brand would be phoning, particularly ship-to-shore, Thompson pressed the receiver to one ear while covering the other with his free hand. He blocked the noise from the wedding feast. He wanted to hear whatever it was Brand had to say.

"Well, Monsignor," Brand continued, "I guess you could say we've had our rounds. You won a big one. And, in all candor, I've got to tip my hat to you. You beat me at the game I play best. However, my victory was not inconsiderable. I think at this point a referee might call our joust a draw.''

"Uh . . ." He almost said something.

"But listen . . ." Brand wanted no conversation; he wanted to complete an offer he was sure Thompson could not refuse. "I think it's time we buried all the hatchets. Life is too short to carry a grudge forever. So I'm issuing an invitation—call it a command performance, if you will."

Brand's tone was light and informal. He knew better than to sound as if he actually were demanding anything from Thompson.

"Sunny and I are on a cruise," Brand went on, "and we want you with us."

Thompson found that hard to believe.

"You may find that hard to believe," Brand correctly surmised, "but as proof"—Brand by now was so lighthearted he was nearly laughing—"just listen to what I've prepared for you.

"As you can well imagine, cabins are about as scarce as dishonest bankers. But I've got one for you—in the luxury class. I'll have aboard all the clothing and gear you'll need for this Alaska cruise. And I'll arrange with the diocese for your absence so you can be with us for the next couple of weeks. Now, how about that, Monsignor! What better way to let bygones be bygones than aboard a cruise through the Inside Passage? You could use a well-deserved vacation," Brand's week-long investigation had revealed the Costa Smeralda trip aborted when Thompson was compelled to await a call from Rome, "and Sunny and I really are eager for your company.

"What do you say, Monsignor?"

In his inner heart, Thompson told himself, he knew he had too much class not to win Brand over eventually.

"You don't mean it!" the Monsignor exclaimed, knowing full well Brand meant it. Several waiters glanced at Thompson.

"But I do mean it." Brand could tell that Thompson had taken the bait. "I had to wait till now to call you, because I wasn't sure I could secure that extra cabin. But we've got it, and we were able to get you all you'll need for your wardrobe.

"We've just left port here in L.A. But we'll dock in San Francisco tomorrow. We'll be there from 5:30 P.M. till 2 A.M.

Monday. That's Pacific time. I've made arrangements for you to join us tomorrow after we dock. I have a Learjet waiting for you right now."

"Where?" By damn, Thompson thought, I'm going to make up for that canceled Costa Smeralda trip and then some.

"The jet is waiting at City Airport. I'd advise you to get there immediately. We can get you to the coast in time for you to get a little rest before meeting the ship. I'll have a car waiting at Frisco Airport and a suite for you at the St. Francis for tonight. How about it, Monsignor?"

"I'll be right there!"

Two waiters looked at each other and shrugged as Monsignor Thompson hurried from the hall after murmuring an excuse to the bride and groom.

Eager to begin this unexpected vacation, Thompson averaged about ten miles above the forty-miles-per-hour limit down Gratiot. Unusual for him. As he turned onto Conner, he remembered that City Airport parking was not completely supervised and that his car would be vulnerable to vandals if left unattended for two weeks. This was particularly true in the case of an Eldorado. He decided to leave it on De La Salle school property. The Brothers surely would keep an eye on it.

He was about to exit the car when he became aware of a sticky substance on his hands. From what he could ascertain by the dim interior light, it appeared to be blood. Damn! It must have been that Spic attendant. Sonofabitch! What else did he mess up? Thompson grabbed several tissues and wiped the steering wheel, gearshift and rear-view mirror. He could see no other stains. If there were any, they would have to wait till he returned.

He locked the car and hurried the short distance to City Airport and the waiting Learjet.

Both he and Lee Brand would enjoy a contented sleep this night.

Lee Brand stood near the canopied gangplank of the *Alaskan Queen*. He had been waiting there since the ship had docked in San Francisco one half-hour earlier. His eyes were in constant motion. They sought the figure of Monsignor Thompson, while also staying alert for any passer-by who might know Thompson. This was one of the plot's most delicate moments.

Finally, there he was, Monsignor Thomas Thompson, unmistakable though disguised in mufti.

Smiling, the two men shook hands.

"I see you used the threads we got you in L.A.," said Brand.

"Yeah," said Thompson, "your chauffeur said he'd have my clericals cleaned and put aboard."

"Not to worry. It will be done.

"Well, Monsignor," Brand continued, his expansive gesture indicating the bustling crowd of passengers and visitors scurrying about the Main Deck, "what do you think?"

"Great, Lee. Really great. You know, I've never done anything like this—just checking out of the diocese without any preparation. It's kind of fun. Like skipping school. Or," Thompson elbowed Brand jokingly, "just saying to hell with the diocese!"

"That's right, Monsignor. Don't worry; I took care of notifying everyone who needs notifying. But then, who deserves a break more than you?"

"Nobody I can think of!" Thompson laughed a little too loudly.

Good, thought Brand; he's been drinking. All that first-class booze laid in at the hotel room had not gone to waste.

"C'mon, Monsignor," Brand took Thompson lightly by the arm and guided him toward the elevator, "let's go up to your cabin."

"Let's."

They were alone on the elevator. It stopped at Boat Deck. The first cabin immediately to the right of the elevators, 301, was Brand's back-up. It was, indeed, a luxurious outside double. Brand found the key and let Thompson into the cabin.

Thompson entered, studied the decor, and whistled. "Say, this really is First Class."

Since Brand's phone call the night before, Thompson had been taking each step with a grain of salt. He was determined not to be blindsided by the wily Brand. Yet, so far, every Brand promise had been as good as his bond. The Learjet had been waiting. Thompson had been the sole passenger on what could only be described as a luxury flight to San Francisco, where he had been met by a liveried chauffeur. The suite at the St. Francis had been opulent, and there was no way he could have complained about the contents of the liquor cabinet.

And, true to his word, Brand had arranged for his vacation from sacerdotal duties. Thompson had been saved the trouble of checking with the Chancery this morning; on waking, he'd been reassured by finding a telegram from Monsignor Iming under his door. It read: DIOCESE WILL TRY TO MUDDLE THROUGH WITHOUT YOU FOR TWO WEEKS. BON VOYAGE!

And now, this, his cabin for the next two glorious weeks. From experience, Thompson knew this must be among the finest cabins on board.

For the first time in this rather frantic nearly twenty-four hours, Thompson began to relax. And, as he did so, the liquor he had somewhat nervously consumed in his hotel suite began to catch up with him. He sat down heavily on the bed.

"Well, Monsignor," said Brand, "now you can relax."

The invitation was unnecessary. Thompson had already begun to relax.

Brand wheeled out of the closet an elaborate liquor service.

"We'll be eating at the second sitting," he said, "so I thought we could lounge over a drink or two."

"Oh, I don't think I'd better. I had a few, at the hotel, you know."

"That's what *this* is for." Brand pushed forward a generously loaded if small plate of cold cuts and cheese. "So the booze won't hurt you."

"Ne potus noceat," Thompson translated. "How nice!"

Although feeling lightheaded, Thompson decided he could withstand a fresh onslaught of liquor. It would not be long till

226

dinner. Food always took the edge off almost any level of intoxication, he had found. Besides, he knew the reputation cruise ships enjoyed for the quality and quantity of their food.

Thompson made an instantaneous resolution. To hell with his diet; he was going to enjoy the food on this cruise. And to hell with his lightheadedness. Another drink or two would only enhance the taste of dinner. He formed an open-faced sandwich with a potpourri of ingredients. The first taste actually did make him feel a bit more steady.

Brand sat on the other bed, opposite Thompson. On the serving cart between them, he placed two glasses filled with ice water. Not many things surprised Thompson any more, but that did.

Brand noticed Thompson's surprised look and smiled. Placing two more glasses on the cart, he poured a solid three fingers of Jack Daniel's in each.

"So the water doesn't hurt the Jack Daniel's," he explained.

Thompson smiled and sipped the whiskey happily.

Three drinks later, Thompson felt little pain. Brand still nursed his original libation.

Thompson chuckled. "I'll never forget it." His speech was noticeably slurred. "All the time you thought we were working on your daughter's case, we were doing nothing about it. I used to think about you, going about your business, confident that we were solving your problems. And then, when you showed up at the Tribunal and you knew the game was over. God, Lee, but you're a poor loser! Oh, you gave the impression you were in control. But I could tell you were just seething. Oh, yes, you are a very poor loser, indeed.

"But, as you say, that's all water under the dam. Or was it over the dam . . . the goddamned dam." Thompson laughed more loudly than his joke deserved.

The smile on Brand's face was frozen. If it had not been for his befuddled state, Thompson would have noticed this. He also would have noticed that Brand's knuckles had turned white around the glass he clutched. Thompson also might have noticed the ominous formation of those parallel vertical lines on Brand's forehead. But Thompson was well past a state of sharp perception.

Brand glanced at his watch. Never did he lose his plaster-of-paris smile. "Looks like it's time for dinner, Monsignor."

"About time, too," Thompson slurred.

Actually, it was 8:30. The second sitting had begun fifteen minutes ago.

Thompson rose unsteadily from the bed. Brand assisted him up and out of the cabin. Thompson protested his ability to take care of himself. But he did not protest too much.

Brand led him onto the open promenade of Boat Deck. "Let's get a little air before we head down for dinner," he urged.

The promenade was empty except for Brand and Thompson. Just as Brand had planned. The diners of the first sitting were watching the first presentation of either the evening movie or the stage show in the lounge. The diners of the second sitting were fifteen minutes into their meal. No one was around. No one but Brand and a handful of his faithful, well-paid employees even knew that Thompson was aboard the *Alaskan Queen*.

"You missed the lifeboat drill, Monsignor," Brand said as he steadied the unsteady priest.

"The what?"

"Boat drill. In case of emergency we get into the lifeboats."

"Lifeboats? Where?"

"Just up there, Monsignor. They're attached to the Navigation Deck just above us."

"Above us." Thompson looked vaguely heavenward. "I don't see any damn boats."

"Well, here, Monsignor," Brand unlatched the railing gate and opened it, "just step through here and we can get a better look."

It was frightening. Nothing separated them from the now foreboding Pacific but a narrow ridge of planking. In spite of himself, Brand was filled with dread. Thompson, a shadow of his usually alert self, seemed oblivious.

"Where? Where?" Thompson continued to scan the skies for the elusive lifeboats.

"Right up there, Monsignor. One deck above us."

Thompson leaned precariously over the edge. "Oh, yeah. I see 'em now."

Thompson was only one small nudge from joining the fish of the sea. Vengeance is mine, thought Brand.

Five very large men dwarfed the room. Four wore guns but no jackets. The fifth was dressed in a black suit and wore a roman collar.

It was a very hot, muggy Wednesday, August 15. The forecast was for intermittent showers with a threat of thunderstorms. It was nearing 9 A.M. The working day, at least for four very vital members of the Homicide Division, was about to begin officially.

"About the only thing we know for sure," said Bill Lynch, "is that on Saturday evening, August 11, Leo Cicero went bowling."

Walter Koznicki and Ned Harris exchanged glances.

"What does that have to do with the disappearance of Monsignor Thompson?" Harris asked.

"Nothing really," Lynch replied. "Except that's the only solid information we have so far."

Sergeants Lynch and Patrick were giving a verbal report to their superior officers.

Father Koesler once more felt like excess baggage. It was true that he had not planned on using this week for vacation, but he was sure there were better ways of using it than by being a superfluous adjunct to a couple of Homicide detectives.

"Cicero left his house a little before nine," Patrick continued. "Several neighbors heard the car leave the driveway, and his bowling partners corroborate that he arrived at or before nine. He didn't return home until nearly two Sunday morning."

"How about Mrs. Cicero's story that she was called to the scene of her daughter's nonexistent accident?" asked Harris.

"No way of verifying it," said Lynch. "None of the neighbors noticed her going or returning. No one at or near the scene of the 'accident' remembers her car. She could have gone there, but there's no way she can prove it.

"One of the neighbors thinks she saw a cab stop in front of the Cicero house sometime between 10:30 and 11, but she isn't sure. We've checked all the major companies and there's no

229

record of a run to that address. If there was a cab, it had to be from a little fly-by-night outfit or a driver who doesn't keep very good records.''

"So it's a brick wall so far, eh?" Harris concluded.

"The one big thing she's got going for her," said Patrick, "is that we haven't got a body."

Something at the back of Koesler's consciousness knocked for attention. The priest could not bring it to the fore. He was unsuccessfully trying to recall Angela Cicero's copy of the Poe anthology. He had planned to check his own copy to try to determine which story she had been reading. But he had forgotten about that, too.

"Bill thinks the kid at the Roma parking lot is holding back," said Patrick. "We intend to get back to him in a couple of days."

"Why the delay?" Harris asked.

"He's stewing right now," said Lynch. "Just want to give him enough time to figure we're done with him. Then we'll bounce him hard."

"What is your assessment of Angela Cicero, Father?" asked Inspector Koznicki.

"Me?" Koesler was caught off guard at being suddenly included in the discussion. "I guess she's a good woman. I really don't know her very well."

Koznicki smiled. He knew that Koesler thought most people were basically good unless he was given more than adequate reason to believe the contrary.

"No, I meant temperament, Father. Would you say she was a shy, retiring type?"

"Oh, no," Koesler responded quickly, "quite the contrary. She is most self-assertive. One of the most self-motivated people I've ever known."

Patrick arched an eyebrow. "I didn't get that impression."

Koesler reminded him of Angela's Roman intervention on behalf of her daughter.

Patrick inclined his head in an "I stand corrected" gesture. "Then she *does* have enough spunk to have actually carried this off."

"Oh, no," Koesler protested, "Mrs. Cicero couldn't murder anyone, especially a priest." Even as he made the assertion,

230

Koesler recalled Angela's confession just before her daughter's wedding and her hatred for Thompson.

"Father," Lynch drawled, "the first rule in a homicide investigation is to remember that anybody can kill anybody. All you've got to do is find the body and the motive. Not necessarily in that order."

"Who's next?" Harris asked.

"Lee Brand," Patrick answered.

"Brand and his wife are on a cruise," said Lynch. "His secretary gave us his itinerary." Lynch consulted his notes. "The ship is going to be docked in Vancouver until 5 P.M. Pacific time today. Want us to go out there and question him?"

In spite of themselves, smiles crossed the faces of Patrick and Lynch at the thought of escaping this oppressive Detroit heat.

Harris looked questioningly at Koznicki.

"Sorry," said Koznicki, "not a chance. We're on an austerity budget. Besides, that's not only out of our jurisdiction, it's Canada. Get the Vancouver police to look into it for us.

"We'll meet again tomorrow morning."

The meeting adjourned. Harris and Koznicki left the room.

"This may be a silly question," Koesler asked, after a brief silence, "and I hope I don't offend you. I mean, one of the surest ways of upsetting a priest is when someone asks him what he does all day after he says Mass . . . but, if the Vancouver police are going to question Mr. Brand, what are you going to do today?"

Lynch leaned back in his chair and closed his eyes. Patrick's crow's-feet crinkled in a smile.

"We're going to continue our investigation into a couple of other homicides," said Patrick. "There are plenty to go around. We seldom, if ever, are working on just one case at a time."

"Oh," said Koesler, "I see."

Lynch sat upright. "And what are you going to do all day, Father? After you've said Mass, that is?"

Koesler laughed. "Actually, I haven't said Mass yet. But I will. This is a holy day of obligation, the feast of the Assumption of Mary. I plan on taking the evening Mass."

Both Lynch and Patrick were Catholic. While each attended Mass quite regularly on Sundays, neither paid much attention to the Church's six holy days of obligation. Now, confronted with the fact that they were obliged to attend Mass, yet having had no previous intention of attending, they felt slightly uncomfortable.

"What time is that Mass of yours this evening, Father?" Patrick asked.

"Seven-thirty."

"We may just see you later," Patrick said.

"Damn, Sam!" Lynch commented.

"I can get up there and be back today!"

"I know you can, but you're not going to!"

The argument was familiar. Only the details changed.

"Come on, Nellie," Joe Cox pleaded, "for the sake of journalistic integrity, let me go to Vancouver!"

"Journalistic integrity! Journalistic integrity!" Kane bellowed, "journalistic integrity be damned! You just want a free vacation day!"

They were now both shouting, and the few reporters who were not busy on assignments were plainly amused. Cox suddenly became aware of the city room's attention. He lowered his voice and his manner. "Easy, now, Nellie," he said, soothingly. "A round-trip to Vancouver is not going to put the *Free Press* into receivership."

"I know that and you know that," Kane lowered his voice to match Cox's, "and we both know that Lowell holds the travel vouchers. There's no way you're going to get on a plane without Lowell's O.K."

"So?"

"So you are currently near the top of his shit list."

Cox knew that. He also knew it was Nelson Kane himself who occupied the pinnacle of that list.

"Listen," Kane continued, "call the *Vancouver Guardian*; Lowell doesn't have to approve that. Get somebody to string for us. Give them the line of questioning you need, and ask them to hop aboard the *Alaskan Queen* and interview Brand."

Cox was not surprised. If he had written a scenario beforehand, this is precisely how it would have read. But it never hurt to try for a free trip.

"Oh, and Cox . . ." Kane had resumed his chair and was unwrapping a very inexpensive cigar, which, fortunately, he would not light. ". . . get me a lead obit for the final."

"An obituary!" Cox seemed genuinely offended. "It's come to this: I'm back writing obits!"

"Get me a lead obit," Kane repeated.

"I think I've been violated!"

"Get off my back, Cox; you've never been integral."

Bob Ankenazy waited in the General Assignments Unit office. His friend, Sergeant Terri Scanlon, was bird-dogging Homicide for him to see what Sergeants Lynch and Patrick were up to today.

Ankenazy was feeling slightly smug. Joe Cox had some kind of edge over him, and the Homicide cops were being no help. But with all those slammed doors, Ankenazy had found an open window. Terri Scanlon, whom he had known for years, was willing to get him the necessary information. In return, all that was expected was that he babysit the phone and take messages.

For every moment the phone did not ring, Ankenazy was grateful. A phone call at GAU could be anything from a mark's complaint to a threatened bombing. The business of GAU was, as its name implied, very general. They investigated bombings, embezzlements, crimes by city employees other than police, and con games. They licensed junkyards and checked pawnshops and hotels for illegalities. And they provided security details for some downtown stores.

Ankenazy was diverting himself by imagining the kinds of calls that could find their way to the GAU and raising the absurdity of the calls to the ninth power, when Scanlon came back.

Returning his expectant look with one of consternation, she leaned back against the outer office door she had just closed. "I don't understand it," she said.

"What? What don't you understand?" Furrows began to form in Ankenazy's brow.

"They're on an entirely different case."

"Lynch and Patrick?"

"Yes."

"What happened to the Thompson case?"

"It's been farmed out."

"Where?"

"Vancouver."

"Vancouver?" The cold fingers of panic clutched at Ankenazy. "What's in Vancouver?"

"A cruise ship . . . and someone named Lee Brand."

"A cruise ship. Which one?"

"I don't know. That's all I could find out. The Homicide people are pretty close-mouthed. About all I can get for you are on-duty rosters or bits and pieces of conversations. Apparently, the Thompson investigation is continuing, and it is proceeding in due course. But today's work is being done for us by the Vancouver police. It must involve someone aboard that cruise ship . . . Brand maybe.

"Sorry, Bob, that's about all I could get for you, at least for today."

Although the gods were no longer beaming on him, they were not entirely hiding behind a cloud. It was a nasty turn. Unless he was able to cash in on these scant leads, he would fall hopelessly behind the *Free Press*.

Ankenazy became overwhelmed at the realization that, on the one hand, he had volunteered to take this story off Pat Lennon's hands and, on the other, that he had then fought the objections of Leon London so that the *News* would pursue the story.

If only I had left well enough alone, he thought. However, at this point there was nothing but to see if there might be a silk purse at the end of this sow's ear.

He thanked Terri reflexively and found a pay phone. Using the *News*'s credit card, he called an acquaintance at the *Vancouver Tribune*.

"Paul Armbruster? Thank God you're in! This is Bob Ankenazy at the *Detroit News*. Could you check something for us, Paul? How many cruise ships are docked at Vancouver today?"

"Just a second while I check." There was a several-minutes

pause. Armbruster's voice came back. "Just one: the *Alaskan Queen*."

So far so good, Ankenazy thought.

"Look, Paul, do me a favor. Can you leave your office right now?"

"For a good reason."

"I think I've got one. There should be a passenger named Lee Brand on the *Queen*. Board the ship and check with him to see if he's traveling with a Roman Catholic priest—a Monsignor Thompson—from Detroit. Just to be certain, check the passenger manifest to see if Thompson or any other Detroit-area people are listed.

"There's a standard stringer's fee with a healthy bonus in this. But time is at a premium. Whatever you find, call me at the *News*. I'll be back there in a few minutes."

"Sure thing."

As Wednesday progressed, Ankenazy would learn that Mr. and Mrs. Lee Brand were the only Detroit-area passengers on the *Queen*. Armbruster, clued to the story and supplied with questions, was able to get an interview with Brand. After which, with Brand's help, he was able to get a copy of the passenger manifest. He was also compelled to inform Ankenazy that this was by no means the only interview Brand had given this day. Earlier, Brand had spoken with a staff writer for the *Vancouver Guardian* who was stringing for the *Detroit Free Press*. Brand had also been questioned by the Vancouver police, who were acting on behalf of the Detroit police. Both the other reporter and the police had secured and teletyped back copies of the passenger manifest.

Well, Ankenazy concluded, it was another day of good news and bad news. At least he could stay abreast of Joe Cox.

But what the hell kind of magic did Cox possess that could give him an apparent advantage over even the police?

Father Koesler, at least, was not working on any other homicide cases. So he decided, just before noon, to go golfing. Since St. Anselm's lay roughly between downtown and St. John's Seminary, he decided to stop at his rectory and change before using the seminary course. He had plenty of time before this evening's Holy Day Mass.

As luck would have it, there was a threesome warming up near the first tee as Koesler arrived at the seminary. Fathers Pat McNiff, Bob Morell, and Mike Dolan, all of whom Koesler knew. As he pulled his cart toward the practice green, Koesler reflected that at his age he now knew almost all the older and middle-aged priests. Only the very youngest were unfamiliar.

Greetings were exchanged. Implicitly, Koesler was invited to complete the foursome. The conversation revolved around Monsignor Thompson's disappearance. To date, it was not widely known outside the Police Department that Koesler was quasi-officially involved in the investigation. Which well-suited Koesler's desire for a low profile; he would not volunteer the information.

"What the pot," said Mike Dolan brightly, "I think Thompson broke away for a quickie vacation. I mean, what's all the commotion for? This is only the—what is it?—fourth day he's been gone. Why, hell, back when I was in the Navy, I could lose four days on a really well-earned hangover."

The others laughed as they continued to limber up, taking practice swings with their drivers. Dolan, singularly, swung all four of his woods. He approached golf in much the same way others prepared for baseball.

"Jeez, I don't know, Mike," said McNiff. "There were a lot of people didn't like Thompson very much. In fact, I think you could say he must have been the most disliked priest in the diocese. And he did disappear under pretty suspicious circumstances."

"It was a bad combination." Koesler swung more vigorously than the others. He was not yet warmed up, but sensed they were nearly ready to begin. "The only tool he had to work with was canon law, and nobody did him any favor handing him that. On top of which, he administered the law very strictly."

"Very strictly!" exclaimed Morell. "More by his whim, I'd say. But you'd have to look to the suburbs to find the people who are really sore at him. He didn't bother us inner-city priests all that much." He indicated himself and Dolan, pastors, respec-
236

tively, of Sts. Theresa and Elizabeth. Very much core-city parishes.

"What the pot he didn't bother us!" contradicted Dolan. "What do you call what he did to poor Shanley? He damn near crucified him!"

Koesler, aware that it had been he who had involved Shanley with Brand, felt a twinge of conscience.

"Ah, yes, Shanley . . . how could I forget?" said Morell.

"You don't think Thompson could continue with his inner-city crackdown?" Koesler asked.

"Not a chance." Morell was confident. "Shanley committed the unpardonable sin. He witnessed the marriage of a couple of Very Important People. The people *we* marry you're never going to read about in the paper. Not even an obituary."

"Say," observed Koesler, "does it occur to any of you that we've been referring to Thompson in the past tense? As if he were dead?"

"Nil nisi bonum de mortuis," McNiff commented.

"Then *nil*," said Morell.

"What's happened to Shanley anyway?" asked Koesler, as they moved toward the first tee. As far as the eye could see, it appeared the foursome was alone on the course. "I haven't heard anything about him since I read in the papers that he accepted the suspension."

"He's disappeared, for all practical purposes," said Morell. "None of us knows where he's gone. He's got till mid-September till his suspension is up. I wonder where the hell they'll send him?"

"A hospital chaplaincy somewhere," McNiff opined. "Probably Mt. Carmel, where they can keep an eye on him."

Mike Dolan nominated himself as first off the tee. He wiggle-waggled very little. He simply stood and stared fixedly at the ball, which he had teed rather high. The muscles in his arms rippled as his animus toward the ball increased. Finally, he exploded with the fastest backswing in captivity. It was probable that at no time, once he began his swing, did he see the ball.

"Where'd it go? Where'd it go?" Dolan scanned the skies, looking in vain for a small white dot.

"It's slicing, Mike, it's slicing." Morell's eye followed the flight path. "Way up high, Mike, way up high! It's slicing!"

There was truth in this description. The ball was way up high and slicing. It descended on the other side of a tall maple and this side of the tennis courts. It would be in very tall grass. The chances of finding that ball before it was cut to death by a mower ran from slim to nonexistent.

At that point, the foursome felt a sprinkle of raindrops. They quickly escalated into a cloudburst.

The three priests who had not yet teed off ran for the clubhouse dragging their clubs behind them.

Dolan, standing motionless on the tee, watched them. Then he picked up his bag, threw the strap over one shoulder and trudged down the fairway heading toward the right rough and the inevitably fruitless search for his ball.

As he disappeared into the rainstorm, he was heard to mutter fervently, "What the pot!"

———

Most holy days originally were conversions of pagan feasts. As they became fixed dates in the calendar, they became, ipso facto, holidays. Whole villages would celebrate the combined feast day and holy day by attending morning Mass and then enjoying a communal picnic.

Through the centuries, this custom, along with nearly everything else, evolved. The Church stuck steadfastly to her holy days of obligation, while the world no longer granted the holiday. The only exceptions were Christmas and New Year's, when church and state still combined the holy day and holiday.

Even though Church law still obliged Catholics, under pain of serious sin, to attend Mass on all holy days, attendance was nothing as compared with Sundays. Only a relatively few Catholics deigned to attend holy day services. Every once in a while, though not often, Catholics voted with their feet on an isolated rule or regulation by simply not observing it.

Dean Patrick and Bill Lynch had not attended holy day services since childhood in parochial school. They would not even have been aware of the event were it not announced from the pulpit on the preceding Sunday. Even then, they never seriously considered attending.

Thus, each felt a measure of surprise to find himself among the thin crowd in St. Anselm's at 7:30 P.M. for the feast of the Assumption into Heaven of the Blessed Virgin Mary.

It was a novel feeling for them to view Father Koesler in his sacramental role of priest presiding over Mass. Until then, Koesler had been little more to them than a millstonelike onus they were forced to carry through the Thompson investigation. From this point on, they would, of necessity, see him, in the specialized view of a Catholic, as their priest.

During the homily, Koesler spoke interestingly enough of the privileges of Mary stemming from God's selection of her for a most special and important role, comparing this to God's selection of us as His children.

As the offertory began, Lynch turned to Patrick. "Is there going to be a collection?"

Without looking around, Patrick replied, "Is this a Catholic church?"

No sooner had the words left his mouth than parades of ushers marched down the center and side aisles, baskets at the ready.

"Lend me a buck, will you?" Lynch asked.

"Is that all you're going to give the Lord after all He's given you?" Patrick chided, repeating a reproof he'd heard uncounted times from various priests in various parishes.

"I'm not giving this to the Lord," Lynch stage-whispered. "I'm giving this to Father Koesler, who will probably mismanage it."

The shoulders of the two men shook with silent laughter.

Koesler had marked the two detectives as soon as he entered the church. The crowd was not so large that a couple of tall strangers would escape notice.

Their presence was a stark reminder of the fact that Tommy Thompson was missing, possibly in peril, possibly dead. Koesler decided to offer this Mass for Thompson, the investigating detectives, and the eventual success of their efforts. To which, if the detectives had known his intention, they would have added a sincere, "Amen."

6

THE ANNOUNCEMENT WAS THERE IN THE *Detroit News*'s August 5 issue. It was there for everyone to see. Monsignor Thomas Thompson would be at a wedding reception at Roma Hall in East Detroit on the evening of August 11. It was unlikely that any of his cronies would be with him. He would be unguarded, unprotected, among strangers, virtually alone, vulnerable.

It was noon on that Sunday, August 5 and Father David Neiss, having read the *Free Press*, was plowing through the comparatively enormous Sunday *News*. He had offered the 9 and 10:30 Masses earlier that morning and needed only to assist Father Cavanaugh with communions at the 11:45 and 1 P.M. Masses, and he would be finished with work for the day. He had about half an hour before he would be needed for the 11:45 A.M. communions.

Wedding announcements ordinarily did not interest Neiss. He was about to turn the page when his eye caught a familiar name. So Tommy Thompson would be at a wedding reception at Roma Hall next Saturday. Neiss could not think of Thompson without reflecting on how the man had mucked up the lives of a young couple Neiss respected and liked.

Somebody should do something about that man, Neiss thought. What Thompson had perpetrated against Harry Kirwan and Mary Ann McCauley was nothing less than a despotic crime.

240

The proscriptions of canon law were bad enough without adding capricious rules of his own.

Just because Thompson posited that Poles were likely to have their invalid marriages convalidated—even though in this case all authentic records indicated the contrary—two very fine people had been driven away from the Church. And, as far as Neiss could discern, it was all Thompson's doing.

But who could or would do anything about Thompson? There seemed no question that Thompson was keeping all the rules and regulations. God, he enforced them beyond the last dotted "i" and crossed "t"!" So there wasn't much chance that anyone in the bureaucracy would do anything about him.

How about some disgruntled petitioner? No; if it hadn't happened by this time—and Thompson had been wheeling and dealing for a good number of years—it didn't seem possible any such person now would lay violent hands on the clergyman.

For a fleeting moment, Neiss considered the possibility that he himself might be the agent of justice. He would have considered this possibility earlier and more seriously had his ego strength not been battered and bruised by continual emotional beatings administered by his emasculating pastor, Father Cavanaugh.

Suddenly, in the manner of a divine inspiration, a favorite Biblical text came to Neiss. He picked up his Bible and found the beginning of the book of the prophet Jeremiah, the man of tears.

God says to Jeremiah, "Before I formed thee in the belly I knew thee; and before thou camest forth out of the womb I sanctified thee, and I ordained thee a prophet unto the nations."

Then Jeremiah says, "Ah, Lord God! behold I cannot speak for I am a child."

But God says, "Say not, I am a child: for thou shalt go to all that I shall send thee and whatsoever I command thee thou shalt speak. Be not afraid . . ."

Be not afraid! Be not afraid to do what?

What, thought Neiss, can I do? What could I do?

He checked his watch. Fifteen minutes before he had to help with communions. He sat back and closed his eyes. As he sat very still, he could envision the coming week. If all these concepts worked out, perhaps he could become God's messenger in time for next Saturday's deadline. I shall not be a child, Neiss decided. And I shall not be afraid. I shall bring Thompson to his knees, so help me God.

To hell with Cavanaugh! To hell with 11:45 communions! I think I'll go fishing. Fishing and plotting go well together . . .

MONDAY, AUGUST 6, 2:30 P.M.

There had been hell to pay, of course, for skipping out yesterday without helping with the distribution of communions at the last two Masses. However, Father Cavanaugh was forced to temper his fury when confronted by a seemingly reborn Father Neiss.

As was the case with Saints Paul and Peter, as recorded in Galatians, Chapter 2, Verse 11, Neiss had withstood Cavanaugh to his face. The air had been thick with acrimony, but it also had been cleared. The two priests had now established the beginnings of a more professional relationship. There was no doubt that Cavanaugh would fall victim to some recidivism. He had too long-standing a habit of treating subordinates like children to turn a decisive and permanent new leaf. The rebirth most affected Neiss, who, for the first time, felt like an adult.

Now, Neiss was headed toward Detroit's east side to check out the first part of his plan. The first peg of the plot rested with the advice and consent of one Peggy O'Brien.

Peggy, now twenty years old, until a year before had been a Divine Child parishioner and a most prized member of Neiss's Young Adult Club. A talented singer and dancer, Peggy had been the star of several of the shows staged by the club. However, last year she had decided on a career change that had had a radical effect on her entire lifestyle. Peggy had become a topless dancer.

For this she had been virtually disowned by her parents. Father Cavanaugh had only barely been dissuaded from denouncing her from the pulpit. Most of the members of the Young Adult Club had seen her perform at the Club Libra at McNichols and

Outer Drive. Some of the girls envied her, secretly. Some of the young men lusted after her, noisily.

From time to time, Peggy visited Father Neiss. She assured him that her job was not sinful. Although regularly propositioned, she never went out with any of the patrons. She did live with a young man. But they intended to get married if it seemed their relationship was working out. And that was O.K., wasn't it, Father?

Somehow, the two had remained friends. And now, Neiss's plan to bring Monsignor Thompson to task depended on Peggy's professional advice and cooperation.

Neiss pulled into the parking lot of the Club Libra. An attendant took his car almost before he could exit it.

Neiss entered the Club. He was in mufti. At first, he could see nothing. The lights were so dim it appeared there were none. So far so good.

Gradually, as his eyes grew accustomed to the darkness, he could see more clearly. He spotted a couple of empty stools at the bar and headed for one.

But most especially, he could see the stage. There, under lights that, due to the dimness that marked the rest of the Club's interior, seemed brighter than they actually were, was Peggy O'Brien. She was wearing a G-string. That's all. Well, there were the strapped shoes with four-inch heels. But one tended to overlook them.

It was true what they said of the Irish and their fair skin. Obviously, all of their skin was fair.

Peggy undulated to the rock and roll rhythm blaring from a nearby jukebox. Her dancing, if anyone cared to critique it, was good.

Neiss surveyed the room. Even now that his eyes had grown completely accustomed to the subdued lighting, he still could see next to nothing. Good, he thought.

Other than the waitresses and dancer, there were no women in the room. Some of the patrons studied Peggy as if she were one of the wonders of the world. Others conducted business conversations as if there were not a ravishingly beautiful nearly nude woman dancing only a few feet from them.

At one point near the end of the final number of her set, Peggy

243

noticed and recognized Neiss. Her eyes widened, and she missed a beat. But then she concluded her dance without further incident.

She stepped from the stage to scattered applause from the studious men. The businessmen continued their conversations. She put on a robe and motioned Neiss to join her in a booth near the kitchen. As Neiss moved boothward, he noticed her successor mounting the stage. She wore a G-string and a halter top. Evidently, at one point in her performance, Peggy must have been similarly modestly attired.

"Well, I must say I'm surprised to see you here, Father."

"Oh, I always said I'd catch you at work one day."

Neiss didn't add he had been surprised to see so much of her today.

"How did you like it?"

"Uh . . . interesting. Very interesting. And very good. Reminded me of when we did 'Guys and Dolls' and you played Adelaide."

"Only it was warmer."

"Warmer?"

"With clothes on."

"Oh."

"But what brings you here, Father? You didn't come all the way over here just to catch my act. Not in the middle of a hot afternoon."

"Well, I do have an ulterior motive. But I don't know exactly how to bring it up."

"Best to come right out with it, Father. We're friends. And besides, I've certainly told you any number of things that weren't easy to confide."

Neiss ran his finger around the rim of his glass. The beer was his ostensible reason for being in the Club.

"I was wondering if you would have any serious objection to having your picture taken with someone in a . . . uh . . . compromising position?"

"Father!"

A few patrons glanced briefly in their direction.

"It's for a good cause."

"Perhaps you'd better explain."

"Yes. You're entirely right. That was too abrupt."

"Well, there's this monsignor, head of the marriage court. He's made life miserable needlessly for a lot of people, and—"

"Thompson."

"You know him?"

"I've heard of him from some of my friends. He's all you say he is and more."

"I'm glad you know about him. I don't want to hurt him, just bring him down to earth so he can know, first-hand, what it's like to be taken advantage of."

"So what do you have in mind?" She was not just interested; she was now involved.

"Well, I thought I could get him in the Club next Saturday night—maybe about 10:30, 11 P.M. I could get him to drink too much, maybe even slip him a Mickey. Then we could get some photos of him, here in a booth, with you or one of the other girls. I think in those circumstances, he might think better of taking advantage of others in the future."

She tapped a finger on the table meditatively. "It won't be easy. That hour the place is jammed." She smiled. "But I'll have a booth waiting for you. And I'll be the one in the photos with him. I know how I can carry this off without being recognized myself. And, as you've said, Father, it *is* for a very good cause."

Neiss raised his glass of beer in salute. They smiled conspiratorially.

THURSDAY, AUGUST 9, 5 P.M.

So far, it had been a satisfying day off for Father Neiss. He had played tennis—not well—and gone swimming.

About a half-hour previous to this moment, he had arrived at his parental home in Royal Oak. In another half-hour, dinner would be served, and he would join his father and mother at the kitchen table.

Now, he was rummaging through a medicine cabinet in the upstairs bathroom.

Finally, he found what he was looking for. The label on the

245

bottle read, Somnos. It was a sleep-inducer. The bottle had been pushed to the rear of the medicine cabinet. A good sign.

Neiss carefully studied the instruction label. He saw what he was searching for. Chloral hydrate. The common ingredient in knockout drops and Mickey Finns. He had looked it up.

He could barely read the faded typed prescription. At last he deciphered the dosage: "Two capsules every three hours as needed."

Neiss tried to estimate how many capsules it would take to render Monsignor Thompson ripe for picture taking. He had to include in his reckoning the fact that Thompson probably would be drinking. But if an older man such as Neiss's father could safely consume two capsules every three hours, the chloral hydrate content could not be very concentrated. Neiss decided on six capsules.

He took a small white envelope from his trousers pocket, opened six Somnos capsules, and, one after another, poured their contents into the envelope.

Later, during dinner, the conversation turned to the type of health insurance Neiss's father had been able to carry with him into retirement.

Spinning off that topic, Neiss was able to segue to, "Say, Dad, do you still take those sleeping pills?"

"Nope," said Mr. Neiss, as he forked loose a tender piece of pot roast, "don't need 'em any more. Sleep like a baby ever since I had that prostate operation."

Father David Neiss knew someone who could use them. He felt a secret thrill that he, a humble parish priest, was actually going to slip someone a Mickey, just like in those detective stories. His one regret was that he could not tell his parents. He could think of no way to help them understand he was doing this for a good cause.

His father neglected to tell him—it just didn't seem material— that the Somnos bottle in the medicine cabinet no longer contained the original prescription. The doctor had increased the dosage. Mr. Neiss had put the new capsules in the old bottle, because he didn't like to fool with those newfangled childproof caps.

The capsules that Father Neiss had emptied into his envelope did not contain 250 milligrams. Each contained one gram, 1,000 milligrams. And the prescription on the discarded bottle had ordered only one capsule before retiring.

SATURDAY, AUGUST 11, 10 P.M.

Even in the relatively short time he had been a priest, Father Neiss was familiar with the wedding routine from rehearsal to reception. He knew that, in all probability, by this hour there was nothing ahead in the evening for Monsignor Thompson but rubbery chicken, reconstituted potatoes, canned gravy, thawed vegetables, and cake baked for quantity not quality.

He dialed and asked for Thompson.

"Monsignor Thompson."

"Monsignor," Neiss, with his newfound self-confidence, had not even bothered to write out the invitation he was about to extend, "this is Dave Neiss—Father Neiss. You might not remember me. I'm the young priest you advised a couple of weeks ago. It involved a Polish first consort in a *defectus formae* case. I was a little reluctant to get that testimony until you made me see the light."

"Uh," Thompson grunted. For the life of him, he couldn't think why Neiss should be calling at all, let alone having him called to the phone during a wedding reception.

"I wanted you to know that I've been doing a lot of thinking about the advice you gave me then. About not getting involved emotionally with clients. I think if I can just put that advice into practice it could turn my whole priesthood around. You may have more influence on me than all the spiritual directors I had in the seminary."

That made sense to Thompson. It had been good advice, damn good!

"So, I've been thinking that if we could get together every once in a while, more of your philosophy could rub off on me. I know I could learn a lot from you. And when I heard you were going to be at this wedding reception, I remembered all the receptions I've had to attend—and you've had so many more—and I thought I could start out by returning a favor, and get you

247

out of the reception and into something more, uh, relaxing for a Saturday night.

"Monsignor, I'd like to take you out to a real neat place I know. It's pretty close to St. David's where you live. The name of the place is the Club Libra. They've got great entertainment; it's dark enough in there so no one will recognize us; I know one of the entertainers who's promised us a good booth, and the drinks are on me."

"You don't mean it!" He spoke loudly enough so that several waiters glanced at him. Neiss had correctly surmised that Thompson was bored with this wedding, which was a carbon of the hundreds of previous weddings he'd been forced to witness, participate in, or suffer through. This sounded like a dandy out. In addition, this young lad could learn a lot from him. Neiss needed him.

"Oh, yes, I certainly do mean it." This was working better than Neiss could have hoped. For once, he was going to carry off without a blemish a goddamn tour de force. "In fact, I have an extra sport shirt you can wear. I can lend it to you when we meet."

"Where?"

"Well, we do want this to be between just the two of us. How about we meet in De La Salle's parking lot?"

"I'll be right there!"

Thompson made hurried excuses, mounted his Eldorado, and hurried down Gratiot. Neiss was waiting at the school's parking lot. Thompson noticed the congealed blood. Muttering a soft curse, he wiped the wheel, rear-view mirror, and gearshift before joining Neiss and donning the proffered shirt, leaving his clerical collar and shirt in Neiss's car.

Even though it was dark outside, the darkness of the Club Libra, complicated by clouds of tobacco smoke, was such that, on entering, neither Thompson nor Neiss could see. But they were seen. Peggy O'Brien, performing on stage, winked at the hostess, and the two priests were literally led to a ringside table. Still the two drinking companions could scarcely see each other. To everyone's way of thinking, it was perfect.

"May I take your orders, gentlemen?" asked a waitress dressed in very little black silk.

248

"A light beer," said Neiss.

"Jack Daniel's neat with water on the side," commanded Thompson.

By this time, they had no trouble seeing the performer who was gyrating only a few feet from them.

"Would you believe it, Monsignor? That girl used to perform in our parish plays."

"Don't call me Monsignor, dummy! Not in here."

Neiss was aggrieved. The music's volume was such to preclude anyone—even at the nearest table—from overhearing them.

Thompson drained the Jack Daniel's in a single gulp and sipped the water. This disappointed Neiss, whose little white envelope was at the ready. He hoped Thompson would order another drink. As it turned out, that was like hoping rabbits would have babies.

The second and third Jack Daniel's went about as unceremoniously as the first. Thompson dawdled over his fourth drink. Peggy O'Brien had captured his interest entirely. She was down to her G-string, and God! like the Grand Canyon— *mutatis mutandis*—she was a wonder. Thompson's dallying gave Neiss the opportunity he'd been waiting for. Into Thompson's drink went 6,000 milligrams of chloral hydrate.

"Say she used to dance at your parish?" Thompson's speech was becoming slurred.

"Yes, Tom." Neiss still nursed his first beer.

"Like that?"

"No. In full costume."

"Pity. You wouldn't have needed Bingo."

The waitress kept coming to their table like the sorcerer's apprentice.

After Thompson's seventh slug of whiskey, his face seemed to flush abruptly and he appeared to sink into a deep sleep. This seemed to Neiss to be about what the doctor ordered. Serendipitously, Peggy finished her set, grabbed a robe, and headed for their table.

Just to assure himself all was well, Neiss found Thompson's wrist, and felt for his pulse. Either he was doing a poor job of locating the pulse, or it was very, very weak. Then—could it be?—the pulse stopped altogether. He felt for an artery in the

249

neck. Nothing. He held a water glass against Thompson's lips. No vapor. Thompson was not breathing.

My God! thought Neiss; he's dead. I've killed him!

Just then, Peggy slipped into the booth very, very close to Thompson. One look at Neiss's face was enough to wipe the smile off hers. She conducted her own study of Thompson's absent vital signs.

"My God!" she said, a bit too loudly, "you've killed him!"

"Shhh!" Neiss admonished. "I'm not sure what to do next, but letting everybody know he's dead is not it."

"Now what?" Peggy waved away the cameraman with whom she had arranged for the compromising photos.

"What do we do next?" Neiss echoed.

"We mustn't panic," Peggy directed. "But we've got to get rid of the body."

"How do you do that?"

"How do *I* do that? It's *your* body!"

Neiss considered that only fair. "O.K., how do I do that?"

"Let me think." And she did.

"Wait a minute," she said at length, "did you read in the paper the other day how that Cass Avenue drunk fell into a dumpster and was loaded into a garbage truck and came to screaming just before he was dumped out?"

"Ye . . . es," Neiss slowly recollected.

"Well, if he hadn't wakened, the guy would now be part of a landfill."

"No kidding! Do you think it would work?"

"Can you think of anything else?"

Neiss shook his head. He was infinitely grateful for even one idea.

"O.K.," said Peggy. "Leave enough for the bar bill and tip. We'll drag him out between us. It won't be the first time a drunk has been carried out unconscious."

Awkwardly, they worked Thompson's body out of the booth. Stumbling frequently, they managed to get him out of the Club with no one the wiser as to his true condition.

"O.K.," Peggy panted, "there's a dumpster out back. With any luck, nobody'll be around it now."

"With any luck, we'd be taking pictures now. And Monsignor Thompson would be dead drunk instead of just dead."

Lurching and stage-whispering encouragements and reproaches at each other, they dragged Thompson's dead weight to the rear of the Club. There was, indeed, a huge dumpster. And, as luck would have it, no one was around.

"I'll climb up and pull," Peggy directed, "and you stay here and push."

That seemed fair to Neiss. Peggy clambered up. Laboriously, Neiss positioned Thompson's bulk and began to push as hard as he could. Suddenly, he felt soft, warm, rounded flesh. It was not Monsignor Thompson's bottom Neiss was pushing. It was Peggy's.

"Father! Please! This is not the time to get fresh!"

"Oh, I'm sorry. Unintentional! Unintentional!"

At long last, Thompson's body tumbled into the dumpster. Neiss climbed up and with Peggy began burying Thompson's body beneath the garbage and bottles. The body well buried, they descended from the dumpster to brush themselves off and catch their breath.

"Now what?" Neiss inquired.

"Tomorrow morning, a garbage hauler will stop here, dump these contents in the truck, compact them, take them out of town, and dump them in a landfill.

"Now you go home and say your prayers that all goes well and no one uncovers the body."

"It was intended to be in a good cause," said Neiss, lamely.

"Father, do me a big favor: next time you come up with a good cause, go check it out with the Salvation Army."

The conspirators parted and went their separate ways.

Yesterday's inclement weather had cleared out of Michigan, and a delightful high pressure system with cool breezes from Canada had replaced the rain. This was the kind of day when it was a crime to be forced to stay inside.

Joe Cox was at his desk wearing a smug smile. On his desk was a copy of today's *Free Press* as well as an early morning copy of today's *News*. Each was opened to the latest installment of the Missing Monsignor story as by-lined by Joe Cox and Bob Ankenazy for the *Free Press* and *News*, respectively.

Today's installment, in each paper, involved an unnamed Detroit banker who had ample reason to be the cause of whatever might possibly have happened to Monsignor Thompson.

To anyone reading both papers, it was clear that the *Free Press* coverage of this mystery was by far the more complete and colorful. Only the accounts written by Cox included, in graphic detail, the mean and nasty things Thompson had done to a suburban housewife and a Detroit banker. The series promised more scandal to come.

Readers of both papers were implicitly invited to join in the guessing game. Who had done what to Monsignor Thompson, whose reputation was slowly deteriorating. So far, readers of the *Free Press* had the better run at the solution.

"Cox!" Nelson Kane called across the several desks that separated them.

Instinctively, Cox rose from behind his desk. He finished reading Ankenazy's last paragraph before attending Kane. Poor slob, Cox thought of Ankenazy, he's crippled without the diary, and the poor son-of-a-bitch probably doesn't even know it.

Kane loved it. He relished mystery stories about rotten monsignors even more than weeping statues in Catholic churches. He'd taken some flak from the Archbishop's press secretary, Father Octavio, who protested what he saw as bad publicity for Monsignor and Church alike. Octavio had threatened to get out a letter to all parishes suggesting that *Free Press* subscriptions be canceled by The Faithful. But Kane could eat priest-secretaries and never know he'd had a meal.

For now, the city editor had other concerns. He wanted to talk to his premier reporter before Cox escaped out into this beautiful day.

"I see," said Kane as Cox reached his desk, "you've been engaged in comparison shopping."

Cox caught the allusion to his study of his own treatment of the Missing Monsignor story as contrasted with that of the *News*.

"Comparisons are odious," Cox quoted with a cherubic grin.

"But when it comes to you and Ankenazy and the Missing Monsignor, they're sweet . . . right?"

Cox merely widened his grin.

"Listen, Cox," Kane worked an unlit cigar from the left to the right side of his mouth, "I've seen this happen a dozen times. You're on top, you get ahead of the competition, and then you start getting cocky. And then the whole thing blows up in your face."

The grin faded.

"And I don't intend for that to happen to us on this story!" Kane asserted.

"Hey, look, Nellie," Cox protested, "I know damn well that Ankenazy is among the best the *News* has. If both of us had the damned diary, I'd be running my ass off trying to find an angle to beat him. But the poor bastard hasn't got it. I don't even know how he's managed to stay even with me so far. But he just hasn't got Thompson's own words. And that's the heart of this story.

"No, Nellie, if I'm cocky about anything, it's just that I'm the one who got on this story early. I'm the one who found the diary. Since then, it's been mostly downhill sledding. Hell, I could practically write this story now without leaving the city room.

"And it was interesting seeing the Cicero woman open up when she realized that I knew about her dealings with Thompson. I wish I could have seen Brand. But at least we've got his statement. It's going to be fun seeing how each one of these suspects reacts."

"Who's next?"

Cox paged through his notepad. "Neiss, a Father David Neiss, at . . . uh . . . Divine Child parish. I've got an appointment with him," Cox checked his watch, "in about half an hour. Damn, I'd better get on my horse!"

"Cox," Kane articulated his most serious and profound concern, "when are you going to get to Lennon?"

"All in good time, Mein Führer. All in good time and in proper order."

In the back of Cox's mind lurked the possibility of this mystery's being solved before Lennon's turn to be interviewed came up. Cox believed there was no need to make enemies needlessly. Especially when the prospective enemy was the woman with

253

whom he shared bed and board. He grabbed his jacket from the back of his chair and breezed out of the city room.

I don't like it, thought Kane. No, goddammit, I don't care: I don't like it. He's too goddamn cocky. This thing is going to blow up, and we're going to have ecclesiastical egg all over our faces.

Kane had been in the city room and the company of volatile reporters too long for him to question an instinct as deeply rooted as this one.

―――――――

"At least he's got an alibi," said Patrick.

"That puts him one up on Mrs. Cicero," said Lynch.

The two detectives, along with Ned Harris, Walt Koznicki, and Father Koesler, were studying the report on the interview with Lee Brand by the Vancouver police.

"There's no doubt," said Patrick, "that on August 11, from 10 P.M. on, our time, Brand was not only on board the *Alaskan Queen*, but the ship had left port and was at sea."

"That pretty well takes him out of the Detroit area at the time of the disappearance," said Lynch.

"Unless . . . unless . . ." Koznicki leaned forward in his chair, "is it possible the Monsignor could have joined Brand later on?"

"Yeah," Harris brightened, "suppose Brand arranged for Thompson to join the cruise at some later port of call."

"But we have the passenger manifest," said Lynch. "Thompson's name is nowhere on this list. Nor is there anyone listed from the Detroit area besides Brand and his wife."

"Can't others besides passengers come on board at a port of call?" Harris asked.

"Yes," said Patrick. "But if anyone stays aboard after the ship leaves port, and if he doesn't become a paying passenger, he becomes a stowaway. And, according to the report, the purser said that eventually one or another of the cabin stewards will always become aware of the presence of a stowaway."

"So it comes down to this," Lynch summed up, "if a passenger's name does not appear on the passenger manifest, he is not a passenger."

"Unless," said Harris thoughtfully, "he's under an assumed name."

"Yes, but," interjected Koesler, a bit self-consciously, "even if he were—even if Monsignor Thompson had left Detroit to join a cruise, under whatever name, I'm sure he would have made provision for someone to cover for him on the weekend at Shrine. To say nothing of his absence from the Tribunal. Monsignor Thompson is just not the type to voluntarily leave his obligations unattended."

"Well, what do you say, men?" Koznicki asked.

"It seems to me," said Patrick, "that Brand had as good or better a motive as anyone on our list for taking revenge against Thompson. But, as of this moment, there seems to be no case against him. His alibi seems to be beyond question."

"All right, then," said Lynch, "we move right along to the next customer, Father David Neiss."

Koznicki caught the sense of discomfort on Koesler's part.

"Something, Father?"

"Oh, nothing. It's just that I find it repugnant to think of a priest committing an act of violence, particularly against a fellow priest."

"These are leads we are following, Father," Koznicki reminded. "Of their very nature, most of them will take us nowhere. But, if we are to be able to find Monsignor Thompson, or discover what happened to him, we must follow every lead we have."

"I understand, Inspector. It's just an instinctive response on my part."

"Well," said Lynch, "every investigation continues with the next lead. Or, GOYAKOD."

"GOYAKOD?" Koesler puzzled.

Harris laughed and decoded: "Get Off Your Ass and Knock On Doors."

"Coming, Father?" Lynch asked.

He was not sure why, but Koesler rose and went off to accompany Patrick and Lynch on the next leg of their investigation.

Joe Cox had not been alone in comparing *News* and *Free Press* coverage of the Missing Monsignor series this bright Thursday morning. The *News*'s Robert Ankenazy and Leon London had been likewise occupied. In fact, the two had had a spirited argument over the wisdom of continuing the series.

Ankenazy had no argument as to the present superiority of the *Free Press*'s coverage. His contention was that once begun, the *News* was obliged to complete the series no matter how apparent it became that they were being forced to march doggedly in the *Free Press*'s footsteps.

London's opening premise had been that the *News* should not have become involved with this story at all. Ankenazy should have perceived and admitted at the outset that all early leads and impetus belonged to the *Free Press*. It was a premise for which Ankenazy had no defense.

In the end, Ankenazy won London's grudging accedence to his assertion that the *News* must continue coverage for the time being. But, London insisted, as soon as the *News* could cut its losses and run, it must do so.

Following the agreement, Ankenazy once again called on Sergeant Terri Scanlon and, utilizing her good offices, discovered the identity of the next suspect to be questioned—Father David Neiss. It was a small trickle of good luck in an ocean of bad. Neiss was a friend of Ankenazy's wife; through her, the two men had met socially a few times. At least he would not have to question a total stranger.

Ankenazy called on Neiss just after lunch, and, as he had come to expect, found that Neiss had had two visits earlier that day. The everpresent Cox had been first, followed by that peculiar threesome of Patrick, Lynch, and Koesler. Ankenazy's discouragement was patent.

"What's the matter, Bob?" Neiss asked as the interview concluded. "Haven't I answered your questions well enough?"

Ankenazy smiled in spite of his feelings. Neiss was a man without guile. "It isn't that," he said. "As a matter of fact, your statement is the most helpful of the three I've had so far."

"Well, I just tried to answer about the same as I did for that other reporter and the police."

"Fine; you did fine. The thing that grinds my—the thing that bothers me is, how did they find you, and how do they know what to ask?''

"The diary, I suppose."

"The what?''

"The diary. The police have a diary that Monsignor Thompson kept, and the *Free Press* reporter has a copy of it.''

A diary. A goddamn diary! Suddenly, as if layers of cataracts were falling from his eyes, the picture began to clear for Ankenazy. The police had found a diary belonging to Thompson. No . . . wait; they wouldn't have let Cox have it. Certainly not without giving the *News* the same break. No; *Cox* must have found the diary, made a copy, and given the original to the police. That *had* to be it.

Ankenazy's problems were by no means over, but it was reassuring just knowing the etiology. How much further could he push this? There was only one way to find out.

"Did either the reporter or police show you the diary?'' Ankenazy had moved to the edge of his chair in Neiss's office.

"No, not the actual diary. The reporter showed me a photostat of what Monsignor Thompson had written about me . . . it was pretty bad.'' He blushed. "The police just asked me questions. But it was obvious they had read the diary. They asked questions about things they could have known only from what the Monsignor wrote about me.''

"Did the reporter show you any more of the diary than just what Thompson wrote about you?''

"No, just that.''

"O.K., Father. Now, just a moment while I try to put this all together.''

This, of course, explained why Cox and the police were checking the same suspects almost simultaneously. Both were undoubtedly following, in succession, the names in the order Thompson had mentioned them in his diary.

There were X numbers—Ankenazy could not know how many—of petitioners or associates of Thompson's who were written about in the diary. Clearly, what Thompson had written about them, the way Thompson had mistreated them, made it obvious that each of these people had adequate reason to wish Thompson ill.

Think now, Ankenazy commanded himself: The people on the list from which Cox and the police are working are the ones Thompson mentions in his diary—the ones Thompson professes to have screwed. But, from what he, Ankenazy, had been able to learn so far, screwing people was something Thompson did well. Maybe what he did best. The people in Thompson's diary are those who Thompson himself would admit have little love for him.

And what about the others? There must be dozens of people who would have reason to wish Thompson ill.

Put it this way: if Thompson has been murdered, perhaps, perhaps likely, one of those mentioned in his diary did it. Maybe it was just as possible that someone whose life Thompson had ruined but had not even mentioned in the diary had done it. They're out there, Ankenazy knew it. But how to find them?

Well, why not begin with this young priest in whom there was no guile?

"Father," Ankenazy returned full attention to Neiss, "neither you nor I know who else is mentioned in that diary. But we know the police are investigating people who have reason to dislike—to put it mildly—Monsignor Thompson.

"As a reporter, I have an obligation to investigate along the same lines. But I don't know who else might fit in this category. Do you know of anyone—not a housewife or a banker; they've already been investigated—who would have reason to dislike . . . uh . . . intensely, Monsignor Thompson?"

"Gee, I don't know if I can answer a question like that." Neiss's inclination was to be helpful. But this request appeared to compromise his obligation to protect professional secrets.

"I know how you feel, Father." Ankenazy's attitude was solicitous. "But as long as the name or names you give me are not protected by the seal of confession, I can keep a professional secret, too. And I would explain to any source you give me that he or she is free to cooperate with me or not. But if I get cooperation, the source would be protected by anonymity. I promise that."

It was Neiss's turn to ask for a few moments for reflection.

None of what he could tell Ankenazy fell under the protection of the seal. If he were to give the reporter a name, the source
258

would be free to refuse the interview out of hand or to cooperate. In some sense, letting out one's feelings about the Monsignor could have a cathartic effect. He had felt better after telling the reporter and police about at least part of his relationship with Monsignor Thompson.

"O.K. But you promise these people will be free not to answer questions if they don't want to?"

"I haven't the power of the police. I can only ask. And, since they haven't been charged with any crime, I couldn't use their names publicly whether they cooperate or not. And the police can't force me to reveal their names."

"Well," Neiss said, "there is this newly married couple . . ." He felt strange using the phrase since they had not been married in the Church. ". . . Mr. and Mrs. Harry Kirwan. I don't have their address, but I think his phone is listed."

"Thank you, Father." Ankenazy felt better than he had in days.

"Oh, and there's one other. Somebody Father Cavanaugh mentioned who was considerably upset by the Tribunal's rules and seemed to take specific objection to Monsignor's position. That would be . . ." Neiss rattled his memory. ". . . a Mr. Janson. Fred Janson. I think he is a lawyer."

Ankenazy thanked Neiss, left the rectory, and drove away.

Today, Cox, you bastard, he thought, I'm going to match you stride for stride. Tomorrow, I believe I'll begin my own investigation.

Oh, yes, this was an extremely beautiful day.

7

FATHER NORMAN SHANLEY GUESSED THAT ANY association whatsoever with Lee Brand had to involve a mixture of good and bad news. Certainly, such was the case with himself.

If it hadn't been for Brand, Shanley would not have been suspended from his priestly ministry for a month. At least not yet. Obviously, there was no way of knowing what the future held. Perhaps his casual approach to canon law would have attracted the hierarchy's attention at some time in the future, perhaps not. But agreeing to witness Brand's daughter's wedding, with all the attendant hoopla, definitely had caught the hierarchical eye and ear.

Still, Shanley continued to be unable to totally fault Brand. His charge of reverse discrimination if Shanley witnessed problem marriages of the poor but not of the rich still rang true. If only Brand had not made the wedding into The Greatest Show on Earth. But, Shanley reasoned, ex post facto, wherever Brand goes, there the media gather.

On the other hand, Shanley had never lived so well. He was now ensconced in a penthouse in the prestigious 1300 Lafayette East high-rise. Brand maintained the suite for out-of-town guests and emergencies. He had insisted that Shanley use the suite for the duration of his suspension. He had made arrangements to provide food and whatever else the priest might want. Shanley had decided to be good to himself for once, put a good face on the matter, and enjoy a lifestyle he had no reason to expect he would ever experience again.

It was now late Sunday morning. He had attended Mass earlier at the nearby and nearly empty Jesuit church, Sts. Peter and Paul. Nondescript churchy music droned from the radio. Shanley relaxed in a comfortable leather chair. The window-wall's southern exposure provided a memorable view of the Detroit River and southwestern Ontario. Alternately, Shanley gazed at the peaceful scene or read the Sunday papers.

Ordinarily, he would not have noticed it, but with nothing but time on his hands, he was reading the papers more carefully than usual. Thus it was that Shanley happened to see the announcement in the *Detroit News*'s August 5 issue. Monsignor Thomas Thompson would be at a wedding reception at Roma Hall in East Detroit on the evening of August 11. It was unlikely that any of his cronies would be with him. He would be unguarded, unprotected, among strangers, virtually alone, vulnerable.

Shanley let the paper slip to the floor. Thoughts and impressions of Monsignor Thompson flooded Shanley's conscious and subconscious. A montage began forming in his imagination. Thompson's face appeared, along with those of Elvira and Leroy Sanders. Faces of others whose fates had been extracanonically repaired blended into the imaginary picture.

There was no doubting Thompson's ultimate goal. In successfully prosecuting Shanley, Thompson had made his first successful incursion against the core-city ministry. Now he would be able to hound the other priests. If Thompson were able to impose strict canonical procedures on the central city, the ecclesiastical ball game would be finished for the poor of downtown Detroit.

All this probably would happen if Thompson went unchecked. And who was there to stop him? No one that Shanley could think of. No one but himself.

But could he do it? He could not even bring himself to think of the word. Murder. He kept thinking of the deed as *it*.

And if he did *it*, what could he possibly do with what remained? The body.

261

Each time Shanley tried to dismiss the idea, the images of those poor people would return to haunt him.

Maybe it would not be all that impossible. All that was necessary for evil to triumph, he reminded himself, was for good people to do nothing.

Shanley leaned back and closed his eyes. As he sat very still, he could envision the coming week. Maybe it wouldn't be impossible.

MONDAY, AUGUST 6, 10 A.M.

Shanley decided to begin at the finale of his plot and work backwards.

As chaplain at several small hospitals, he had become an integral part of many of the hospitals' successes as well as their failures. At times, he was able to rejoice with the families of the rejuvenated patients. At others, he grieved with the bereaved. Bereavement, in most cases, led to a cemetery.

Shanley, as was his habit, had become friendly with the employees of these cemeteries. So his call earlier this morning to Rick Fox, in charge of the crematorium at Woodward Cemetery, had been enthusiastically received.

Damn few priests or ministers even acknowledged Fox's existence, let alone showed any interest in him. Shanley had been the exception. As often as they met at the cemetery, the priest would greet Fox, inquire as to his family's health and, most of all, ask after family members who from time to time might be ailing.

Fox happily anticipated Shanley's visit, and assured him that 10 A.M. would be a good time. It would be between funerals.

Located near the West Seven-Mile Road fence a far distance from the Woodward Avenue front gates, the crematorium building resembled a chalet. It comprised an impressive vaulted A-frame interdenominational chapel, mausoleums and, of course, the retorts—two of them.

Shanley arrived for his visit promptly at ten. He exchanged greetings with Fox, and learned that, for once, all members of Fox's family enjoyed reasonable health.

262

"But you didn't come all the way out here just to find out how we was," Fox said, smiling.

"No, you're right, Rick. There is something more. I've got a problem. Or, rather, I'm going to have a problem."

Fox's smile quickly segued into a concerned frown. "Oh? Anything I can help with?"

"Yes, I think so, Rick. But something I don't want you to get involved in."

"How we going to do that, Father?"

"What would you say, Rick, if I asked to borrow your keys to this place for just this Saturday night?"

Fox paused and considered. "Geez, I don't know, Father. I shouldn't ever leave these keys out of my possession."

"Well, this way you don't know what I'm going to do here. I suppose you read about me in the paper?"

"Saw it on TV." Fox seemed embarrassed that he knew of Shanley's disgrace.

"Then you know I can't priest in a church for a month."

Fox nodded.

"Maybe I'm going to conduct a service in the chapel here."

"Is that what you're going to do, Father?"

"I said maybe that's what I'm going to do. The whole thing is, you trust me enough to lend me your keys for Saturday night. And you help me out a whole lot. If anyone sees me here, I'll take full responsibility."

Fox paused and pondered again. "Geez, I don't know, Father. I'll have to think this over awhile, O.K.?"

"I guess I can't ask for any more than that. Sure, Rick, I'll get back to you later in the week." Shanley looked around the room. "That casket over there," he indicated a wooden coffin resting on a four-wheel cart, "are you going to cremate that now?"

Fox nodded.

"Mind if I watch?"

"Oh, no, Father. No problem." Fox was pleased to have the company.

Shanley studied Fox's every move, asking questions at nearly every step. Along the way, Shanley learned that: metal caskets must have their lids removed; the cremation process requires anywhere from one to three hours, depending on the container type; the temperature in the retort reaches approximately 1700 degrees Fahrenheit; the body simply dissolves; the process can be viewed through any of three openings in the rear of the retort; viewing is not physically uncomfortable since a downward draft pulls the heat out the bottom of the retort; only the white dust—calcium—is retained; the rest is brushed aside. And that when frozen bodies come from the morgue, they must be defrosted prior to incineration.

Apparently, even crematoria are not exempt from gallows humor.

Shanley thanked Fox for the crash course in cremation. Fox thanked Shanley for his interest in an unpopular subject. Shanley promised Fox a call later in the week. Fox promised Shanley serious consideration of his request for keys.

MONDAY, AUGUST 6, 1 P.M.

On his way back to the apartment, Shanley made a slight detour. He stopped at a U-Haul outlet on Gratiot, where he purchased a garment box, 24 by 21 x 48, for $6.79. He had no difficulty bringing it up to the apartment on the service elevator. People were forever moving things in and out at 1300 Lafayette East.

WEDNESDAY, AUGUST 8, 2 P.M.

It was as easy as he had been told. Anybody could get cyanide.

A pharmacist friend told Shanley that if he needed cyanide to kill some of the more stubborn weeds in his mother's garden, all he had to do was find a garden supply store, preferably one of the old-time ones.

Shanley had selected Kowalski Lawn Supplies on Joseph Campau in Hamtramck. He was waited on by none other than Mr. Kowalski himself, who warned Shanley to dilute the cyanide or he would have trouble. Shanley assured the proprietor the cyanide would be put into liquid form.

Shanley was required to sign for the cyanide, but he was not required to produce identification. He signed the first name that occurred to him: Mark Boyle.

WEDNESDAY, AUGUST 8, 4 P.M.

On his return to the apartment from Kowalski's, Shanley phoned Rick Fox.

Against his better judgment, but because he could not conceive of a priest's doing anything seriously wrong, and because Shanley had always been so friendly and solicitous, Fox had decided to let him borrow the keys that would admit him into the cemetery and the chalet. But only for Saturday evening. Shanley thanked Fox profusely and assured him he would pick up the keys Saturday afternoon and return them no later than Sunday afternoon.

SATURDAY, AUGUST 11, 10 P.M.

From his own experience, Shanley knew this was the time to call. The wedding dinner would have just begun.

"Monsignor Thompson." The voice and tone were unmistakable.

"Monsignor, this is Father Norm Shanley."

That was odd, Thompson thought; he sounded friendly.

"The more I think about what happened—and I've had a lot of time to think lately—the more I'm convinced I was wrong, and you were doing no more than your duty in upholding the law."

"Uh . . ." Thompson was about to strongly suggest that if Shanley wanted to apologize, he might better do so during business hours. However, the next name Shanley spoke caught Thompson's ear and interest.

"Lee Brand is really the cause of my being in this predicament. Brand and my own poor judgment. I don't suppose you

265

know this, Monsignor, but Brand has me staying in his downtown penthouse, probably to salve his own conscience. Well, I've decided that Brand owes both of us something. Me, for getting me in all this trouble with his damned publicity. And you, for flaunting his flouting of your authority. So I've decided to throw a party here in his apartment tonight that will go a long way toward breaking his lease—if you know what I mean!''

"You don't mean it!'' Thompson definitely knew what Shanley meant and was getting enthusiastic about the possibilities. Several waiters glanced at him.

"We ought to enjoy ourselves at Brand's expense, Monsignor. We've got just time to get you here and settled in before the party begins. But, I was thinking, there's no place to park here and it wouldn't be smart to leave your Eldorado on the street in this neighborhood. And it might look funny to the priests at St. David's to have your car parked there and your not being in the rectory. So I thought I'd meet you and drive you here.''

"Where?''

"How about the parking lot at De La Salle, say in about half an hour.''

"I'll be right there.''

And he was. Shanley preceded him to the parking lot by only a few minutes. Shanley was puzzled that Thompson remained in his car after parking it. He seemed to be wiping the steering wheel and rear-view mirror. But Shanley thought little of it.

They used the service elevator to reach the penthouse. As Shanley had figured, at that hour and in the service elevator, they met no one.

"Not a bad place," said Thompson, inspecting the rooms after taking in the view. "Undoubtedly the scene of many a Brand nookie party." Thompson was particularly stimulated at the thought of making it where Brand had—sort of a violation of Brand himself.

"When does the party start?" Thompson called out.

"In a very little while," said Shanley, returning to the living room. "We'll make sure we get you out before the police are called . . . but have a slug of this while you're waiting, Monsignor." Shanley offered him a glass containing a dark golden liquid. "It's Frangelico, a really pleasant liqueur."

Thompson took the glass and passed it beneath his nose. "Smells nutty," he commented.

"Yes."

Shanley left the room as Thompson tossed down the drink in a single gulp.

From the kitchen, Shanley could hear the gasps, the staggering, the crash of a lamp and then, silence. He returned to the living room. Monsignor Thompson was on the floor. He was blue. The reason Shanley had decided on poison to do *it* was to avoid the necessity for being present when death occurred. He had succeeded.

Shanley was able—with some difficulty—to get Thompson's body in the garment box. The trip in the service elevator and in Shanley's station wagon was without incident. Nor had he any problem entering Woodward Cemetery and Crematorium. But since the retort portal was sized for coffins, Shanley had to—with much tugging—drag the body out of the garment box before he was able—with much shoving—to get it in the retort. After which he dismantled the box and pushed the sections in after the body for good measure.

Remembering all he had seen Fox do, Shanley closed the heavy door, turned on the oil pump, flipped the switch and set the timer for an hour and a half. Instantly, three jets of flame shot out of the retort's inner walls.

Shanley sat down to wait.

Lee Brand might wonder about that white ash that covered the earth in his flower pots. Shanley would tell him it was fertilizer.

Getting married sensitizes one to the institution. That was the only reason Harry Kirwan could think of to explain his reading wedding announcements in the *Detroit News* on this sleepy first Sunday of August.

He and Mary Ann would be wed this coming Thursday evening at a candlelight ceremony in St. Stevens Episcopal Church in Farmington Hills. It would not be an unmixed blessing. From all indications, very few of her relations would attend. Her parents were attending, but under protest, and only because they had found a priest who was lenient enough to give them a permission—which was not, in fact, his prerogative to give. But then, some priests were forever giving, or withholding, permissions, in matters that should be settled by the individual's conscience.

These thoughts were passing through Kirwan's stream of consciousness when his eye caught Monsignor Thompson's name.

So, according to the August 5 issue of the *Detroit News*, Monsignor Thomas Thompson would be at a wedding reception at Roma Hall in East Detroit on the evening of August 11. It was unlikely that any of his cronies would be with him. He would be unguarded, unprotected, among strangers, virtually alone, vulnerable.

Later this Sunday afternoon, Kirwan would take his fiancée for a drive to his parents' home on the shores of Union Lake. He and Mary Ann would be happy to be together but, as happened often lately, there would be an emotional cloud of unhappiness shadowing their good times. And that cloud was due to none other than Monsignor Thompson. He and his silly Polish rule had changed their lives, probably for all time to come.

If no one but Kirwan himself were affected, he might have been able to forgive and forget. But the life most directly affected was Mary Ann's. This injury he could neither forgive nor forget.

He briefly pictured a confrontation with Thompson. But what good would a sound thrashing do? It might just possibly improve Kirwan's disposition. It certainly would do nothing to save future victims of Thompson's capriciousness.

Was he, Harry Kirwan, Public Relations Manager of Michigan Bell Telephone Company, then called to the beau geste? He pondered that one a while. Ubiquitous arguments against the ultimate involvement poked their heads up. Only one consideration surfaced on the opposite side of the question. If he did not do something drastic, no one would. In the end, the latter argument prevailed.

He gathered and stacked the Sunday papers and checked his watch. He still had a couple of hours before he was to pick up Mary Ann. Perhaps time enough to plan the extraordinary events of the coming week. As he sat very still, in his mind's eye he could envision these events unfolding. He was amazed at how simple it all seemed.

MONDAY, AUGUST 6, THROUGH THE DAY

It was as Kirwan had suspected. He and Thompson had several mutual acquaintances. Among them were quite a few local politicians and businesspeople.

It did not take long to learn many things about Monsignor Thompson. And this time, Harry didn't even have to call in any markers. His sources spoke freely and easily about Thompson. He was fairly well liked by some fairly prominent people. Where there was antipathy, it ran deep. He enjoyed lavish vacations and tagged along on such junkets with wealthy friends quite regularly.

It would be an understatement to say he liked to gamble. He was, indeed, just this side of being a wagerholic. He particularly favored card games, especially poker. He played with priest buddies but preferred the company of VIPs with whom there seldom was a ceiling on stakes.

Kirwan was confident he had more than enough information to act.

FRIDAY, AUGUST 10, 1:30 P.M.

Kirwan was visiting the site of a planned Bell office building in Dearborn within sight of Ford World Headquarters, more familiarly known as the Glass House. Ranged about the landscape were very large trucks, a variety of mammoth construction vehicles, and building materials. The formation of the new building had scarcely begun. Kirwan approached the foreman, Bill Dowd, a Bell employee Kirwan had known for years.

"Hi, Harry," Dowd greeted him, "when's the cornerstone laying?"

"August 24," Kirwan consulted a pocket calendar. "Just two weeks from today."

Dowd surveyed the chaotic scene. "Well, we'll be ready for them. Should have most of the foundation done by then."

Dowd, accompanied by Kirwan, began walking toward the actual site of the building.

"Who's going to be here for it?" Dowd asked.

"Oh, the Mayor of Dearborn, a few other local politicos, the guys from the appropriate Congressional districts, a clergyman or two."

"Not the Mayor of Detroit?" Dowd asked, chuckling.

Kirwan smiled ruefully. "Not likely. He raised enough hell when the company decided to build in Dearborn instead of Detroit. But we'll probably get a gang of protesters complete with picket signs."

"Oughta get jobs!"

"What?"

"If they had jobs," Dowd expatiated, "they wouldn't have time to waste our time. See 'em every night on TV. I think that's why they're there, mostly: to show up on TV. Sick of 'em."

Dowd came to a halt. They were at the actual site where the building would be erected. He looked into the excavation fondly. He loved to see new buildings rise. It was his raison d'être.

"Pouring the foundation?" Kirwan asked needlessly. It was obvious.

"Yeah. We got about half the concrete in. Should finish it Monday."

"Who's standing guard nights and weekends?"

"McNamara. You know Mac."

Kirwan nodded.

"Figure we can get by with just one 'cause we've got the area fenced." Dowd's sweeping gesture took in the encircling metal fencing topped by several strands of barbed wire.

"Looks pretty secure," Kirwan observed.

"Yeah. We'll get 'er up and to hell with the goddamn protesters. And that goes for their goddamn signs too."

It was fortunate the newly wedded Mr. and Mrs. Harry Kirwan had delayed their official honeymoon. It allowed time for what had to be done tonight.

Two evenings ago, when Harry and Mary Ann had been wed, Harry had taken careful note that one and one-half hours elapsed from the beginning of the ceremony until they and their guests began the dinner. Casually, through that evening's celebration, Kirwan had asked the caterer, cook, photographer, and anyone else who regularly serviced weddings about the average time these events took. There was general agreement that the times varied. But in a Catholic wedding where there was a Mass—unlike the Kirwans' case—the average time was about two hours. So Kirwan waited until exactly ten to place his call.

There was a slight delay while Thompson was summoned to the phone.

"Monsignor Thompson."

Kirwan had never before heard the voice. It was easy to dislike the tone of put-upon, overbearing annoyance.

"Monsignor, we haven't met. My name is Harry Kirwan."

"Uh . . ." Thompson disliked being called away from a party. He disliked being called by people he didn't know. He disliked this phone call and thought to terminate it as quickly as possible.

"Several of your friends," here Kirwan dropped names of VIPs he'd learned were card-playing chums of Thompson's, "are getting together tonight for a *major* poker game to be followed by some entertainment they know you will appreciate. Al Braemar and Tony Vermiglio were particularly eager that I get in touch with you. They wanted me to assure you this would be an evening you would not soon forget."

"You don't mean it!" Thompson spoke with such enthusiasm that several waiters glanced at him.

"None of them will be driving there, and they thought it unseemly that your car be parked in the area. They suggested I meet you and bring you to the game. Would it be satisfactory for us to meet?"

"Where?"

"I thought the parking lot at De La Salle. It's close to your residence so you won't have far to drive after the party."

"I'll be right there!"

And he was. Kirwan was waiting for him. Thompson seemed to fumble with several things inside his car after parking. But it didn't matter. At this stage of the game, Kirwan knew he'd won; he was in no hurry.

Thompson entered the passenger side of Kirwan's car. As he did, Kirwan called on his training as a Ranger during the Korean War, and with the hard edge of his hand chopped Thompson behind the ear. The Monsignor crumpled like a rag doll. Kirwan covered Thompson's face with a pillow, and smothered him. It was quick and painless. With the body covered on the floor of the back seat, Kirwan drove to the Dearborn site of Ma Bell's new edifice.

As anticipated, Kirwan had no difficulty getting past McNamara. They knew each other well, and Kirwan was going in to gather some additional data for a publicity release that had to be turned out tomorrow for the early Monday editions and broadcasts.

The building site was dark. But Kirwan could see well enough by the light from distant Michigan Avenue. In the trunk of his car he had a mix of cement, sand, and gravel the equivalent of that being used in the building's foundation. There was plenty of water. He donned coveralls and mixed a batch of concrete. Dumping the body in a shallow section of the foundation, he poured the concrete over it to a depth of several inches.

Kirwan tidied up the area and prepared to leave. With comparatively little preparation, this had been completed seemingly without a hitch.

There must be, Kirwan thought, a lot of bodies in building foundations. And they remain there because the police are not likely to tear down an entire building to find out if a sought-after corpse is there.

Kirwan returned to his new bride with a special and gratifying sense of accomplishment.

Friday, August 17, and comparisons had lost their malodor at the *Detroit News*. At least for the moment.

Bob Ankenazy had his third installment locked in the CRT. It featured a nameless and purposely mislocated suburban priest who had been given ample cause by Monsignor Thompson to do him ill. For the first time in this series, Ankenazy's story presented the lurid and gossipy details that heretofore had been a Joe Cox exclusive.

Ankenazy and his managing editor, Leon London, were celebrating the breakthrough with coffee while relaxing in the editorial conference room.

"Who would believe a grown man would keep a diary in this day and age?" asked Ankenazy, not expecting an answer.

"Johnson and Nixon kept tapes," London observed. "Any chance you can get a copy of the diary?"

"I don't think so," said Ankenazy. "There's no way the cops would have let Cox have a copy—at least without letting us have a copy. They don't need the kind of trouble the *News* would give them if they tried something like that. No; Cox had to discover the diary first, the lucky bastard—and then give it to the cops. However, I have something else up my sleeve."

He told London of the leads given him by Father Neiss and of his theory that if Thompson was indeed murdered, he did not necessarily have to have been killed by someone mentioned in the diary. Although Ankenazy had to admit probability lay with the diary characters.

"So," Ankenazy continued, "I'm having lunch with Harry Kirwan today. It never fails; ask for an appointment with anybody in P.R., and you're having lunch."

London smiled, then became serious. "You know, Bob, if you can get not only a story, but permission from any of your sources to reveal his or her identity, we may have a bargaining tool."

"For what?"

"I'm not sure. Just try it. Something may come of it."

It was as if Yoda, the Jedi Master, were speaking. Ankenazy decided to follow instructions if at all possible.

"Cox, goddammit, he caught you!"

Nelson Kane was in a state of borderline rage.

"Now take it easy, Nellie; it isn't that bad." Cox said it, but beneath the surface he didn't really believe it.

"Like hell it isn't! Haven't you read the morning edition of the *News*? Ankenazy got everything you got out of Neiss and more. You think that isn't 'that bad'? Cox, the *News* climbed up your ass and over your head. For all we know, Ankenazy may be ahead of you this minute!"

Cox felt as if he were backpedaling to defense a full court press. "Now, wait a minute, Nellie. I checked with Father Neiss this morning. Ankenazy's wife happens to be a friend of his. Neiss volunteered information none of these other people have or will. For these most recent suspects, Ankenazy has got to go back to Go and try to catch me."

"Does he know about the diary? Did Neiss tell him about the diary?"

"Yes," Cox admitted.

"Goddammit then, Cox, he's going to try to get it!"

"How? I'm not going to give him the time of day. And the cops have no reason to give him a copy. If they were going to, they'd have given him one the first time he asked for a break. They gave him nothing then; they'll give him nothing now. He's dead in the water."

Apparently, Kane was beginning to see the theoretical logic of it all. The thumping vein had settled back into his neck, and his blood pressure seemed to be cruising close to normal.

"Now I've got to get over to interview Father Shanley," Cox continued, "1300 Lafayette East. Not bad. Should be quite a story. The only problem will be to mask his identity after all the publicity of the Brand wedding. But," the cockiness had returned, "I can do it." Cox turned on his heel and was gone.

Kane hitched up his pants. I don't care, he thought; that son-of-a-bitch is getting too complacent. This story isn't in our back pocket yet. Kane's teeth unclenched. But damn, it's a good story. It had readers all over Michigan playing amateur detective.

What does a missing monsignor do? Sell newspapers.

274

"It's just strange, is all I'm trying to say," said Sergeant Lynch.

"What's strange about it?" asked Father Koesler.

"That Father Neiss should claim to have received a sick call to a nonexistent address last Saturday night."

"And that he spent almost two hours trying to find the place," added Sergeant Patrick.

"I don't find it all that strange," said Koesler, who, with each hour of this day, was becoming more and more actively involved in the investigation.

"You don't?" Lynch persisted. The three were en route to 1300 Lafayette East for an appointment with Father Shanley. They would arrive only minutes after Joe Cox had left Shanley.

"No," said Koesler. "Things like that are always happening to priests. People trying to get a handout give hard-luck stories to priests. If the priest asks for some identification, frequently he is given a fictitious name and address. There are always sick people—I mean emotionally—who will send a priest out on a false alarm. Finally, there are those who are in a genuine emergency and in their confusion they give an incorrect address or wrong directions.

"There is always the possibility that the sick call Father Neiss took fell into the third category. If there actually was someone suffering or perhaps dying and he had been given a wrong address and directions, I think it only natural for him to spend some time looking for the right house."

"Maybe you're right, Father," said Patrick, "but it has an artificial ring to me. And, as far as this investigation is concerned, it has no value, since no one can corroborate it."

"Yes," added Lynch, "as far as we're concerned, Father Neiss remains on a front burner."

As they drove on in silence, Koesler wondered just how many front burners this investigation could hold.

———

Sergeant Terri Scanlon of the GAU was conscious of the fact that her old friend Bob Ankenazy had not been in yet today to discover, through her, who it was Lynch and Patrick were investigating. She missed him. She'd grown accustomed to his questions.

8

PAT LENNON HAD ALWAYS READ THE *DETROIT News*, even when she was employed by the *Free Press*. Now that she was an employee of the *News*, she read it more carefully.

It was due solely to her more complete reading that she happened to notice Monsignor Thompson's name in the Newlyweds column of the August 5 issue. The announcement stated that Thompson not only would witness the wedding but that he would attend the reception at Roma Hall on the evening of August 11. It was unlikely that any of his cronies would be there, Lennon thought. He would be unguarded, unprotected, among strangers, virtually alone, vulnerable.

At this point, Lennon could not fight off the distraction, so she ceased reading and leaned back, gazing out the apartment window at Detroit's east side. She allowed her thoughts to pile themselves one atop another. Joe was still sleeping, so she could afford the luxury of uninterrupted thought. And her thoughts revolved around Monsignor Thomas Thompson.

It was a crime, maybe one of those crimes that cried to heaven for vengeance, the kind the Sisters in school used to tell her about, for someone like Thompson to represent the Church. The treatment he had given her he had intended to be shaming and degrading. Thompson had succeeded only in making Lennon very, very angry.

277

It would have been one thing for her simply to learn that according to the rules and regulations of the Catholic Church, she could never marry again. But to have placed between herself and a declaration of nullity nothing but a clerical casting couch routine was nothing less than sacrilegious. She wasn't kidding herself. She'd been around too long to miss the bald-faced, albeit adolescent innuendos and all-but-open invitation to bed that Thompson had thrown at her.

If this was his conduct toward *her*, what self-indulgent evils might Thompson inflict on others? Lennon was aware that she was wise to the ways of the world. If she could handle the high-pressure blandishments of Karl Lowell and his *Free Press* bedchamber he kept in constant usage, she certainly could deal with a clumsy if insulting amateur such as Thompson.

But what of other women? What about women who might be lured into a relationship that gratified Thompson only in hopes of getting what passed for justice at his hands? What about young women with no experience in such matters? They could be scarred for life by someone like Thompson.

And who was doing anything about it? Where were the signs that anyone was heading Thompson off at the pass? Even Father Koesler, whom Lennon greatly respected, gave no indication that anyone could invade this unassailable fiefdom Thompson had created.

Well, what, indeed, could anyone do about Thompson? He was protected by the Church whose reputation he defiled.

Suddenly, another image began to form in Lennon's mind. Maybe it would be possible for her to do something definitive about the problem. Several possibilities came to mind. Considering each carefully, she shook each off in turn. Then one scheme presented itself that seemed, at first blush, foolproof. The longer she scrutinized it, the more it held up. She really thought she could pull it off. And easily do so within this week.

As she sat back absently watching the freighter traffic on the Detroit River, she envisioned her activities during the coming week. The details grew increasingly clear.

Lennon had managed to wangle an assignment to check on some of Michigan's summer resorts and see how business was doing now that half the season was over. The assignment was part of her plan. Today she would check on some of the resorts in the Port Huron area. Ostensibly, that was why she had requisitioned a Volare from the news desk, gotten the keys from the watchman, and also reserved the car for the coming weekend. She was to check out the resorts on a weekday afternoon and again on a theoretically busy weekend evening.

Having completed the first part of this assignment, she drove some twenty-five miles north of Port Huron. The site was just as she'd remembered it. A long disused driveway led from U.S. 25 through the trees to a cliff overlooking a barren beach against which beat the relentless waves of Lake Huron.

She descended the rickety steps built clinging to the cliff. She looked around fondly. This was probably the most sheltered beach on Lake Huron. At one time, in their younger moments of madness, she and Joe had converted this into their own private nude beach.

She removed her shoes and stockings and stepped into the waves. The water too was just as she had remembered, outrageously cold. Lake Huron became what jokingly might be described as warm for about two weeks in the average summer. And those usually were the last two weeks of August. It was not quite time for the old lake to warm up. Good. She checked her watch; it had taken just an elapsed hour and a half to drive here from Detroit. Good. As far as she could see, all was in readiness for Saturday night.

Saturday night, she thought, live or dead.

SATURDAY, AUGUST 11, 10 P.M.

She had had alternate plans to get Cox out of the apartment but hadn't had to use them. It was Cox's turn on night desk at the *Free Press*. Bitching all the way, he'd gone off to work it.

Lennon had no idea at what stage the reception would be now. But she was sure that by this time the wedding party had at least made it to Roma Hall. She didn't care what stage the reception had reached; she was about to make Thompson an offer he could not refuse.

"Monsignor Thompson."

She suppressed the impulse to hang up. "Monsignor, this is Pat Lennon. You may remember meeting me at the Tribunal a week or so ago."

"Uh . . ." Indeed he remembered. He took this opportunity to let a combination of recollection and imagination take off.

"I guess our meeting didn't end all that well. But I've been thinking about it, and maybe I was hasty. I've always kind of liked men who were forceful, who had the courage of their convictions. To get to the point, I must admit you really turn me on."

Thompson smiled. His suspicions regarding the effect he had on her were confirmed.

"I can't think of anything more boring than a wedding reception, especially when you've been to as many as you have. I'll lay it on the line," she had let her voice drop an octave; it was seductive. "How would you like to make it with me tonight?"

"You don't mean it!" Several waiters glanced at him.

"Oh, yes I do. But we can't make it at your place or mine for that matter. The rectory is dangerous, and I have a madman reporter living with me. So I thought we could go out to a cottage I have on Lake Huron. How about it? Do you want to meet me?"

"Where?"

"How about the parking lot at De La Salle? It's close to your place and not all that far from mine."

"I'll be right there."

And he was. Fussing with something for a few moments after parking his car, Thompson got in the passenger side of Lennon's company car. He wore a silly grin as he removed the vest with his Roman collar and tossed it into the back seat.

She drove toward the I-94 Freeway that headed north.

The breeze from the air vent lifted her soft summer skirt, revealing an attractive thigh. Clumsily, Thompson pawed her.

"Time enough for that when we get there, lover; we don't want to cause an accident, do we . . ."

If that was the way she wanted to play it, that was fine with him. He could wait. Waiting would just make it better.

They exchanged small talk while she drove, though the conversation remained strained. As they neared Port Huron, Lennon produced a 1.5-liter bottle of Paul Masson Golden Cream Sherry with an alcoholic content of 16 percent. It should be enough, she thought, to get him tipsy without being drunk. They passed the bottle back and forth. Beyond the first sip, she faked drinking the wine. He continued to swallow it in great gulps.

It was difficult to see the obscure driveway, but Lennon found it on her first try.

"This it, honey?" Thompson seemed ideally tipsy.

"Follow me, lover." Lennon exited the car and started down the rickety steps.

"Hey wait! I don't see any cottage. This is just a goddamn bare beach."

But Lennon was better than halfway down the steps. Thompson, tripping and stumbling all the way, followed. When he got to the beach, he found that Lennon had reached the water. The usually restless Lake Huron was smooth and reflective. Lennon was busy doing something. Thompson focused more carefully. By God, she was taking off her clothes. By God, she was . . . yes, she was naked! Thompson could see moonlight reflecting off her curves. He lurched toward her. She eluded him and went splashing into the surf.

"Hey, what the hell—?"

She glanced at him over her shoulder. "Haven't you seen 'From Here to Eternity'? Before we wrestle on the beach, we've got to get wet."

It was the damndest thing he could think of. But there was that gorgeous Lennon body undulating under the surface of Lake Huron. He could think of no reason to remain on shore.

He stripped to his boxer shorts and undershirt. Embarrassment about his flabby body kept him from removing all his clothing.

My God, this is cold! he thought as he stumbled into the water. My God, this is really frigid! he thought as he arrived at chest-deep water. My God, he thought, this is breathtaking! For the first and last time in his life he suffered a stomach cramp. And, as Red Cross instructors will attest, when you get a stomach cramp in the water, you are very likely to drown. Which is what Monsignor Thompson did.

"Where are you, lover?" Pat Lennon was in deep water, treading, prepared to drown Thompson. But if he didn't reach her soon, she would become an ice float.

She looked in vain. The surface was unruffled. But she had seen him enter. There was only one conclusion. He had drowned. An eventuality she could only have hoped for.

She swam back to shore. His body might or might not be found. He might be devoured by the fish. It didn't matter. There was no way he could be linked with her. Besides, he had drowned all on his own. She could pass a polygraph on that.

She reached shore and collected his clothing, including the vest and collar from the back seat of the car. She set it all afire, warming herself slightly at the blaze.

She could go home now with only one problem: she had the beginnings of one hell-of-a cold.

"Fred, dear, here's the name of that Monsignor Father Cavanaugh was talking about."

Pauline Janson was reading the Newlyweds column in the August 5 issue of the *Detroit News*. "Monsignor Thompson, it says, is going to marry some couple at St. David's and then attend the reception." She looked over at her husband. "Isn't that odd, Fred, to hear of a person for the first time and then right after that, to read his name in the paper?"

"Yes, dear," Janson agreed inattentively as he read the financial page, "that *is* odd."

Shortly thereafter, Pauline went off to the kitchen to prepare the standing rib roast that would be the piece de resistance of Sunday dinner.

Fred stopped reading the financial news to gaze at the society page his wife had laid near her chair. He never read any part of the social section of the paper. If Pauline had not read that notice to him, he never would have seen it. This, in itself, he thought portentous. Retrieving the social section, he returned to his chair to read the item for himself.

Monsignor Thompson would attend the wedding reception at Roma Hall in East Detroit on the evening of August 11. It was unlikely that any of his cronies would be with him. He would be unguarded, unprotected, among strangers, virtually alone, vulnerable.

Fred Janson recalled his reaction on learning of all the rules and regulations surrounding the granting of a Church annulment. As a lawyer, Janson was familiar with the exquisite details of law, but the ecclesiastical annulment regulations went well beyond anything he had encountered in civil law. The deck was stacked against the petitioner, unlike civil law. And, while some of the regulations represented universal Church law, others were the product of Monsignor Thompson's repressively legalistic brain.

Janson recalled concluding that Thompson had virtually the power of life and death on the cases that came before him, and to Janson's way of thinking, Thompson should not have all that power.

Janson recalled actually meeting the man. Was it in Lee Brand's company at the DAC? Janson had taken an instant dislike to the Monsignor. Something Janson seldom did with people newly met.

Apparently, there was no movement afoot to do anything about this medieval situation. To the contrary, if one cared to believe Father Cavanaugh, Thompson's administration was sliding toward a more liberal stance than some in the Church would prefer! If that were true—if Thompson were "liberal"—Janson wondered what horrors a *conservative* Tribunal would inflict on its petitioners.

What was needed, Janson reflected, was some stunning, perhaps violent action that would attract the attention of the hierarchy to the injustice both of Church law and of the system that implemented it. Something the Church simply could not overlook or sweep under the carpet. Something like . . . the murder of an officialis.

The thought, though it seemed a logical culmination to all else he had considered, startled Janson. He had never before considered murdering anyone. Yet, it did seem to be the only action that could bring the desired reaction.

Clearly, however, Janson could not conceive of himself in the role of a murderer. It was simply out of the question. Then, what of hiring someone to do the deed? There would be no more involvement than the payment of money. He thought he could be comfortable with that.

But how does one go about hiring a murderer? Where does one look? What does it cost? Where does one start?

As he relaxed in his favorite chair, comforted by the savory aroma of the rib roast, he thought he could see the beginning of an answer to all these questions. He envisioned what the coming week would bring.

TUESDAY, AUGUST 7, 7 P.M.

Victor D'Agostino and Fred Janson had been in law school together. They had passed the bar together. After that, their legal careers had split and gone in widely divergent directions. Janson had become a highly paid specialist in corporation law. His firm handled many of the big business accounts in the Detroit area. D'Agostino had specialized in criminal law. He had established every bit as solid a reputation in his field as Janson had in his. However, D'Agostino's specialty brought him into the company of some of the most notorious criminals in the Detroit area. And that is specifically where the two men's lives separated. Janson regularly could be found in the company of automotive and finance tycoons, while D'Agostino palled around with Detroit's top hoods.

Thus, it was to D'Agostino that Janson turned in this his hour of criminal need.

The two had just finished a most satisfying dinner in Topinka's on the Boulevard. They had met at Janson's invitation so, D'Agostino understood, it would be Janson's business that would be discussed. And, as was the usual understanding with get-togethers such as this, whatever the business was would be discussed after dinner over coffee.

Coffee had been served. Janson carefully packed his pipe, a prelude to lighting it. D'Agostino lit an exotic panatela.

"So, Fred, what is it I can do for you?" D'Agostino would have been taken aback if Janson had merely wanted advice in a corporate business matter.

"I'll come directly to the point, Vic. Do you know anything about murder for hire?" Janson lit his pipe; his visage disappeared behind the smoke. He'd done this purposely. He did not want D'Agostino to see his countenance on broaching the question.

D'Agostino stirred cream into his coffee. Short of being asked for corporate legal advice, he would be next most completely surprised by Janson's interest in murder for hire. "I've heard of it," he answered at length.

"I'm interested but at sea. Where would one begin if one wanted to hire a killer?"

"One might begin at any of several places. The appropriate bartender, the appropriate cabbie . . ." D'Agostino was more than comfortable using impersonal designations. He preferred it. If he were forced to guess, he would have supposed the intended victim to be Janson's wife. D'Agostino knew nothing of Janson's marriage. But, a man in his position . . . an elderly wife . . . a young secretary . . . a refusal to divorce . . . it was common enough.

"It is all, then, in knowing the appropriate person?" Janson sipped his coffee.

"That's correct."

"And would a person in your position know such a person?"

"He could."

"This person, if contacted, could contact a professional killer?"

"He could."

"And what would the professional charge?"

"Five thousand dollars."

"That's all?"

"Five thousand dollars for each contracted victim."

Suddenly, the fog cleared from Janson's head. Until this moment, since last Sunday afternoon, he'd been living a dream, a quixotic dream. It didn't matter how evil he perceived some person to be, there was no possible way he could kill or have anyone killed. It was preposterous.

It had taken this moment to awaken him to reality. The knowledge that he could, indeed, if he wished, arrange for someone's murder. He could easily afford it. He was talking to a man who could set it up. He was one relatively minor financial transaction away from arranging a murder. It took this—the matter-of-fact reality of it—to open his eyes. There was no possible way he could continue on this path.

"Well, Vic, I just wanted to know. I'm surprised that such an arrangement is so inexpensive."

D'Agostino sensed, from Janson's expression and manner, the change of heart that had taken place. In truth, he was as relieved as Janson.

"Well," said D'Agostino, "perhaps they make it up in volume."

Men of the world, they both laughed, and concluded their dinner with B&B and reminiscences of law school days.

As they parted, Janson experienced an enormous sense of relief. He had almost done something for which he could never have forgiven himself.

———

Copies of the *Detroit News* arrived at police headquarters before the *Free Press*. Even though the *News* was basically an afternoon publication and the *Free Press* a morning paper, the order of arrival today was not unusual. On Saturdays, the *News* published only one edition, and they got it out early.

Koznicki, Harris, Patrick, Lynch, and Koesler each picked up copies of the *News* and looked immediately for the latest Robert Ankenazy-by-lined episode in The Case of the Missing Monsignor. They found it at the bottom of page one. They expected to read the saga of a priest who has the full and ancient sanction of the Church lowered on him for his disobedience to

286

canon law. Instead, they read an even more fascinating story involving someone in management at a Detroit utility whose life had been practically destroyed by the caprice of Monsignor Thompson.

"Management?" said a startled Patrick.

"A Detroit utility?" said Lynch.

"Where the hell did he get that?" asked Harris.

"It's not in the diary, is it?" asked Koesler. He was never sure he read things as thoroughly as possible.

"No, but I'm damn well going to find out where he got it," Patrick vowed.

"Before you do that," said Koznicki, "what did you find out about Father Shanley?"

"Nothing terribly unusual," said Lynch. "Thompson gave him ample reason to strike back, just as with the others. However, he has no alibi, although he comes close to having one."

"How's that?" asked Koznicki.

"Well, Shanley claims he spent all Saturday evening and night in the penthouse Brand put at his disposal," said Lynch.

"But," continued Patrick, "he claims he was supposed to have had a visitor that evening, a Father Robert Morell. Morell didn't show. Morell says he got an unexpectedly long visit from a stranger in need and when he tried to call Shanley, Shanley's phone was out of order."

"So," Lynch returned, "Shanley almost had an alibi, but he doesn't. There isn't anyone who can testify to his not having left the apartment all night."

"Interesting," said Harris, "so he remains a live one."

"Yup," said Lynch.

"And now," said Patrick, "Bill and I . . . and Father," he had almost forgotten Koesler, "will go over to the *News* and find out what we can about a put-upon utility exec."

———————

"A manager in a Detroit utility!" Nelson Kane stabbed the words out. "Do you appreciate how superior this story is to yours?"

"Well, you know, Nellie," Joe Cox shrugged, *"de gustibus non est disputandum."*

"De gustibus, shit!" said Kane bitterly. "Look at these stories. *You've* got a priest who broke the law. O.K., so Thompson dumped on him a little heavily. Thompson again proves himself a functional son-of-a-bitch. But the guy *did* break the law.

"Now look at Ankenazy's story. Here's a guy who abided by all the rules! Not even a Catholic, but he's going to play by all the Church rules. Then Thompson throws a brand new one at him from out of left field. A Polish rule. A *Polish* rule! Do you realize how angry the Poles get when they're singled out for this sort of prejudicial attention? This goddamn Polish rule is going to sell papers, Cox. I'd rather have a Polish rule than a goddamn weeping statue!"

"Nellie," Cox protested, "I don't know where the hell Ankenazy got this guy!"

"He got this guy, you turkey, by doing some leg work. He didn't get handed a diary on a silver platter. He had to go out and develop his leads like a newspaper reporter is supposed to do! My advice to you, fella, is to get the hell out of here and come back with a goddamn winner. We wrap up this series tomorrow, and we'd goddamn better come out on top, or I'm going to have your ass! Is that clear?"

It was clear. Cox backed away from Kane nodding his appreciation of the situation. It would be a few minutes before the blood returned to his cheeks.

Damn him, thought Kane for the umpteenth time. I knew he was getting too goddamn cocky!

————

Patrick, Lynch, and Koesler met with Ankenazy and London in the *News*'s conference room.

"I want to lay it on the line, Ankenazy," said Patrick in his best threatening demeanor, "I want your source on your story in today's paper. And, if necessary, I'll go to the Grand Jury to get it."

"A bit of overkill, I think," Ankenazy replied. "I can give you what you want if you give me what I want."

"A quid pro quo," Koesler Latinized. "That sounds fair."

"Exactly," said Ankenazy.

"Let me do the negotiating, O.K., Father?" admonished Patrick.

Koesler felt chastened.

"If you can give me your source's identity," Patrick addressed Ankenazy, "then I want it. No deals."

"No deals," Ankenazy responded, "no name. Go to the Grand Jury. It could take weeks, maybe months, to get what you can have right now. If we make a trade."

"What do you want?" asked Patrick.

"The diary."

All of them had known it all along. There was silence for a few moments.

"Cox has got it," Lynch reminded.

"O.K.," Patrick agreed and dug the diary out of his briefcase. "Give me the name, and you can make a copy of this."

Ankenazy revealed Harry Kirwan's identity and photostated the diary.

The police and Koesler left. Ankenazy smiled at London. "Just as you said: the source's identity came in handy. I'm just grateful Kirwan agreed."

"I had a hunch you'd be able to trade the name for the diary, either with the cops or with Cox. I'm only glad it was with the cops. What, by the way, happened with that second lead?"

"Fred Janson? Dead end. Compared with the others, he got benevolent treatment. He didn't like the procedures, but then I guess nobody does. Janson just wouldn't have fit in this series. He doesn't qualify as an especial victim of Monsignor Thompson."

All the while he was speaking, Ankenazy was paging through Thompson's diary. He was grateful to whoever, undoubtedly Cox, had underlined the relevant passages.

"Aha!" Ankenazy read aloud. "The victims—or suspects—in Thompson's chronological order are: Angela Cicero, Lee Brand, David Neiss, Norman Shanley—the not-too-well-disguised suspect in today's *Free Press* story—and—brace yourself—Pat Lennon."

"Lennon! Why, she's at work just outside this office. In editorial!"

"Correction," said Ankenazy, "she *was* at work. She is about to be interviewed."

———————

Patrick and Lynch had decided the trio would interrogate Harry Kirwan before tackling Pat Lennon. Kirwan was new to them, and they hoped to strike while a subject was still willing to talk. Not only did they know exactly where Lennon would be, they had an appointment to talk with her later in the afternoon.

In the back seat of the police car, Koesler sat silently. Mentally, he was tracing his contribution—or more precisely, lack of it—to the resolution of this case. He had been with these detectives five days. He would be with them two, perhaps three, more. So far, he had given them his pastoral opinion a couple of times. That had been of little practical value. And now he had compromised Sergeant Patrick's bargaining position with Bob Ankenazy simply by speaking out of turn.

It was an unaccustomed feeling. This was not his métier. He was utterly untrained in police procedure. Yet, in some way, he felt he was failing. But how can one fail at something one has no business trying?

He decided to stick it out for the full week he had promised his friend Koznicki. He had already made arrangements with the Jesuit who had been covering Masses for him. Koesler would take the afternoon and evening Masses today at St. Anselm's. The Jesuit would take the three morning Masses tomorrow, Sunday.

The only silver lining he could find at this moment was that the routine business of St. Anselm's was coming along fine. Regular calls to and from Mary O'Connor revealed that Deacon Schroeder had neither built his pagoda nor sold the rectory.

Now, if only Les would continue to stay out of Mary's way and let her run things.

———————

Ankenazy explained to Pat Lennon what it was he was about to give her to read. Then he handed her a copy of that section of Thompson's diary that dealt with her. After which Ankenazy stepped back a considerable distance. Fortunately, it was a Saturday afternoon, and only a skeleton editorial staff was in the newsroom.

As Lennon began to read, her eyes widened, and her facial muscles tightened.

" 'Sexy bitch,' " she quoted. " 'Sexy bitch'! Where does he get off calling me a bitch, that bastard!

" 'A light, clinging dress,' " she continued. " 'All the curves are there'! 'Enough to exchange for a bishopric'! All this goddamn son-of-a-bitch needs is to become a bishop! He's already got a goddamn swollen prick!

"I had 'a workable case'! Can you believe this? I had 'a workable case'! The bastard admits it right here!'' In her rage, tears began to flow freely down her cheeks.

The few reporters who were at their desks looked up, startled. They did not know what Lennon's problem was. But whatever it was, obviously this was an explosion of emotion that none of her co-workers would have believed Lennon capable of.

She had always exuded an air of the self-possessed professional. Other women—occasionally even men—in the newsroom had, from time to time, brought their emotional problems to her.

Whatever it was she was reading had stripped from her every veneer of the image of the constantly unruffled, calm, cool woman of the world that Lennon had carefully created. Fellow employees who witnessed her current uninhibited, uncontrolled emotional explosion did not so much lose any of their respect for Lennon and her professionalism as they grew in wonderment at what the document she was reading could possibly contain.

"I wanted that case to go through so damn badly. And it could have! It didn't have to depend on him; it was my right! And he withheld it from me!

"And look at this! Just as I suspected: the bastard just wanted to go to bed with me! He would have dispensed justice if only I had laid him! Oh, that son-of-a-bitch! 'Tit for ass' is it! Thinks he could turn my answer into 'another kind of passion,' does he! 'Tit for ass' is it! Let me get the bastard! I'll kick him in the balls and cut off his goddamn prick! I'll cut the fat off his ass and feed it to the pigs!''

Suddenly, she looked again at the pages Ankenazy had handed her. "Wait a minute," she said, slowly, "this isn't Thompson's diary. It's a copy. Where did you get it?" Before he could answer, she went on, "You got it from the cops who were here, didn't you?"

Ankenazy nodded, afraid to speak.

"And they're not the only ones!" The entire picture was flooding in on her. "Joe Cox has a copy, too, doesn't he? *DOESN'T HE*!" She was nearly shrieking.

"That's why he's been ahead of you on this story, isn't it? It's true, isn't it?"

Again, Ankenazy nodded.

"Damn! Damn, damn, damn, damn, *DAMN*! Joe! Why wouldn't he tell me? Half the city's been reading the filthy things that dirty old man wrote about me, and Joe didn't even tell me."

Ankenazy felt no inclination to come to Joe Cox's defense.

"I've been left naked for the whole city to leer at. And the guy who's supposed to love me just left me there! He didn't even tell me! He didn't even *tell* me! Just who the hell does he think he is? How much does he think he can get away with?"

Ankenazy considered these to be rhetorical questions.

By now she was throwing things. At first, nothing significant. Papers, pencils, ballpoint pens. Then in her rage, she escalated to notepads, paperweights, and books. Ankenazy did not step in until she was about to pitch her CRT unit to the floor. At that point, he took her firmly by the shoulders, then held her tightly.

For a while she continued screeching imprecations and threats. Finally, fury spent, she slumped in Ankenazy's arms, shoulders shaking under the force of silent sobs. He assisted her back into her chair.

"Oh, Bob," she said, haltingly, "it's so terrible. It's like going to communion and finding garbage. I wanted that marriage case to go through so badly. And he toyed with me. Oh, Bob . . ." She dissolved once more in silent sobs.

Ankenazy waited with her until she gradually regained her composure. Several reporters walked by her chair to do no more than put a solicitous hand on her shoulder.

She was still a professional. She realized Ankenazy had a job to do. She gave him his interview. After which, he sent her home. Then he wrote his story, the culmination of the series and, he thought, the most effective of the lot. At one point, he almost described her as the "social companion" of a *Free Press* reporter. But he eschewed that. He didn't give a damn about Cox, but he respected Lennon too much to give anyone a means of identifying her.

———

After what she had gone through that afternoon, it was not unexpected that she didn't have much left to give Joe Cox.

Besides, it took Cox the better part of an hour to try to explain why he had not told her about Thompson's diary. And, in the face of her verbal and literal missiles, his effort never quite reached a level that could be described as successful.

It was not her fault. It was not his fault. But tomorrow morning there would be Nelson Kane to face.

———

Now here's a break in routine for you, Koesler thought.

Ordinarily, he spent the better part of Sunday mornings in church. But, here he was at police headquarters with a man he'd come to know pretty well over the past few years and three others he'd come to know pretty well over the past few days. Sergeants Lynch and Patrick were summing up for Koznicki and Harris what had been gleaned from yesterday's interrogations.

"On the whole," said Patrick, "I'd say we have two more people to add to the four we've already questioned, who had very good reasons to be very angry with Monsignor Thompson."

"Did both Kirwan and Lennon open up?" Harris asked.

"Pretty much," said Lynch. "Kirwan seemed to have nothing to hide. The Polish angle was kind of funny. I didn't know that anyone thought the Polish were more Catholic than, say, the Italians or the Irish."

"Oh, but they are," said Koznicki, smiling. "It comes from the national experience, I believe. There is no doubt the Irish have been persecuted for their Catholic faith for some 800 years. But even that does not compare with the brutalization of the Poles over the centuries. Even today the Church in Poland is under Communist siege. In the face of such opposition, you either become a virtually unshakable Catholic, or you simply abandon that for which you are being persecuted. And the Poles in this country tend to identify and empathize with their compatriots in Poland. So, perhaps, requiring added proof that a Polish person has not had a marriage blessed is not entirely out of the question.

"What would you say, Father?"

Koesler was jolted out of a semi-distracted state. He hadn't expected to be questioned. "I'd say it's a bit of a belt-and-suspenders approach. All that you say is true, Inspector, but the proof of a defect of form presented by the Kirwan couple was sufficient. At least it was sufficient to fulfill all the demands of canon law. The additional required proof represented Monsignor Thompson's demand alone. I had never even heard of that requirement until I came across the reference in the diary, and even then, I didn't know what it was until I read about it in Bob Ankenazy's story in yesterday's *News*. It must be a very recent addition Monsignor Thompson has made in the annulment regulations."

"I stand canonically corrected," said Koznicki.

Koesler felt slightly more relevant.

"What about Lennon?" Harris asked.

"A very testy lady," said Patrick. "Of course, I don't much blame her after what Thompson wrote about her and the way he treated her. I think we were lucky that we were not the first ones to confront her with the diary. She was still hot about it when we questioned her at her apartment. Evidently, Ankenazy showed her the diary right after we let him copy it. And, evidently she got so furious about it, he sent her home early."

"What were these two suspects doing the night of the eleventh?" Harris asked.

"Kirwan says he was home with his wife all evening and all night. She corroborates," said Lynch with a grin. "It figures; they were married only two days before."

"But," said Harris, "that's it: there is no witness other than his wife?"

"That's it," said Lynch.

"How about Lennon?" Harris asked.

"She's in trouble for an alibi," Lynch answered. "She was scheduled to go to Port Huron on the second of a two-part feature she was working on. But she claims she got a call about 9:30 or 10:00. An anonymous tip regarding a local dope ring story she's also been working on. She figured the resorts could wait. She says she was told to drive to Memorial Park, leave her car, and walk down the block to the Detroit River where she would be met by someone who would give her names, dates, and places of the ring's dealings. She claims she waited almost three hours, pacing, and no one showed up. She says all she got out of it was a bad cold that she's still recovering from."

"Can she substantiate any of that?" asked Harris.

"Just the cold," said Lynch. "Her roommate, Joe Cox, was at work at the *Free Press* most of the night. Apparently, no one remembers seeing her leave or return to her apartment building. And, of course, there's no traffic in the park down by the river at that time of night."

"Gutsy gal," commented Harris. "O.K., Patrick, Lynch: see if you can tie this in with the other investigations."

"Other investigations?" Koesler reacted almost involuntarily. He had no idea to what Harris was referring.

Koznicki smiled. "I'm afraid, Father, you have thought that you and Sergeants Patrick and Lynch have been the exclusive investigators in the Thompson case. In reality, you have been part of the principal investigation. But while your investigation has been going on, other officers, some from the Fifteenth, some from Homicide, have been following up, checking alibis, looking into the activities of these suspects during the week leading up to the disappearance—things like that."

The things I don't know about police work, thought Koesler, could fill volumes.

"Tie up all the loose ends this afternoon, if you can," Harris continued, "I'd like to wind this up tomorrow. Tuesday, at the latest."

Patrick and Lynch began putting their papers together preparatory to leaving. Koesler simply sat. Again he felt like excess baggage.

Harris noticed his inactivity and smiled. "Father, why don't you take the rest of the day off? They're just going to be doing routine work."

"Want to come home with me, Father?" Koznicki suggested. "Wanda and the children would be delighted to see you."

"No, thank you, Inspector." Koesler took a deep breath. "It's such a nice day, I think I'll just go out to the lake."

They parted, some to work, others to play.

If anyone felt like a puppy that had misbehaved, was repentant, and contrite, yet feared punishment at the hand of its master, it was Joe Cox.

Before even looking at Bob Ankenazy's story, Cox had strongly suspected it would be better than his. Reading the account in Sunday's *News* confirmed his fears.

Then the call had come from Nelson Kane summoning Cox to the *Free Press*, even though it was Sunday and his day off. As he left the elevator and entered the city room, Cox felt as if he had a tail and that it was between his legs.

In the large, rectangular, nearly deserted city room, Kane sat at his desk, his teeth working an unlit cigar. Cox slunk into the chair adjacent to Kane's desk.

"You've read the *News*?" Kane did not look at Cox.

Cox nodded. Then, realizing Kane was not looking at him, he articulated his response. "Yes." He almost added, Sir.

"You realize Ankenazy interviewed the woman you live with?" Kane's voice was remarkably restrained.

"Yes."

"You realize his interview was better than yours?"

"Yes."

296

"Lots better?"

"Yes."

"In future, when I tell you you're getting too goddamn cocky and to get off your ass and dig up some leads, will you listen to me?"

"Yes."

"And will you do what I tell you?"

"Yes."

"O.K. Now get off your ass and dig up some leads. I want to give this series a decent burial. Got it?"

"Yes."

In the elevator, Cox wished Kane had yelled at him as was the usual treatment dished out when he'd been less than perfect. He felt worse now than he had before.

In the city room, after the elevator door had closed behind Cox, Nelson Kane picked up a huge ancient dictionary. He held it above his head with both hands and brought it crashing down against his desk. The impact sounded like an explosion. The heads of the few copy editors and reporters present popped up. It would be a few minutes before their hearts would resume a normal beat.

Kane had broken the binding of the dictionary.

But he felt better.

The Casey children had gone downtown to take in the Greek Ethnic Festival at Hart Plaza. Thus, given the usual chaotic commotion in the Casey yard, things now seemed sepulchral. Joe and Irene and Father Koesler, each with a Stroh's in hand, sat at the picnic table near the shore of Green Lake. The rowboat bobbed in the gentle current. Sailboats tacked in wide arcs searching for a breeze.

Each had a beer, God was in His heaven, all was right with the world.

"How's everything at the paper?" Koesler asked. He did not want to mention or discuss his quasi-police work of late, so he tried to steer the conversation down other paths.

"Oh, pretty much the same," said Irene. "Jim Pool is working on getting out a back-to-school supplement for the end of this month.''

Koesler shook his head and chuckled. ''Jim and his supplements. One of these days, he'll probably suggest an atheists' supplement.''

''We shouldn't make light of Jim's supplements,'' said Joe. ''They bring in much-needed revenue from the advertisers they attract.''

''That reminds me,'' said Irene, enthusiastically, ''we've got a new advertiser.''

''For the supplement?'' asked Joe.

''Nope, for the paper. Just signed a six-month contract. This one looks like he might become a permanent advertiser. The man even took me out to lunch.'' Irene made the announcement triumphantly.

''Who is this knight in shining money?'' asked Joe. In an oversight rare for her, Irene had neglected to mention the new advertiser to her husband.

''Leo Cicero. He owns Cicero Construction.''

''Leo Cicero?'' asked Koesler. ''You wouldn't happen to know if he belongs to Divine Child parish?''

''As a matter of fact, I do know. And he does. It's amazing what you learn over a luncheon.''

Koesler was surprised at the apparent coincidence. ''You wouldn't also happen to know if his wife's name—''

''—is Angela,'' Irene supplied. ''Is that the right name?''

Koesler nodded.

''They must be an extremely close couple. He mentioned her frequently.''

It was an amazing coincidence, Koesler thought. Strange how often the cliché, it's a small world, proved true.

''You know what I found really surprising?'' Irene enthused. ''Here this nice Mr. Cicero owns a construction company. And yet he does most of the work around the house himself. Things like wiring, plumbing, gardening.''

''Most of those guys do,'' observed Joe. ''If they came up the hard way, they like—''

''—to keep their hand in,'' Irene concluded.

''You know, Leo—he told me to call him by his first name—''

298

she blushed, "Leo said that just last week he and his wife finished some work in their basement. Seems one corner had been bricked off during the original construction. To hide some pipes, I guess. Well, the Ciceros bricked off the other side just to make it symmetrical. Isn't that great of them? To build their own brick wall in their basement? And him with his own construction company!"

"Well, that's the way it is with those guys," Joe drained his can of beer. Fortunately, there were many more where that came from. "If they came up the hard way, they like—"

"—to keep their hand in," Irene again assisted.

Koesler could not recover from his surprise at this coincidence. Imagine, he thought, here I am, a member of an investigative team that interrogates Angela Cicero as a possible murder suspect, while, in the very same week, her husband has lunch with Irene and signs an ad contract with the *Detroit Catholic*.

It is, he thought, a small world indeed.

It came to him while he was showering early Monday morning.

That frequently was the case with Father Koesler. Showering involved such a series of repetitive, automatic actions that, aided by the soothing flow of hot water, his mind tended to wander freely. Often, some of his best ideas came during his morning shower.

Memories of chance remarks tiptoed tantalizingly through his consciousness. What was it Sergeant Patrick had remarked about Angela Cicero?—"Maybe she's building a Panama Canal in her basement like that crazy nephew in 'Arsenic and Old Lace.'"

Then that earlier conversation when Lieutenant Harris said something about the investigation running into a brick wall. To which Patrick had commented regarding Angela, "The one big thing she's got going for her is that we haven't got a body."

All these thoughts had been exhumed by the memory of what Irene Casey had said just yesterday. "The Ciceros bricked off the other side just to make it symmetrical. Isn't that great of them? To build their own brick wall in their basement?"

Brick wall. Body. Panama Canal in the basement. Brick wall in the basement. It all fit together like yin and yang. There was only one missing piece to his puzzle—the item he had been promising himself he would check but had been constantly postponing.

He would postpone it no longer. Half-showered, he stepped out of the stall, wrapped a towel around his middle, and scurried down the hallway to the living room bookshelf.

A startled Deacon Schroeder watched openmouthed as the dishabilléd Koesler peered myopically among the shelves. Finally, he found the volume he was seeking and returned with it to his bedroom.

As Koesler left the living room, Schroeder commented, "That must be *some* book!"

Koesler sat on the edge of his bed, balanced the huge Poe anthology on his towel-clad lap, and slowly opened it to the middle. To the point where he remembered Angela's bookmark appearing in her own volume.

He knew it! There it was. "The Cask of Amontillado," Poe's tale of vengeance wherein the victim is sealed behind a wine cellar wall.

Koesler was agog. He was also undecided as to whether to complete his shower before phoning Inspector Koznicki. He decided he could shower anytime. It wasn't every day a simple parish priest could solve a murder.

He dialed Koznicki's home. The Inspector had not yet left for work. The priest carefully explained all the clues that had led to his conclusion. He could feel the Inspector catch the enthusiasm of putting the puzzle together.

"All right, Father, it seems to make great good sense," said Koznicki. "If you are correct, then Monsignor Thompson has been behind that wall for more than a week now. Haste is no longer necessary."

For the first time, Koesler wavered. He had drawn all but the final conclusion—that if his theory were correct, his classmate had been long dead. His mind rattled: if Thompson's body were behind the Ciceros' wall, wouldn't there be—an odor? But, maybe . . . maybe it was zipped into one of those heavy plastic bags that— He was brought back from his macabre musings by

Koznicki's voice. "Which means," the Inspector concluded, "that we proceed by the book. I will pick up the court order for search, and we will pick you up on our way over. You do want to be in on the end of this, don't you?"

Koesler pulled himself together.

"Oh, yes. But I think it might be better if I drive myself. That way I'll feel more free to stay around in case there is any counseling needed."

"Very well, Father. Figure on meeting us at the Cicero house in about an hour and a half."

That was more than enough time for Koesler to finish showering and shave. There was enough time left over to get through both the mail and the *Free Press*. Which he would have done if he hadn't been so excited.

———————

Leo Cicero had been called home for the event. He stood in his basement, a bewildered man. Angela had passed bewilderment minutes before. She was in full fury.

Koznicki, Harris, Patrick, Koesler, and the Ciceros stood by while Lynch let fly with a sledgehammer against the newly erected brick wall. With his long, deceptively slender but strong arms as a lever, it took Lynch only four blows before a sizable section of the upper wall crumbled.

Lynch stood back. Koznicki stepped forward with a large flashlight. He waited a moment for the dust to settle, then he peered into the space behind the wall. He drew back with a noncommittal expression. He handed the flashlight to Harris. Harris peered behind the wall. He, too, stepped away from the wall with a noncommittal expression. The identical routine was followed by both Patrick and Lynch.

Koesler's by this time overwrought brain was no longer functioning reasonably. Visions swam before him of the rotting corpse in the exhumation scene of Dumas's "Lady of the Camellias," of the taxidermically preserved mother in "Psycho"—he could only imagine the similar horror that must rest behind that brick wall. Probably a skeleton strapped to a chair, the skull fallen back, sockets staring blindly into the torch's bright beam.

Lynch handed the flashlight to Koesler. With considerable trepidation—he did not have a strong stomach for this sort of thing—Koesler moved to the jagged hole and peered in.

The tomb was empty. Thompson had not risen. He had never been there.

Koesler was speechless. Which did not happen often.

One by one, they filed by the stunned priest. Each patted him on the shoulder.

"You can't win 'em all," said Lynch.

"It did sort of make sense," said Patrick.

"Well, Father Clouseau, you've done it again," said Harris.

"We all make these little mistakes from time to time," said Koznicki.

The Inspector addressed the Ciceros. "Please accept our apologies. The city will pay for the damage, of course. You may send the bill to my office at headquarters."

"Who's going to pay for the humiliation of it all is what I want to know!" spat out the furious Angela. "Who's going to pay for my husband's having to take time off from his work! Who?"

"No payment can be made for any of that," Koznicki explained. "But we will pay for the property damage. And, of course, again, we do offer our sincere apologies."

The four policemen started up the stairs.

"Why did they think somebody was in there?" asked the still bewildered Leo.

"You think you can just come in and break up people's homes and just walk out? Well, we'll just see about that!" Angela hurled her words like harpoons at the four backs ascending the steps.

Koesler now bemoaned the fact that he had driven over himself. Originally, he had intended to stay if counseling or support were required. If anyone now needed support it was Koesler, who, as the author of this fine mess, was now left to pay the price.

He spent the next hour and better being gaped at by Leo Cicero, who never quite comprehended the event, and being bawled out by an unflaggingly enraged Angela Cicero.

Unbloody but bowed, Koesler finally departed the Cicero residence with one predominant thought: Methinks the lady doth protest too much.

———————

It was Tuesday morning, August 21. Father Koesler considered his participation in the Thompson investigation finished. As of yesterday, he had given the full week asked of him by Inspector Koznicki. And especially after yesterday's performance at the Ciceros', he had decided to retire from police work defeated.

In order to get back in the routine of parish life, Koesler was making some remote preparation for next Sunday's sermon. The Gospel text included the passage wherein Jesus asks His followers, "Who do men say I am?"

He was consulting H. L. Mencken's *A New Dictionary of Quotations on Historical Principles from Ancient and Modern Sources*. Under the category of "Reputation," he came across a Spanish proverb: *He who has lost his reputation is a walking corpse.*

Koesler marveled at how aptly that seemed to describe Tommy Thompson now. Thanks to his absence, the discovery of his diary, and the ensuing publicity in both metropolitan daily papers, Thompson might just as well be a walking corpse, if not a corpse in actuality, for he surely had lost his reputation.

At that point, the phone rang. Mary O'Connor informed him that the caller was Inspector Koznicki. Koesler could think of no reason the Inspector would be calling this morning. And then he wondered if the city had decided to stick him with the bill for the Ciceros' basement wall. It was with some misgivings he picked up the phone.

"Father, we're going to tie things together this morning in the Thompson case. We should be able, after that, to determine whether to continue our investigation and, if the answer is affirmative, what kind of manpower we should afford it. Can you be with us?"

"You mean after yesterday . . ." In the wake of the Cicero fiasco, the last thing Koesler expected was to be invited back into the fray.

He could hear Koznicki chuckle.

"When yesterday becomes sufficiently a thing of the past, you will find humor in it. Trust me.

"In the meantime, you have been a part of this investigation. And I would appreciate any insights you might have."

Reluctantly, Koesler agreed to attend the meeting.

Before leaving for downtown, he glanced again at Mencken's reference book. *He who has lost his reputation is a walking corpse.* Poor Tommy.

Koesler felt as if he were going to a wake.

———————

Father Koesler was surprised at the number of police in attendance. There had to be twenty-five or thirty.

All who had been in any way involved in the Thompson investigation were present. Some were from the Fifteenth Precinct, some from Headquarters, and some from Homicide.

A spokesperson for each team of officers reported on what they had discovered. After all the reports had been presented, Lieutenant Harris summed up.

"The most significant new information comes from Lynch and Patrick. Yesterday, they returned to Roma Hall and questioned the parking attendant again. He now admits that he cut himself on the cartridge casing. He picked it up from the floor and left it on the car seat. Where it came from and why it was in the car we don't know. We do know that at least some of the blood on the tissue is his. Whether any of the blood is Thompson's is doubtful; unfortunately, both the attendant and Thompson have the same blood type. The Monsignor's pistol is still missing, and we have no explanation for the lack of prints inside the car.

"Mary Alberts, Thompson's secretary, could think of only one out-of-the-ordinary incident in the time frame we're dealing with. At one point, she found some of the Tribunal files out of order. She mentioned this to Thompson, who did not seem to consider it of any importance.

"Now, let's consider our suspects.

"We know from Thompson's diary and from their own statements that all had ample reason to seek revenge if they were so inclined. So, let's take for granted there is sufficient motive in each case.

"First, there is Angela Cicero. From our interrogation of both Mr. and Mrs. Cicero, we know she was responsible for her husband's joining a bowling team. She alone arranged for him to be out of the house and thus for her to be alone during the crucial hours Saturday night, the eleventh of August. She has no alibi for that night. She claims she was called to the scene of an accident involving her daughter—an accident that turned out to be nonexistent. No one can substantiate this claim. However, we do know she did not bury Thompson behind the wall in her basement.''

A hoot of laughter came from the assemblage. Koesler blushed. This was his first intimation that he had become notorious throughout the department.

"Next," Harris continued from his notes, "we have Lee Brand. Obviously, Brand was aboard a ship and not in this area at the time of Thompson's disappearance. So he begins with a pretty good alibi. Something out of the ordinary does seem to have occurred midway through the week before Brand sailed. According to his travel agent, he ordered another cabin in addition to the one he and his wife would occupy. Brand did not give the name of any individual who would be occupying this cabin, which is listed in his name. However, according to the agent, this sort of extravagance is not unusual for Brand, who frequently will provide for a possible business traveling companion. The provision does not always work out. In addition, we have the results of the investigation carried out at our request by the Vancouver police, which indicated there are no Detroit-area passengers other than the Brands; the passenger manifest substantiates that finding.

"Next, we have David Neiss, a Catholic priest. The only unusual event we found regarding Neiss during the week of August 5—and this we have from his own voluntary admission during interrogation—was a visit to Club Libra, a topless bar."

There was an undercurrent of snickering.

"Evidently, this was entirely out of character for Neiss. One of the dancers there is a former parishioner and was a member of a parish club Neiss moderated. She states that Neiss was not

305

in the club the night of Saturday the eleventh. His alibi is tissue-thin, however. He claims he was summoned to a sick call, the address of which turned out to be nonexistent.

"Next, we have Norman Shanley, another Catholic priest. He is in temporary residence in a penthouse leased by Brand at 1300 Lafayette East. During the week of August 5, he visited the crematorium of Woodward Cemetery. Our source is the manager of the cemetery, who happened to see him enter and leave the crematorium." He looked up from his notes, grinning. "We had a bit of luck here; the manager happens to be a resident of 1300 Lafayette East. His apartment is on the floor directly beneath the penthouse. We got his testimony during a routine questioning of neighbors of the Brand apartment.

"However, the maintenance operator of the crematorium states that Shanley did not return there again and undoubtedly was not there the night of the eleventh, since the cemetery was locked, and he would have needed keys. Shanley has no substantial alibi for the eleventh. He states he was in the penthouse alone, expecting a visit from another priest. The other priest states he received an unexpected visitor at his rectory, tried to call Shanley, but the phone was temporarily out of service."

Koesler was taking notes assiduously on a large legal pad he had brought with him. Occasionally, he made additional notations in the margins.

"Next," Harris intoned, "is Harry Kirwan. During the week of August 5, he made an unscheduled and unexpected visit to a Bell Telephone facility under construction in Dearborn. This we have from Kirwan himself in his accounting for his whereabouts during that week. However, the night watchman states Kirwan was not at the site on the night of the eleventh. Kirwan's wife states they were together all that night. They were married just two days before."

More snickers.

"Finally, we have Patricia Lennon. During the week of the fifth, she took a *Detroit News* auto on a story assignment to Port Huron. This is confirmed by the logs kept at the news desk. On the night of the eleventh, she again checked out a *News* vehicle. She claims she was called to a meeting with a news source who did not show up. The odometer figures in the log indicate that she did not drive far enough to leave the corporate limits of the city of Detroit.

"There is one more consideration. From the testimony of the waiters at Roma Hall, we know that Thompson appeared to have been enticed; he was in a hurry to leave the hall, and he went willingly, even eagerly."

Harris looked up and paused. He had spoken a long time, and his voice sounded harsh.

"Well, ladies and gentlemen, any ideas?" Harris opened it up to the floor.

"From what Thompson wrote in his diary," offered one officer, "it doesn't take much imagination to figure what the two women could entice him with."

General laughter. Koesler continued to write as if Harris had not finished speaking.

"Brand and Kirwan could have offered him something of value," said another officer, "but I can't see either of those two priests coming up with anything that would get him to come out. I would, for the moment, discount the priests."

There was a murmur of agreement. Koesler, who had stopped writing, seemed lost in thought.

"That odometer reading on Lennon's car that indicated she hadn't left Detroit," said a third officer, "well, odometers can be adjusted—and rather easily."

This comment launched general subdued conversation. Koesler's eyes were closed, but his lips were moving silently. He seemed to be having an argument with himself.

"That Cicero woman," said a fourth officer, "she deliberately cleared the way to do something she didn't want anybody to know about on Saturday night. I'd go back and lean on her story again."

The murmur following this opinion seemed equally divided between agreement and disagreement.

Koesler cleared his throat. First hesitantly, then more loudly.

Conversation came to a stop; all eyes turned toward the priest. After his blunder the previous day, no one could believe Koesler would dare offer another hypothesis. Only Koznicki smiled confidently. He had the deepest respect for his friend's mind. The very fact that Koesler would speak at this meeting after what had taken place yesterday reinforced Koznicki's confidence in him.

In the strained silence, Koesler's voice sounded strange even to himself. "I think I know," he said, "where Monsignor Thompson is."

9

KOESLER FOUND HIMSELF STANDING; HE WAS not sure why. It was almost as if he were a child again, reciting in school.

There was no doubt he had his audience's attention. Either incredulously or credulously, the police officers were listening so intently one could have heard the proverbial pin.

"Now I'm sure I can't answer all your questions just yet. We don't even know all the questions yet. But let's look at what we do know and what, from this knowledge, we can safely infer.

"When I sat here listening to Lieutenant Harris summarize the result of everyone's investigation, a pattern emerged. It sounded as if each suspect seems to have made a plan for the week in question—during which it was generally known *where* the Monsignor was going to be on the eleventh and approximately *when*. Perhaps each suspect's plan revolved around Monsignor Thompson, perhaps not. But, if we assume that each had something in mind, each seems to have carried out what could appear to be only half a plan, which is very strange.

"One makes sure she is free to do whatever she wishes on the night in question but claims to have been sent on a wild goose chase that can be neither proved nor disproved.

"Another reserves an extra cabin on a ship. Now, there's a definite plan of some sort there. But, apparently, he does not use the cabin, which is listed under his name.

309

"Another visits a topless bar for, as far as is known, the first time in his life. Did he intend to meet or take Monsignor there on the eleventh? As far as we know, the suspect did not even go to the bar on the eleventh, nor did the Monsignor.

"Another visits a crematorium. Ominous by anyone's standards, particularly if we are looking for a missing person and cannot even find his body. Yet, the suspect appears not to have returned to the crematorium.

"Another visits a construction site. A marvelous place for a body; who's going to tear down a building to see if someone is buried in its foundation? But the suspect does not return to that site.

"Finally, a suspect drives a good number of miles to reach the locale of an assignment. A locale to which she is scheduled to return on Saturday night. What is in the vicinity of that locale? For one thing, the desolate shoreline of Lake Huron. Another handy place to deposit a body. And on the night of the disappearance, the suspect again checks out a company car, which she had reserved earlier in the week. But she does not go to the locale earlier planned; instead she ends up, she says, in a fruitless wait for a news source and, according to mileage records, does not leave the Detroit city limits."

"Wait a minute, Father," Patrick interrupted. "You're limiting your consideration to each of the suspects separately. What if they were acting in consort? What if it's a conspiracy? What if each carried out only part of the entire plot? You know, the whole is equal to the sum of all its parts. What if they are all in this together, like the characters in Agatha Christie's 'Orient Express'?"

Ah, thought Koesler, another mystery buff. You never know where they're going to pop up.

"That's an interesting notion, Sergeant," said Koesler. "But, with all due respect, I don't think it will hold up. In 'The Orient Express,' not only did all the suspects know each other, they were all on the same train. Here, at least five of the six suspects share only one thing—inclusion in Monsignor Thompson's diary. And since there is no indication they had known of the diary or had the opportunity of reading it prior to the disappearance,

310

most of them, at least, would not even know of the others' existence."

Koesler returned to his previous line of conjecture. "So, you see, each seems to have, in effect, carried out half a plan. But if each carried out only half a plan, then where is Monsignor Thompson? He should be here among us. But obviously, he is not. If he were, he certainly would not stand idly by while his reputation was being destroyed.

"First of all, I believe he is alive. I believe this for several reasons. First, and least of all, is his constant and rather annoying habit of telling everyone that nothing ever happens to him.

"Second, I don't think any of our suspects would make a very good murderer. And, I think that the fact that—to all appearances—one plan after another was not carried through is an indication of that. Now, of course, there is always the possibility that a person or persons unknown could be responsible for whatever has happened to Monsignor Thompson. Obviously, if he provokes a spirit of vengeance from six people we know, he is quite capable of provoking such a spirit from any number of people we don't know.

"However—and here I come to the third and most important point—I don't think the person responsible for Monsignor's mysterious absence had to kill him to get revenge. I call your attention to the Spanish proverb . . ." Koesler quoted the proverb as if it had only suddenly occurred to him; he thought he would allow himself a flamboyant touch at this point. " 'He who has lost his reputation is a walking corpse.' If Monsignor Thomas Thompson's reputation has been destroyed—and I think we all would agree that it most certainly has . . ." Here and there around the room, heads nodded. ". . . then there is no need to kill him physically. The man is already a walking corpse.

"But, we have said that if Monsignor were alive, and if he were here, he would not have allowed the destruction of his precious reputation. So, obviously, either he is not here—or if he is, he is not able to do anything about what is happening. And, I asked myself, who was in a position to arrange for such a circumstance—to remove Monsignor Thompson from the scene and yet keep him alive?

"Lee Brand, of course. He began the actualization of his plan

311

far from the Detroit area and has remained far, far away throughout.''

There was a good deal of tumult among the officers.

"Wait a minute," one shouted above the others, "Brand sailed with his extra cabin empty and as late as last Wednesday, five days after Thompson disappeared, he still was not aboard the *Alaskan Queen*!"

It took Koznicki almost a full minute to quiet the group.

"Let's postpone considering Mr. Brand and his empty cabin for a few minutes," said Koesler, when comparative quiet was restored. "Let's go back in time to when I first met the Brands. It was at the Fourth of July party at their home. Somebody, I think it was Brand's wife, expressed the fear that something might spoil their daughter's upcoming wedding. Brand said something about how that couldn't happen, not with Monsignor Thompson as part of their game plan.

"I mention this only to emphasize how dependent Lee Brand had made himself upon the Monsignor. We all know, from reading his diary, how the Monsignor manipulated and abused that dependency.

"The next time I met Brand was in his office. In the short time I was there, I was amazed to hear him make two very questionable business rulings. He ordered an extremely low prime rate given to a man who, apparently, was in a position to grant Brand special favors. On the other hand, he denied a letter of credit to a man who obviously had every right to it, only because Brand disliked the man's wife, who had gotten drunk at a Brand party.

"To me, this is an indication that Mr. Brand does not just talk a good fight, he fights the fight. He is a mover and shaker, a wheeler and dealer. He is wily and ruthless. And he is not the type to be satisfied with half a plan. With, in effect, no more than a daydream.

"Now, I'd like to bring up a couple of incidents that occurred, I think a week ago, Monday, when this investigation began.

"The first took place in an office just down the hall. Joe Cox brought in Monsignor's diary. Cox went from the defensive to the offensive when you began pressing him on his having taken the diary. I believe he said something to the effect that you guys—
312

meaning you police—passed right over the diary earlier in the afternoon. Now, apparently, the officers in Homicide did not get to St. David's rectory before Cox. Their involvement did not begin until the day *after* Cox found the diary. Homicide officers assumed Cox had been preceded by officers from the Fifteenth Precinct.

"However, later that Monday morning, I was privy to a conversation between Inspectors O'Hara and Koznicki. As they were parting, Inspector O'Hara said something about the Fifteenth and Homicide starting out even. And Inspector Koznicki pointed out that it was officers from the Fifteenth who had found the car. In turn, Inspector O'Hara responded that it was Homicide who had turned in the missing person report on the Monsignor. At which point, Inspector Koznicki agreed that the two departments were, indeed, starting even. There was utterly no mention of anyone's having searched St. David's rectory before Cox got there.

"At the time, I remember wondering if there were a third police force in this somewhere. Apparently, someone giving the semblance of police searched Monsignor's belongings before Cox did. Now, St. David's housekeeper mistook Cox's press credentials for police identification. Who else, I asked myself, carries credentials that could resemble police identification?

"When I was in Brand's office, I remember expressing some amazement at what the man could accomplish. He replied—and he did so so confidently that I recall his reply verbatim—'Private investigative agencies are good at quietly gathering information and arranging things that need to be arranged.' And I recall thinking about what he said and how he said it, 'My God, you've got your own police force.'

"So, it's my theory that it was Mr. Brand's private investigative agents who found Monsignor's diary. And I suggest that when they entered the rectory, it was not to take anything, but to put the diary where it would be certain to be found.

"Brand knew who was mentioned pejoratively in the diary. However, Brand's knowledge of this leads me to at least a partial solution to another part of this puzzle. Of the six suspects, only two have seemingly satisfactory alibis. Brand is one. The other is Harry Kirwan, the only suspect not mentioned in the diary.

Which leads me to the hypothesis that somehow Brand is responsible for the fact that the four others mentioned in the diary do not have alibis. He could not arrange the same fate for Kirwan for the simple reason that he did not know of Kirwan's existence.

"But I have no idea how he managed this. This is one of the unanswered questions.

"Finally, we come to the *Alaskan Queen* and the empty cabin, which, I believe, is filled with Monsignor Thompson."

By now, none of his audience was dubious; they were all taking notes furiously.

"A good percentage of the clergy are, from time to time, invited to be chaplains on a cruise. Even I have had such an invitation. As you can guess, the chaplain does not pay for his voyage. He is remunerated. However, as an employee of the cruise, his name does not appear on the passenger manifest. It is on the crew manifest.

"That, in conclusion, is what I think happened to Monsignor Thompson. Mr. Brand made him an offer he couldn't refuse. Probably via ship-to-shore phone. Brand arranged for the Monsignor's transportation to a subsequent port-of-call. Once the Monsignor got aboard, Brand arranged for him to become ship's chaplain. That would have pleased the Monsignor. He wouldn't have to be beholden to Brand. You asked the Vancouver police to send you a copy of the passenger manifest. I think you will find his name on the *crew* manifest."

Koesler sat down. He had talked himself out. He was exhausted. But so sure was he that he had solved the mystery that he also was on an emotional high.

There was a pause while all that Koesler had conjectured was absorbed.

"There's one way of checking this out," Harris broke the silence. "Lynch, call the *Alaskan Queen*. Tell them to check the crew manifest!"

Lynch left the room at a brisk gait. The air buzzed with murmured conversation. It was about fifteen minutes before Lynch returned.

"Thompson is a member of the crew," he announced. "The ship will dock in Vancouver tomorrow morning."

The murmurs grew louder.

"All right," said Koznicki, "enough! Patrick, get a plane to Vancouver. Take the diary and the newspaper clippings with you. Get on that ship and get to the bottom of this. Lieutenant Harris and Inspector O'Hara will handle the clean-up investigation."

The room was a hubbub.

A now-beaming Koznicki approached Koesler still seated in the rear of the squad room.

"Father," said Koznicki, almost scooping the priest up, "come with me. I would like to buy you a very good lunch.

"Now, tell me: what gave you your first inkling? What was the tipoff?"

"Well," Koesler answered, "when we discovered it was the parking attendant's blood on the tissues, I started with the supposition that maybe Tommy was alive and well. Then I just went on from there."

The two had a delightful and extended luncheon.

10

MEANWHILE, BACK ON THE *ALASKAN QUEEN*

IT WAS FRIGHTENING. NOTHING SEPARATED THEM FROM THE now foreboding Pacific but a narrow ridge of planking. In spite of himself, Brand was filled with dread. Thompson, a shadow of his usually alert self, seemed oblivious.

"Where? Where?" Thompson continued to scan the skies for the elusive lifeboats.

"Right up there, Monsignor. One deck above us."

Thompson leaned precariously over the edge. "Oh, yeah. I see 'em now."

Thompson was only one small nudge from joining the fish of the sea. Vengeance is mine, thought Brand.

No, rather vengeance *will* be mine, Brand amended.

He was like the hunter who stalks his prey only for the sake of the hunt. Only to prove to himself he could have killed. It was too easy. Only Brand's most trusted employees knew Thompson was aboard. Had Brand pushed ever so slightly, only the fish would have known that Thompson had left the ship.

But no; Brand far preferred his original plan. Thompson would go on living while, unbeknownst to him, his reputation was slowly swirling down the drain.

Instead of launching Thompson on a brief but terminal underwater adventure, Brand helped him toward sobriety. It was not difficult. Alcohol passed through Thompson at a remarkable rate, aided by the meal Brand had sent to the cabin.

Had his hand been forced, Brand would have arranged for the ship's Catholic chaplain to be called away—or induced away. But, as fate had it, the Coastal Line had only a minister and a rabbi for this cruise. The priest had had to cancel at the last minute, and there had been no time to book a replacement.

Thus, the Captain was delighted to learn that Monsignor Thompson would be willing to act as Catholic chaplain. Catholics aboard had already missed Mass on Sunday once, and many were uneasy about it, even though it was explained there was no sin involved since it had been impossible for them to attend. The Captain never had that problem with Protestants or Jews, only Catholics. He was particularly pleased his new-found chaplain who would offer Mass daily held the rank of monsignor. It added a touch of class.

Thompson, for his part, did not mind in the least. Having the status of ship's chaplain and being, in effect, a member of the crew, freed him from obligation to Brand.

Thompson had not known what to expect from Brand in this new relationship Brand had engineered. His uncertainty had been the cause of Thompson's bringing his pistol along on this trip. He did not mind offering Mass daily; although ordinarily, on vacation he preferred ridding himself of all occupational hazards. But the minor inconvenience of spending thirty-five to forty minutes daily on Mass was little enough to pay for the supreme luxury of a cruise.

Brand had provided all the clothing Thompson needed. There was no reason not to suppose that Brand had also made all necessary provisions for Thompson's absence from the Detroit diocese, particularly in view of Monsignor Iming's telegram. All was well.

For Brand, the only fly in the pie occurred while the ship was docked in Vancouver en route to the scenic Inside Passage. First, it had been the Vancouver police, who had politely requested a copy of the passenger manifest from the purser's office, and just as politely questioned Brand. Could he give them his whereabouts from the time he'd left Detroit the previous week, why were two cabins listed in his name, and could he tell them anything of the whereabouts of one Monsignor Thomas Thompson.

He hadn't needed many lies to answer them. He'd been on the ship since leaving Los Angeles, the extra cabin was for private cocktail parties he liked to throw—the public rooms are so . . . public; and no, he had no idea where Monsignor Thompson might be. Which, at that moment, was exactly true: Thompson could have been in any of a dozen activity rooms on any of six decks.

However, the police visit did put him on the alert. By the time the reporters from the two Vancouver papers came on board, Brand had arranged for Thompson to have a lengthy private tour of the entire ship, including the bridge. There Thompson became fascinated with all the gadgetry, the one sonar and two radar scopes, the port and starboard automatic pilots. And there Thompson was able to bother the navigator with so many questions—maximum speed? Twenty-five knots. Cruise speed? Twenty-one knots—to the point where the navigator considered abandoning ship.

Fortunately for Brand, the reporters came to him first. He was not only able to lie glibly, as only Brand could, but he was also able to play the cooperative and concerned source, accompanying each of the reporters, in turn, to the purser's office, where he requested and received for them a copy of the passenger manifest.

In actuality, Brand would not have considered his caper a failure even if Thompson had been discovered in Vancouver either by police or reporters. He was sure that if even part of Thompson's diary reached the public eye, the consequences for Thompson would be ruinous. But the longer Thompson's whereabouts remained undiscovered, the more time there was for Brand's plan—that the whole story be told.

And it was. Day after day, Brand received reports on what the *News* and the *Free Press* were publishing. While the rest of the passengers got a daily news bulletin containing only capsule resumes of major national and international news stories such as quakes in California and unrest in the Middle East, Brand alone received the juicy gossip from Detroit.

As the ship cruised the Inside Passage, docked at Ketchikan

and Juneau, and went through Glacier Bay, all went well. Thompson made new friends among the very wealthy and took notes to add to his diary on his return. Lee and Sunny Brand seemed happy and relaxed as they ate well and frequently, jogged in the morning, and danced late into the night.

All the while, and known only to Lee Brand, in Detroit, Monsignor Thompson was becoming a walking corpse.

It was in Sitka, Alaska, on August 21, with only five days left in the cruise, that the idea of having his cake and eating it too reoccurred to Lee Brand. Things had been going so well for him and his cause, he decided he could, with impunity, destroy Thompson's reputation and the Monsignor to boot.

It would happen as the result of an unfortunate accident. But it would have to wait till August 23, after the ship left Vancouver and cruised down the coast toward San Francisco. Once out of the passage, on the open sea, the entertainment director could once more stage the skeet shooting contests. Brand was familiar enough with skeet shooting to know exactly what he wanted done.

Each shooter is permitted four consecutive shots at each turn. Brand need only reach the officer in charge of the ammunition. He, in turn, would make sure the third shell would have an inadequate supply of powder, thus jamming the barrel. The fourth shell would hold an inordinately heavy supply of powder. On the fourth shot, the skeet bore would explode in Thompson's face and the poor Monsignor would die. Accidentally, of course.

Brand was well-aware that in bribing a ship's officer to rig the ammunition, he would be moving out of the safety of his own tightly knit organization for the first time in l'affaire Thompson. He was also cognizant of the element of great jeopardy in such a movement. Neither of these considerations was of sufficient weight, in Brand's mind, to deter him from arranging for Thompson's demise.

For one, Brand found the jeopardy itself attractive. Part of what motivated him finally to have Thompson killed was that Brand had become bored playing cat and mouse. Like Henry Higgins, once Brand knew he'd won, the game grew deadly dull.

Secondly, he did not fear moving beyond his circle of trusted employees and, in effect, placing himself in a vulnerable position as far as a mere ship's officer was concerned. His supreme faith in the power of Money far outweighed any fear that the officer might implicate him.

If the officer were to take umbrage when propositioned, why, it would be his word against Brand's. No contest. However, once the officer decided to play along, he would be as deeply implicated as Brand. His own participation would ensure his silence.

But the most substantive reason for Brand's confidence was Money. It was Brand's basic philosophical approach to life: all one needed to do was ascertain how much a person demanded for whatever it was you wanted him to do. Pay the sum. And watch the deed get done. It had worked too perfectly in the past for Brand to have any serious qualms about its effectiveness now.

The *Alaskan Queen* docked in Vancouver August 22 at 9 A.M. It was scheduled to leave port again at noon. After which Brand could begin putting his ultimate solution into operation.

However, a few minutes after docking, a tall, handsome, disheveled man boarded the *Queen*. He identified himself as Sergeant Dean Patrick of the Homicide Division of the Detroit Police Department. A member of the Vancouver police accompanied him to substantiate Patrick's official status and to provide jurisdiction if such were needed.

Patrick asked to be directed to Monsignor Thompson.

A deck steward took both officers to the Lido Terrace on Promenade Deck. Patrick instantly recognized Brand and Thompson, who were seated at the same table, drinking coffee. Patrick had seen too many pictures of both men to mistake either of them.

It was odd seeing Thompson in the flesh. Patrick had come to take so for granted that the Monsignor was dead, the detective had never expected to see him alive.

Patrick introduced himself and pulled up a chair. Brand seemed more startled than Thompson by Patrick's presence.

As Patrick explained his mission and began showing the newspaper clippings to Thompson, Brand relaxed and smiled. The game was over. There would be no ultimate solution tomorrow. But he had won the game going away and had been saved from committing a murder that already in hindsight would seem to have been a disastrous mistake. Besides, had he had the

Monsignor done away with, Brand would never have been able to enjoy the cleric's woe at learning what had happened to his reputation.

And woe it was. As Thompson read the clippings, presented in chronological order, his face took on a progressively deeper hue. It was a combination of embarrassment and rage. As he neared the final clipping, he grew livid and began to sputter.

"What is the meaning of this outrage! Who is responsible for this! Where did this come from!"

The other passengers on the terrace looked on, evidencing awkwardness over the disturbance. This was not good form. Some of the onlookers were among the wealthy new acquaintances Thompson had cultivated. They began to question the as-yet tenuous ties that bound them to this person.

"We don't know the answers to all the questions, yet, Monsignor," said Patrick, "but as to where these stories originated . . ." He handed Thompson the diary.

"My diary! Where did you get it?"

"It's a long story, Monsignor, but I think the gentleman sitting next to you can tell us most of the answers."

Thompson turned to face Brand, who gazed back with a look of serene contempt.

"You!" Thompson spat out. "You did it! You've ruined me!" His eyes blazed. "I am no stranger to revenge, Brand. But this is more than un-Christian, it is devilish!"

Thompson clearly was on the verge of tears. Patrick feared he might possibly be near a stroke or something equally catastrophic.

"Why don't you get your things, Monsignor," he said, gently. "You can come back to Detroit with me."

Silent now, tears of anger and shame brimming his eyes, Thompson rose slowly from the table and stumbled in the direction of his cabin. "Yes, yes, Sergeant. I'll be right with you."

He spoke so quietly Patrick could scarcely hear him. As he left them, the Monsignor somehow seemed to have shrunk and aged.

"Are there any charges against me, Sergeant?" Brand, unconcernedly sipping coffee, continued to look smug.

"Not just at this moment, Mr. Brand. But you are returning to Detroit, aren't you?"

"Right after we finish this cruise on the twenty-fifth."

"We would appreciate it if you would make yourself available on your return."

"Certainly." Brand did not rise. But as the policeman got up to leave, Brand looked up, "By the way, Sergeant, who told you where to find Monsignor Thompson?"

"You may find this a little unusual, but it was Father Koesler."

Father Koesler. Who would have thought it? Brand recalled the priest's visiting briefly on the Fourth of July and then again in his office when Brand was looking for a nonconformist priest to perform his daughter's noncanonical wedding.

Father Koesler, who seemed so bland. Who would have thought it? Well, Brand concluded, I owe him one. Their finding Thompson now is an unimagined stroke of luck. One more day and I would have been responsible for what, in the light of what happened today, would have been a most foolish murder.

As of now, the police have no criminal charge to bring against me. If tomorrow's planned incident had taken place, they undoubtedly would have brought a charge of suspicion of murder.

Well, all's well that ends well. Sunny and I can enjoy the remainder of our cruise.

He did not bother bidding farewell to Monsignor Thompson.

———

This would be Father Koesler's final appearance at police headquarters, at least in connection with the Thompson investigation. Koesler breathed a small prayer that it would be the absolutely final visit. The few times he had participated in police investigations, he had never felt comfortable about his involvement. Left to his own devices, he would be happy to be just a parish priest. That was all he had ever wanted to be.

Not that he did not enjoy his relationship with Inspector Koznicki. But the pleasure of their friendship could be enjoyed without the big gray building at 1300 Beaubien.

The meeting between Koznicki, Harris, Patrick, Lynch, and Koesler had concluded only minutes ago. Patrick told them of his finding Thompson and Brand together and the ensuing confrontation. The detective also told of his trip back with Thompson. It had been pretty grim.

As far as the police were concerned, the case was closed. No one involved had broken any laws for which the police cared to file charges. And unless Thompson intended to bring charges, which, under the circumstances, seemed unlikely, Brand would be subject to no legal action.

When Koesler wondered about Brand's having lied to the Vancouver police, Harris had explained that although lying might be a sin, lying to an investigating officer was not a crime.

Now, Koesler and Koznicki were enjoying *kafe* in a Greektown restaurant.

"I'm sure I don't need to tell you, Father, how proud of you I was last Tuesday," said Koznicki.

Koesler smiled. "I had to come up with something after the Cicero caper."

"Nonsense," said Koznicki, returning the smile. "I have done the same type of thing more often than I care to remember. Particularly with unpredictable human nature, every logical bit of evidence can point in one direction, only to prove a false lead."

"To err is human, eh? No, I think I just had a different set of experiences that led me to suspect Brand. I could see how determined he was that Monsignor Thompson should solve his problem. And then I witnessed Brand's arbitrary, almost vicious behavior toward bank clients. He was simply not the sort of man who could rest without revenge.

"Then there was that private investigative agency that seemed to be an extension of his right arm. And I don't know why any of your officers should know that a priest might be a member of a ship's crew.

"But Brand had more than his share of luck, which frequently happens to damn-the-torpedoes types. At any point along the way his scheme could have fallen apart . . . if Thompson hadn't been in such a rush to leave the reception that he didn't notify any of his associates of his planned absence . . . if the Vancouver police had asked the purser for Monsignor Thompson, instead of merely asking for a manifest . . .

323

"But, of course, at that time no one had any reason to even suspect the Monsignor was onboard; their assignment was merely to ascertain whether Brand had an alibi for the time of the Monsignor's disappearance.

"And even then, unless they had questioned the purser himself, they still probably wouldn't have known of the Monsignor's presence—it isn't like the good old days of luxury liners when the purser was a seagoing watchdog. Nowadays, the purser spends most of his time sequestered in his inner sanctum, leaving the day-to-day passenger contact to his assistants in the outer office. Frequently, these assistants speak or understand only basic English and might not even have known of the Monsignor's presence or status. Or, if they did, could have had trouble either comprehending the police questions or communicating the answers.

"There were so many ifs. But, as Louis Pasteur said, chance favors the prepared mind. And Brand was prepared. And lucky." He smiled. "As I was in coming up with the solution."

"As usual, you are being modest, Father. If the thought had occurred, it is certainly logical to expect a clergyman to get at least a free trip in exchange for his services. No, one of us *might* have reached the correct conclusion sooner or later. The fact is, you *did*."

"Well, at least there are no dead bodies around this time." Koesler finished his *kafe*. "By the way, Inspector, did you get an invitation to a banquet this Sunday at the Pontchartrain Wine Cellars?"

Koznicki mentally checked his appointment calendar. "I don't think so. No, I'm sure I didn't. An invitation from whom?"

"None other than Lee Brand. The invitation came from his social secretary, who followed it up with a confirming phone call. I have no idea what it's all about. But I think I'll go and find out."

"Wait a minute," Koznicki raised a hand, "the Wine Cellars is not open on Sunday."

"Apparently it is for Lee Brand. Everything opens for Lee Brand."

"I am surprised he invited you. You are the one who found him out."

324

"I'm sure Mr. Brand does not intend to give me an award."

"If I were you," said Koznicki, solemnly, "I'd be on my guard. Lee Brand may have wreaked vengeance on Monsignor Thompson, but I fear he is like a killer shark: his thirst for vengeance is never entirely satisfied."

―――――――

"How did you like my wrap-up on the Thompson case?" Cox called from the living room.

In the bedroom, making final preparations for an evening at the Fisher Theatre, Pat Lennon smiled. All Joe Cox needed to stay happy was infinite love and literary reassurance.

"You did swell, sweetie," she called out. "Almost as good as Bob Ankenazy."

Silence. Then, "What do you mean, 'almost as good'! My 'Monsignor Under a Microscope' was yards better than his 'The Money Man Did It'!"

Lennon emerged from the bedroom. She was stunning in a loose fitting white gown. "Sure it was, lover. You've just got to get used to the fact that my loyalties are divided. Between the company that pays me very well and the man I love."

"Speaking of the man you love," Cox put down the magazine he'd been paging through, "have you given any thought to that marriage case of yours down at the Tribunal?"

"Please, Joe, not after what I've been through!"

"O.K., O.K.! Too soon! Too Soon! But keep it in the back of your mind. The only problem you had in that process was Thompson. And, given the fact that that was a serious problem, it seems he's not going to be around much longer."

Lennon looked at Cox sharply. "Is that a fact, Joe? Has it been announced?"

"Not officially, mind you, but the word is out. I was talking with Father Octavio and, while he's still kissed off about the series on Thompson, he still wants to be friends. Anyway, he said some kind of transfer is in the works."

"Somehow," Lennon said thoughtfully, "I don't think a lateral arabesque is what the Thompson problem needs. Something more drastic is called for."

"Well, if the scuttlebutt is true, there'll be a new man at the top in the Tribunal soon. Probably that Father Oleksiak. And you got along well enough with him.''

"Maybe . . . maybe." She adjusted her stockings. He admired her legs. "I need some time."

"While we're making plans for the future . . ." Cox rose; they were about ready to leave. ". . . how about some golf this Sunday? I'm sure you'd like to renew acquaintance with that phlegmatic phenomenon, Nelson Kane."

"That would be nice, seeing Nellie again. But not this Sunday. I've been invited to a banquet by none other than The Money Man Who Did It."

"He not even back from the cruise yet!"

"His social secretary made the arrangements. I have no idea what it's all about, but I can't wait to find out."

"Where's it going to be?"

"Pontchartrain Wine Cellars."

After a pause, Cox remarked, "But that's not open on Sundays."

"Apparently it is for Lee Brand. Everything opens for Lee Brand."

His entire life had turned around and was now headed in the wrong direction. It had gone steadily downhill since last Wednesday when he'd first discovered what Brand had done to him.

Monsignor Thompson had returned directly to Detroit, where he had found his career in shambles. There weren't even that many people who seemed happy to see him alive. Mary Alberts was about it. She had known all along, what he was and had tacitly forgiven each abuse or indiscretion as it occurred.

Al Braemar and Tony Vermiglio had not even returned his phone calls. He had gone down to the Tribunal on Thursday, but it was like a tomb. No one called. No one, with the exception of Mary Alberts, talked to him. He had just gone through the motions, then returned to St. David's where he spent a quiet evening with scotch and TV.

But Friday had been the nadir. Monsignor Iming had called early Friday morning to inform him that the Archbishop would see him at 10 A.M. It was during that meeting he'd learned that all the rungs on the ecclesial ladder he'd been climbing had been removed.

Thompson had been impressed with the fact that when Lee Brand got angry, two parallel vertical lines formed in his forehead. But when the Archbishop became angry, his forehead furrowed, and his heavy eyebrows seemed almost to meet. And Boyle had been angry—with that extremely rare but controlled anger that was typical of only a highly self-disciplined person.

The conversation between Boyle and Thompson had not treated of ecclesiastical sanctions of any kind. It had to do with scandal and effectiveness. Public relations. The effect the recent incidents would have on Thompson's functioning as a priest and officialis. Never once did Boyle refer directly to Thompson's diary or the contents of the news stories. As far as Boyle was concerned, a diary was like a confessional. An internal forum that Boyle, at least, would never drag into the external forum.

For a time, Thompson had fought the inevitable. He argued that he could regain a good reputation. Boyle remonstrated that at least in the area where his conduct and thoughts had been made public, this would be impossible, at least in the foreseeable future.

Thompson suggested a lawsuit against Brand. Boyle argued that such litigation could not possibly obliterate Thompson's own written words. Words that had been turned against him. Such a trial would only lead to more scandal, washing the Church's dirty linen in public, dragging all the nastiness out again, perhaps even more spectacularly. And, Boyle warned, Thompson's last state would be worse than his first.

Gradually, Boyle led Thompson to the inevitable conclusion: that if Thompson were going to continue to exercise his priesthood, it could not be in the Detroit Archdiocese. At least not in the foreseeable future. Once Thompson was able to accept this, it came time for Boyle to inform him where he would be going. The Archbishop handed him a letter of official appointment. Thompson would keep it always. It read:

For the care of souls, I have it in mind to assign you to St. Mary of the Sea Seminary in Mundelein, Illinois. There you will assume the duties of professor of canon law. The matter of ex-

327

cardination and incardination has been settled. By the consent of His Eminence, William Cardinal Hitchcock, you will be a priest of the Archdiocese of Chicago.

The appointment was effective August 27—Monday. Thompson had just two days to pack and clear out of town.

At first he had been almost literally in a state of clinical shock. After reading the letter of appointment, he sat silent for a lengthy period. That he must leave Detroit he had come to accept during his conversation with Boyle. But out of state? Teaching in a seminary? What a profound, radical change. Only the Church would expect her ministers to change from black to white overnight and never break stride. The supportive words of a solicitous Boyle eventually pulled Thompson from his melancholy.

Now, Saturday, August 25, Monsignor Thompson was packing. He would take the plane to Chicago and have his belongings picked up by the movers. Odd, he thought, according to his original plans, today he would have been docking in Los Angeles with the Brands. In reality, he was being run out of Detroit. Only the rail was missing.

Late the previous night, Thompson had finally managed to purge his mind of the last evil thought about Lee Brand. Such thoughts were a waste of time. There was no way he could strike back at Brand. It was time to dismiss him and look to the future. He must rebuild his ecclesial career from its present state of ashes *Ex cineribus*.

They might think he was buried alive in the Mundelein seminary, but he would show them how wrong they were. Every seminary held some students from wealthy, influential families. It was only a matter of finding and cultivating them. Then there was the Cardinal Archbishop of Chicago. Thompson was not unfamiliar with "Wild Bill" Hitchcock, as he was known in Washington. Their past casual friendship undoubtedly was the basis for Hitchcock's having accepted Thompson for incardination into the Chicago archdiocese.

Hitchcock, unlike Boyle, was a man who could understand Thompson. Hitchcock and Thompson had a similar appreciation for the finer things in life. Thompson could envision evenings to be spent with Hitchcock over gourmet meals, fine wine, stimulating conversation, and a carefully reconstructed future in

328

the hierarchy. Surely a word from a Cardinal of Hitchcock's importance to the Apostolic Delegate would mean a hell of a lot more than a recommendation from the Archbishop of Detroit.

Thompson felt himself back on course. They would hear from him again, by damn. They would be sorry, all of them, that they had abandoned him when he hit bottom. God, thought Thompson, never shuts a door that He doesn't open a window.

God's in His heaven; all's right with my world.

Next to the justly world-famous London Chop House, perhaps the most prestigious—less posh, more class—Detroit restaurant was the Pontchartrain Wine Cellars.

The dark, mahogany decor was subdued and elegant; the food uniformly excellent. The Cellars management bent policy to open this Sunday afternoon for two reasons: Lee Brand was a man of position and clout in the Detroit area. And Lee Brand had relied again on his four magical words, Money Is No Object.

Gradually, the guests began to assemble. They were few in number. First came Harry Kirwan, then Pat Lennon. They had never met, so they exchanged greetings and fell into an awkward silence. Next to arrive was Father Norman Shanley. Now there were three who had never met, and the silence intensified. Angela Cicero arrived; then there were four strangers. Next came Father David Neiss. He knew both Harry Kirwan and Angela Cicero so those three formed a clique, while the other two remained on the fringe. Then Father Koesler arrived. He knew everybody. Besides having known all but Kirwan prior to their entanglement with Thompson, Koesler had sat in during the police interrogation of each. In addition, Koesler was the only one of the six present who had read Thompson's diary in toto.

It quickly became evident to Koesler that he was the only one who understood their connection. But the time had obviously come for them to know.

"You," he pointed to Angela, "are 'The Suburban Woman.'"

"And you," he indicated Harry, "are 'The Utility Official.'"

"You," Neiss, "are 'The Suburban Priest.'"

329

"You," Shanley, "are 'The Urban Priest.'"

"You," Pat, "are 'The Paper Woman.' "

"And I," Lee Brand stepped out from behind a room divider, "am 'The Money Man.' "

The five continued to look at each other blankly.

Sudden comprehension reached Pat first. "We're the suspects!" She was almost squealing. "We're the suspects in The Case of the Missing Monsignor! This is a party for the suspects!" She shook her head. "Isn't this the damndest thing!"

"That is correct, Ms. Lennon," said Brand. "And thank you all for coming. Now, won't you all be seated? You'll find place cards at the table."

And so they did. Their names were engraved on cards shaped like a monsignor's biretta.

"I hope you don't mind," Brand said as they seated themselves, "I ordered for everyone."

Nobody objected to surf and turf.

"I think you'll like the wine," Brand continued as the sommelier presented him the cork. "It is Montrachet by La Romanée-Conti '64, a white Burgundy that should assist both viands." Brand smiled at the cork and tasted the wine. "And," he nodded approvingly at the sommelier, "it is properly chilled."

Kirwan knew enough about wine to realize this Montrachet would go for a couple of hundred dollars per bottle. He was impressed.

Conversation remained stilted at best. Only Brand seemed entirely at ease.

About halfway through the meal, Pat Lennon suddenly looked across the table at Father Koesler. "Wait a minute; you're not one of us. You weren't a suspect. What are you doing here?"

"I expect Mr. Brand will let us know all the answers in his own good time." Koesler sipped the wine. It was nectar.

Brand's own good time came during the sherbet course.

"Ladies and gentlemen . . ." Brand stood. His guests continued eating, but fell silent and attentive. "I know we all have things to do today, even though it's Sunday. So I thought I'd begin the proceedings now so the proceedings and banquet may end together."

330

A bit formal, Koesler thought. There are only six guests. He sounds as if he's addressing a Republican convention.

"As you know," Brand commenced, "you share the distinction of having been suspects in the case of the strange disappearance of Monsignor Thompson. I am of your number. Father Koesler is the odd-man out. He is with us this afternoon because he was not only part of the investigation of this case," Brand bowed in Koesler's direction, "he solved it. And to the victor goes the spoils. Or, at least a very decent meal."

Brand smiled. His guests, with the exception of Koesler, laughed politely. The priest was locked in a close study of his host.

"Since you all suffered varying degrees of inconvenience by being suspects in this case," Brand continued, "I thought I owed you an explanation of just what happened."

Showboating, an insufferable ego play, a touch of class? Koesler couldn't decide.

"There was, in this drama we played out three weeks ago, a certain amount of luck and coincidence," said Brand. "This was to be expected since coincidence is an integral part of life, just as 'Isn't it a small world?' is a cliché, true because it is so often appropriate.

"Perhaps the fundamental coincidence is that all of us were mentioned in Monsignor's diary."

Brand turned to Pat Lennon. "This is, by the way, Ms. Lennon, off the record. Understood?"

Reluctantly, Pat nodded.

Brand smiled graciously and continued. "Your first question will undoubtedly concern the diary.

"As was the case with each of you, I had my problems with Monsignor Thompson. The Monsignor supposedly was expediting the marriage case of my daughter's fiancé. However, as time went on, the Monsignor gave me more and more reason to doubt his sincerity—moreover, to doubt he was giving this case any special treatment at all. So I had some private investigators see what they could find out about the matter. It was rather simple for them. They were able to go through the Tribunal files several times."

Mary Alberts' messed-up files, thought Koesler.

"During one of these searches, one of my more inventive agents stumbled across the diary. Sensing there might be some use for this in the future, he photocopied each page and brought the package to me. Earlier diaries were never found. They may have been locked away in some secret archive. But, as we all know, the diary we were able to produce was packed with relevant dynamite.

"That diary became the skeleton on which I fleshed out my plan of taking Thompson on the cruise. All I had to do was get the contents of the diary into the public domain, so to speak, and I would have achieved two very vital things: I would create five instant suspects, and I would let the public know what kind of monster Thompson really was.

"So, when Monsignor Thompson came to join me on the *Alaskan Queen*, it was a simple matter to have the diary transferred to his desk in the rectory, where it would be quickly found. We were prepared to tip both *News* and *Free Press* as to its existence and whereabouts Monday morning, before the investigation began, and let the reporters vie for it. But, as it happened, Joe Cox found it Sunday afternoon. For our purposes, that worked just as well.

"Once the diary was found, all of us became suspects.

"I did not much care what you all did through the week of the fifth while I put my plan into preparation and action. I wouldn't need you until the night of the eleventh when Thompson would be at the wedding reception, and my plan would begin."

Angela remembered what she had done during the week of the fifth. She remembered both envisioning her plot and the moment she had called it off. Sunday morning, the fifth of August, she had seen, as on a movie screen, everything she would have to do. As if patterning herself after the movie, she had lived every step until the morning of the day she was to kill Thompson. For the first time, she realistically considered what it would take to hit a man with a board and knock him unconscious. She could not do it. She could never bring herself to physically assault another human being. It had been precisely that quality she had hated in her father. At that moment, she had called a halt to her plans. Then came that crazy phone call . . .

332

David Neiss recalled his daydream. Even in his own fantasies, he had been a blithering idiot. When he saw, in the daydream, where his own maladroitness could lead—to a dead instead of dead-drunk Monsignor—Neiss had been very careful at his parents' home to ask detailed questions about the sleeping potion. But shortly after leaving his parents, he had realized the professional care needed for the administration of a dangerous drug. How could he tell how much the Monsignor would drink and how it would affect him? He could not abide bungling this and having it end as it had in his daydream. At that moment he had canceled his plan and called Peggy to tell her. Then came that crazy phone call.

Norman Shanley relived his canceled plan. He remembered his rationalizing the necessity for Thompson's death. He had seen his friend at the crematorium and all still was well. But when he actually held the poison in his hand, he knew he could not go through with it. At that point, he simply terminated his plan. Perhaps there would be some other way of doing something about Thompson. Although, before his disappearance, Shanley could not think of one. Then there was that night when his buddy Bob Morell didn't show up . . .

Harry Kirwan well remembered his plan. He had not had the slightest doubt that he could carry it out. Not until after he had visited the site of the new building and after he had purchased the sand and cement. Not until then did the realization strike that he would be unable to be at the site after burying Thompson. And who knows what might have happened? The foreman might have noticed an unevenness and ordered that area dug out and repoured. Or the grave might have been uncovered by some workman's mistake. Exigencies Kirwan could have obviated if he had been able to work at the site until the foundation was complete. But nothing could be protected in his absence. At the moment that realization had occurred to him, Kirwan had dropped the plan. Instead, he spent a quiet and delightful night with his wife.

Pat Lennon would never forget her activity during the week of the fifth. It was a week that had brought her closer to actually committing murder than she ever would have thought possible. It was not until after she had visited that deserted beach and her

333

scheme evolved from speculation to the practical sphere that she knew she could never do it. Unlike her fantasy, wherein Thompson merely slipped beneath the surface of Lake Huron and his death seemed somehow utterly beyond her responsibility, in reality, she, of course, would be directly responsible for his death. In reality, she might even have to actually hold his head under water. To actually kill him. Involuntarily, she shivered whenever the plot reoccurred to her. She had, indeed, checked out a *News* staff car for the eleventh, intending to cover the Port Huron weekend resort story. But when she got the phone call about the drug story—which proved bogus—she had decided to postpone the Port Huron trip to Sunday instead of Saturday night. She had not wondered much about the phone call. It was by no means the only false alarm she'd ever received. She regretted only the cold she had caught.

"By the way, folks," Brand continued, "I feel I have two things for which to apologize to you. And one is more egregious than the other." He looked more charming than contrite. "My first apology is, of course, for revealing the contents of Thompson's diary. While I was certain the news media would not dare disclose your identities, you were subjected to a police investigation, and I apologize for that.

"But more, I apologize for taking from all but one of you your alibis for the eleventh. Mr. Kirwan, of course, I did not even know you would be on the list, so I did nothing to try to take away your alibi. But Mrs. Cicero and Father Neiss, I'm afraid my agents were responsible for your wild goose chases.

"And Ms. Lennon, I'm afraid the same is true regarding your missing drug source. With you, Father Shanley, it was not a case of getting you out of your residence as it was with the others. We had to find a way to keep you home. Once we discovered you had a date with Father Morell, we arranged for the long-winded visitor to your friend, as well as putting your telephone temporarily out of order."

Cicero, Neiss, Shanley, and Lennon silently weighed whether Brand's apology and even this expensive feast were worth their inconvenience. When each added the revelation of Monsignor Thompson's darker side made possible at least partially through their inconvenience, each felt prone to forgive—or at least to hold no grudge.

"A question, if one is permitted, Mr. Brand?" Kirwan asked. Brand smiled and nodded. "Thompson's car; why was it parked at De La Salle?"

"Good question—and another odd coincidence.

"We flew Thompson to San Francisco from Detroit City Airport. I took it for granted that Thompson would park at the airport. I had men there who were to move the car from the airport parking lot. I didn't want his disappearance to be linked with air travel. But Thompson saved us that trouble by deciding to leave his car at De La Salle. He thought it would be safer there."

Brand smiled at the memory. There was appreciative but nervous laughter from all but Koesler.

"And," Brand continued, "when he found blood, he wiped the car clean of prints. He couldn't have helped more if he'd been working for me. By the way, he was able to take his pistol with him—he didn't trust me much—because he was traveling by private plane, then cruise ship.

"Which reminds me: I was puzzled when I heard about the empty cartridge found in his car. Some circumspect questioning revealed that Thompson himself had fired that shell. The fool took a potshot at a pheasant while waiting for a funeral at Mt. Olivet Cemetery. He had wondered what happened to the casing but never did find it."

"Another question, Mr. Brand," said Lennon. "If Thompson trusted you so little he brought along his gun, what made him trust you to arrange for his leave of absence from the diocese?"

"Oh, I don't think he did. But my phone call Saturday was too late for him to reach anybody at the Chancery, nor would he have needed to; after all, he had no obligations until noon Mass Sunday at Shrine. I'm sure he would have phoned from Frisco were it not that he got a telegram from Monsignor Iming early Sunday telling him all was clear for him to be away for a couple of weeks. Of course," he smiled slyly, "Monsignor Iming never sent such a telegram."

335

"What's going to happen to Monsignor Thompson now?" asked Angela Cicero of no one in particular.

Brand shrugged and turned his palms up. "I couldn't care less. I'm done with him."

"I believe he's being sent to a Chicago seminary to teach canon law," said Koesler, whose clerical gossip source was unimpeachable.

"He's going to teach young men studying for the priesthood to be like him!" Father Neiss's horrified reaction was instantaneous.

Silence fell on the group. One by one, after speaking a word or two with Brand, they left, undoubtedly retaining visions of their aborted plans, possibly each glad he or she hadn't carried them out . . . but possibly wishing someone else had—or would.

Finally, only Brand and Koesler, along with a couple of waiters, remained.

"I guess you think you won, don't you?" said Koesler.

"I don't *think* I won," said Brand, in instant ill humor; "I won! I *did* win! It's just as Machiavelli said . . ."

Machiavelli, thought Koesler. Wouldn't you know Machiavelli would be his patron saint!

". . . 'Men ought either to be indulged or utterly destroyed, for if you merely offend them they take vengeance, but if you injure them greatly they are unable to retaliate, so that the injury done to a man ought to be such that vengeance cannot be feared.' "

"So you fear no vengeance?" asked Koesler.

"Not hardly. Not from Thompson."

"There is another kind of vengeance, Mr. Brand. The way the Bible puts it, *Vengeance is mine. I shall repay, saith the Lord.*"

"So?"

"So I am not burning any candles for Monsignor Thompson." Koesler spoke firmly. "But you managed to tear his reputation to shreds by using his diary. By using more his evil thoughts than his evil deeds. Even born-again Presidents admit they occasionally lust in their hearts.

"Monsignor Thompson may have run roughshod over a good many people by maladministering bad law. And that is some-

336

thing the Church should have been alert to and should have corrected. You might have been instrumental in effecting that kind of solution. But Mr. Brand, you deliberately and completely destroyed the man's reputation."

For the first time, Koesler witnessed the storied deep vertical parallel lines forming in Brand's forehead. He had to admit it was a threatening sight. But Koesler plowed forward in what he considered a priestly obligation.

"Mr. Brand, as a Catholic you must know that it is the teaching of our Church—*your* Church—that each person has a right to a good reputation whether such reputation is deserved or not, unless the person himself or herself publicly destroys that reputation. But you have taken it upon yourself to destroy a man's reputation by innuendo and the revelation of his most private thoughts.

"Mr. Brand, I really don't know if you won. I wonder if your act of vengeance is the final act of vengeance. Or whether the final act of vengeance is the one the Lord reserves to Himself. And whether the Lord's vengeance may be directed at you. For the good of your soul, I urge you to consider this."

"All right, now you listen to me!" Brand's anger was impressive. He had been transformed from gracious host to snarling despot. "Nobody talks to me like that! Nobody! And especially not you! I owed you one, Koesler, but this is it! We're even! Never, never cross me again!" He flung down his napkin. "You may leave!"

Koesler shrugged and left.

During his drive back to St. Anselm's, he continued to wonder what Brand had meant. What had Brand "owed" him? Finding Father Shanley for his daughter's wedding? No; Brand had discovered Shanley without Koesler's help. What could it be? Koesler sensed he would be pondering that remark for a long time.

He entered his office in the rectory. There was still a considerable pile of unopened mail on his desk. Testimony to the amount of time he had lately spent away on detached duty with the Detroit Police Department. He sat down and shuffled through the pile.

One rather bulky business-size envelope with the return address of the Tribunal caught his eye. What now?

The envelope contained the considerable but incomplete documentation Thompson had ordered Koesler to send regarding his parishioner's petition for permission to separate. The covering letter was signed by Thompson. This, thought Koesler, must have been one of the last bits of Tribunal business for the Monsignor. Funny thing; Koesler no longer heard those three menacing Scarpia chords.

The letter read: *Why did you send the Tribunal this documentation on a petition for permission to separate? It is incomplete.*

Koesler threw back his head and laughed. "That it was incomplete is what I've been trying to tell you, you dumb bastards!" he said aloud to no one. Deacon Schroeder, in the living room, heard him. First running through the rectory near-naked, now this. Schroeder wondered if Koesler were coming unglued.

Oh, Tommy, Koesler thought; Chicago survived Mrs. O'Leary's cow and Mayor Daley. What are *you* going to do to that toddlin' town!

Then Koesler thought of Cardinal "Wild Bill" Hitchcock and his reputation for living high off the hog. Hitchcock and Thompson—they deserved each other. Wouldn't it be odd if Tommy Thompson got his bishopric through Hitchcock? So that once more, Tommy Thompson, after the football game, could accompany the rich kids into the mansion.

Stranger things had happened.

ABOUT THE AUTHOR

William X. Kienzle, author of the highly acclaimed *The Rosary Murders* and *Death Wears a Red Hat*, was ordained into the priesthood in 1954 and spent twenty years as a parish priest. For more than twelve of those years he was editor-in-chief of the *Michigan Catholic*. After leaving the priesthood, he became editor of *MPLS Magazine* in Minneapolis and later moved to Texas, where he was director of the Center for Contemplative Studies at the University of Dallas. Kienzle and his wife Javan presently live in Detroit, the setting for all three of his novels, where he enjoys playing the piano and organ and participating in sports as diversions from his writing.